ALL IS NOT ENOUGH

After her beloved mother's death, Regan Trent realises with mounting disbelief that she is totally at her stepfather's mercy – but mercy is a foreign concept to Sherwyn Huntley. To this ruthless man, Regan is simply an obstacle between him and the Trent fortune. Denied a place at her mother's funeral, cruelly separated from her younger brother, promised in marriage to a sadistic pervert, Regan prefers to take her chance in the wide world – but Huntley will stop at nothing to achieve his cruel ambitions...

Please note: *This book contains material which may not be suitable to all our readers.*

ALL IS NOT ENOUGH

ALL IS NOT ENOUGH

by

Meg Hutchinson

Magna Large Print Books
Long Preston, North Yorkshire,
BD23 4ND, England.

British Library Cataloguing in Publication Data.

Hutchinson, Meg
    All is not enough.

    A catalogue record of this book is
    available from the British Library

    ISBN   978-0-7505-2766-8

First published in Great Britain in 2007 by Hodder and Stoughton
A division of Hodder Headline

Published in Large Print 2007 by arrangement with
Hodder & Stoughton Limited

Magna Large Print is an imprint of Library Magna Books Ltd.

Printed and bound in Great Britain by
T.J. (International) Ltd., Cornwall, PL28 8RW

1

'Now I understand. Now I know why it was my mother begged me to leave this house, to go somewhere far away and not return, I know why it is that the very thought of you has always filled me with revulsion... Now I know why my mother took her own life!'

Each word an arrow of hate, Regan's voice flew across a room almost devoid of light, heavy velvet drapes drawn together barricading windows against the intrusion of day.

'So now you know!' Sherwyn Huntley was tall and sparely built, a neatly pointed metallic grey beard following the line of his jaw to fuse with sideburns leading into flat brushed hair. The colours merged with the grey of the room until it seemed only his eyes remained, hard, black as the coals sitting unlit in the firegrate, eyes Sherwyn Huntley fixed on the pale drawn face watching from among courted shadow. 'Now, as you say my dear, you know, and as you must also know I will be making no changes, though in the case of yourself I admit to a certain temptation.'

Why had she not seen? Why hadn't she realised?

Regan Trent watched the supercilious lift of her stepfather's mouth above the casing beard and felt a cold self-condemning anger course through her veins. How could she have been so blind, so stupid?

9

'*You* will be making no change!' Anger flashing into brittle life, Regan stared at the man she detested, the man who ruled her life. 'But I will, I intend to stay here in this house just long enough to see my mother laid to rest and then I shall leave!'

'Leave?' The smile, urbane and mocking, was masked by the dimness of the room but the tenor of the voice carried it clearly to its listener. 'I don't think you fully understand, my dear, you will not be leaving this house.'

'You can't prevent me!'

'Oh but I can.' It purred above the anger. 'You forget I am your legal guardian. It is my word and my word only says what you may or may not do and I say you will remain here at Woodford.'

'No!' The word cracking from her lips, Regan took a step forward into the light of a lamp at the further side of the room.

Pretty? Having lit the lamp Sherwyn Huntley blew out the match and threw the spent sliver of wood onto the bed of unlit coals set in the grate. He returned the matchbox to the pocket of his silver-grey silk waistcoat and swept a glance over his stepdaughter. Pretty? The thought asked again, another answered in quick refrain. No, that had been his thinking two years ago, when his marriage to her mother brought him into closer proximity to a young girl he had vowed to care for and protect.

At eighteen years of age, slender as a willow reed, the promise of that body had still to be realised but the passage of time had fulfilled that promise in every detail. And his pledge? Sherwyn

Huntley's smile remained; time had changed that also.

'I won't, I won't stay under the same roof, I despise you for what you did to my mother...' Repugnance flashing cobalt darts to where her stepfather stood, Regan's whole body shivered with loathing and with sudden fear. What he had said was true: he was her legal guardian, he could dictate her life, keep her here until she was of age. A whole year! It rang like the knell of death. A whole year of living in the same house as the man she would hate forever, a year before she could escape his evil. Yet there was a way: her mother's funeral. There would be people there, people she could turn to for help.

'My parents have friends,' she said, the knowledge of their presence on the day of her mother's burial lending her strength. 'I will tell them what you put her through, what you are, I will ask they take me away with them.'

It had shocked him, he had not expected that! Regan's small chin lifted in an echo of defiance, a quick flush of triumph warming through her veins. 'Make no mistake, they will take me from this house.'

A fall of lamplight skeined fine threads of silver interwoven among grey, and touched his temple and brow with a halo of pale gold, which served to intensify the ebony hardness of eyes glinting with cynicism. She thought she had him. Sherwyn Huntley's inner smile deepened. This slip of a girl thought to have bettered him, but she would learn – as her mother had learned. No one, and especially not a woman, could outwit Sherwyn

11

Huntley. Watching her now, the rapid breath of anger lifting breasts small and firm above a tiny waist, honey-gold hair capturing the spill of citron until it glistened as if sprinkled with yellow diamonds, their delicate touch caressing intimately a face Michelangelo might have sculpted from purest alabaster, he reaffirmed that which had been decided so many months before: Regan Trent would belong to him. *'Make no mistake!'* She had thrown the words with vehemence, a warning? Silent mockery touched against his throat. His stepdaughter had much to learn, but then he was an excellent tutor.

'I fear, my dear, I have already made a mistake, that of oversight.'

What did he mean? Regan felt the sharp pull of tightening nerves. This man had destroyed her mother's life; like some great spider, he had woven his web of lies, spinning threads of deception, drawing them ever tighter until they bound with the tenacity of drawn steel; he had given precious little thought to the misery he caused the woman he had professed to love, and doubtless he would give even less account to the discomfort of one he knew hated the very air he breathed.

'I ask your forgiveness...' He paused, savouring his choice of word. That was the one thing in life he could be certain of, as certain as every man must be that life, however cherished, would in time be snatched away. He was certain Regan Trent would never grant Sherwyn Huntley forgiveness; but what did that matter? He could live as well with her hatred. 'I should have mentioned to you...' He spread long-fingered hands in an

12

expression of apology, the single shake of the head adding no sincerity, '...you will not be present at the funeral of my wife, neither will there be any other mourners. After all, my dear, we could hardly embarrass the friends you spoke of by inviting them to attend the burying of a woman who has taken her own life, I cannot incommode other people with the onus of having to manufacture an excuse for not attending the burial of a *suicide*.'

Emphasis drove the knife blade of grief so deep into her heart that Regan gasped with almost physical pain. He knew the agony she would undergo at seeing the coffin which held that worn-out, defeated body being passed not through a door but from a window, lowered by means of a broad plank of wood, then carried to the stone gateway of the house; there to suffer the further indignity of being lifted over the surrounding wall. The ignominious departure decreed by society! Regan felt the knife blade twist. No matter her mother had been driven by a cruelty no woman could with stand, she had committed the ultimate sin. The consequence was the shame of such a removal from her home, but even more shameful was the burial which church and man declared could not be graced by holy service, nor could the departed be given a resting place in consecrated ground; suicides must be laid in an unmarked spot beyond the boundaries of any churchyard.

'Please, you can't mean...' It was a sob echoed in her eyes.

'Oh but I do!' His voice a perfect match for the hardness of ice-cold eyes, Sherwyn Huntley overrode a cry that was food to his soul. Marcia

13

Trent had broken under his yoke; now her daughter would be harnessed to the same. That air of defiance, that haughty lift of the head would very soon give way to the droop of defeat; Regan Trent would acknowledge there could be only one voice at Woodford and that voice belonged to Sherwyn Huntley! 'I mean it in all sincerity.' The flow of words was chilled as a mountain stream. 'My wife chose to bring this degradation upon my name – that I can neither prevent nor erase. But I can shield you from a little of it by not having you subjected to the stares and remarks of bystanders.'

'No!'

'Yes!' Long fingers brushed the air with the snap of finality. 'I repeat, you will not be present at the funeral of my wife.'

'*My wife…*'

Regan stared at the door as it closed with final significance behind her departing stepfather.

'*You will not be present at the funeral of my wife.*'

Those words shouted in her mind, each of them crystal clear. He had deliberately chosen the phrase, chosen not to say 'your mother'. That was the cruelty of the man her mother had married, a man whose vindictive streak she knew would be made ever more clear to the girl who had discovered his secret.

She was to have been married. Standing before the open wardrobe, Regan looked at the gown that had been delivered two weeks before. It was of heavy white satin, with tiny crystal beads, worked in a pattern of lily of the valley, glinting in the soft gleam of the oil lamp beside her bed.

Reaching out, she touched the silky cloth, the folds of it rustling against her fingers, the crystals shimmering like specks of ice on virgin snow. This was her bridal gown. In this she was to have been driven to the church, walked to the altar; in this gown of purest white she was to have been given in marriage to the man she had loved.

'Be happy my darling.'

Soft as they had once been spoken the words returned. Her mother's words. They had gone together to the dressmaker's for a final fitting of the gown. Regan, excited and happy as a child on a first visit to a spring fair, so full of her own happiness that she had not noticed how quiet her mother had been, how drawn into herself. But then she had seen the tears. Regan's hand dropped back to her side, the brush of movement sending crystal-tipped ripples glistening over the lovely skirt to brush against the satin bodice. The dress was cut in the style adopted by Alexandra of Denmark for her marriage to the Prince of Wales, a beautiful Princess Royal-style creation which lent itself perfectly to the veil of delicate Brussels lace. It was the veil her mother had worn as a young bride. 'Something borrowed,' her mother had said with a smile, taking the froth of lace from its box, 'we must not forget the traditions.'

Why had she not seen it then? Why had she not recognised the pain in those tired eyes? But she had not. The tears which had trembled in them she had taken to be a mother's tears of joy at seeing her daughter dressed as she would be for her wedding. Regan's throat tightened, fighting the surge of her own tears. How wrong that thought had proved. Now there would be no wedding.

Ignoring the still-open door, the box with its spill of blue tissue paper and Brussels lace left unregarded on the shelf that ran the width of the wide mahogany wardrobe, Regan crossed to a window obscured by drapes custom decreed could not be opened for several days following a death in the house. A holding to the grief of parting from a loved one? A statement to the world announcing the sorrow of the house? For any other family of the town she would have agreed the gradual return to normality was just that, but here, for Sherwyn Huntley, it was no more than a pretence of grief, a lie. Like the lie that Regan was too stricken to attend the burial. Lies! Teeth clenched against an invasion of tears, Regan breathed deeply. There had been so many lies. Not all of them told by Sherwyn Huntley.

From the hall below, the sound of a long-case clock striking the hour reached the bedroom but for Regan it went unheard against the tumble of thoughts filling her mind.

She had been so impressed by the young man introduced to her by a smiling Sherwyn. Myles Wentworth was the son of a boyhood friend of Huntley and as such had been welcomed at Woodford, not least by a young girl dazzled by the man's charm and good looks. Twenty-four years old, a few inches taller than herself, his skin tanned by the touch of a foreign sun, hair an unruly wealth of copper, he had pretended to lavish attention on her. But that was all it had proved to be, pretence. An act, a mockery! And she had been duped by it.

16

A tap at the door brought her sharply about, one hand dashing moisture from her lashes with a fierce determined stroke; she would not give Sherwyn Huntley the satisfaction of seeing her weep, nor would she voluntarily give permission for him to enter her bedroom. Unaware she was holding her breath, Regan stood in mute defiance, the quiet tick of the small gilt-cased carriage clock on the mantel above the grey dead fireplace sounding like the boom of cannon in her ears. How long would he stay listening at her door? Would he presume to enter? Blood pounded her temples from pressure of pent-up breath as her gaze locked onto the door. Maybe he would think her in bed, even already asleep? Maybes were dashed with yet another subdued knock. If only she had thought to turn the key, to lock herself in!

'Miss Regan...'

A flood tide of relief swept over her, washing the tension from her nerves, the drumbeat from her ears. She ran to the door and threw it open to a slightly stooped grey-haired figure.

'I'm sorry to have disturbed you, Miss Regan, but the master said to bring a tray to your room, seeing as how you didn't come down to supper.'

She did not want supper, she never wanted another meal in this house.

'Thank you.' She nodded to the man who had lived at Woodford House some twelve years, who had been butler to her parents from before Saul was born. 'Thank you but I do not wish supper, please take it away.'

'But the master ... what will I tell the master?'

Regan bit back the reply she wanted to make.

Sanders was not responsible for her feelings and did not deserve the words choked in her throat.

'To refuse will perhaps bring the master here to your room; he is bound to want to ensure you are not ill.'

He was offering a route through the jungle of her thoughts. To return the tray untouched would give Sherwyn Huntley a perfectly reasonable excuse for coming to her room. Looking now at the man who had always treated her with the regard he might have for a daughter, Regan allowed her relief to show.

'Will I leave the tray, Miss Regan?'

'Yes ... thank you.' He placed it on the small table her mother had given her to provide a means whereby Regan could sit to write her journal or press the flowers she sometimes gathered from the garden or adjoining countryside; her mother had been aware of the needs of a girl awakening to adult life, the need for moments of privacy teenage years demanded. She had recognised her daughter was becoming a woman and had accepted it with gentle consideration until Sherwyn Huntley had 'corrected' his wife. It would not do for his step-daughter to grow to womanhood believing her wants and desires to be all that mattered, that her requests take preference over all else.

He had smiled when speaking but Regan had sensed the deeper intention behind his words. He was master now at Woodford and everyone beneath its roof would conform to his wishes. But those wishes had very quickly taken the form of dictates, orders her mother had attempted to soften only to arouse anger in the man she had

18

married, anger which brought subjugation and in its wake a defeat that had turned Marcia Huntley from a happy, smiling mother to the tired, nervous woman almost afraid to speak. What had caused so drastic a change? Regan's hands clutched as they had a few minutes before. She would never have to ask herself that question again, for now she knew the answer.

'Mr Sanders...' She addressed the manservant in the manner required of her by both parents, who had taught that, though paid domestics, servants were people deserving of respect. 'Mr Sanders,' she repeated as he straightened from setting down the tray, 'would you please inform the master I have retired for the night and that there is no need for concern.'

She had seen the understanding in those grey eyes. Sanders knew the loathing she felt for the man who termed himself not only stepfather but friend, but did Sanders understand it? Could he possibly guess the cause of that emotion? No, he could not; nobody ever could.

2

'Perhaps it would be better if I leave.'

'Leave?' Sherwyn Huntley's glance was sharp above the rim of his brandy goblet.

'Just until things are ... well, you know ... until things have settled down.'

'By "things" I presume you mean the girl.' The

thought lay in Sherwyn's mind like lead. The girl was an encumbrance, a hindrance to his life here at Woodford. She had come with the wife, a part of the bargain without which there would have been no Woodford, no easy living off another man's labours, but then one did not always have to keep all that was included in a bargain.

'You are thinking of Regan of course.' Above the heavy cut glass polished ebony eyes gleamed a half smile. 'That is commendable but I would have thought as her fiancé she would prefer that you stay. The support of the man she loves can only help ease the pain of losing a mother.'

Placing a refilled decanter on an elegant mahogany sideboard, Sanders' white-gloved hand rested fractionally on the heavy glass stopper. *'Ease the pain.'* Like acid the words burned in his mind. Whose pain would that be? That of Regan Trent or the so-different pain of her stepfather!

'But what might be thought?' At the butler's back the smile answering Huntley was almost coquettish. 'I mean, what will other people think of my being here during the period of mourning?'

'People!' Sherwyn Huntley's half-hidden smile broke across the stage of his face. 'Which people would they be, Myles?'

'You know ... people.' A sheen of copper glinted red-gold, the slight shake of Myles Wentworth's head catching light spilling from crystal-drop gasoliers. 'Friends of the family, business associates, might they not think it a little distasteful a young unmarried man staying in the home of a young unmarried girl with no mother to chaperone her?'

Tapping the base of his goblet on the sofa table set beside a scroll-end couch, both a match to the sideboard, Sherwyn's imperious summoning of another drink showed little respect for the beautiful inlaid surface.

'Friends of the family.' The smile remained fixed. 'You need have no qualms on that score. They have already been informed I wish the funeral to be strictly private, and as for business associates, again you need have no qualms for I keep business and family matters very widely apart.'

You didn't have to look far to find reasons for that! Sanders filled the goblet held by his employer, then turned to the younger man. Sherwyn Huntley kept visitors to a minimum and those who had known Marcia Trent before her marriage to him had not been welcomed at all. Nor would they be now. Supporting the decanter on the palm of one hand, the other holding the graceful curve of the fluted shoulder, he glanced briefly at the handsome face. Myles Wentworth was the only visitor welcome to this house, one Marcia Huntley would prefer had never come here at all.

'You are certain my remaining here is what Regan would wish?' Myles asked, sampling the brandy almost before the decanter was lifted clear.

'Quite certain.'

The answer followed Sanders across the room, a sequel to it coming sharply to his mind as the door closed behind him. Yes, Sherwyn Huntley was certain but was that certainty expressed on behalf of his stepdaughter or for himself? Business partners. That was how the younger man had first been introduced into Woodford, his father's business was to be joined to that of Huntley, but of all associates of that man only Myles Wentworth had become a regular guest, staying first a week and then gradually increasing his length of visit until now he was an almost permanent resident. Permanent! Reaching the butler's pantry, a room he looked upon as his own private space, he sat heavily on a stout wooden chair. Marcia Trent had held a definite dislike for that man, she had not once voiced that opinion but years of working in this house, of speaking with and serving the woman, he had come to sense what she felt, and one of the strongest feelings had been that of dislike for Myles Wentworth. And now her daughter, the child she cherished, was to become the man's wife.

Why? He stared at the oak bureau at which he did the household accounts. Why, when Marcia Trent disliked Wentworth so much, had she agreed to his marrying her daughter? The question might be asked by any who did not know the mistress as well as Edward Sanders and he need not ask, because he knew the answer! Hands he had unconsciously rested on the small table gripped at the chenille cloth, rumpling it until the deep red fabric spilled like blood over his fingers. Fear! His breath hissed softly between tightly clenched teeth. He had seen it in her eyes, heard it in her voice, watched it in the tremor of her hands. Marcia Trent had been afraid of her husband; but even the fear she could not truly hide had not deterred her from attempting to prevent a marriage between Wentworth and her daughter. He had overheard that discussion. As

22

he remembered, his fingers dragged at the cloth, tightening and squeezing as if around the throat of some hated enemy. He had been bringing afternoon tea to the sitting room when the raised voice of Sherwyn Huntley had made him pause outside the door. Although not an eavesdropper – he had sometimes chastised staff when catching them lingering a trifle too long and too close to a door – that time he had listened.

'*You say Regan has professed love for him.*' Huntley's voice, edged with its normal irritation, had carried clearly. '*That she has conveyed to you her wish to marry.*'

'*Yes.*' Marcia Trent's voice had trembled in a sudden stillness and he had waited, God in Heaven, he had waited! Then she had gone on. '*But I believe Regan's feelings to be those of infatuation. Myles Wentworth is the first man she has met and therefore...*'

'*Therefore?*'

Huntley's one word had cracked out with a snap of breaking ice. He should have gone into that room then. A pulse drummed in the base of his throat while Edward Sanders listened to the voices he knew would never leave his memory.

'*Therefore...*'

It had come softly, apologetically, beneath it that tremor of fear. '*... I think it best she wait a while before taking so serious a step and so I cannot agree to the marriage.*'

'*You think!*'

It had been the snarl of an animal seeing its kill stolen beneath its nose.

'*You cannot agree! But then you never could think,*'

could you, Marcia, or you would know your agreement or otherwise is totally irrelevant. Only mine is necessary and that agreement has already been given.'

'Regan will listen, she will...'

'She will listen to me and so will you! Remember the ultimatum: confinement to a mental institution for the rest of your life is not the most pleasant of prospects but it is one which most decidedly will be yours should you dare to disobey me. And Regan? She will remain here at Woodford with Myles Wentworth for a husband.'

'No Sherwyn, I beg you...'

The plea had ended abruptly, cut short by a choleric bark which had reduced the woman to silence. Menace edging every syllable, Huntley had continued.

'I have already spoken of your mental condition to an acquaintance of mine, an eminent doctor. He is of the opinion your mood swings, those erratic changes from smiles to unfounded anger, are characteristics of madness; they will, so he assures me, become more violent and recommends you are admitted to an institution now before anyone suffers harm as a result of your failing reason. It is an action I would regret but one I will not hesitate to perform; after all the well-being of my stepdaughter is paramount, I must take every precaution to see no hurt befalls her.'

'That is not true, my reason is sound.'

Why had he not gone into that room? Entering then would have prevented...

'Truth is what I say it is!'

The interruption barked again in Sanders' brain and with it the sharp sound of a slap followed by a low frightened cry, then...

24

'If I choose to say I fear not only for your sanity but for the threat madness poses to the safety of a young girl you have already attacked on two occasions, then who is there to gainsay you should not be certified?'

'That is a cruel lie, Sherwyn. I have never, would never, harm my daughter.'

Seated in the quiet solitude of the butler's pantry Edward Sanders winced at the echo of a remembered laugh. Out of everything he had heard said that one statement rose clear above the rest, a trumpet sound of truth among an orchestration of lies and falsehoods. Marcia Trent would never harm her daughter and if what his heart told him was true then Marcia Trent had taken her own life rather than watch that daughter come to know the same unhappiness she herself suffered. The action of a broken woman, one whose agreement or silence was gained by use of the fist, and the man who used that fist sat now with his protégé in the drawing room. Yes, Huntley would teach Myles Wentworth business procedure, pass on to him the skills necessary for keeping oneself in the comfort recently acquired, and if those skills included the physical and mental domination of a wife? Edward Sanders' hands jerked, involuntarily pulling the cloth half from the table. Yes, Sherwyn Huntley would teach that also.

He had kept his word. Regan Trent stood at her bedroom window peeping between closed curtains at the sad cortège passing along the drive towards the gate of Woodford House. Four sable-coloured horses, tall black plumes on their tossing heads, drew the chased glass-sided hearse which

25

held the coffin of her mother. It would be taken out of the hearse at the gate, passed over the wall and then replaced in the hearse to be taken to its final resting place against the church wall. Against but not within that boundary! Tears blurred the scene into an amorphous wash as she pressed her fingers to her mouth. Marcia Trent had been spared the ignominy of being taken from the house on a handcart, that usual procedure for removing a suicide to his or her burial place, but she was not to be spared unconsecrated ground. Marcia Trent could be given no place within the church's boundary: that institution denied her holy sacrament or permission to lie in sacred ground. She had committed a sin so great it found no forgiveness in the eyes of the church.

'My mother committed no sin!' Her hands moved against the window as if to snatch her mother to her, to hold her back from that ultimate disgrace, Regan's cry echoed in the quiet evening. 'She does not deserve this, she does not deserve...' She sank to her knees, choked by sobs. Her mother had not deserved the life marriage to Sherwyn Huntley had brought. Those early weeks had seemed so full of promise for her mother, filled with a secure future which would erase the sorrow of years of widowhood, but it had been a false promise; one which had lasted only a short time after the ceremony which placed her mother under the yoke of domination. It had been made painfully clear. Sherwyn Huntley had married not for love, not for companionship, but for money, the money Marcia Trent would bring him. And he had taken control in its entirety. His word had become the all in Woodford from that first day, he had taken no account of her mother, much less consulted her upon any matter. For Sherwyn Huntley she had merely been the means to an end, the purse he had so swiftly cut from its strings, then uncaringly tossed aside as one might an empty package.

And what of Marcia Trent's daughter? Crouched beneath the window Regan pressed both hands to her face. Why was Sherwyn Huntley so determined she marry Myles Wentworth? But that was a question she had already found the answer to. A wife could not testify against her husband. She was being given to Myles Wentworth as a sacrificial lamb. By becoming her husband he became stepson-in-law of Huntley and as such a member of the family ... and families kept their secrets.

Secrets! Regan's stomach churned with the thought. She would have to keep them as her mother had kept them; but could she? Did she have the same strength of will her mother had shown? And if not, what then would become of her?

Had it been because of her? Apprehension surged through her and Regan dropped her hands. Had her mother accepted blindly all that had happened in order to shield her daughter? Would she ever have married Huntley had it not been in some way a provision for Regan? But what? What could Sherwyn Huntley have had to offer in exchange for marriage?

There had to be something! Rising to her feet, she peered between closed curtains seeing now only an empty driveway slicing between lush green lawns edged about with low box hedges.

Deep in the mists of memory something stirred. The garden. She had been in the garden. She frowned and forced her brain to concentrate. The garden to the rear of the house ... the summer house, she had been in the summer house. Huntley and her mother had not known she was there, had not suspected they were being overheard. Guilt brought a touch of colour to Regan's cheeks. She ought to have called to them, to have informed them of her presence, but caught in the golden summer afternoon she had lain half asleep.

'My daughter has no part in this...'

Clearly, as if just spoken, the words of her mother seemed to ring in the silence of the room, but it was the laugh which followed that set Regan's nerves tingling. A quiet sound, it had not caught her attention, but hearing it now, its fullness revived by memory, she heard it for what it had truly been, the menacing snarl of a predatory animal preparing for the kill; that had been Sherwyn Huntley.

'On the contrary my dear, Regan plays a great part.'

She had not meant to listen, but the drowsiness of the afternoon... She should not allow that overheard conversation to return, it was wrong of her to have stayed silent then and it was wrong to recall it now. What passed between her mother and the man who at that time was no more than a friend, a visitor to Woodford, had been private, it had not concerned an eighteen-year-old girl. Yet it had concerned her. Turning away from the

28

window she went to sit on the bed. She had heard those words, heard Sherwyn Huntley speak her name, yet still she had not truly listened to the voices that had gone on.

'You have no claim upon me and certainly you will never have any upon my daughter.'

There had been an undertone in that, a tremor of uncertainty ... no, not uncertainty. Realisation forged a path through the shroud still holding memory at a distance and with its coming the touch of warmth in Regan's cheeks became a flood, a hot tide of self-reproach. It had not been uncertainty she had heard in her mother's voice, it had been fear. She had been afraid of Sherwyn Huntley and she, Regan, had ignored ... but that was unfair, she had been given no reason to believe her mother was anything other than happy, yet the next words should have told her that was not how it was.

'What you say is true, Marcia ... at the moment. But ask yourself this.

What if Regan should become pregnant? It is not such a ridiculous flight of fancy. A young girl, flattered by the attentions of a more mature sophisticated man, gives herself to him.'

'Regan would never...'

'Perhaps not willingly, but not all things are a result of willingness. There are other ways, Marcia, and you cannot keep watch on your daughter every moment of the day. Then of course there is your son. I offer you marriage and with it the pledge to safeguard your children as I would were they my own, but should you refuse then I see no way other than the one I have already placed before you.'

'*I see no other way!*' The words exploded in Regan's mind, the shattering implication leaving her stunned. He had wanted Woodford so badly he had threatened to seduce – even rape – an eighteen-year-old in order to get it; that had been the hold Huntley had had over her mother, that had been what he offered, marriage with the mother or a daughter shamed into the same, and whether by seduction or rape had not mattered to Sherwyn Huntley. Regan stared blindly across the room. He had known her mother would not refuse, known Marcia Trent would accept anything in order to keep her children safe. But as with all promises made by the man she had taken as a husband Marcia Trent had seen that one crumble, brushed away with the coming of Myles Wentworth.

Why had she, Regan, not seen? Why had she not recognised the man behind the smiling handsome figure ... the man Myles Wentworth truly was?

3

'*To safeguard your children as I would my own...*'

In the semi-darkness Regan let the words run again in her mind.

Was this how Sherwyn Huntley would care for a child of his own? Would he give a daughter of his to a man like Myles Wentworth? Knowing the misery such a marriage would bring? But she was

30

not the daughter of Sherwyn Huntley, she had been simply a pawn in his game of deception. All games had an ending, a conclusion, and marriage to a man she loathed equally as much as she loathed Sherwyn Huntley was the ending destined for her.

Only if she allowed it! Like a sliver of light it crept into her mind. He could not drag her to the altar, he could not force her to say the words; unlike with his wife he had no stick to beat her with, no daughter to keep from the hands of a potential rapist. In fact Sherwyn Huntley had no hold over her save that of guardian, and that for just one year. It would feel like eternity! Regan stared into shadow. But one year was not an infinite span of time; one day she would be free.

Determination lent her courage. She lit the lamp set beside the bed and then the one kept on the small table, preferring their softer light to that shed by the gasoliers mounted on three of the four walls. She had been so happy in this house. Watching ripples of radiance touch the walls with a wash of pale gold, Regan followed the shadows back into childhood. She had been cherished but not spoiled. One day she would be a woman with a home, family and household, and as such must be taught the responsibilities that went with it. This had been her father's thinking. But he had taken her practical education a step further, teaching her the intricacies of business. Perhaps, as her mother had declared in trying to spare her this onerous task, a woman had no need of such tuition. Nevertheless she had enjoyed being with her father, delighting in his praise whenever she

31

got a long column of bookkeeping figures correctly added, or spotted an imbalance between
reported import and actual delivery of goods.
Those had been her special times, sharing her
father's company with no other person. Had he
secretly wished she had been a boy? Another son
to whom he would pass a share of his business? If
so, it had never been apparent in word or deed;
her father had shown her only love.

'Regan, my dear.'

The voice, the soft tap at the door, made the
memory fade as in a flash of lightning, froze the
very blood in Regan's veins.

'Regan, I wish to speak with you.'

She had no wish to talk either to him or to his
house guest. Regan held her breath and stared at
the shadow-enshrouded door. Remain silent and
he would presume her to be sleeping, he would
go away. But a second tap followed the first,
louder, more demanding.

'Regan...' Hard and brittle, Sherwyn Huntley's
words seemed to hurl themselves against the
locked door, to crash into it as if they would break
it down. 'Sanders told me he spoke with you only
minutes ago so you see it gains you nothing to
pretend to be asleep, and it will certainly gain you
nothing to sulk. You will join me in the drawing
room in five minutes or I will be obliged to bring
you there myself, forcibly if need be.'

He would do that. Regan listened to the silence
which fell after the last word. The man who
called himself her guardian would drag her from
this room, embarrass her before the servants, but
then her embarrassment would mean nothing to

32

Sherwyn Huntley.

Crossing to her dressing table she stood a moment staring into the oval mirror at a face streaked with tears. To see the distress he had caused would give Sherwyn Huntley great pleasure.

'You will not get that from me!' The words edged between her clenched teeth as Regan went into her bathroom. Plunging both hands into a basin of cold water, splashing it over her face, she whispered again, 'You will get no pleasure from me ever again!'

'Ah my dear, how good of you to join us.' Sherwyn Huntley rose as Regan entered the drawing room. 'Myles was worried the events of the day had left you feeling unwell.'

Why should she feel unwell! Regan let the acid of contempt eat into her mind. The day had only seen her excluded from her mother's funeral, prevented her from attending that last goodbye, why would that affect her health or her feelings!

'I am perfectly well, thank you.' Pointedly ignoring Myles Wentworth's offer of a chair Regan crossed to the further side of the room before sitting down.

'My dear, Myles and I...'

'Please.' Head lifted high, aquamarine eyes cold as iced water, Regan looked directly at her stepfather, 'There is something I wish to say to Mr Wentworth and also to yourself. First, I will never marry Mr Wentworth; he, I am positive, is well acquainted with the reason for my decision. Second, to you, Mr Huntley, though it grieves

33

me, I accept the fact that as my legal guardian you can prevent my leaving this house, that you have jurisdiction over my life until I am of age, but that day will come and when it does I will see you pay for what you have done, be very sure Mr Huntley, I will see you pay!'

A smile bland as that which had welcomed Regan into the room touched Sherwyn Huntley's mouth but the lips it edged were taut, the line of them pale against the iron grey of his neatly trimmed beard.

'I understand your feelings.'

'You understand?' Grief and anger mixing explosively hurled Regan's interjection across the room, 'You understand nothing of my feelings! You know only your own, *you* are all you care about, all you have ever cared about; you married my mother for just one thing: Woodford. Well you have that, but that is all you will get. Bear in mind Marcia Trent's daughter is no part of that takeover!'

'As I was about to explain...' Sherwyn Huntley's smile remained but found no reflection in the ebony eyes. 'I understand your feelings, the sadness at the loss of your mother combined with the cruel circumstances of her death have profoundly affected your emotions, one could expect little more. It is because of this, and of course to help you the more quickly to overcome your sadness, that Myles has agreed to my proposal to allow your marriage to go on as planned. It will take place two weeks from today. Oh yes...' He paused, the momentary silence hanging in the room. 'The observation of mourning, but you must not worry what people may think of your cutting that period so short, I myself will assure them it was done solely at my behest, my hope being that the happiness of becoming the wife of the man to whom you have given your heart would alleviate, in some measure, the pain of losing your mother.'

'You hope for my happiness, the happiness you afforded my mother!' Scorching contempt blazed at the smiling Huntley before Regan turned her glance on the younger man lounging easily on a brocaded sofa. 'And you, Mr Wentworth,' she breathed hard to quell the revulsion she felt, 'you have consented to the marriage going ahead as arranged. How very considerate of you! Considerate but not surprising, seeing you are an accomplice in all that has been done, that you are as guilty as the man who drove my mother to take her own life and as such need to take steps to protect yourself. But do not think to do that by marrying me. You are as sickening as the man beneath whose roof you committed so despicable an act, the man you call your partner, and that is what you are, partners in evil, Mr Wentworth, evil which will be told to the world. It will learn the truth of you both.'

'And also of your brother?'

Though spoken softly the trumpet call of threat resounded in every word, blazing a warning as Regan turned to look at Sherwyn Huntley.

'Ah!' He nodded. 'I see you had forgotten him. Self-pity is a strong emotion, Regan, an emotion which can bring harm to others ... as it can to your brother.'

'Saul?' Regan stared into the soulless eyes of her stepfather.

'It would not seem so strange.' He smiled coldly. 'A father needs the comfort of his children during this time of grief, what then would be more natural than bringing a son home from school?'

'Saul is not your son, you are not his father.'

'Correct, my dear.' He inclined his head slightly and beams of gaslight caught the icebound eyes, polarising into lambent darts. 'Biologically I am not the father of Saul, but in law that is not relevant. As stepfather I have the same responsibilities a natural father would have and as guardian the same powers. You have said now and previously you are subject to my will until you attain majority and so, I remind you, is your brother, a child I can bring back into this house tomorrow.'

He had been right. Back in her own room Regan gave way to despair. In grief for herself she had given no thought to her brother Saul, who had also not been present at their mother's funeral. Remaining in school would spare him the hurt of seeing his mother laid into the ground, while there he need not learn the method of her death. It had been one decision she had agreed with, that Saul should be spared the knowledge of that suicide, at least until he was older.

Until Saul was older! Would their mother not have thought of that? Would she not have realised the effect her death would have upon a boy as young as Saul? Yes, of course she would. Breath catching in her throat, Regan sank to the bed. She had thought her mother's suicide to be the result of the unhappiness awaiting a daughter ... had she also feared for her son? Had she feared the vile

36

practices of Sherwyn Huntley would be turned upon him? Was that what had finally tipped the balance? Had Sherwyn Huntley made a threat against Saul? That same threat he had intimated a few minutes ago in the drawing room? But facing such as she had known her husband capable of, Marcia Huntley would not have killed herself, she would not have left her son without any sort of protection. Clutching her fists so tightly her fingernails dug deep into her palms Regan stared at the horror forming in her mind. Could it be their mother had not been responsible for her own death?

Blood which had turned cold in her veins nevertheless continued to flow, feeding life into her brain, into the horror forming there. If not suicide then...! She choked on the thought yet still it persisted, resisting all effort at denial, allowing no doubt, continuing to grow, to strengthen, drowning out all else save for one word: murder. But that was a stupid thought, too ridiculous to contemplate. Desperately Regan tried to fend off the chaos in her mind, but each effort proved vain; time and again the notion returned, found a way to counter reason, to answer question with question until her brain reeled.

But it could not have been murder! Regan grasped at straws. Who could possibly have wanted her mother dead? Who would be in a position to commit such a deed?

From the room below a laugh harsh and loud broke the stillness. Sherwyn Huntley! Wreathed in the shadows of her unlit room Regan stared toward the door. Sherwyn Huntley had been in such a position, he could enter and leave his wife's room at any time. But murder! It was too wicked even for him. Was it though? Heedless of the pain of her fingernails stinging her palms, Regan let the thought ride. He had known his wife knew of his behaviour, would that have provided a reason? Had that man been so afraid his odious doings would be brought to light that he had to murder her?

The official finding had recorded poison taken while the balance of the mind disturbed. But disturbed by what? The poison administered by whom? Had anyone else thought as she was thinking now? Seemingly not. It had all been done so quickly, the doctor giving his diagnosis, the coroner confirming it, everything going so smoothly. If Sherwyn Huntley had killed her mother then it had been sublimely easy for him. The grief-stricken husband! He had played the part well, too well to arouse any hint of suspicion that all was not as it seemed. In the darkness of her room Regan's insides twisted. Deception was the forte of Sherwyn Huntley, it masked a practice that was sickening. Did it also mask a murder?

'You handed over the package?'

Sprawled half across a couch upholstered in rose velvet perfectly matched to floor-length drapes echoing the same delicate colour in an exquisite Bukhara carpet Myles Wentworth waved an indolent hand. 'As instructed, but then don't I always do as instructed?'

So far yes! Sherwyn Huntley's face retained its impassive look but beneath the façade of satis-

38

faction a shrewd brain worked. Myles, the handsome biddable Myles, the docile agreeable Myles, always following instruction, always accepting the business he was partner in be headed by another. But for how much longer?

Pouring brandy into a pair of exquisite Royal Brierley crystal goblets he handed one to the younger man, then took his own to a chair beside an elegant fireplace. Myles Wentworth was a man given to easy living: fine food, expensive clothes, carriage and matching pair, he liked the finer things of life and had no qualms as to how they were come by. Definitely averse to work of any description other than the collection or delivery of the occasional package, he spent his days between racetracks and gambling houses. And his evenings? Brandy glass held beneath his nose Sherwyn Huntley breathed the delicate bouquet. Just where did Wentworth spend those evenings he was not a visitor to this house? And more to the point, with whom did he spend them? The last question honed an already sharp suspicion. Huntley sipped, rolling brandy over his tongue.

'Payment,' he asked after swallowing, 'it was given in full?'

Myles Wentworth smiled to himself. That was not the question Huntley wanted to put, what he truly wished to ask was what took so long? Well well! A mouthful of brandy added warmth to an inward smile. So Sherwyn did not entirely trust his partner, but which area of activity promoted that mistrust? Was it that of business, or was it more the social aspect? Holding the ebony stare with an open smile Myles Wentworth knew he need not ask. Sherwyn Huntley was a man jealous of power both in business and social spheres, he would do all he could to hold onto it ... but sometimes all was not enough.

'Cash.' Myles waved the glass, a lazy half-interested move hiding the quickness of his thoughts. 'That is the way you prefer, is it not?'

'It is the best way.' Choosing a chair Huntley settled into it. 'Cheques, transactions on paper, they can be traced.'

'Whereas cash can be claimed to be settlement of a wager, a gentleman's agreement.'

'Can you think of a better way!'

That was not an enquiry, but a rebuke, a slap on the wrist for the less worldly wise. Drinking again, Myles felt the fire of alcohol add to the flame of resentment beginning to burn in his stomach. Sherwyn Huntley really should be more considerate of who he treated to sarcasm, for one day he might find out which of the two of them was actually the more worldly wise. Savouring the thought, he watched the older man. The light of gasoliers played on strands of silver among steel-grey hair, the so dark eyes seeming to see past the flesh into the mind, the mouth firm within the expertly trimmed beard, the body lithe and well kept. Handsome? Yes, Sherwyn Huntley was all of that on the outside, but on the inside? Myles drained his glass. On the inside the man was ugly, twisted with a greed for money, distorted by a need to dominate. Need and greed, one fed the other, but while both fed money into his own pocket Myles Wentworth was not disturbed by it.

Laying aside the empty glass he withdrew a

40

Moroccan leather wallet from an inner pocket of his jacket, counting several banknotes onto a table set beside Huntley's chair. 'Two hundred.' He returned the wallet to his pocket.

'Questions? Bargaining?' A glance at the spaced banknotes was enough to show him the amount was as stated; Huntley took half, handing them back to the younger man.

Accepting the money, tucking it once more inside the expensive wallet, Myles gave one brief shake of his head. 'No questions. As for bargaining you know they always try. You would think they would give up trying for it never gets them anywhere.'

'That is the way it is to remain, relax the rule once and you spell the end. The buyer as well as the seller wants to make maximum profit on every deal, hence the inevitable quibble.'

'Well, the quibble brought him no extra profit this time nor will it on the next.'

'The next?' Huntley placed his share of the banknotes in a small cash box also on the table. 'This is a reorder?'

'Isn't there always?' Myles paused in the act of refilling his glass. 'Those people are hungry for the goods, they would take two, three times as much, so why not supply what they want? Take advantage of the market while it lasts?'

Locking the small metal box Sherwyn Huntley deposited the key in his waistcoat pocket before answering. 'And the goods, Myles ... where do we procure the extra supply?'

'There are other places.'

'And there are precautions!' Huntley's eyes

signalled irritation. 'One being not to flood the market. Goods which are easily obtained become cheaply obtained and I, Myles, do not intend ever to sell cheaply. Some here, a little there, maintain the hunger and the market you speak of will also be maintained and so will the style of living you presently enjoy.'

Some here, a little there! Myles replenished his drink and thrust the stopper into the neck of the decanter. From now on there would be a trifle or two more than the little, and the profit? That would go solely to Myles Wentworth!

4

All week it had been impossible to believe yet impossible not to believe. Murder! The word plagued Regan, tormenting her every waking moment. Had her mother's life been ended not by herself but by the man she had married? At last able to draw the curtains of her room fully apart Regan looked out over the garden. Bathed in the light of a heavy golden moon, its radiance gilding the leaves of bushes and trees so they glistened like sequins against the darker fabric of night, it breathed of peace, of love she had thought could never end.

As her glance wandered over it she felt its quiet beauty call to her soul. So many times she had strolled there with her father, played there with her brother, sat with her mother. The family she loved. But now her parents were gone, lost forever. Suddenly stifled by the closeness of the room she opened the window, breathing deeply of air perfumed with the scent of many flowers: roses, evening primrose and the delicate night-scented stock her mother had had planted beneath the windows of the house to further enhance the pleasantness of warm summer evenings. How different it had been then. Resting her brow against the window frame Regan stared into the play of light and shadow turning the garden into a stage on which she saw again those beloved faces.

'...listen to advice, weigh it carefully in your mind, then act for yourself...'

Within the warm stillness of the garden the words of her father echoed from the past and Regan's throat thickened at their whisper. They had sat together those long pleasant evenings, her father discussing new business ventures with an eagerly listening daughter, her mother smilingly admonishing him for burdening a young girl with such boring conversation. But she had not been bored, she had loved every minute of being with them. Now those minutes would be treasured, gems of life safely guarded in her heart.

'You are sure she will do as you say?'

Those words were not imagined, they were not echoes of the past! Instinctively Regan pulled back from the window.

'Be under no illusion, Myles, she will do exactly as I say.'

'And should she refuse?'

Beneath the partly opened window Sherwyn

43

Huntley's hard laugh scratched the soft night.

'She knows the consequence of refusal.'

'The brother?'

'The brother!' Footsteps crunched on gravel as Huntley's answer abraded the peaceful stillness. 'Regan knows I can bring the boy home, keep him here in this house, do with him as I please ... and she knows the sort of thing that pleases me, so in order to protect him she will have to do as she is told.'

'...*in order to protect...*'

Regan pressed her lips tight together to prevent the cry escaping them. That was the threat Sherwyn Huntley had made to her mother. She had kept silent, said nothing of his cruelty for one reason only, to protect her children. Now he was employing the same tactics with herself: do as I say or your brother will suffer.

'Do as you say!'

Cynicism thick as paint coated Myles Wentworth's reply the sarcasm of it not lost on Regan.

'Which poses the question, what is in this for Myles Wentworth other than a marriage he does not want and a wife he most positively does not want? Both will be a burden I prefer not to carry.'

'You will not carry it for long.'

'But why carry it at all, why not do as before?'

Pressed to the wall inside the window Regan heard the hiss of irritation, then Sherwyn Huntley voice cold and deprecating.

'Why?' An icicle snap, it echoed in the golden stillness. 'The matter of a will is why! The terms laid down by Jasper Trent. These say that upon reaching the age of twenty-one years each of his

44

children shall receive in their turn one half of his estate; however should either die before attaining majority then their half is to be given to the surviving child, and I, my dear Myles, intend that child to be the daughter.'

'And how is that intention to be achieved?'

Soft and insidious as a slithering snake Sherwyn Huntley's laugh slid in the shadows. 'There are ways and there are ways, we have simply to choose. Perhaps the boy suffers an accident while being brought home from school, maybe a kidnapping resulting in his being found dead. It is as I say merely a matter of choice.'

'Then Regan becomes the sole inheritor.' Myles nodded. 'And Regan will be my wife, how very fortunate.'

Greed informed every syllable. Sherwyn Huntley smiled inwardly. Myles Wentworth had an appetite for money, an appetite Sherwyn Huntley would feed just so long as it suited him.

Quiet as before, his tone revealing nothing of the thoughts coiled like a serpent in his mind, Huntley answered. 'Yes Myles, Regan will be your wife.'

'And her money will be mine.'

Greed again! The smile spread to Huntley's lips. Let it grow and develop until like a drug the need became addiction, and the supply of that drug would be controlled by Sherwyn Huntley. Careful to erase all trace of satisfaction occasioned by his thoughts he answered.

'Regan will be yours but her inheritance may not be.'

'What the hell does that mean! The law states

the property of a woman becomes that of the husband.'

'Agreed.' Huntley gave a brief nod of assent.

'So why say her inheritance might not be?'

Urbane, suppressing the gratification of hearing the other man's poorly hidden alarm, Huntley's reply drifted to the girl listening above.

'I do not say it, Myles, it is a condition imposed by JasperTrent; a clause which requires that Regan sign for her inheritance.'

'Another bloody stumbling block!' Anxiety becoming anger, Myles Wentworth kicked savagely at the pathway, the scrape of boot against stone advertising a growing irritation.

'A stumbling block maybe,' Sherwyn Huntley answered quickly. 'But not an insurmountable one.'

'Not insurmountable!' Wentworth laughed hollowly. 'Not bloody insurmountable! I don't see how you can climb over that one; you can hardly grip her hand and force her to write, not with a lawyer looking on.'

She would have to sign! Regan's breath caught. *She* would have to sign in front of a lawyer. But she would not, and as Myles Wentworth had said she could not be forced.

'Of course I cannot grip her hand, that was never my intention.'

'Then how?'

Accompanied by another kick at the pathway the question spat at shadow, shadows which answered with Sherwyn Huntley's voice.

'It is really very easy. Unfortunately the health of your wife's mind, sadly impaired by the circumstances of a mother's death followed by that of a brother, will deteriorate. Despite all of your care her mental capacity will weaken to the point where doctors will advise admittance to an institution, and once there of course you, her husband, will be granted leave by the courts to sign on her behalf.'

'But what if the doctors do not agree?' Myles's doubt resurfaced. 'What if they refuse to certify her as incapable mentally? If she is not committed to an asylum?'

It seemed the answer had needed to be thought over, but in Sherwyn Huntley's mind there was no need for further thought. Letting the silence hang he breathed deeply before saying quietly, 'The doctors I consult will say what they are paid to say, but then every eventuality, however remote, should, I agree, be considered. This I have done. Should it be Regan is not confined to a mental asylum then she will follow the path taken by her mother.'

'Suicide?' Myles Wentworth's return echoed his anxiety. 'Won't that prove a trifle awkward? I mean two of them taking their own life?'

Sherwyn Huntley's cold laugh bruised the gentle night. 'The human mind is a fragile thing, Myles, a very complex part of the body not even the most proficient members of the medical profession fully understand. Who then will protest? Who will there be to deny your wife's balance of mind became so disturbed she took her own life?'

'Like mother, like daughter.' Myles Wentworth's relieved laugh spilled into the garden. 'And once she has gone then everything will

47

belong to me; the brother's inheritance and hers, all mine.'

'Not all, Myles.' Sherwyn Huntley's response cut quietly across the jubilant laugh. 'Half will be yours, the other half you will give to me.'

He had it all worked out. Sherwyn Huntley had planned it to the last detail. The moon having deserted the sky, Regan looked into the well of shadows mantling a garden silent now the two men had returned indoors.

'*...she will follow the path taken by her mother.*'

Sherwyn Huntley's words burned in her brain and with them another: '*suicide*'.

Suicide! Hands clenching together Regan swallowed hard on the constriction risen in her throat.

'*...the doctors I consult will say what they are paid to say...*'

Was that how it had been with her mother? Had Sherwyn Huntley paid doctors to say her mother's mind was failing? Had she been so terrified by the thought of being locked away in an asylum she *had* taken her own life? No! No tumult followed that denial, no swirling chaos of emotion depriving Regan of rational thought. It had not been suicide. Her mother had not taken her, own life. Murder! Long and slow it rang in her mind. Murder! And Sherwyn Huntley was the killer. The man her mother had once thought loved her, the man she had married ... he had killed her! Cold and heavy as stone, suspicion pressed heavily in Regan's chest. Closing the window she walked slowly across the shadowed room. Sitting on the edge of

48

her bed, the lamps unlit, she stared unseeingly into the gloom. Suspicion. That was all she had, but it was not enough; only proof would bring that man his deserts and without proof who would believe her? But not to try, not to attempt to make him pay for his crime...

From somewhere in the darkness it seemed a voice answered, a voice though not entirely unsympathetic yet nevertheless firm, the voice of authority. There has been no crime. Yours are the beliefs of a grief-stricken heart, of a mind disturbed by stress.

Regan's fingers twisted in her lap. That would most certainly be the conclusion of any magistrate and it would prove exactly the opening her mother's killer looked for, the one he had already spoke of to Myles Wentworth: a perfectly valid reason for having her confined to a mental institution.

And he would have succeeded once again. Thoughts closing like a trap from which she could see no means of escape, Regan sat motionless except for the constant twist of fingers. Sherwyn Huntley was devious; more than that he was clever. In the company of others his manner was impeccable. If listening to a man bemoan or extol a business venture while in the company of ladies he would expertly turn the conversation around to become more socially acceptable. Charming, witty, attentive. That was only part of Sherwyn Huntley's character, the other half being sly, deceitful and totally without morals. One face, but hiding behind it two very different personalities! Two men in one body. ... and she hated both. But hate, like suspicion, was useless against a man like Huntley, a man who let nothing and no one stand in the way of what he wanted.

No one! Regan's senses jarred. Huntley wanted not only her gone from his path but Saul also. He was already speaking of some awful happening, something contrived to bring about the death of her brother.

Perhaps if she agreed to marry Myles Wentworth, to place no obstacle in the way of Huntley taking her inheritance, then he would not harm Saul. But even as the thought came the hope of it died. Sherwyn Huntley knew Saul was to inherit half of everything and he was not a man who would settle for the rest. She could promise to make everything over to him the moment she became twenty-one but that would not solve the problem of Saul, and the lawyer their father had entrusted with his will would never agree simply to hand over the boy's share to his stepfather.

Sherwyn Huntley wanted it all. Alone in the darkness of her room Regan felt the trap tighten. But for Huntley all was not enough. Taking money, business and property would satisfy his greed, but to satisfy his lust for evil he would take the life of Saul, and then her own.

'Oh God.' Despair made Regan cry out. 'Oh God, what can I do?'

5

'So I have decided Saul shall come home for your wedding.' Sherwyn Huntley smiled briefly but the eyes watching Regan were black ice. 'A page in attendance, what could look more appealing, and following that celebration he will be tutored here at Woodford.'

Seated opposite a large walnut desk which had belonged to her father Regan felt her nerves leap. Saul would not be returned to school but tutored here at Woodford! But tutored in what? Her brother was little more than a child, he would not know the potential evil that threatened a life in this house, he would have no knowledge of the sordid activities his stepfather engaged in.

'I trust having the boy as the bride's attendant pleases you my dear.' The suave voice, so sickly false, cut through Regan's thoughts. 'I am sure your brother will be proud and honoured to be with you on your special day.'

Forcing her hands to lie still in her lap, to keep her gaze steady on the face of the man who was prepared to kill to take what was not his, Regan felt fear flow like a cold tide along her veins.

'...*perhaps an accident while being brought home from school.*'

The words she had heard being spoken to Myles Wentworth resonated in her brain. Saul was to be taken from school? Her marriage would provide the perfect alibi for murder. Despite her efforts to show no reaction her fingers clenched tightly together. She had prayed so hard for a way to be shown whereby she could save Saul, sat long into nights striving to think of an answer, of a way of protecting him, but it had all proved futile. Sherwyn Huntley had complete control of both her own and her brother's life; neither could do anything, or go anywhere, without his permission.

'I shall write to the head of the school this evening informing him that a carriage will be sent to collect Saul on Friday week. That will allow time for him to be instructed in the duties of attendant.'

A carriage would be sent. Regan's fingers bit harder into each other. Much easier to arrange an accident with a carriage than with a train or public coach! Huntley might as well have said it out loud for his intention was clear. Oh God ... what was the matter with her mind! Why could she not think of something – anything – to save her brother?

'That, I think my dear, takes care of everything, however should there be something I have forgotten...'

'There is.' Regan's reply came quickly, the thought barely half formed. 'If my brother is to act as pageboy he will need the appropriate clothing.'

'Ah yes.' Huntley nodded. 'A school uniform would hardly serve the purpose. So my dear, what will you choose?'

'That depends entirely upon the choice of fabric the dressmaker will have. She may not have exactly what I want and that will involve sending away for materials.'

The ice which had glinted in his eyes during the whole of the conversation deepened visibly as Sherwyn Huntley shook his head. 'I trust there will be no need for that, my dear. I am sure you will find the dressmaker will already have available all that will be necessary.'

In other words she would take what was there. Regan knew he was aware of her attempt to gain time as she was aware that behind that bland mask Sherwyn Huntley was laughing.

'Perhaps.' She answered defiantly, refusing to allow the one thought which had come to be defeated before it was fully formed. 'But should that prove to be so we will still need time for the suit to be made.'

'Made or not the marriage will take place on the day I have arranged; there will be no further discussion on the matter.'

The ultimatum had been given. Regan's heart sank. It was not negotiable.

'*...think ... act for yourself...*'

Like a small voice the words said so long ago murmured plainly in her mind as if once more her father was instilling confidence, willing her to trust in herself. Rising from her chair, with a small nod of agreement, she said, 'With time so restricted then I should visit the dressmaker today.'

'I cannot escort you today, I have business which cannot wait.' Opening a drawer of the desk Huntley withdrew a sheaf of papers.

She could guess what business. Regan repressed the thought, answering tartly, 'That is my good fortune.' Then at the sharp lift of Huntley's head added, 'I shall take Ann with me. I trust you have no objection to my maid accompanying me.'

'You were with your mistress the whole of the time?'

Lips edged white with anger, eyes flaming like black torches, Sherwyn Huntley barked the question.

'Yes sir.'

'The *whole* of the time?' A fist hitting the desk added to the emphasis as Huntley glared at the trembling maid.

'I ... I stopped with 'er sir, just like you told me.'

'You are quite sure of that? Be warned, I will find out if you lie, and depend upon it the consequence should you not speak truthfully will be very hard for you.'

'I don't be lying, sir.' The girl met the cold threatening look then immediately lowered her gaze to the carpet.

No, she was not lying, she would not dare lie to him. Sherwyn Huntley swept a contemptuous look over the girl he had summoned to the study. No one in this house would risk the result any untruth would bring down on their head, yet still he must ask.

'Listen to me carefully.' He spoke more quietly but threat beat like a drum in every word. 'And answer even more carefully. You went with my stepdaughter to the town. You remained with her all of the time she spent in that dressmaker's shop and upon leaving those premises you returned immediately to Woodford?'

'No sir, beggin' of your pardon but that don't be right. The mistress an' me, we didn't come

54

back 'ome right off.'

This was what he wanted. Sherwyn Huntley's mouth tightened with satisfaction. This would confirm what he suspected. Every inch the Grand Inquisitor he stared a moment at the figure shuffling uncomfortably a few feet from his desk before saying, 'If you did not return straight away, then where did you go?'

Once more lifting her gaze, meeting that of her master, the girl replied unhesitatingly. 'Why to the glovemaker, sir. Miss Regan said o'course her brother would be needin' of new gloves so we called at that shop an' all while we was about it.'

The glovemaker! Huntley's fist drummed the desk, a hard tattoo of frustration. He had been so sure ... after all who else would have done it?

'Was that all?' The demand crashed like falling ice, causing the girl to shake noticeably.

'Yes sir, that were all, Miss Regan 'er said it were no use to call on the shoemaker for 'er were unsure as to the size of shoe Master Saul would be needin', said her would have to ask you to request his school to furnish that information.'

It seemed it had not been Regan's doing, but if not her, then who? Huntley's eyes narrowed as he looked at the girl.

'Will .. . will that be all, sir?'

The girl bobbed a nervous rapid curtsy, almost running from the room at the snapped dismissal.

'Why did Mr Huntley ask to see you?' Regan Trent's glance met that of the young woman turning now from folding freshly laundered linen into the drawers of a tall mahogany dresser.

'Reason we both knowed he would.' The maid's cheeky grin flashed. 'Asked had I been alongside o' you all o' the time we was gone from the 'ouse? Did I go everywheres you went?'

Regan had guessed the girl had been called to the study when Sanders, not Ann, had come to her room in answer to her summons. He had no knowledge of what the master wished to speak to Ann about, he had said in answer to her queries. But she had already known; what, other than wanting to know every detail of that outing, could be the reason for Huntley sending for her maid?

'Did ... did you tell him?' Regan's eyes followed the trim figure crossing to a wardrobe.

'O' course I did.'

Muffled by the gown she took from the wardrobe falling partly over her face the maid's reply brought a chill of disappointment to Regan. She had trusted Ann, trusted her to say nothing of what had gone on yesterday; she had believed her promise not to divulge their secret, yet that was what she had done.

Once the cream tulle gown had been laid carefully on the bed the maid turned to face Regan. '"You were with your mistress the whole of the time?"' Her mouth tight, her eyes glaring in perfect parody of the master of Woodford, she repeated his words. '"Be warned, I will find out if you lie ... you remained with her all of the time she spent in that shop and upon leaving those premises you returned immediately to Woodford?"' Well, I 'ad to answer, and knowin' 'im to be a man who don't take no heed to the harm he might cause to such as me, then I 'ad to say how, a'

56

beggin' of his pardon, that d'ain't be as how it was, that we called to another place after finishin' with the dressmaker.'

Regan tried to swallow her disappointment. But then Sherwyn Huntley was not a man to gamble with, one sliver of doubt as to what Ann said and he would root out the truth, fair means or foul it would be one and the same to Sherwyn Huntley; nor would he hesitate to put the girl from the house, to dismiss her without a reference. Like so many others dependent upon him for their living Ann could not risk that.

'It's all right, Ann.' The words had to be forced out. 'I realise you had to tell Mr Huntley the truth.'

Mr Huntley! Tidying brushes and combs on the dressing table Ann Searson missed none of the bitterness with which the name had been spoken. Sherwyn Huntley had married the girl's mother, he had become stepfather to both of Marcia Trent's children, yet no affection accompanied the relationship. Regan Trent despised the man who for the next year would rule her life. But would it be only a year? Fingers stilled, Ann gazed at the brush she held, its mother-of-pearl back gleaming in the light streaming in through the window. In spite of Edward Sanders' strict rule on gossip and eavesdropping, talk below stairs had it that Sherwyn Huntley was like not to want to share the running of Woodford Business Enterprises with Regan Trent, neither would he take happily to having control of that business passing completely out of his hands once Saul Trent attained his majority. Fancy words was them! Ann set the brush down. But fancy or no they was clear to 'er, they meant bein' old enough to manage your own affairs and that to Sherwyn Huntley was most like to be as a red rag to a bull. A whole year! Ann drew a slow breath. How much of that time would pass before this particular bull charged?

'Ann.' Regan spoke softly, seeing in the maid's short silence worry for the breaking of a promise. 'You must not feel badly, you had to tell Mr Huntley the truth.'

There it was again ... *Mister.* Ann Searson were not the only woman who disliked Huntley! A faint smile hidden inside, Ann turned, answering brightly, 'Oh I told 'im the truth all right, it were just I d'ain't tell 'im the all of it!'

'Not the all?' Regan frowned in puzzlement.

'No, miss. I answered truthful ... what was asked.' The maid's hidden smile became a giggle. 'I said as how we called at the glovemaker and that it were no use a' callin' at the shoemaker cos you d'ain't know your brother's size foot.'

'And?'

'An' nothin', miss.' Ann grinned. 'The master he d'ain't ask no more questions, an' me? Well, I d'ain't have to answer that which weren't asked, now did I?'

6

They had called nowhere else. The maid had been with Regan Trent the whole of the time she had been absent from the house, she had vouched her mistress had spoken with none but the dressmaker and the glovemaker. So who had contacted the head of that school? Who had arranged the boy's leaving? Fingers tapping the desk, Sherwyn Huntley stared angrily at the opposite wall. No one would presume! Nobody would dare! Yet someone had; someone had taken the boy. *'I have your letter here in front of me.'* The aggrieved tone of the headmaster's letter stared up from the page of heavy cream vellum, the bold strokes of each word seeming to add to the ire of their content. *'It quite clearly states you wish your earlier instruction be altered to comply with those contained within this second, and more relevant, communiqué, namely that the boy, Saul Trent, be put upon the train for Woodford on the twelfth day of this present month of June. The letter bears your signature. This request was duly observed with a senior member of my staff personally seeing him off at the station.'*

Bearing your signature! The words throbbed in Huntley's brain. Who was the author of that letter? His first thought had been Regan, but even had she dared write such it had not been sent from this house; of that at least he was certain for he assiduously checked all outgoing mail himself and

59

there had been nothing except envelopes bearing his own handwriting; they had included no second message to that school. A letter carried from the house to be posted elsewhere? Fingers continued to beat their tattoo of anger. Regan could have done that, written a letter in that room of hers then given it to that maid to send for her. She might even have carried it herself hidden in some pocket or other; it was not an impossibility. But she had visited no post office while on that outing to the dressmaker, for had she done then that fool of a maid would have said so, and as for forging his signature ... an inward shake of the head denied the suspicion. His stepdaughter had a will of her own but she would not dare go so far as that. A new thought, incisive as a razor, cut through the rest. Regan Trent had not been present when he had spoken of an incident possibly befalling her brother, she had not known. Who then had written that letter instructing that the boy be removed from his school? His eyes darkened, the hand drumming the desk curved into a hard fist. Only one person other than Sherwyn Huntley knew of that proposition. Myles Wentworth!

That had all gone rather well, better in fact than he had hoped. Myles Wentworth gazed admiringly at the figure reflected in a long mirror. It had been easy taking the boy, rather too easy. He smiled at the reflection. A man of his talents would rather have welcomed at least a small challenge, but there had been none, the boy had been handed over without the slightest hesitation. But then who would question so obviously respectable a fellow?

A handsome, cultured and above all intelligent fellow such as was Myles Wentworth. Self-praise added further depth to the smile. Whoever would suspect a gentleman of his standing?

'If I might suggest, sir, two buttons on the coat instead of three ... it would allow a slightly higher line of trouser to be seen, most becoming to a gentleman with a physique such as you are fortunate enough to possess.'

Flattery! His thought interrupted, Myles again studied the reflection. Flattery; but true none the less. He did possess an enviable figure. Arms outspread to each side while the coat was pinned back to the suggested line, he returned to thoughts of a moment ago.

The dealer had tried quibbling over the price. It was too high ... he would never get a customer to pay such a sum ... he would be out of pocket ... you can't expect a man to be out of pocket. He had trotted out all of the usual reasons for paying less than the asking price, and so the bargaining had gone on, the dealer complaining of a drop in the market, bemoaning the fact that trade wasn't what it had been a year or so previously, yet all the time his eyes had never strayed far from the young lad sitting in the corner of the dingy room. He should have tried harder to keep his glance from returning to the boy, but the softly curling hair and wide eyes, the face attractive as a girl's, had him already counting a profit he claimed he would not make. It was the threat of losing that profit which had brought the business to an end. Myles smiled at the picture arising in his mind. Apparently unconcerned at not securing a sale he had taken the boy by the arm, then turned for the door, saying over his shoulder he had another buyer eager to take the goods. That had the money appear quicker than a rabbit out of a magician's hat.

'There, sir.' After he had secured the pins the tailor stepped aside. 'Of course what we see does not have the refinement of the correctly tailored garment, but I think sir will agree that even at this stage the style proposed lends itself well to the figure. If I might be permitted...' With a light touch of the hand patting the drape of the coat more neatly into position the tailor stepped behind Myles to look at the reflection. 'It is of course a completely new style, but one very becoming to a gentleman as athletic in appearance as yourself, and I venture to say that once it is brought to the attention of cultured society it is bound to prove most popular, for as sir will have noticed the removal of one button lifts the line of the coat thus emphasising that of the leg, and the longer, narrower sweep of reveres, again very new, succeeds in drawing the eye to the waist and once more to the graceful line of a more closely fitting trouser. All in all it provides a picture of unmistakable elegance.'

With a price tag to match! Outside the shop Myles raised his silver-topped cane, then stepped into the hansom which had quickly answered his signal. But what had the price mattered? The money acquired from selling a boy had more than covered the cost of the clothing ordered from his favourite tailor. Leaning into the comfort of the upholstered carriage he smiled. The dealer had paid what was asked ... and he would pay again next time.

'I have received a communication from the headmaster of your brother's school.' Sherwyn Huntley's glance displayed nothing of the fury burning in him since reading that tersely worded letter. 'It informs me that in compliance with my own written instruction, Saul was placed on a train for Woodford on the twelfth of this month, that was three days ago.'

The sitting room which her mother's touch had graced with elegance and comfort seemed suddenly to close in on Regan. 'Three days!' Nerves quickening, she stared at the man in the winged armchair which had proved her father's favoured choice of seat. 'Then why is he not here?'

'That is precisely the question I ask myself.' Sherwyn Huntley's gaze remained even. 'Why, if he was put aboard the train, has he not arrived? My second question I put to you. Are you responsible for his disappearance?'

'Me!' Regan's fingers clenched and unclenched in her lap. 'How could I be? I have not seen my brother since Christmas last, when he was on holiday from school.'

Huntley's lips tightened. That was so yet one did not necessarily have to be face to face with someone one wished to remove from a particular place; that could be arranged in a variety of ways. 'Quite so,' he answered, 'yet you did call at your brother's school the day you supposedly visited only your dressmaker and glovemaker, is that not so?'

Had the maid told her of his further interrogation about the occurrences of that day? Had she gone to her mistress despite his warning her not to? Sherwyn Huntley's cold glance remained on the girl perched on the edge of a graceful Hepplewhite couch. Was the look of worry which had come so swiftly to that pretty face a dupe designed to have him believe she knew nothing of the boy's removal from school? Was it merely pretence? Still not entirely convinced she had played no part in that abduction he watched the colour drain from Regan's cheeks, the flash of sudden fear dart quickly in her eyes. If this was play-acting, it was very good. But then had he expected tears? A trembling denial in answer to his question? Or perhaps a fainting fit? There might have been one or all of those reactions, typical tricks employed by a woman caught out in deception. But Regan employed none of those feminine tricks. Instead her features and body displayed only fear.

'Ann?' Regan's voice shook on the words. 'Ann told you?'

'There was no need.' Sherwyn Huntley's long fingers lifted expressively. 'The letter I have spoken of tells me also that you were a visitor to the school on the afternoon of the day of your outing to your dressmaker. It also states you asked to take your brother from the premises so that you might indulge him in some small treat. That is so is it not? Ah, I see your eyes have answered for you, but that was not your sole intention, was it, my dear? You and that slut of a maid planned to run away taking the boy with you.'

'Ann!' Eyes wide in her blanched face, Regan met the ice-cold gaze. 'Where is Ann?'

'Where?' Huntley's hands lifted again, this movement one of dismissal. 'If she has any wit at all, which I most seriously doubt, then she will have followed my orders and left Woodford far behind, for as I told her, should she be here come morning she will never again be able to leave for anywhere. I will deal with her like any other vermin found on my property, destroy her in the fullest sense of the word.'

Across from him, Huntley watched Regan's anxiety become a blaze of anger, the fury of it spitting in her words 'That sense no doubt being some lethal accident! Is that also the reason for Saul not reaching home? What have you done to him! What have you done to my brother!'

'Done?' Frowning slightly, tight-lipped, Sherwyn Huntley faced the accusation. 'Why would you think I have done anything to Saul? He is my stepson, a boy I would safeguard with my own life.'

A boy he would safeguard with his own life! Staring into the cold impassive features of the man who had brought so much unhappiness into her life Regan felt all remaining fear of him melt in the furnace of anger.

'Why would I think you have done anything to my brother, to a stepson you would safeguard with your own life! Was that what you were doing with the young boy I saw you with here in this house, were you safeguarding him? Now I see *your* eyes answer for you. You are more than a liar, you are a menace. Listen, listen to your own words. "There are ways, we have simply to choose. Perhaps an accident while being brought

65

home from school, maybe a kidnapping resulting in the boy being found dead." Those are your words spoken to Myles Wentworth. Yes I heard your explanation of how my brother could be disposed of, how you could murder the stepson you would safeguard with your own life – you hypocrite! Saul's death will see me become sole inheritor of my father's estate and with my marriage to Myles Wentworth you will have it all. *That* is why I think you and no one else is responsible for my brother's disappearance, you want the inheritance but not the inheritors. Marriage brought you an easy living, one which you intend to maintain though murder be the only way, but I tell you, Mr Huntley, unless Saul is brought home alive and well you will get nothing, for I will not marry Myles Wentworth and regardless of what you might do to me I will see the world learns of your despicable behaviour.'

They had been careless. Behind a mask of complacency Sherwyn Huntley's thoughts seethed. That business of the boy should not have been discussed outside closed doors. The girl had overheard so who could say no other person might also have done so? Regan Trent would be no problem. The solution he held to her threat would ensure her silence and her cooperation for just as long as was necessary; but had anyone else overheard? If so, who? The maid Ann? Sanders? It could be any of the staff, any of whom might try their luck. Blackmail! Like a hammer blow the thought struck but no trace of its acid wake showed on the indifferent mask-like expression. Blackmail was a dirty business, one which did not always bring the desired result. But he could take no chances of being exposed, he would have to pay even though payment would be death!

'So you overheard.' Huntley's reply came smoothly, not a flicker of an eyelid of the faintest change of tone to hint at the thoughts which had raced in his mind. 'Then no doubt you will have heard the rest of what was said.'

'Yes!' Regan's stare blazed into granite-hard eyes. '"Doctors I consult will say what they are paid to say ... should it be Regan is not confined to a mental institution then she will follow the path taken by her mother..."'

Sherwyn Huntley smiled. 'You listened well, my dear.'

The hatred inside her forced Regan bolt upright, clenching her hands which wanted to strike that supercilious face. 'Yes!' she breathed from taut lips. 'Yes I listened well, and what I heard convinced me my suspicion as correct.'

'Suspicion!' Huntley raised an eyebrow. 'What suspicion might at be, my dear?'

'Suspicion that my mother did not take her own life ... that she was murdered and yours was the hand that did it.'

In the seconds of silence following the accusation Sherwyn Huntley drew his thoughts together. The son was gone where? The daughter was at the limit of endurance and any moment could blurt out that which would damn him in the eyes of society for the rest of his life. That he could not, would not, allow. The time to play his trump card was now.

'I congratulate you, my dear.' Voice like silk, he

smiled again. 'Perception is yet another of your attributes, and of course it is correct. Yes, I killed your mother, I gave her the poison which ended her life. It was not at all difficult to accomplish. I was her husband and so what more natural than that I should want to see my wife before retiring to my own bedroom? Every member of the household knew Marcia needed a little laudanum to help her sleep. What they did not, and will not, know is that I administered a little more. I went to her room after the house was settled for the night and there gave your mother a further dose, not of laudanum but of aconite, or as it is commonly termed "monk's hood". The plant grows quite liberally in the hedgerows and given its extremely poisonous qualities collecting sufficient for my purpose proved a simple enough task. After assisting my dear wife in the taking of the potion I had distilled from this most deceptively attractive little flower, all that remained was to dispose of the contents of the laudanum bottle and replace it upon her nightstand. So very simple yet so very effective. No one suspected anything other than suicide, no one, that is, except you, my dear.'

Though she had suspected her mother's death had not been self-induced, listening to that blatant confession to murder, watching the smile that revealed his self-congratulation, Regan's mind reeled. This man had killed her mother!

'Why?' It was a whisper.

'Why did I poison my wife?' He laughed, a sneer soft in his throat. 'Oh come now, my dear, you already know the answer to that. I could not take the risk of Marcia revealing my little peccadilloes just as I cannot risk your doing the same. No, I had to make certain my ... shall we say indulgences remained private, therefore...' he shrugged, 'Marcia had to be silenced, permanently.'

He had murdered her mother in order to shield himself! Killed her so she could never speak of the vile practice he took pleasure in, and Saul, had the man smiling so confidently at her also murdered him? But Saul knew nothing of what had gone on in this house, he had not been here when– The thought halted abruptly, her mind refusing to acknowledge the rest; he had been at school ... yet not every day – or night! There had been holidays, weeks when her brother had been at home. Had Saul seen? Too shocked to speak of it to anyone had he held the horror of it deep inside, or had some other horror made him draw into himself? She had not given much attention to his reticence following the last holiday, putting his quietness down to a reluctance to return to school. But had it been that? Or had it been something worse? She closed her eyes at the awfulness of the thought. Had Sherwyn Huntley found Saul knew his secret, had he threatened her brother also with death?

She gasped, 'Saul ... what has happened to Saul?'

'Another pointless question.' Huntley shook his head. 'Really, my dear, must you be so naïve?'

The very heartlessness of the look, the inexorability of those black obsidian eyes smiling contemptuously into her own steadied Regan's reeling mind. Rallying every atom of will she forced a stillness to her voice.

'Forgive me, Mr Huntley.' She spoke calmly though her fingers twisted agitatedly about each other. 'I will be more blunt. Is my brother also dead? Have you killed him as you killed my mother?'

It seemed for a moment he would not answer, then with a superficial laugh low in his throat the reply came. 'Yes, my dear, your brother is dead, though not in quite the same way your mother died. It was not myself carried out his murder.'

'But you were behind it, you ordered it!'

How come she was so calm? Did she know he was lying about the boy being dead? That he had no idea where Saul Trent was or who had withdrawn him from that school? Was she herself lying when she said she had no knowledge of her brother's sudden disappearance? Had she somehow managed to orchestrate it? Sherwyn Huntley ran rapidly through the minefield of possibilities. He could not as yet prove or disprove any of the questions posed by his mind; better then to play the charade through.

'Yes.' He nodded, giving an inconsequential shrug. 'I, as you put it, was behind your brother's demise. I admit I was not prepared for you visiting his school, that was very shrewd of you my dear, though unfortunately not quite shrewd enough, for as you found out I had forestalled any action you thought to take. In fact the boy was already dead before you got there.'

He had known Saul was dead! He had known that all the time! Shock acting like a brake on her senses Regan sat motionless, her eyes seeing yet not seeing, her brain empty and unmoving. Only

70

her heart felt alive, a heart screaming its pain.

'I see you are slightly confused.' Smiling, Huntley moved to sit beside Regan, placing a long-fingered hand over hers bunched together in her lap. 'You are asking yourself why, when I knew the boy to be no longer alive, did I ask if you were responsible for his being taken out of school; there is no great mystery, my dear, those questions were designed to have you believe your brother a victim of some unfortunate circumstance in which I played no part, the belief any magistrate will uphold. A young boy travelling alone is prey to an abductor, and when no word of him reaches us, no ransom note asking an amount in exchange for him, then the law can only presume a case of kidnap with intent to murder. However...' He pressed the tense fingers beneath his own. 'Since that was not your belief it seemed kinder to tell you the truth.'

Kinder! The trenchant cynicism of the smile, the mock-sympathetic touch of the hand cutting through the vacuum that was her mind, Regan's senses returned with the suddenness of an explosion.

'Kinder!' Eyes wide with blue fire, she jumped to her feet. 'You think it a kindness to tell me that in addition to murdering my mother you have had my brother killed! You call that kindness! Well I too can show kindness, Mr Huntley, I will show it twice: first by telling the world you are a lecher, an obscene defiler of children, and second that you are a murderer. The kindness of that will be having you hanged, make no mistake.'

Huntley was on his feet with panther-like

speed, his hand closing viciously on Regan's wrist, his eyes bottomless twin pits of venom. 'I make no mistakes, my dear,' he breathed through taut white lips. 'But you have, so now I must take steps to ensure you make no more!'

7

Wrapped in the cloak of night Woodford House lay in silence, its occupants sleeping. All except for one. Naked, her whole body quivering with sobs rising from deep within her, Regan Trent huddled on the floor of her room, a tiny island among silver streams of moonlight.

'No ... you have made the mistake...'

In the arid desert of a mind gripped with shock the voice of Sherwyn Huntley rasped like wind-blown sand.

'...you have made the mistake...'

'...you have made the mistake...'

Again and again the words grated against a brain too numb to resist and with each repetition Regan's bent head jerked as from a blow.

Beyond the window, its drapes left open to the night, a high moon drifted across a clear sky, its brilliance making the stars pale while beneath tiny puffs of cloud played hide and seek, casting a soft drift of shadows along the walls and over the garden.

'...you have made the mistake...'

The memory of the fierce jerk accompanying

the words snapped Regan's head back on her neck, the pain of it at last making itself felt among the frozen wastes of her senses. But she did not want to feel, she did not want to move, she did not want to live! Folded into herself she tried to fight off returning reality, to close her mind to the flood of memory, but still it came washing over her in icy waves.

He had gripped her wrist with one hand, the other striking her face, sharp stinging blows that rocked her head on her neck. Then he had hauled her behind him up the stairs and into this room.

'No one defies Sherwyn Huntley, that is a lesson you have long needed to learn and now I am going to teach it.'

Pain, physical now as well as mental, clawed at Regan yet still she remained unmoving, tightly curled against the horrors encroaching into a brain rapidly becoming alive to their nightmare.

She had tried to speak but another blow to the mouth had halted her words. Half-conscious, she had felt the tug tip her almost from her feet as he had snatched at her gown, ripping it from her shoulders.

'A woman is not my preferred choice of entertainment but for you, my dear, I make an exception.' It had been said with a laugh caught on a turbid breath, a corruption of sound, a cohesion of spite and lust as he had torn away the rest of her clothes. *'You should have kept your threats to yourself.'*

Trapped in the misery of memory Regan's arms tightened about her trembling body but the effort of barring the words from her brain proved futile.

'But then...'

The eyes devouring her body had become an obscenity, a dark glittering bestial stare empty of compassion. They had lifted, their look of pure lechery driving into her dazed mind, his breath rasping harshly as his hands closed on her upper arms.

'...had you done so I would not be enjoying the pleasure of this moment...'

'Please...' She had sobbed painfully through bleeding lips. 'Please...'

'Nicely asked, my dear.'

He had pushed her backwards from him, sending her sprawling across the bed, that same carnal laugh resonating in his throat; and all the while those raven eyes dancing with black flames of lust had watched her as slowly, a vile gloating obvious in every move, he had stripped away his own clothes.

'But it is too late for "please".'

He had stepped close to the bed...

Crouched in a puddle of silver moonlight Regan pressed her hands to her broken lips feeling nothing of their sting, nothing but the fear and revulsion she had felt those hours ago.

'Girls as well as boys have to be taught to obey, they have to know their master, and I, my dear, am your master...'

Late-afternoon sunlight had filled the room, golden fingers touching chair and table, blessing the dainty porcelain figurines on the mantelpiece with a soft warmth. But there had been no warmth in the look that had swept her, no tenderness, no compassion, only the venal exultation of the victor.

'*Yes, my dear ... your master, to do with you as I please, and this is merely a proof of that fact.*'

He had stepped even closer, his legs thrusting her own apart, then catching both wrists had pulled her to a sitting position, the jerking column of swollen flesh brushing against her mouth.

Folded into herself, wanting to merge with darkness and never come out again, Regan retched as she had retched then, felt the sickness rise to her throat as it had risen when with a slow swing of the hips he had slid that column back and forth over her lips, blood from her injured mouth trailing a line of scarlet across her face, while with lips clenched she had twisted her head in an attempt to avoid the touch of the throbbing flesh.

'*No my dear...*'

The low grating sound, half laugh, half growl, which had rolled in his throat, drummed again in Regan's mind. It was so real, so real! Lifting her hands to her ears she pressed tightly trying to stop the words, the laugh, yet still they came.

'*Not this way, no, with you I will take my pleasure the way I prefer.*'

With that he had snatched her to her feet in one rapid movement, twisting her about and flinging her back onto the bed. Face down on the coverlet she had tried to scream for help, but the pressure of a hand pushing her face into the cloth had prevented any sound except his harsh warning that a gag might add even more pleasure to his moment.

Seconds later she had felt the pain, pain without ease as he drove on and on and all the time that venomous laugh reverberated low in his throat, a laugh which became a harsh, strident animal cry, suddenly subsiding into a long drawn-out moan. Then she was free of him.

He had stepped away from her but though her body was released she remained unmoving, the quiet sounds of his dressing sending waves of fear jangling along her every nerve. Then the sounds had stilled. Face down on the bed, eyes tight shut against the horror of his assault, she had held her breath, sensing him come to stand once more beside the bed. Was it to happen again? Was he about to enter her again, to repeat that act of degradation?

'That was quite agreeable, my dear.'

Regan shrank even closer to the floor as though to escape the hand which had stroked her buttocks, as if in an effort to escape that which had followed. But there was no escape, there never would be any escape from the words now ringing in her brain.

'I might even say it was a pleasant deviation, and one which will most certainly be repeated.'

The stroking had gone on, fingers tracing from waist to bottom and on to the moist vee between her legs, Huntley's laugh coming thickly as she shrank from the touch.

'I shall recommend Myles try the same, though I doubt he will, his taste does not run to the pleasure of female bedfellows; but seeing your child will bear his name then fair play dictates he be given the opportunity; Oh yes, my dear, there will be a child, I shall make sure of that. Imagine the scandal then of refusing to marry Wentworth. I shall let it be known, discreetly of course, of your coming to my bed in the middle of the night, of how my brain, fuddled with

sleep, mistook you for my wife, of my mortification over what transpired. Think of that, Regan, a young girl seducing her own stepfather! Think of the shame of that before refusing to become Mrs Myles Wentworth!'

'Oh God!' A soft cry of pure pain whispered in the stillness, beams of silver touching the face lifted in despair. 'Oh God, help me!' She had cried those same words over and over as she had scrubbed at her body, washing again and again, trying to rid herself of the touch of his flesh; but no washing had taken away that feeling of revulsion, of sickening repugnance. It had stayed with her throughout the repeated scrubbings and it was with her still: it always would be.

'Mrs Myles Wentworth!

Her mind revolting at the thought, Regan pushed herself to her feet, the ache of muscles kept too long in one position drowned by the pain in her mind. She couldn't! She couldn't marry that man knowing what she did!

'...there will be a child...'

A child! A bastard child! 'Oh God!' The cry stifled between clenched lips was siren-loud in her brain.

'...I shall make sure of that ... most certainly be repeated...'

Huntley would commit the same crime again and then again for as many times as it took until she became pregnant. And after that?

'...I might even say it was pleasant...'

Regan shuddered. So pleasant he would continue in that abuse even though she became Myles Wentworth's wife? But hadn't he said a woman was not his preferred choice of entertainment? Hands twisted together Regan watched luminescent silver beams criss-cross the room, radiant children of the moon playing tag with the shadows, but she saw only the cold dark eyes of the man who had raped her. Yes, he had said that, but then Sherwyn Huntley had said so many things which had proved to be lies. He had said he loved Marcia Trent, then had killed her. He had professed to care for Saul as tenderly as for any son of his own, then had arranged the boy's murder; and herself, a stepdaughter he declared he wished only to protect, he had raped in order to force her into a marriage she did not want. It was a crime he would repeat if only for the satisfaction of degrading her. But rape did not provide Huntley's ultimate satisfaction: that would come only with her death and the transfer of every penny of her inheritance into his hands.

Below, from the hall, the chime of a long-case clock drifted through the darkness of the silent house, floating up the staircase and sounding at each door before passing on; but the sonorous ring did not come alone. Its warning chased thought from her head while at the same time adding fresh frissons of fear to nerves strung taut as wire. Regan held her breath.

Yes, there! Her teeth bit painfully into lips swollen and bruised, her ears strained to catch every nuance of sound. There! Regan's nerves screamed and a sob escaped her. There again, a half second behind the fading resonance, a brush of sound ... the brush of fingers against her door.

He had threatened to repeat what he had done that afternoon, he was here to carry out that threat! Heart hammering in her chest Regan stood transfixed. He had come to rape her all over again! Bunched fingers repressing the scream of mounting fear, she stared towards a door lost in shadow. The key! She should turn the key! But he had taken it with him when he left, had locked the door saying she would not leave her room until the day of her wedding.

Perhaps if she screamed it would wake the household, others would hear, Mr Sanders would come. For a moment hope flared but as quickly died. Huntley would declare he had dashed to her room thinking an intruder had entered the house but it was no more than a bad dream, a nightmare.

Aided by a capricious flick of a chasing moonbeam Regan's stare found the door handle, watched it begin slowly to turn before again it was swallowed by shadow. This was her living nightmare, one that would go on and on.

The final strains of the clock chime had died away into silence, the faint brush against the door had stopped. Forced to breathe Regan gasped against the tightness in her lungs. Why did he not come in? Was this some new mental torture Huntley had concocted to further his sadistic pleasure? Why? It was not that he could see her fear while he stood out there. But Sherwyn Huntley would not need to see, he would know the horror was designed to build slowly until his victim cried for mercy; only then, with this appetite for evil momentarily appeased, would he stop.

'Please.' Unaware she had spoken what was in

her heart Regan continued to murmur in a whisper, the soft words barely penetrating the silence. 'Please don't let me scream, don't let me give him that satisfaction.'

Moments became seconds, seconds became eternity, an eternity of waiting, until unable to bear the tension Regan fell to her knees with her face pressed into her hands, another soft cry for help escaping through her fingers. It was then the Fates listened. High above the house a resplendent moon bathed the earth with a flood of light. Silver-gold, it swept through the window of Regan's room, shimmering over furniture, gleaming on fabric, irradiating every corner, its lustrous glory touching a kneeling figure, stroking the naked body with soft translucent tenderness. Was it a sign from the Fates with no time to listen longer? There was no telling, yet at that instant Regan raised her head, her glance fastening on the door painted with the brilliance of moonlight. Her brain almost numb from fear she stared uncomprehendingly. Then she realised. The handle was no longer turning! Had Huntley tired of his game or was this a furtherance of it? Breath sucked into her throat, afraid that even the removal of her hands from her face would somehow become known to the man standing at the other side of her door, Regan remained motionless, the dance of her pulses the only movement of a body still trapped by fear. Then a further prance of moonbeams caught her attention, directing it over the linen-panelled carving of the door, down to the carpet where, clearly displayed in tinsel brightness, lay a sheet of white paper.

8

Still gripped by fear Regan stared at the tiny patch. Faint against the expanse of carpet, it lay barely visible in the dimness of the room suddenly deserted by a fickle moon.

Who had pushed it under her door? What was written on it? Shivering as much from tension as from the chilled night air she sought answers in her mind. It had to be Sherwyn Huntley, no other person in the house would write to her. Yet whey had he not come into the room? Question countered answer. Was this another of his sadistic pleasures? Had making the threat of rape written as well as spoken afforded him extra satisfaction?

She would not read it! She would not even pick it up! It would lie there until he returned to this room and picked it up himself!

A quick surge of defiance along her veins released senses fear had rendered almost powerless, Regan's thinking became more logical.

Huntley had the key to her room. Given his detestable mind he would not have remained outside it, would not have left a note for her to read in private; he would have wanted to witness that reading for himself, to see the humiliation his words would produce. He had the only key, so why had he not used it? The thought broke as, like a shaft of light, another flashed across her brain, one that had Regan catch her breath. No one but Huntley had the means of entering her room. Yet he had not! No one save Huntley would write her a note. But he would not forgo the self-indulgence of watching her read it! Perhaps her assumption that he was the one responsible was incorrect. With a tight sob, Regan stared at the small pale patch.

Had she been wrong? Would someone other than Huntley send that note? Ann? But Ann was gone. Mr Sanders? Yes, he might have. But to tell her what? Was that note a message concerning her brother? Hope becoming a desperate need to know, Regan ran to where the sheet of paper showed in the dimness, snatched it up and carried it to the window.

It was no use. Twisting the paper, trying to distinguish the words she could see written on it yet could not read in the poor light of a rapidly clouding sky, frustration tingled in Regan's veins. She could not wait for dawn, for a new day to afford light enough by which to read the note; she had to read it now.

But someone had delivered this letter, someone other than herself had been, perhaps still was, awake in the house. Anyone standing even now in the corridor beyond her door would not know she was reading it, but should that person have gone into the garden they would notice if she lit her table lamp.

Slowly, her heart beating rapidly for fear of making a sound, Regan drew the heavy drapes across the window.

It did not speak of Saul. It made no mention of her brother. Disappointed, Regan read the words through again. Clear, precise, written in a neat strong hand, each word correct in its spelling, the one sentence they formed stared blackly from the lamp-illuminated paper.

One sentence! Hope which a moment before had flared with vivid life became a lifeless weight pulling her with it into despondency. One sentence which conveyed nothing, which told her nothing! What senselessly cruel trick was this? What had the writer hoped to gain by playing it? Dejection gave way to disgust; she threw the letter aside. She had been right after all, this was one more scurrilous act perpetrated by a despicable man.

She had so wanted the note to concern Saul, to tell her he was alive, that what Huntley had said of having him murdered was yet another of the man's lies. But that had not been realised, nor the endless prayer in her heart that her brother would be brought back to Woodford safe and sound. That hope was dead, as her mother was dead ... as Saul also was dead.

She must face the truth! A wave of coldness engulfing her, Regan trembled. Sherwyn Huntley was her guardian. For a year more he was as much her master as he was master of his servants. But where a member of the household staff of Woodford could end their term of service, where they could leave this house, its daughter could not; she was trapped here, held under lock and key, a prisoner in her own home. Huntley held undisputed sway over her life, he could use her as he wished and when he no longer derived satisfaction from his cruelty, when her father's wealth and business was safely in his grasp so his need of her no longer existed, he would, as with an animal past its use, have her killed. But wouldn't that be a relief? Death would bring freedom from his threats, it would end the odium of being forced to live alongside a man she detested; it would bring release from that terrible promise. Rape! It snatched at her, gripping her throat. Rape! It rang in her brain. Rape! It shouted in her mind, the roar of it beating along her veins, crashing against her ears until with a cry she sank onto the bed.

Cold which had numbed her brain now revived it. Her body cramped with being huddled tight against itself, Regan shivered, only then realising she was still naked. Rejecting the idea of a nightdress she reached for her clothes, then drew her hand back. They were the clothes he had touched, those he had ripped from her; they were clothes she would never wear again. Mouth set tight, holding off memory hovering at the edge of her mind, she crossed to the wardrobe.

'Pick from the cupboard of flowers.'

Regan felt the tears rise. Her mother had often used those words, saying her daughter looked so pretty she must have picked a gown from a cupboard of flowers.

Regan's hand stilled against the dress she reached for. Her mother's words, the words written on that paper! But why would Huntley have chosen to write that particular expression? To taunt her? To remind her of the happiness of childhood? Childhood! Memory surged. Her mother had not said those words since ... when? Regan stood, gown in hand, while she racked her brain.

There had been so much, sorrow following the death of her father, the long months of mourning; then had come Sherwyn Huntley. Regan gasped at the sudden light of clarity. Her mother had not once used those words after the death of Jasper Trent! She had not once spoken them in the presence of Huntley; yet he had written them on that paper.

She could have been mistaken. Regan hesitated. Her vision could have been blurred with tears, she could have read something she *wanted* to see rather than what was really written. Across the room the sheet of paper gleamed in the light of the bedside lamp. After hesitating a moment longer she picked it up.

Pick from the cupboard of flowers.

She had not read wrongly. Regan stared at the note held in shaking hands. Her mother's words. She held the paper closer to the lamp. The letters were neat, the writing strong and clear yet something did not sit easily. Then she realised; the note she held had not been penned by Sherwyn Huntley, whose handwriting she had so often seen on letters laid out for the morning post. So whose handwriting was it?

Who else could have heard her mother's smiling words? And why choose to write them now? Regan shivered as she turned again to the wardrobe.

The question returned again and again, each answer rejected as Regan dressed. Saul? Had that note come from him? No, his writing was not yet the sure hand of an adult. Ann then? No, no that was not feasible, the girl could not place herself in danger of being caught by Huntley simply to deliver a note, especially when that note made no sense at all.

Who? The question buzzed in her brain like a persistent fly, plaguing, eluding all effort to brush it aside. Why? Regan gazed past her reflection in the dressing-table mirror letting it rest once more on the sheet of paper lying on her bedside table. Of course! At the base of her throat a pulse beat rapidly. It could only have come from him!

'What do you mean by that?' Sherwyn Huntley's angry glance swept from a letter he was reading to the man standing a few feet from the wide-topped desk.

'Just what I have said.'

Huntley's grasp had tightened on the paper, his eyes repeating the warning signalled by the grip of tense fingers, a warning that no respect was offered in that reply, none of the deference expected from a paid menial.

Seated in a hansom driving him to the railroad station Edward Sanders' thoughts returned to that moment. He had never held respect for Sherwyn Huntley, and as for deference that would never be observed again. He had remained as butler to that man for one reason only, but with Marcia Trent's death that reason had been removed. So why had he not left Woodford immediately? Why stay at that house for as long as he had? The thought followed his glance across wide fields clothed with wheat, the yellow heads swaying to the music of a gentle breeze sighing among heavily leafed branches of trees decked in the greenery of summer, a thought which demanded an answer. Why had he stayed when his love was gone? For the sake of her children, for the daughter and the son. But he could do no more for them.

'Station, Mr Sanders.'

The hansom had drawn to a halt, its driver already placing a travelling box on the roadside.

'Thank you.' Edward Sanders' smile held a genuine warmth as he alighted from the carriage.

'We be a' goin' to 'ave the missin' of you Mr Sanders sir, bless me if we ain't.' The cabbie shook his head. 'I were a' sayin' of my Bess only t' other day, Edward Sanders be the only true gentleman along o' Woodford 'ouse, an' now you be a' goin'. It be a cryin' shame an' I don't 'ave no carin' of who might hear the sayin' of it; it were a bad day that there 'Untley set foot inside that 'ouse.'

A bad day! Handing several coins to the man who made again to carry the box, Edward bent to pick it up himself, using the moment to hide the look which had come to his eyes. So it had proved for Marcia Trent, and for Edward Sanders.

'You journey safe to wherever it be you're goin' Mr Sanders.' The cabbie touched a finger to the cap worn low on his brow. 'God willin' we might 'ave the seein' of you again.'

'God willing.' His reply partially submerged beneath a blast of steam and the shrill sound of a whistle, Edward turned for the station and ran onto its one platform, throwing box and self into the second-class compartment whose door was held for him by a stationmaster chuckling something about 'the skin o' the teeth'.

Placing his box on the overhead luggage rack he sank onto a seat of the compartment breathing a prayer of thanks for its being empty. Few of the village folk ventured far from Putley and those who did most certainly did not journey by train, viewing the money it cost as extravagant waste when a farm cart or carter's wagon would serve equally well, albeit the time taken would be longer; and as for Huntley and his like, they would travel in nothing less than first class so Edward Sanders was unlikely to be observed by anyone who might recognise him. Relaxed at the thought he settled more comfortably in his seat. Yet even so, Edward Sanders would stay in his second-class compartment.

'*What do you mean there was no reply!*'

Edward's thoughts returned again to that scene in the study, Sherwyn Huntley's snapped words seeming one with the clipped rhythm of the train wheels passing over the points. Huntley's expression had held traces of accusation as he had looked up from a letter he had been reading.

'*I mean that Miss Regan gave no answer to my knock.*'

'*Has she been served breakfast?*'

Clever! Edward remembered the smile which had almost surfaced. That was Huntley's way of finding out if there was a key to that bedroom other than the one held by *himself*.

'*A tray was taken up.*' His reply was smooth. '*But with Miss Regan's room being locked it could only be left outside her door. It was still there when I went to tell her you wished to see her in the study.*'

'*Very well.*' Huntley had taken his gold pocket watch from his waistcoat, a glance at the clock on the stone fireplace confirming the time. '*If my stepdaughter has not come downstairs in one hour you will repeat my message to her.*'

'*I will not be in this house in one hour's time, I am leaving Woodford.*' Edward savoured the words as he had savoured them when speaking. They had been like wine on his tongue.

Huntley had replaced the watch in the pocket of his waistcoat, a deliberately drawn-out process, then without even glancing at Edward had snapped harshly, '*You will leave Woodford when I choose!*'

It had been obvious Huntley had seen that terse reply as the end of conversation, that he had expected his servant, duly reprimanded, to return meekly to his duties. But he had thought wrong. Eyes closing, Edward allowed his thoughts to run on.

'*Your days of dictating what I may or may not do, of choosing what or how, are over.*' Said quietly, over a head already bent once more to the letter, his remark caused Huntley's fist to slam down on the desk, the ferocity of it jangling ink wells in their brass containers. Almost slowly as when returning the watch to his pocket Huntley had lifted his glance, eyes black as winter ice snapping with the malevolence of Arctic wolves.

'*Are you aware...*'

'*I am very much aware...*' Edward's own eyes had glittered frost, his lancet-sharp response cutting off Huntley's question. '*Aware of all that has gone on, is going on in this house; now you be aware, should any harm befall Regan Trent, or her brother, then you will answer for it.'*

'*You dare to threaten me!*'

Acid had spewed in that exclamation, the hand holding the letter crumpling the paper into a ball. It had been an action devised to bring fear to a servant dependent upon a master for his living, to bring about an abject apology followed by a servile withdrawal. That was the second time Huntley had thought wrongly; but whatever the man had expected his look on hearing the reply had proved it not to be the answer he had actually received.

Beyond the window of the train, fields of crops gave way to meadow, cattle grazing on velvet-soft grass turning to look at the train as its steam whistle disturbed the peaceful stillness, but Edward heard only his own quiet reply to Sherwyn Huntley.

'*You might think of it as a threat. I however view what I say as advice, advice I now repeat. Should you wish the activities of yourself and your friend Wentworth to remain a secret then take care no harm befalls Regan Trent or her brother.*'

He had left Woodford an hour later.

9

She had remained in that room more than twenty-four hours. Sherwyn Huntley consulted his pocket watch. She had not emerged from the moment he had dragged her there, since their shared pleasure.

Replacing the watch he smiled to himself. Shared was hardly the description Regan Trent would place upon it, but then what did her feelings or any woman's count for? He patted the pocket holding the watch. For Sherwyn Huntley a woman's feeling mattered less than naught. Regan Trent had taken no food or liquid unless she had drunk water already in her bedroom. The cook had reported, 'Miss Regan, her don't be tekin' of 'er meals.' But then how could a tray be taken when that door was locked and he alone could open it? He alone! Reaching for the decanter of claret set beside him on the supper table, Sherwyn Huntley's smile registered satisfaction. That was how it would be for the rest of the short period he intended Regan Trent should live. Of course she would become Wentworth's wife, but like the woman he married Myles Wentworth was of little consequence; he also, should it prove necessary, would be dealt with accordingly.

'You say she has not left her room since yesterday, does that not concern you?' His own glass filled, Myles Wentworth squinted through the delicate glass admiring the deep rich colour of the wine.

Huntley sipped slowly then replaced his glass on the table before answering. 'Concern me ... why should it?'

Above the glass held now to his mouth, Myles Wentworth regarded the other man blandly. 'Well,' he shrugged, 'I mean, if she hasn't eaten...'

'I have ensured trays have been taken up to her,' Huntley interrupted. 'If she refuses to allow them into her room, if she refuses to eat then there is no one to blame except herself.' Huntley reached again for his glass. What he had not told the man sitting opposite was that he had not unlocked that door, and while he held the key then neither could anyone else.

'Perhaps we should ask her to join us.'

Huntley shook his head. 'Not at present, we have business to discuss, business best concerning no other ears.' With an impassive wave of one hand while the other reached for the decanter, Wentworth uttered an apathetic, 'Not tonight, I'm not in a mood for business tonight.' This brought a sharp rebuff from his host.

'Tonight, or any night I choose! Remember Myles, your very comfortable style of living depends upon my goodwill.'

This bastard had ordered him around long enough! However, all things had an ending, and this relationship would have *its* ending; but not yet. Myles Wentworth swallowed slowly. Not quite yet!

'Oh I remember.' His equable reply concealed a riled mind. 'But then you should also remember your own dependence, should I refuse to wed the delightful Regan.'

'Then someone else will!' It snapped across the table, ringing against delicate glass.

'Mmmm.' Wentworth nodded but the amiable smile forced to his mouth hardly compensated for the glint of irascibility darkening his eyes. 'I imagine you will find someone to play your game; but what of that other game, the one you are so fond of? Will they play that also? But that takes me from the point in question about your remembering your own dependence. It is a fragile thing, a thing

92

it would take no more than a word to shatter.'

Each movement slow and deliberate, Sherwyn Huntley took a cigar from a silver humidor. Clipping the end, lighting it with a match he then flicked toward the fireplace, he sucked deeply, tasting the flavour of tobacco on his tongue before exhaling a cloud of lavender-grey smoke.

'Dependence, as you say, is fragile.' He smiled through the faint haze, a poisoned smile, the smile of a serpent. 'But then, my dear Myles, so is life, that too can be so easily destroyed.'

As he had destroyed Edward Sanders? Huntley felt the ache of his clamped jaw. That man also had hinted at exposing him. It was a risk he should have ended there and then ... an accident while cleaning a pistol! No one would have questioned, yet as it was Sanders had left. But it was not too late, the man could be found and when he was he would be eliminated as would anyone standing in the way of Sherwyn Huntley.

Myles drank again. No smile could hide the warning implied in Huntley's words: their warning of death. But death carried a two-edged sword, one of which could as easily strike Huntley.

'But then you understand all about the fragility of life, do you not, Myles?' Huntley returned to the conversation. 'How one must be made to serve another? The weaker sacrificed to benefit the stronger? Which returns me to the question of business. But that will be discussed more privately in my study.'

Bloody business! Myles Wentworth scowled moodily. That had been the last thing on his mind when accepting the invitation to visit Woodford

House; he had thought more along the lines of a quick supper then the pair of them whiling away the rest of the night in the delightful confines of Mrs Langley's establishment in Worcester. His mood darkening rapidly, Myles followed his host into the study immediately helping himself from the decanter he had carried with him.

From where he had gone to stand before the stone fireplace, Sherwyn Huntley watched the younger man swallow a generous mouthful of wine. Myles Wentworth was a handsome man; his cultured background held a positive appeal for prospective clients, and when not the worse for drink, his wit and charm proved a definite advantage. But handsome is as handsome does! The adage lingered in Huntley's mind. Looks and charm were positive attributes but they were of use only so long as they served a profitable purpose.

'Well!' Slumped into a winged leather armchair, a refilled glass in hand, Myles Wentworth was churlish. 'What business is so important it cannot wait?'

'The business of Saul Trent. What have you done with him?'

Saul Trent? Several glasses of fine claret had made Myles Wentworth's reaction a little slow. Saul Trent! Why was Huntley asking about him? Wasn't it the sister he was having problems with? Wine rolling over his tongue, Myles took time for his brain to catch up. The girl was here in the house and the boy at school.

'I asked, what have you done with Saul Trent?'

Though quietly put the interruption left little doubt as to the ill humour provoking his question. But what was the cause of this interrogation? The snatched seconds benefited his brain; Myles's thinking clarified, his churlish mood evaporated allowing a more efficient concentration to take its place. Huntley had wanted the boy dead, he wanted no prospect of his ever returning to lay claim to Woodford and all that went with it; but sold instead of slaughtered! That one chance, slender almost to extinction, had nevertheless existed.

'What have I done with him?' Myles played his cards carefully.

Black ice in a frozen face, Sherwyn Huntley's eyes regarded his guest, the reply cracking across the room seeming to resound through the silent house. 'That *is* what I said!'

Careful, Myles! His own eyes now reflected an indolent smile, masking the attention sharpening in his mind. Wentworth followed the path of caution. Quietly, giving no hint of his mounting interest, he laughed. 'You wanted him out of your hair, didn't you?'

There were several people he wanted out of his hair and this asinine coxcomb was one of them! Long and slow, Huntley's exhalation was a song of irritation. He would like that particular job done now but it would have to wait a little longer; postponed but not renounced; most certainly not renounced!

'As you say,' he answered, watching the other man twist the stem of the glass between long, expertly manicured fingers, 'I wanted him out of my hair–'

'So what's the problem?'

The interruption threatened to ignite the fire of anger in Huntley. Dousing it with an indrawn breath he answered curtly. 'The problem is a letter sent to the boy's school requesting he be put on the train for Woodford; a letter signed with my name, a signature forged by you, correct me if that is not so.'

'Naughty of me I admit.' Wentworth smiled disarmingly. 'Did it on the spur of the moment, should have spoken to you first old chap; but the damn ruse worked, didn't it; I mean nobody suspected.'

No, no one had suspected. The boy had been put aboard the train with no questions asked. But he had questions to ask. Watching the slender hands play with the wine glass, hands which had never known a day's labour, the acid of contempt bit deep in Sherwyn Huntley, something he made no effort to keep from showing in his next words. 'It was thoughtless, but then logical thinking has always been beyond you.'

My ... my! Spiralling the glass, Myles appeared to admire the myriad points of colour exploding from the deep red contents, yet he realised the true fireworks were those exploding in Huntley. The master was annoyed. The thought provoked a laconical smile. But then that was not exactly earth-shatteringly new.

'It proved most embarrassing!' Huntley snapped. 'A second letter arriving on the heels of one I had written only a few days previously had me looking like I didn't know my own mind!'

Ahh, the so-competent Mr Sherwyn Huntley had been made to look a little less competent!

That was the source of his annoyance, the star of his efficiency had been ever so slightly dimmed. That was a wound indeed; one which gave so much satisfaction in the delivering.

'Sorry.' He held the glass a little higher, a motion of atonement.

'So why did you do it?'

Mouth pursing, Myles Wentworth contemplated the snapped question.

'I mean taking the boy from the train! Wasn't that risky, had you been seen, if someone had recognised you!' Impatient with the seeming apathy to answer, Huntley snapped again. 'Bloody thoughtless Wentworth, totally bloody thoughtless!'

'But I wasn't seen.' Myles shrugged affably. 'You have not been approached by anyone claiming to have seen me take the boy, have you?'

Less affable, his answer a grudging 'no', Huntley moved to sit in a replica of the chair Wentworth lounged in.

'There you are then.' Myles refilled his glass, then swallowed half the contents with a satisfied gulp, and went on. 'You've been chewing on a bone when there was no need; waste of energy, my friend, now what say we adjourn to Mrs Langley's?'

Not yet content that he had been told all there was to tell, Huntley shook his head at the suggestion. First things first; play could come later.

'Did the boy object to leaving the train before it reached Woodford?' A sudden doubt followed the question; Huntley leaned forward in his chair, his glare fastening on the man sipping wine as if it was his last chance to do so; which it might well be should the answer to the next question prove the wrong one. Lips tight, he said, 'You did leave that train prior to its reaching here?'

Waving a languid dismissal of the query Myles subdued his flourishing displeasure. Huntley took him for a fool, but then there was no fool like an old fool and Huntley had the seniority!

'Of course.' The answer deceptively serene, he returned a look of composed assurance. 'I made out it was nothing short of coincidence we should both be on the same train, both bound for Woodford House. The lad was a little reticent at first, but when I suggested a detour by way of Ross-on-Wye would afford the opportunity for him to acquire a gift for his sister and also a pleasant meal at some hotel bordering the river, he agreed right away.'

'And where is he now?'

Where indeed? Myles emptied his glass into his throat before answering. 'That you should not know. What you wished has been done; should enquiries be forthcoming then you can answer, in all honesty, that you have no knowledge of why Saul Trent was not on the train when it pulled into Woodford, and that you have no idea of his whereabouts. Now, Sherwyn, I am off to visit Mrs Langley and her delightful entourage, something I suggest you also should do.'

The note could only have come from one person. Regan glanced again at the paper left on her bedside table while she dressed. One other person who could have been present when her mother had said those words, one man who could have heard her say 'picked from a cupboard of flowers'. Mr Sanders! It had to be Mr Sanders! But why choose to write that? Was it meant to comfort, to tell her she had a friend here still at Woodford? No. An involuntary shake of the head dismissed the idea. He would have no need to assure her on that point; what then? What was that message meant to tell her?

'Pick from a cupboard of flowers.'

The words imprinted like a brand on her mind, Regan had no need to read them again.

Repeating like the chorus of a song it trilled in her brain until she wanted to cry out, pick what? The wardrobe holds nothing but clothes and I have already taken a dress! Breath held, Regan tried to sort through the torrent of thoughts, to separate reason from emotion.

It was more than an attempt to comfort her. Regan grasped at logic. An instruction ... written as it was, using the word 'pick' rather than 'picked' so not a perfect quotation of her mother's words, the note could be an instruction. But to do what? Frustration made her utter a sob. What did it want her to do?

'Think, Regan...'

Across the space of time other words reached out, another voice whispering in her mind, the much-loved voice of her father.

'Think, my clever little girl...'

Soft, gentle, reassuring it played like the waters of a brook, soothing, easing.

'Listen to advice, weigh it carefully in your mind then act for yourself.'

That note was advice, it was saying to pick something from the 'cupboard of flowers'. That surely meant to imply there was something other than clothing in that wardrobe. If indeed that note had come from Mr Sanders, and she was certain now it had, then he was telling her to search. Carrying the lamp across the room she set it carefully on the floor beside the tall cupboard.

She had felt in every pocket of every dress. Some ten minutes later, dispirited at finding nothing, Regan sank to the ground, her shoulders slumping with disappointment. Whatever she might have been intended to find she had failed.

'*Think.*' It seemed the voice of her father spoke again. '*Flowers are a product of a garden, they are not the soil, not the ground, not the all.*'

Not the ground! Not the all! Warmed by hope, Regan rose quickly. Dresses were something housed within the wardrobe, they were not the wardrobe itself. That was what she was meant to do, to search the fabric of the wardrobe itself. Swiftly she ran her hands over shelves, her fingers probing every corner. Nothing! Choking on tears of despair she stared at an interior she had stripped of clothing, of hatboxes, of every last shred. She had felt in every part of that cupboard. She stared at the wardrobe gleaming in the mellow light of the lamp set beside it on the floor. No, she had not run her hands over every part of it. She had not felt above the inside of the door.

10

An evening at Mrs Langley's! The prospect was pleasing. Sherwyn Huntley nodded agreement to Myles's proposal. The fact that Wentworth had taken it upon himself to write to that school had angered him, but it had gone by with no serious consequence, and Wentworth had dealt with the problem of the boy. Following the younger man from the study, Huntley breathed satisfaction. The problem of Saul Trent was no more. The police of course had been informed of the boy's failure to come home. 'A boyish prank.' The local constable had smiled assurance. 'He'll sharp be 'ome once he be 'ungry.' That had almost had him smile in return; Saul Trent would never know hunger; Saul Trent would never know anything ever again for the dead don't feel. In the event he had restrained the smile, adopting the seriously worried mien of a loving stepfather. Loving! That did raise a smile, a sly voracious twist of the mouth quickly banished as Myles Wentworth turned from entering the hall. Saul Trent, like his mother, had never been loved by Sherwyn Huntley. They had been stepping stones to a fortune, stones which had been removed after he had stepped over them, as Regan Trent would be removed.

Regan Trent! He glanced at the staircase. He should go to that room, see that food was taken in to her, warn her that obstinacy was not going to be of any use.

'Are you coming? We've wasted half the evening already, I don't intend wasting what's left of it!'

As Myles Wentworth's petulance registered, a discordant note sounded in Huntley's thoughts and he glanced to where the man stood, already halfway to the door leading from the house.

'I was thinking to speak with Regan.'

'Speak!' Wentworth laughed coarsely. 'Or is it that other pastime you have in mind ... saving yourself the cost of paying for your entertainment, is that it? Well you amuse yourself as you wish, Huntley my friend, I prefer the delights of Mrs Langley's house.'

Had entertaining himself with Regan Trent been somewhere in his mind? Had he subconsciously intended to rape her again using the taking of food to her room as an excuse for going there?

'You have already availed yourself!' Myles Wentworth's vulgar laugh vanished, a look of surprise taking its place. 'I would not have expected that, seeing your preference leans the other way, but then...' he shrugged, '...variety is the spice we might all enjoy should we taste of it.'

'Not that you intend to taste of it!'

'True Sherwyn, true.' Myles Wentworth ignored the acid of Huntley's response. 'But then why spoil the palate with a dish you have no real desire for? However I would like to know why you decided to taste of it.'

Huntley glanced again at the staircase and when his look returned to the other man it was hard as black stone. 'Necessity!' he said, the word grating between lips barely parted. 'Regan Trent needed to be reminded who was master in this house; also she needs to be pregnant.'

'Needs! I don't quite follow you, Sherwyn. Regan *needs* to be pregnant?'

No, he wouldn't understand! Disdain thick in his throat, Sherwyn Huntley surveyed his partner. Wentworth understood no needs other than his own, those of having money enough to maintain an expensive style of living, and to indulge his passion for pretty young bedfellows. Nostrils drawn tight with irritation, concerned the conversation might be overheard, Huntley threw a swift look in the direction of the servants' quarters. It was unlikely anyone would venture into this part of the house unless summoned, but without Sanders to keep his eye on the others. . . Sanders! The name rang like an alarm bell. He really must have the man found and then got rid of permanently.

'So!' Myles Wentworth's gross laugh issued again. 'Do I get an explanation, or is the truth of Regan's *need* simply that it is *your* need?'

Coming from lips which might have been painted by Botticelli, a face Michelangelo could have carved, the coarse smile following that laugh was strangely out of place, but the look in those deeply attractive hazel eyes was not. The look of the devil. Huntley breathed through locked teeth. It was entirely in accord with the nature of the man whose whole posture was a sneer. And like the devil, Myles Wentworth would have you dance to his tune.

'The truth, Myles,' he answered, ice crisping each word, 'the truth is, Regan Trent refuses point blank to marry you, and as you are – or should be

– aware, without that marriage her entire inheritance is lost to us. Getting her with child is the only certain way of forcing her into marriage, but you, my friend, could not be trusted to do that; therefore I have to be prepared to do it for you.'

'How very kind!'

'Isn't it.' Huntley ignored the sarcasm while his own came thickly. 'But you know what they say, Myles, needs must when the devil calls.'

'When the devil calls, could that be the devil rising between your legs?' Myles's half laugh was pure derision. 'Do you take me for a fool? You think I will accept the responsibility, the consequence of your rape. It was rape, wasn't it, Huntley? I cannot believe she received you with open arms, much less with open legs.'

'Coarseness becomes you, Myles, but then you know that. It is the reason you practise it so regularly. But yes, as you perceived, Regan did not welcome my attention, or indeed my intention, yet I could not let that stand in the way of what had to be done, and what might yet need to be repeated.'

'Repeated?' Myles Wentworth raised a quizzical eyebrow. 'I recognise your taste for rape; after all I have witnessed it often enough, when you have had a lad not so ready to partake of your bedroom games, but with a woman! Is it so delightful an experience you lust for it again?'

Jealousy? Sherwyn Huntley watched the expression in those eyes, watched the devilish gleam darken to an envious glare. Wentworth could not do the job himself yet resented its being accomplished for him.

'Lust, Myles!' He smiled deprecatingly. 'No. Impregnating Regan Trent is requirement, not enter-tainment. It is the way to bring her to heel. A bastard child is not to be desired, she will not allow that slur to follow the name of Trent, there-fore she will marry you; but be assured ... you will not be required to fulfil the more delicate duties of a husband. The marriage, for you, will be in name only.'

'I don't see why I need to marry her at all!' Myles Wentworth's handsome face puckered in a frown. 'With her dead or in an asylum for the insane then all she was to inherit must come to you as next of kin.'

'You don't see because you don't look further than the next card game or the next suit of clothes!' Caustic as acid, the reply burned from Huntley's tongue. 'Jasper Trent was a shrewd man, one who, unlike yourself, valued his money. He took care it remain with his family; to ensure it did just that he included a further precaution in his will.'

Angered by the older man's derision, Myles Wentworth's frown deepened, his eyes smoulder-ing with renewed pique. 'Precaution?' The near snarl twisted the handsome mouth. 'What bloody precaution is that? Or is it just one more deception that devious brain of yours has dreamed up? An-other thimble rig designed to lead me along the path laid out by you? Well I warn you, Huntley, make sure that path doesn't fall away beneath you!'

He was the one should be warned! His path was crumbling already and once Regan Trent's inheritance was well and truly in the possession of her stepfather then this pedantic coxcomb would no longer be of use; and things which prove no longer of use were best disposed of.

Finding that the thought calmed the anger aroused ever more quickly in him by Wentworth's attitude, Huntley nursed it a moment longer, cradling it in his mind before saying with forced calmness, 'The precaution I speak of, Myles, is a codicil Jasper Trent added to his will. It states quite clearly his estate was "given only to the children of his blood"; adding "in the event Marcia Trent marrying again, her spouse, then stepfather of Saul Trent, my son, and of Regan Trent, my daughter, the said stepfather would have Woodford as a residence together with an allowance here specified until the day my first born child, the said Regan Trent, attains the age of twenty-one years. On that day all allowances and residency at Woodford House enjoyed by any aforementioned stepfather will cease, and she, Regan Trent, will assume guardianship of Saul Trent."'

'That is clear enough even for you to understand. I may be Regan Trent's guardian but I am not of Jasper Trent's blood, and the law cannot alter that, nor would it countenance any contest I might bring against a will signed and witnessed in the presence of Jasper Trent's lawyer. But with the girl coming of age, with her signature witnessed, the terms laid down by Jasper Trent become fulfilled, and his will invalid. Everything will then be the property of his daughter, and in law the property of a wife becomes the property of her husband. And you, Myles, *will* be that husband.

The situation you find to be so much a grievance is nonetheless required if we are to gain what we both hope for.' The scornful look gleamed again. 'Perhaps marriage might cause somewhat of a change to your preferred way of life, but you have my word it will not last. Things will proceed exactly as we planned. A little while only and then a mental institution or death! Either way Regan Trent will no longer be an impediment. Marriage makes a spouse next of kin, the law has no argument with that. So you see, my dear Myles, like it or not, the bridegroom must be you.'

He didn't like it! Myles Wentworth drew on a pair of fine pigskin gloves, the action conveying the sour feeling rising in his stomach. Sherwyn Huntley was to get half of everything while doing nothing. It was Myles Wentworth who had the onerous task, Myles Wentwórth who must marry! Therefore... He smoothed each finger of the gloves in turn. Therefore, it was Myles Went-worth who should take all of that inheritance. *That* he did like, just as he liked the notion of getting the better of Sherwyn Huntley. And he would. Reaching to take his silver-topped cane from the urn in the hall, Myles hid a smile. He would take every stick and stone, every last farth-ing, not even a pebble from the garden would be handed over to Huntley; and the man would make no claim, he would not risk being accused of killing a wife and also a stepson. Maybe that could not be proven, but the slur in the eyes of society would hurt Huntley in all the right places. The sweet taste of gratification surged, soothing the sourness, and Myles tapped the slim cane

107

against the palm of his hand.

'So be it!' He glanced at Huntley, the hidden smile now evident on a languid mouth. 'Now, I am off to partake of the delights of Mrs Langley's house before the shackles of marriage are fastened; are you coming?'

He had thought of visiting Regan, of using the excuse of taking her a supper tray, then once in her bedroom of repeating what had happened the last time he was there. But he needed no excuse. Huntley nodded to the man already halfway through the door. A few hours spent with Mrs Langley's lackeys, those talented courtesans whose subtle skills in the arts of lovemaking could leave a man breathless, would be amusing; but the truly sensual pleasure, the voluptuous hedonism that had Sherwyn Huntley ascend to the realms of ecstasy, lay not in the act of sexual intercourse, but in domination: total and absolute domination. That and that only was true passion and he would indulge it on his return. The obstinate Miss Trent would again be subjugated. Following Myles Wentworth, Huntley paused a moment to glance back towards the house. The so-naïve Miss Trent. With an insidious Medusa smile he entered the waiting carriage. She would learn all of the arts of a mistress; yes, like it or not Regan Trent would learn ... and Sherwyn Huntley would be her instructor.

Why had it been placed there? By whom? Questions rained like hailstones in Regan's brain. Mother? Had her mother put it there? If so to what purpose? And if there were a reason why had her mother not spoken of it? No, it could not have been her mother. Ann, then? One question answered another, took its place but always asking the same, echoes ricocheting around her mind. Had it been Ann? What would induce her to place it yet make no mention? 'Pick from a cupboard of flowers.'

The wording of the note provided an answer. Ann had not been at Woodford House in those early years, she had not heard them spoken, she had no knowledge of them, therefore Ann's was not the hand responsible. Not her mother, not Ann, and most definitely not Sherwyn Huntley; that left only one other. The writer of the note and the person who had secreted that key in her bedroom could only be Edward Sanders.

If only she could have thanked him.

Seated on a stool near to a horse-drawn caravan, Regan stared vacantly across fields wrapped in the gentle mists of early morning. She had thought, in the flood of jubilation on finding a key, to write a note of thanks; but joy had almost immediately given way to fear, fear of Sherwyn Huntley coming to her room, of discovering there was a key, other than the one he kept, that would open the door of her bedroom. Almost the same moment she had realised should the note be found by Sherwyn Huntley then Mr Sanders would lose his position; he would be dismissed from Woodford House. So she had written no thanks and had burned the note that had been thrust under her door. Edward Sanders had been a trusted servant, she would not be the cause of his losing employment. But the feeling of guilt at not thanking him lay heavy. Once she found a place to live she would write to him, sending the letter to Woodford.

'There you be my racklie, you drinks that down, it'll warm the cockles of yer 'eart.'

'Thank you.' Regan tried to smile at the woman handing her an enamel mug filled with steaming hot tea.

'You be lucky not to 'ave dropped in the brook; it don't do to be walkin' 'alf asleep as you was, the Teme be naught but a little 'un compared to some rivers, but it meks just as cold a bed.'

The remonstrance was gentle yet there was enquiry beneath the concern. Taking the mug Regan sipped gratefully. The woman was asking the reason a young woman was out alone so shortly after dawn.

'I ... I could not sleep.' Regan sipped again, this time with the added gratitude of not having to meet the other woman's eyes. It was the truth but another truth she did not add, that of being afraid to rest more than a few minutes at a time.

'It don't tek no dukkerin to 'ave the knowin' o' that,' the woman said, a shake of her dark head lending emphasis. 'Don't 'ave to be no palm readin' to tell you've 'ad no comfort of a bed in more'n one night.'

'I ... I had to...'

'You needs be sayin' no more.' The response came quickly, cutting off Regan's choked attempt at reply. 'A Romany asks no whys nor wherefores, we seeks no reason afore a good turn be done nor is the 'and we reaches out to 'elp done so for gain; reward comes from the Rai, the Lord of all.'

110

Taking the mug from Regan the woman glanced across fields bathed now in the soft pink pearl of sunrise, their leaves glittering with a thousand diamonds of dew. 'The Rai of heaven gives all of this,' she murmured softly. 'He gives freely, can we do less?'

Across the hedge the bark of a dog disturbed the moment and the woman moved back to stand beside a fire of sticks over which hung a pan filled with sizzling strips of bacon, the aroma mixing with the scent of blossom and budding fruit.

'There be marikli...' She paused, nut-brown eyes fastening on Regan, 'I forgets you be gaujo and not Romany, you don't 'ave the language; what I be sayin' is there be bread to go along o' bacon an' you be welcome to the sharin'.'

Bread and crisply cooked bacon. Regan felt her mouth water. She had not realised how hungry she was. There had been food left outside her bedroom but with no key to open the door she could not have taken it had she wanted to. Another of Sherwyn Huntley's abominable tricks? Had he thought to starve her into submitting to his will? Submission! Despite the shawl the gypsy woman had placed about her shoulders Regan shivered. There had been no submission when he had come to her room, it had been force, Huntley had struck her until she was barely conscious, then slowly and deliberately raped her.

Setting a thickly cut slice of bread along with several rashers of crisp fried bacon onto a tin plate the gypsy woman saw the shudder rip through Regan. This gaujo were more than just hungry and tired, she were feared. Straightening from the task of placing more bacon in the pan hung above the fire the woman's thoughts ran on. The girl were feared, an' if truth were the same as thought then it were rape had her trembling at every sound, had her eyes constantly watchin' field an' hedgerow. Yes, rape were Rosa Mullin's thinkin', for only such melalo, such filth, would bring the look of horror which crossed the girl's face at every sound; that were what this racklie were runnin' from, a melalo mush, a filthy man.

The bark which had pierced the soft hush of morning moments before, became a throaty growl as a dog, its hair bristling, came at a run towards the caravan followed by a tall man.

11

'It grieves me to hear such news, Mr Philbert was a most sociable man.' Social and accommodating. Myles Wentworth sipped delicately, swallowing his distaste at the cheap sherry served in a tumbler rather than a schooner. Philbert had indeed been accommodating; how so would this new governor of Burnford Home for Orphan Boys prove?

Behind an imposing desk the other man nodded agreement, the movement settling heavy jowls wobbling like jelly. 'Indeed he was, Mr Wentworth, indeed he was. I can only hope I can follow his example, tread in his footsteps as you might say.'

Amen to that! The thought flitted quickly. It would be a bore finding another supplier, and he could not risk following the same course again. 'Mr Philbert set an example many would find difficult to follow.' Myles smiled, a smile hollow as it was brief, 'but I am sure if anyone can achieve it then that man is yourself, Mr Ulrick.'

'I can but try, Mr Wentworth.' Heavy jowls wobbled again. 'I can but try; but as you so rightly says it be a difficult task and one made the harder in trying to secure employment for a boy, there don't be many calls for young stable hands and kitchen places always goes to girls. I tell you, sir, the situation don't be an easy one.'

Waving away a further helping of sherry, watching the other man refill his own tumbler to the brim, Myles felt anticipation filter along his veins. This new governor had a liberal liking for alcohol and the size of his paunch attested to an equal fondness for food; perhaps he also had other likes, those which called for a certain amount of extra money!

'Yours is an onerous duty.' Myles smiled again, this time allowing sympathy to show. 'It is not my place to advise...' He paused as if reluctant to go on. 'But nevertheless I will do so if only to give myself the satisfaction; I say you, Mr Ulrick, must allow yourself periods of leisure, you must give yourself time to relax away from this most demanding position.'

Swallowing half a tumbler of sherry in one gulp, the governor wiped his mouth on the back of his hand. 'True,' he said, eyes beginning to water, 'how very true, but a position of governor, though it be a responsible one, don't have a salary of the same proportion; no, Mr Wentworth, it don't allow for the taking of them pleasures a man might care to indulge in.'

Those pleasures no doubt being a whorehouse! Myles's feeling of anticipation became one of satisfaction. This man he could do business with.

'Fortunes can change,' Myles pointed out. 'For yourself as for the boys in your charge.'

'Ah yes, the boys.' Ulrick tipped off his drink then reached again for the decanter. 'I hope, Mr Wentworth, you don't have another to add to the number here at Burnford.'

'Quite the reverse.' Myles watched a generous amount of sherry disappear into the other man's gullet. 'I am here to enquire as to the taking of a lad. I have an avenue of employment should one prove satisfactory.'

'You've come to hire a lad.' The governor wiped his mouth, smoothing mutton chop whiskers with the damp hand. 'Well now, Mr Wentworth, that be the gesture of a real gentleman, a real gentleman indeed. Come with me, sir, I am sure when you views the lads you will find just the one you be looking for.'

'Heel!' The cry had been one of absolute command and the dog had halted in its tracks, the hairs standing high on its neck. Sitting at the door of the moving caravan Regan let her thoughts wander back over the past.

'A fine jukel be Star.' The gypsy woman had glanced at the animal standing statue-still. 'Won't nobody get nowheres near, not with Star a' guardin', he be the best watchdog in all the land.'

The dog belonged with the caravan, and the

114

man with it... Regan had felt relief swamp her veins, he was the same man who had brought her to this caravan. After he had pacified the dog by a low word the man had approached asking as he reached the tiny clearing, 'Do the jacks be filled?'

The question had been for the woman standing at the fire of sticks but the glance of black eyes had come to herself. The man who had asked it, the man who had watched her with a penetrating stare, was the same man who had found her stumbling almost asleep along the river bank. He had not touched her, had simply spoken quietly, saying should she be of a mind to rest and break her fast then his wife would welcome her. Watching him now leading the horse Regan saw what her exhausted mind had earlier failed to register. Black hair sleeked back from the forehead fell thickly to touch the collar of a rough jacket beneath which a bright yellow neckerchief enhanced the deep bronze of a strong chest visible below. Tall and rangy, he moved with a lithe, easy step but it was, Regan recognised, a deceptive ease, the illusory, relaxed step of a panther; like that animal, she realised, he could flash into action the moment it was needed.

'They be filled and set to the wagon.' As though reinforcing her answer the woman had glanced to where several leather bottles were strapped to the side of the beautifully painted caravan; black with pitch that rendered them waterproof they had gleamed like jet in a sudden stream of sunlight. 'There be water enough to last 'til we reaches Worcester an' the river Severn.'

He had taken the plate held out to him, settling

cross-legged a little from the fire, the dog moving closer to his side, then as his wife settled a tin mug of scalding tea beside him he had glanced again at the stranger to his camp.

'I don't be askin' where it is you be mekin' for, I just be sayin' we go to Appleby Fair.'

Appleby Fair? Regan had never heard of it. But a fair indicated lots of people and Sherwyn Huntley had many contacts, he would have people searching for her. If not Appleby then where? Was there any place she would be safe?

Across the space of the fire the man's black eyes had gleamed with diamond brilliance.

'Appleby be a long ways off,' he said quietly, 'an' the fair sees a great gatherin' o' folk comin' from far an' wide.'

Had he read her thoughts? Had he seen past the fear in her eyes to see that in her heart?

'I ... I have never been to Appleby.' Regan had known the reply was inadequate, but how could she tell this couple what it was had her running from her home?

Flounced skirts rustling, the woman had bent to take the smoke-blackened kettle from the tripod spanning the fire. Pouring tea into a second tin cup, then handing it to Regan she had said, 'What Joab be sayin' is should you be wantin' to travel along o' us then you be welcome.'

Gratitude had thickened her throat as it thickened now. She had tried to smile her thanks but doubt had kept it from her lips. To travel with these people, to perhaps be found with them by Huntley ... he would not see their sheltering her as an act of kindness, and who could guess what

116

course his anger would take. She only knew it would not be pleasant.

'Thank you,' she had forced the words, 'but I could not, the risk...'

'The risk!' Of a sudden Rosa's voice had become soft and remote, almost as though she spoke from a far distance, from a world only she could see. Head raised high on her neck, eyes staring at a different time, a different place, she had spoken through barely moving lips. 'The risk be a man; he be tall an' spare of build, his face be bearded an' 'andsome, but the eyes, the eyes speak of a soul 'eld by Satan. He searches for a young woman, a young woman he raped and whose mother he murdered.'

Huntley! Regan had gasped. The woman had described Sherwyn Huntley!

'He searches for a woman.' The gypsy woman had spoken on, the gasp not reaching her distant place. 'He looks for 'er now, 'im and one other, one who would marry with 'er but be no husband, one whose soul be also teken by the devil. Together they searches ... they will not stop ... they will not stop 'til the Angel o' Death be satisfied.'

'The Angel of Death be satisfied.'

That death would be hers. Clasped together in her lap, Regan's fingers tightened painfully. Rosa's words uttered in that strange trance-like state had fitted perfectly the happenings at Woodford, she had described the appearance of Sherwyn Huntley, spoken of deeds of which she could not possibly have had foreknowledge. Coincidence? No. Regan shuddered at what she felt must be true. Those who searched were Sherwyn

117

Huntley and Myles Wentworth, and the young woman they hunted for was Regan Trent.

'Be you cold?' At Regan's side, Rosa had caught the shudder.

'No.' Though her reply was truthful Regan drew the gaily patterned shawl loaned by Rosa closer about her body.

'That don't be full truth, your limbs be warm but your mind be cold, it be frozen from loss of a mother an' a brother.'

There it was again! Regan's breath caught in her throat. Saul! This woman had spoken of Saul! It was not a wild guess. Regan refused the explanation springing in her mind. She had been with this woman and her husband for just a few days yet she trusted them and their word completely; neither Rosa nor Joab would cause her any hurt, neither mental nor physical. But how could Rosa have known about Saul?

Placing the peg she had fashioned from a twig of hazel along with several dozen others in a rush basket held between her feet, Rosa paused. 'I knows what be in your mind as I knows what be in your 'eart. Your first askin' be 'ow do Rosa Mullin know what 'er eyes 'ad no seein' of? An' your second askin' be can 'er tell more of the brother? The answer to one be, that from the earliest of my days, I've "seen" things other folk don't see; they be looked at not through the eyes of the 'ead but with them of the soul. "The Sight" were what my grandmother an' my mother afore me were blessed wi', though it don't always seem a blessin' for there be no choosin' of when it will come, nor choosin' o' what you would 'ave it

118

reveal. That, my racklie, must be the answer to your second askin'; I be knowin' only that a lad of not many years be teken from a train...'

Ahead of the caravan Star's warning bark had Rosa break off her explanation, replacing it with a curt, 'Into the wagon, mek you no sound!'

Huntley? Myles Wentworth? Inside the caravan Regan strained to hear above the thudding of her own heart. Had one or other of them somehow managed to track her down? Did they know she was hiding in this caravan? Had she been spotted and news of her whereabouts given to Huntley? Was it him out there talking with Joab? He would be demanding she be handed over to him, if necessary he would bring the local constabulary, accuse Joab of kidnapping his stepdaughter. That would certainly mean a long term of imprisonment for Joab, for no magistrate would believe the word of a gypsy over that of a gentleman. Gentleman! The magistrate would have that wrong; Joab Mullin might be a gypsy, but he was more of a gentleman than Sherwyn Huntley or Myles Wentworth would ever be. Suppressing a sob. Regan threw open the caravan door.

'Where do we be goin', mister?'

Driving the carriage he had hired for the day, Myles Wentworth repressed the quick rise of repugnance. Rough 'peasant' speech was always offensive to his ear; but then correct speech was not of importance in the type of employment in mind for this boy.

'What be it you've teken me from that 'ome to do? Be it you be wantin' a lad for the stables? I

119

wouldn't mind 'avin' the carin' of that there 'oss.'

'Not the stables.' Myles answered, a smile curving his handsome mouth. 'Your duties will be in the house.'

Eyes of summer green shone in a pale under-nourished face. 'The 'ouse! I be goin' to be workin' in the 'ouse! Cor, I d'ain't never think to that, do it 'ave a uniform? The job I means, do I get to dress like a gent?'

A uniform! Myles hid the humour the question aroused. There would be clothing, but not the brass-button type. 'You will be suitably dressed.' He smiled again, this time into the summer-green gaze. 'But right now I think you would ap-preciate a bite to eat and a drink more than hearing of your future employment. You will find a hamper under the seat, help yourself.'

'This don't be water.' A gulp at a leather-cased flask had the boy choke, his eyelids closing and opening in rapid succession.

'No it is not, one does not drink water when on a picnic; the liquid you have swallowed is claret.'

'Claret.' The lad frowned at the flask still held between fingers not wholly clean from the scrub-bing he had been subjected to prior to leaving Burnford Home for Orphan Boys. 'What be that, mister?'

'Wine,' Myles answered simply.

'Wine!' His exclamation soft with wonder, the lad held the flask with reverent awe. 'Lor, I ain't never 'ad wine afore.'

Myles touched the flask with a gloved finger, urging it to the boy's mouth. 'Drink it down, it is good for the health. Prove satisfactory in what

120

you are required to do and you will be given a glass of wine each day.'

Needing no second bidding the lad drank deeply, not lowering the flask until it was empty. It would take no more than a few minutes. Myles glanced surreptitiously from the corner of his eye. Very little food, a flask full of claret and a feeling of freedom from that Home, a heady combination in anyone's book, but the more so when wine contained a little opium as that claret had. The lad would sleep soon, he would not wake before their destination was reached. But getting there without the lad being seen was crucial; there must be no evidence to link them together. Ulrick? No! Myles dismissed the supposition. The man had been paid well and with the promise of more to come he would keep his silence. But then who cared what became of orphans, where they went or how they lived? They were a burden upon the nation, a thorn in the side of society. No, there would be nobody enquiring as to the whereabouts of such and that was the very reason behind the choosing. Even so, it was best to exercise caution. There was less risk if the lad were inside the carriage rather than sharing the driving seat, and that were best done here where hedgerows restricted what could be observed. Moving quickly he helped the boy, already half asleep, settling him comfortably inside the carriage then lowering the window blinds before once more climbing into the driving seat.

No one cared about orphans. That was the reason he chose from among them. Myles's inner smile was one of pure satisfaction; this particular choice would prove a very good one.

12

'We notified colleagues along of Hereford, Ross-on-Wye, Malvern and along of Worcester asking they keep a lookout for a boy answering the description of your stepson, but as yet there have been no reports of a sighting. We can of course widen the field of search, request the assistance of other counties.'

'I am in your hands, Inspector.' Sherwyn Huntley's face creased with apparent stress. 'I must leave that decision with those trained in dealing with matters of abduction, though I will, if you deem it appropriate, offer a substantial reward, any amount, for the safe return of my stepson; placed in the newspapers that could cover a far broader field.'

'I don't think you should take that step, sir, not yet. I suggest you wait until some word be received, or you are otherwise contacted by who-ever might be holding the boy.'

'Wait?' Brows drawn together, Huntley rose from his chair, and moved impatiently to the further side of the tastefully furnished sitting room. 'But surely a handsome sum of money...'

'Could do more harm than it might do good, sir.'

Sunlight streaming in at the high arched window turned strands of Huntley's dark grey hair to spun silver as he wheeled about. 'I don't follow,' he said. 'Surely a reward will see the boy brought home.'

'Maybe, but then again...'

'Again!' Huntley snapped.

'If I might explain. We have, Mr Huntley, not yet abandoned the idea of this whole business being a boyish prank, a lad grabbing the opportunity of having himself a bit of an adventure. Should you post the offer of a reward, anyone reading that in a newspaper then seeing your stepson might very well kidnap the lad and hold him to ransom for an even higher price: believe me sir, there are such felons, and should the boy simply be playing a prank then the offer of a reward for his return could place him in danger. No, Mr Huntley, it is my opinion we should wait a little longer.'

Drawing a long breath, pausing as if pain was too strong to speak, Sherwyn Huntley walked slowly back to stand before the fireplace and waited several moments more before asking, 'That is your advice?'

'It is, Mr Huntley, it is.' The inspector of police stood as he answered. 'I realise this is torment for you, but I recommend you wait before offering any reward.'

'It is, as you say, Inspector, most harrowing; the more so for my stepdaughter. She I have sent to stay with family on the Continent until this dreadful incident is brought to a close and her brother once more safe at Woodford.'

'A wise decision, Mr Huntley.' The inspector held out a hand. 'It is a thoughtful man spares a woman a care he can shoulder himself.' Then as a servant appeared in answer to the tug at the bell pull which hung alongside the fireplace he shook hands adding, 'We will of course notify you the moment we know of any further development.'

Of which there would be none! Once his visitor had departed all trace of supposed stress and worry vanished from Sherwyn Huntley's face. Myles Wentworth knew how much was riding on that boy being dead; he would have ensured that particular job had been done. And Regan Trent? It had been a brilliant move telling that inspector she had gone to the Continent, it would allay any suspicion and prevent questions the police might have as to why she was not present at Woodford should they wish to speak with her. All well and good, except Regan Trent had not been despatched to the Continent. But that was no insurmountable problem; a girl used to the finer ways of life, how long could she go on now she had nothing? He had searched that bedroom, had left nothing untouched. The jewellery belonging to her was still in its satin-lined casket, dresses hung still in the wardrobe, her more intimate garments remained in the chest of drawers; so far as he could maintain, Regan Trent had fled with only the clothes she stood up in. Money? He hesitated in his thinking, for seconds only. Then like a tide flowing back up a beach the thoughts resumed. He had never allowed her cash, he had paid the bills for every item of clothing, every sundry need she had; that had been the way of things from the moment he had become master of Woodford. No, it was a safe conclusion Regan Trent had no money and without it she would get neither food nor shelter; that if naught else would bring her creeping back to this house.

'I will not be the cause of trouble for you or for Joab.' Standing at the door of the caravan Regan looked into the deep brown eyes as they met hers. 'I will go with them, Rosa.' She came down the steps. 'Tell them I asked to be allowed to travel with you, that way there can be no blame attached to Joab and yourself.'

'Hold you there my racklie.' Rosa Mullin smiled. 'There be no blamin' o' Joab nor none o' me neither, least not from them you sees a' talkin' wi' 'im; they be lovari, they be Romany.'

Hearing the two speaking together, Joab came toward them bringing two men with him to the fire he had built for Rosa to roast the rabbit Star had caught, and by which they would camp for the night.

'There be a diddikai, a gaujo, a man not of Romany blood an' he be askin' questions along o' the next town.' Joab looked at Regan but made no introduction as the two men simply settled themselves cross-legged on the ground. 'He be askin' o' a juval ... a woman; askin' o' everyone he sees an' the description he gives be of a young juval with eyes o' blue an' hair the colour o' honey, a description fittin' yourself. He be also a' visitin' o' gypsy camps an' chance be he'll a visit o' this one.'

'It will be a man employed by my guardian to search for me.' Regan glanced at the men accepting tea from Rosa.

'There be no call for worritin' that word o' you

be teken from this place.' Joab caught the glance, interpreting it correctly. 'They two be o' Romany blood an' Romany be family, we talks wi' one another but says naught to diddikai, especially one we senses be kalo, an' it seems that one along o' Leigh 'as a black 'eart. Like I tells,' Joab forestalled the question rising to Regan's lips, 'a true Romany don't need words to see what a diddikai be truly thinkin', they reads the eyes, an' eyes be the way they sees into the mind, an' that one had a mind set only on money, no matter the pain caused to any other in the gettin' o' it.'

'We can tek another way, tek the road along of Bromyard an' Leominster, that'll mean we won't meet up wi' that gaujo mush.'

One of the men sitting a little back from the fire touched his lips with a blue spotted neckscarf, then with a shake of the head answered Rosa.

'Don't just be one. Chavvies out kettering coshties ... children collecting firewood,' the explanation came with a glance at Regan, 'they was questioned by a man along o' Broxwood, an' the women sellin' pegs an' brooms along o' Bromyard were asked the same, 'ad they 'ad sight o' a young woman travellin' alone, a juval wi' honey-gold hair an' eyes the colour o' a summer lake?'

'Same word be spoke by the Lee family.' His tea drunk, the second man rose nimbly to his feet, his companion doing likewise. 'They says that on the way through Callow End they was stopped by a diddikai who were askin' of a young woman, an' if one be sniffin' along o' there then it don't tek no figurin' there'll be others along o' Worcester.'

Handing their tin mugs to Rosa the two men

126

turned again to Joab, the taller of them saying, 'whoever it be a searchin' o' that juval be wantin' the findin' o' 'er pretty bad.'

Sherwyn Huntley would be desperate to get her back. Regan watched the three men, coal-dark hair emphasised by the bright colours of cotton cloths tied about the neck. They had walked to the edge of the small clearing, their low voices not carrying back to the caravan. But Regan did not need to hear to know the subject of their quiet conversation was herself, and the trouble Joab and Rosa would be in should she be found in their company. But she would not be! Removing the pretty shawl from her shoulders she handed it back to Rosa. 'Thank you.' It was a half whisper held a few moments on a breath. 'Thank you and Joab for your kindness, I just wish I could repay it in some way.'

'What be this?'

No sound had heralded Joab's return and now he stood, the flames of firelight revealing the frown in his dark eyes. Had she not travelled these past days in his company, not witnessed his kindness, Regan knew she would be in fear of him, that she would have taken that stern gaze to be one of threat.

'What be talk of repayin'? 'Ave you not been told a Romany teks no payment 'ceptin' the grace of God?'

'I'm sorry, I did not mean to offend.' Regan looked from one face to the other. 'But you do not know my guardian, he will do all he can to harm you should he find out I have been helped by you; that would cause me more unhappiness than returning to Woodford House, so...' She swallowed the choking sob rising in her throat. 'So I will be leaving at once.'

'There'll be no surprisin' o' this camp, not while Star be 'ere.' Joab touched the head of the dog standing at his side. 'He be set to guard all in this camp an' you be a part o' it; there'll be no leavin', not this day nor any other 'til we be o' a certain mind you be in no danger o' bein' teken by them diddikai.'

'But–'

'No buts,' Rosa cut in briskly. 'Don't go a' arguin' wi' Joab, he knows what be best.'

'An' that be for you to remain along o' Rosa an' me.' Joab settled once more on the soft grass, Star lying alongside him. 'You wouldn't get no more than a mile afore news o' you reached them as searches for you should you be seen walkin' alone.'

'But should I be seen with you! Think of the consequences, Joab, Sherwyn Huntley would not rest until you were put in prison.'

Taking a twig from the fire, Joab held it to the clay pipe he had packed with tobacco. 'Sherwyn Huntley.' He poked the smouldering twig into the fire, sending a shower of brilliant sparks shooting toward the purpling sky. 'Sherwyn Huntley o' Woodford House be well known among the Romany, he would rob a man o' the last penny then come back for the purse; an' robbin' don't be all he likes doin' to a man!' His lips tightening, Joab jabbed the twig viciously into the heart of the crackling sticks. 'Huntley be the worst kind o' mush, 'e kalo an' melalo, black-hearted, filthy-minded, through and through, a varmint the

128

world would be better should 'e be dead!'

'Then you must see, you must both see the danger you will be in if I am found with you.'

'I sees two men.' Rosa held the shawl but her gaze had gone from it, gone beyond the fire, beyond the present. 'One be bearded, the hair an' beard be the grey o' metal an' the eyes be the black o' ebony; the other be younger wi' hair the colour o' polished copper an' eyes o' hazel: he be clean shaven, 'andsome o' face but like the older 'e be evil of heart.' Her head lifting slightly, Rosa paused as if the picture she looked at had faded, but then with a rasp of indrawn breath went on. 'They be watchin' o' a lad, a fair-haired lad sleepin' in a wooden building, it be within sight o' a fine house built o' stone an' surrounded by fields. There be a rose garden...'

Woodford! Regan almost cried aloud. Rosa was describing the grounds of Woodford House, the summer pagoda set near the rose beds, and Saul – Saul was returned home!

'The scent o' roses be strong,' Rosa continued in the soft trance-like tone, 'but there be another stronger smell. It don't be sweet, it be acrid an' a catchin' of the throat.' She coughed, her nostrils wrinkling as though a strong odour invaded the air around her. 'The lad be waking, now 'e drinks from a glass held to his mouth by the grey-haired man, and 'e sleeps again. The two they smiles, they smiles at the sleepin' lad but they speaks o' a girl, a girl they be searchin' of, a girl they say must go the way of her mother.'

Joab had watched Regan the whole time Rosa had been speaking, had watched recognition

129

flash across her face, the relief shine in her eyes at mention of a lad; now he said, 'You knows who it be Rosa were shown. You knows the men 'er talked of, the truth o' that be plain on your face.'

'Yes.' Regan could only whisper. 'Yes, I know them. The older man is Sherwyn Huntley, my stepfather, and the other is Myles Wentworth, the man I was to marry.'

'An' the lad?'

Regan smiled, her voice regaining strength from the surge flooding along her veins. 'That can only be Saul, my brother.' Then, her voice lowering again to a murmur, she added, 'I was told...' She broke off. She had been told her brother was dead; had that been more of Sherwyn Huntley's mental torture of her?

Her back toward them, Rosa was snatched once more into that world beyond sight, the cry rising to her throat lost among the crackle of flames, flames only she witnessed.

'I realise you are thinking of my safety, and I am grateful, Joab, but I must return to Woodford, I must get Saul away from there; he...' Regan's voice broke as she looked from Joab to Rosa. 'He could be in the most awful danger, please try to understand.'

I understand more'n you thinks. Stirring a smoke-rimmed pot suspended on a tripod over the fire, Rosa kept her counsel. The racklie could go to where she had come from, the girl had true feelings for her brother, but evil lurked at the house she had been shown by the 'sight', an evil which would not be denied.

130

The clay pipe between his teeth, Joab stared silently at the fire. His wife had the gift of second sight, though not always did her speak all that were revealed; Rosa had a kind heart and that, he was certain, had ruled her tongue.

'Rosa.' Regan glanced at the figure bent to the bubbling pot. 'Rosa, you must know how I feel, Saul is still so young, and Huntley...'

Spoon in hand Rosa straightened, her figure silhouetted against a rapidly darkening sky. 'I knows the ways o' a woman. Be 'er young or old in years meks no difference to what be in the 'eart, an' your 'eart calls to your brother; but what is longed for don't always be what be got.'

'I don't understand.' Regan frowned. 'What are you telling me?'

A stirring of wind sighed among the branches of tall willows fringing the campsite, their multitude of leaves rustling like so many whispering voices, then reaching the fire the wind teased the smoke, sending it billowing around the figure of Rosa until it seemed to enshroud her in a swirling veil of purple – grey, its edges glittering with myriad sparks. Regan, her emotions already taut with thoughts of what could happen to Saul, caught her breath, the moment seeming almost unearthly. But it was Rosa's face which made her hold that breath in her throat. Eyes closed, brows drawn, lips held tight, it showed someone fighting against a will stronger that its own. Then Rosa was speaking, her soft remote words audible in the quiet left by the suddenly immobile leaves.

Rosa's murmur whispered across a fire which too seemed caught in the surreal moment, its

131

crackling flames reduced to silence in Regan's mind.

'Fire and water!' Rosa's head arched back on her neck, the spoon falling from her fingers. 'There be fire an' there be water ... a man an' a boy, a boy looked on by the Angel o' Death, a man an' a boy ... fire ... there be death in the fire!'

As suddenly as that strange hypnotic trance-like state had come upon her it dropped away. The smoke surrounding her was already dispersing; Rosa picked up the fallen spoon, washing it in a tin bowl into which she poured water from a leather jack.

'What do you mean, fire and water? Does this allude to Saul?' Regan broke the pressing silence. 'Rosa, please! You said a man and a boy, were they Sherwyn Huntley and my brother?'

'I told you times afore.' Rosa turned from washing the spoon. 'I says only what be sent me.'

'But fire!' Regan persisted. 'You said there was death in the fire ... whose death, Rosa?'

Highlighted by the once more crackling flames of the camp fire, Rosa Mullin felt pity for the young woman watching with fear-filled eyes, a young woman whose life a strong inner sense told her had seen many an unhappy day and would see many more yet. But life were life, it were given and it had to be lived. Pulling in a breath she shook her head, setting large hooped earrings swinging, the gold of them glittering in the firelight. 'I don't 'ave the choosin',' she said quietly. 'I don't be given the choice o' who, nor the knowin' o' them that be shown, neither do I be told the purpose; the "sight" comes when it will an' leaves when it be of

132

a mind to, an' it leaves no reason behind.'

There had to be more than that! Tears of frustration linked with fear clutched again at Regan. Rosa 'saw' clearly, she had described Sherwyn Huntley and Myles Wentworth as accurately as had they been standing in front of her. Surely then her 'vision' had revealed which figure met his death in a fire; she must know was it adult or boy.

'Rosa.' She was forestalled by the woman's sharp glance.

'It tells what it will, I don't 'ave the sayin' o' it.' Snapping the roast rabbit into three pieces Rosa set them on tin plates then threw the head to the waiting Star before adding turnip and boiled potato to each meal. Then, set lips showing that what had or had not been disclosed to her was no longer to be discussed, she carried her own plate over to sit beside her husband.

'It tells what it will.'

Unbidden and unwelcome the words returned to Rosa's mind. But she had not spoken the all of it, not said all the 'sight' had brought. The words of the racklie sitting across from her, they had been silent as the words of that 'seeing', words formed only in the girl's heart, yet Rosa Mullin had had the hearing of them. Yes, she had 'heard', unspoken words asking were the figures seen along of the fire the same two people talked of a moment or so afore? Words askin', were it the fire took the man, or did it take the boy?

13

'I trust my gift has proved to your liking.'

Myles Wentworth watched the older man adjust his clothing. The question was superfluous, there had been little doubt of the satisfaction Huntley had felt in the taking of that lad. Receiving no answer Myles smiled to himself. Huntley had tried to disguise the exhilaration of being the first, of being the one to bring innocence to an end; but the tension holding that tight-lipped mouth, the look which had gleamed in those dark eyes, the look of pure carnal lust had spoken for itself.

Helping himself to a glass of wine then settling once more into a comfortable garden chair Myles Wentworth gazed out over the spacious grounds of Woodford House. He had brought the lad here to the summer house, then making sure he was drugged enough to sleep at least two or three hours had returned the hired carriage and driven his own to the front entrance of the house. It had gone well, he had met no one, seen no servant as he had come and gone, no one to witness what had been left here in the summer house. The thought of that possibility had Huntley apprehensive, the risk of the police calling again at the house was a chance he had been unwilling to take. But reticence had not been long-lived. Sipping the wine, holding it in his mouth, Myles's inner satisfaction deepened. The agreeableness he was

134

experiencing was not all due to alcohol, not by any means; that delightful feeling was entirely the result of what he had just witnessed, and what that witnessing would afford him. The wine sliding luxuriously over his throat, he glanced at the man now lighting a cheroot with a match taken from the box set beside the lamp occupying the centre of a small round table. The 'gift' Sherwyn Huntley had so avidly enjoyed had, though he might not suspect it, not been given freely. Oh yes, the first tasting, the delicious thrust into the bent-over boy, the gasp coming from the so-young mouth, that had been Huntley's pleasure, but pleasure had its price and to relive this particular one would cost the man more than the few pounds required to avail himself of the Elysium of Mrs Langley's establishment. But would Huntley pay the asking price? His glance showed him the other man drawing deeply on the cheroot, eyes closed in appreciation of the taste of fine tobacco. Myles returned to his study of the ground stretching away towards the house obliterated by trees and tall shrubbery, which afforded the summer house seclusion. Yes, Huntley would pay the price of privilege and privilege was what Myles Wentworth would continue to ensure he had.

The Burnford Home for Orphan Boys would supply the goods. Myles sipped again, the warmth of assured and unlimited funds adding to that of Huntley's vintage claret, and if that particular source should prove less than profitable there were plenty of other orphanages in the country.

He had driven back to Woodford House, made a great show of ordering his horse and carriage to be taken care of. There could be no question as to his arrival, no notion of his already having visited the summer house, and none but himself and Huntley were to know what had taken place within its walls. Watching the shadows of evening begin to flit among breeze-ruffled greenery, Myles allowed self-satisfaction full rein. Sherwyn Huntley was a man with a vice, that which should it be brought to public notice would destroy him completely, and that was the ace in Myles Wentworth's hand. True, he himself also indulged in that particular vice, he also ran that risk of public damnation, but who was there would inform? Not Huntley, for by doing so he brought about his own downfall. That was the cord by which Huntley was bound, the cord Myles Wentworth would pull ever more securely.

'You approve of my little venture?' Myles broke the silence.

Relaxation disturbed, Huntley laid aside the cheroot with an impatient gesture. Wentworth was taking too many risks.

'You can hardly deny it has lived up to promise.' Myles laughed. 'Not after the performance you have just given.'

Across the small room Sherwyn Huntley felt the distaste which of late had become more pronounced. Wentworth was a gentleman of breeding by birth but not by nature. Though elegant in dress and graceful of manner in the company of other people, when solely with Sherwyn Huntley as he was now then the man showed his other self, the half that was not simply crude but exhibited vulgarity.

136

'I do not deny my appreciation,' Huntley answered tightly. 'But I do decry the risk you took in bringing him here. You ought not to have done so!'

'Oh!' Myles glanced over the rim of his glass. A languid, deliberately provoking look. 'Isn't that rather like shutting the stable door *after* the horse has bolted? But then that is you, isn't it, Huntley ... you take advantage of what another man offers, you do not refuse the pleasure of it, but then censure him for having presented it. I call that hypocrisy.'

'And I call what you are doing lunacy!' Picking up the cheroot Huntley ground it viciously into an ashtray. 'How many more times do I have to remind you, going to different sources widens the risk of being found out.'

'What risk?' Myles waved the half-empty glass, a carefree indolent movement.

'What risk?' Huntley's temper flared. 'You ask what risk–'

'Yes!' Myles interrupted, the same indifference loud in the reply. 'I ask what risk. Our suppliers are amply rewarded, I can't see any one of them reneging on that agreement, it would be like opening their own veins.'

'You can't see!' Sherwyn Huntley pushed to his feet, his chair scraping noisily on the wooden floor. 'You can't see! But then you can't see past money, can you, Wentworth!'

Tipping the remnants of wine into his mouth, Myles swallowed before smiling, a lazy amiable smile that masked his contempt. 'Like yourself my dear Sherwyn,' he placed the glass on the table then glanced at the watching man, 'I cannot see past money and you cannot see past a boy's backside.'

Damn Wentworth! Pacing about his bedroom Sherwyn Huntley let the fire of anger burn in his mind. The man was a positive fool. Why bring those goods to Woodford, especially at a time when the constabulary might take it upon themselves to call again, why not have taken him some place else? But that would not have entered the realms of Wentworth's thinking. They had argued the point of Wentworth removing the boy from Woodford, their conversation waking him, but a full glass of claret enhanced with a deeper draught of opium had quickly seen him asleep again. That had been when Wentworth suggested a return to the house in order to avoid servants' speculations as to why they would linger in the garden after dusk.

And so the 'goods' rested where they had left them. The boy remained asleep in the summer house, but for how long would sleep hold him? Thoughts taking a different turn, Sherwyn paused at the window to stand looking out over night-hidden grounds. If he awoke, no ... *when* he awoke! A frisson of alarm dispelled his anger, leaving Sherwyn Huntley's mind once more clear and incisive. There must be no awakening.

'You can tell the staff they may retire, I shall not return until tomorrow.' Taking a cane from Edward Sanders' replacement, Sherwyn left the house, stepping into the driving seat of his carriage without word or glance to the ostler handing him the rein. He had listened, his heart beating at every sound during the hours after coming in from the summer house, gone repeatedly during dressing for the evening to stare out of the window of his room, searching for any sign of movement. But there had been none. Did that mean the lad was still sleeping or that he had woken and fled? Not the latter. Sherwyn flicked the rein. Please heaven not the latter. Answering the rein the horse moved at a steady pace and in the darkness Sherwyn smiled grimly. That he, with his penchant for a child's body, should ask the assistance of heaven! But that body had been so sweet. With his hands relaxed on the rein Sherwyn's thoughts returned to late afternoon. He had, after some misgivings, accompanied Wentworth to the summer house. The boy, still partly drugged, had smiled at them. Smiled. Sherwyn felt his senses leap as they had leaped then. The clothes had been of poor quality and though assured the lad had been well scrubbed before being brought from that orphanage, another bath, one perfumed with scented oil, would have had him more presentable. But all idea of that had flown from the mind the moment those intensely green eyes had lifted to his and that pretty mouth had smiled.

The lad was handsome, even though of such tender years he was handsome. Beneath his clothing, Sherwyn felt his flesh harden. And the opium in the wine had kept him agreeable, the smile remaining while he had been stripped of his clothes; and the touch of him, the excitement of that young body beneath his hands. Flesh jerked against the stricture of trousers, desire raising its head as Sherwyn relived the moment.

The boy had tried to talk but the opium-laced wine given by Wentworth and drunk so quickly had the desired effect. Eyes glazing over, the boy had quietened, the smile continuing to play over that so-desirable mouth; it had played the whole time through! He had run his hands over every part of that thin body, felt the soft mounds between the legs, stroked the penis, teasing it into arousal. Wentworth had laughed at that, asking should he or Huntley bend over to receive it.

Caught by his own exigency, a sharpening of the appetite he must satisfy, he had ignored Wentworth's coarseness. Dropping to his knees he had taken the boy's manhood between his lips, rolling his tongue over the swollen tip before sucking. The young stomach had tightened. Sherwyn guided the horse between the pillars of the entrance to Woodford. It had been his first experience of the delights of sexual activity. But the game had not been over, not for Sherwyn Huntley. He had released his mouth sliding it slowly over the taut flesh, then with one swift move had regained his feet, twisted the small figure so its back was towards him, then bending it double he had thrust his own palpitating flesh deep into the boy's rear. There had been a gasp, a sharp cry of surprise but no opposition, and no refusal when Wentworth repeated the process.

The lad had slept while Wentworth and he talked. Pulling gently on the rein Sherwyn guided the horse from the road to follow along the high wall surrounding the grounds of Woodford House. He had wakened only briefly, murmuring softly as he drank yet more drugged wine. That had been when the idea had kindled in Sherwyn's brain. Wentworth had objected, but as was pointed out to him, who would possibly question, who could voice doubt? *'As you wish...'* had been Wentworth's response to the man taking his leave.

And it would be as Sherwyn Huntley wished. Bringing the carriage to a halt beneath a dense group of trees Sherwyn dismounted. With the bundle of clothing he had hidden beneath the cloak held fast he slipped through a half-over-grown gate, pausing at the other side to listen for any sound emanating from the night-shrouded grounds. Satisfied no one was around he went quickly to the summer house. His sight had adjusted to darkness so finding his way about the room proved no difficulty. The boy was still deeply asleep, his regular breathing attested to the fact. Relieved, Sherwyn reached for the matches he knew were on the table. But a light, any light, coming from here would be seen; there was little chance of any of his staff being out in the grounds at this late hour, but such a chance, however small, was too great a risk: what was to be done would be done in darkness.

Moving quietly he crossed to the wicker chaise. The boy lay there naked beneath a silk cover. He could taste that flesh again, thrust deep into that delectable orifice. Senses flaring, Sherwyn gazed at the figure just discernable in the shadows. He could ... but no, common sense must come before desire; there would be other young lads, other bodies to satisfy his appetite but only this one could guarantee no more police enquiry.

The thought calmed the turmoil at the base of his stomach as he placed the clothing he carried on the floor, then, as quickly as the drugged figure allowed, dressed it. He had guessed correctly. What fitted Saul Trent fitted the nameless youth. But clothes alone would not be proof enough. This he had realised when collecting trousers and jacket. There would have to be something more. That was when he had remembered the ring. He had forbidden Saul to wear the gold signet ring engraved with the initials S.T., citing the possibility of its being lost or stolen. A shrewd move as it transpired. Congratulating himself, Sherwyn slipped the ring onto the finger of the unmoving boy. Now there could be no question! Satisfied all was as he would have it, the boy's own drab clothing put at the door ready to take away with him, Sherwyn reached for the lamp he always insisted be kept filled with paraffin oil. Removing shade and funnel together with a fitting securing the wick he held the wide-bellied glass bowl in both hands. There would be enough; after all the long days of hot summer sunshine the wood of this building would be tinder dry. Returning the lamp to the table, his ears attuned to catch every sound from outside, he returned to the chaise. Needing no light to guide him he lifted the unresisting form, carrying it to the centre of the room, there to lay it alongside the table. That done he reached again for the lamp.

After dousing the unconscious body with oil he then sprinkled the rest over table and chairs, spreading it across the floor, shaking the last drops from the bowl, then he threw it to the ground smashing it a few inches from the boy's outstretched hand. It was done. All except for the striking of a match. With a smile Sherwyn picked up the box. One match was all it would take.

'But you must realise … you are a wise woman…'

'Yes, I be a woman, I knows the feel o' a heart set nigh to breakin'.' Rosa Mullin stirred the stew of mutton bones got in exchange for reading the palm of a farmer's wife further along the valley. 'I also knows that hastiness brings no benefit, a day more will mek no difference.'

'But it could!' Regan caught at the woman's arm. 'It could make all the difference, should Saul be in danger.'

'What can you do?' Rosa's return was sharp. 'You don't exactly 'ave a regiment o' soldiers at your back nor yet a policeman who would believe your wildness. You bargin' back to that 'ouse will serve only to put you back in the 'ands o' that black-'earted villain that be your stepfather. My Joab says to wait an' that be what we shall do.'

'But…'

'No!' Rosa shook the restraining hand away. 'There'll be no buts, least not 'til Joab be back an' we've 'eard what 'e has to say.'

She had hoped Rosa would understand, would recognise that she, Regan, must return to Woodford, that she must know for herself if the young lad Rosa had 'seen' in her vision was Saul, and if so that he had to be taken away from the threat that was Sherwyn Huntley. But how to accomplish

143

that? Rosa was right in saying there was no one to help, no one who would believe the claim that Huntley was a danger to herself and her brother. But that could not be allowed to influence the decision already firm in her mind. No matter the consequence, she would return to Woodford House.

14

Lying in the bender tent, a construction of bent hazel twigs Joab had made for her to sleep in and over which he had thrown blankets of coarse horsehair before covering the floor inside with rush mats Rosa had woven, Regan lay awake. It had felt so strange, those first couple of nights; the first time in her life she had slept out of doors, so strange she had thought never to sleep again but weariness had overcome her and she had rested. But tonight sleep was again a stranger.

The tent was warm and dry, the bed of fresh bracken she had helped Rosa collect was soft and sweet-smelling, yet still she was restless.

Was she being foolish believing in Rosa's visions ... in believing any person could have that kind of 'sense'? Staring into darkness Regan analysed the possibility. 'It is not given for us to know all things.' The phrase she had once heard preached in church rang now in her mind. Was that not telling her that no one could know the future nor yet the past other than that which they themselves had witnessed? Yet Rosa had described perfectly Woodford House, Sherwyn Huntley and Myles Wentworth. Gypsies travelled all over the country, so it was not inconceivable Rosa had seen that lovely stone-built house, or the two men she spoke of; they both rode every day, and often together. But she had spoken also of Saul.

Beyond the tent a breeze ruffled the long grass, making the leaves of hedgerow and trees ripple, lifting their earth song to the stars. But Regan heard only the cry of her heart.

Rosa had spoken of Saul!

'...*a lad teken from a train...*'

Saul had been taken from the train bringing him home from school!

'...*a fair-haired lad a sleepin' in a wooden building...*'

Fair-haired...

Saul had fair hair. Rosa was describing her brother! But chances were she had never seen Saul; he was almost constantly away at school.

'...*sleeping in a wooden building...*'

The summer house at Woodford was constructed of timber. Each thought a fresh thorn driving into her mind, Regan moved restlessly, bringing a low rumble from the throat of the dog set to guard the tent.

It had to be Saul! But Huntley had said he was dead. Which was true?

Argument and counter-argument clashed like swords. Rosa couldn't ... yet Rosa had described him.

Lifting an arm across her face Regan tried to shut off the chaos of her mind and it stilled, the

145

thoughts were gone. But in the space of half a breath a new one forced itself into her tired brain.

'"There are more things in heaven and earth ... than are dreamt of in your philosophy."'

Where had she heard that quotation? Why remember it now? Lowering her arm Regan stared again into velvet darkness. Where or when did not matter. The words themselves were saying to have faith when she could not understand; the deepest regions of her innermost self had conjured the phrase, so that like a balm it would soothe her.

But belief could not be attributed to just one part of what Rosa had said. It had to be all or none.

All or none! It seemed Regan's heart ceased to beat.

All or none!

Far from calming, the words rocked in her brain.

It had been so accurate, so convincing, so truthful! Like the bow wave of a passing ship thoughts flooded into her mind washing away question, erasing contradiction.

To believe any she must believe all, and all included the mention of fire.

'Fire and water...'

Out of the warm darkness of night the words of Rosa returned, soft but perfect in their clarity.

'...there be fire an' there be water ... a man an' a boy, a boy looked on by the Angel o' Death ... death in the fire.'

Death! Regan's nerves jangled. Whose death, that of the man or of the boy?

And could that boy be Saul?

146

'I was not here.' Sherwyn Huntley looked at the man sitting opposite him in the study of Woodford House. 'I was away on business and did not return until an hour ago when my butler informed me of a fire in the summer house. He also informed me the place is burned beyond repair.'

'Yes.' The police inspector nodded.

'So.' Sherwyn looked solidly at the policeman though his pulses throbbed. 'What brings you to Woodford ... news of my stepson, you have found him?'

A moment's silence in which the inspector looked at the hat resting on his knee. Then lifting his glance he said, 'In a manner of speaking, sir, we think we might.'

'A manner of speaking!' Sherwyn frowned. 'What does that mean? Either you have found my stepson or you have not! Which is it, man?'

'Did your butler say anything else?'

Hidden behind the body of the desk Sherwyn Huntley's hands curled tightly. Had he overlooked something? Had he in his haste to get the thing over and done left some clue, something which would point to him?

'He said only what I have told you, Inspector, but perhaps you would have me bring him to the study where you may ask him for yourself.'

'That will not be necessary, sir.' The inspector answered coldness with politeness. 'But I would ask you accompany me...'

Sherwyn's nerves jolted. Accompany him! Arrest! Blood pounded with each word. Then he had made some mistake! Perhaps the body had not burned, maybe there had been insufficient oil, then it would be seen the victim was not Saul Trent.

Like silence after a thunderclap Sherwyn's whole body tensed, waited as for lightning to strike.

'...to the summer house.'

Lightning had struck. The police had found some reason to suspect him! Despite his best efforts, Sherwyn's hands trembled. But there was still a chance, the police had to prove any suspicion. Making a supreme effort he rose to his feet, his hands forced to lie steady at his sides. No trace of the quake inside showed as he spoke evenly.

'Is that really necessary? The place is, so I am informed, burned almost totally, I see no reason to go poking among the ashes.'

The inspector too stood, his hat in his hand. 'I am afraid it is necessary.'

Watching him, watching the brush of fingers against the hat, Sherwyn felt his chest tighten.

'With your stepdaughter being absent ... but then again I could hardly ask a woman, especially so young a woman...'

'Inspector!' Trepidation flung the interruption across the desk, 'what on earth are you talking about? What possible reason can you have for speaking of my stepdaughter?'

'A reason of identification.'

Identification! The body had not burned. Sherwyn's nerves jumped again, yet, apparently composed, he continued to stare evenly at his caller.

'You see, sir,' the inspector went on, 'the summer house was not empty when it caught fire.' Sherwyn

Huntley frowned in puzzlement; the explanation continued. 'There was somebody in there.'

'Somebody? A tramp, you mean?'

'Maybe.'

'Maybe!' This voice sounded harsh with anxiety. 'Have you questioned the fellow, asked how he came onto these premises?'

The inspector's head shook once. 'No, the person has not been interrogated.'

That had to mean something! Was the boy injured so he had been unable to speak? Sherwyn pushed the thoughts aside, snapping with a pretence of irritation, 'This person has not been questioned ... why not, Inspector? Is trespass not a crime to be answered?'

Glancing toward the uniformed constable who had stood throughout the proceedings at the door of the study, the inspector signed for it to be opened before looking again at the man he had been speaking with. 'Yes, Mr Huntley,' he said quietly, 'trespass is a crime, but unfortunately the dead cannot be made to answer for it.'

'It be your own decidin' as to whether you believes what was shown to me or whether you don't, same as it be none but your own decidin' you goes back along o' where you comes from.' Rosa Mullin looked up from the basket she was filling with pegs made from twigs of willow. 'There be but one thing I ask.'

Not that I change my mind, please not that! Regan's eyes spoke the words.

Rosa read the expression and she shook her head, hooped earrings dancing against her neck.

'No, ain't I asks you changes your mind, I asks you comes along o' me into Abberley, gossip might 'ave it that what Joab 'eard from the Turleys might 'ave the addin' o' more.'

Joab had visited another Romany encampment at first light, returning at breakfast to tell of talking with a gypsy family camped near Orleton. *'They had passed through Putley some days back,'* Joab had related, *'there 'ad been talk there of 'appenings along o' Putley, a fire in the grounds of a big 'ouse.'*

Woodford! Regan's senses had jarred. Woodford House was the only large one near to Putley.

'Seems the same were being spoke of along o' Stoke Lacy, for Jake Turley 'eard the same gossip when comin' through there.' Joab had paused, then looking at Rosa had said quietly, *'Seems that fire burned a buildin' med o' wood, an' a body burned to death along o' it.'*

A body, burned to death! Regan's stomach had lurched. Had it been a boy? Had it been Saul?

'Were others at the Turley camp.' Joab had turned to look at her. *'They be of the same family. They be mekin' for Gloucester an' will call at Pulley on the way. They leaves tomorrow dawn; says if you be o' a mind to travel along o' 'em then Rafe, 'e be the oldest lad, 'e will see you safe back to Woodford.'*

'Where be it Jake Turley be mekin' for?'

The question had been Rosa's.

'Kidderminster.' Joab's eyes had remained with Regan. *'They goes to Kidderminster, Jake also offers a place along o' them should be you wants to take that direction.'*

She had been given the choice, to go on or to return to Woodford. Regan watched the last of

150

the pegs being laid neatly in a willow basket. But there was only one choice she could make: she must return to Woodford.

'Well?' The basket filled, Rosa looked up. 'Say what it be you've decided.'

A few hours more! Regan hesitated. But then the people Joab had spoken of as travelling on to Gloucester would not be leaving before tomorrow, and she would feel safer having their company.

'I...' She smiled. 'I will come with you to the village.'

'Be wisest.' Rosa nodded. 'But not dressed as you be, don't see no Romany a wearin' o' velvet, nor o' silk petticoats.'

'But this is all I have.'

Rosa laughed at the forlorn answer. 'That it be my racklie, but Rosa Mullin 'as that which will see you lookin' every bit the Romany, except you be fair of skin an' yellow of hair an' that don't be usual among gypsy folk; but,' she paused, bottom lip pulled wryly between small white teeth, 'a colourin' o' this sandy earth mixed wi' the juice o' them berries will darken face an' 'ands while a neckerchief'll tek care o' the rest.'

An hour later, the dried sand brushed from Regan's face and hands, Rosa stood back to survey her handiwork. 'There,' she laughed, 'tek a Romany to know you don't be one, an' they ain't like to say.'

Regan touched the flowing dark skirts, one side caught into the waistband displaying the hem of a red flannel petticoat, then at her hands stained light brown from the deeply red earth of the countryside Rosa had mixed to a paste with the

151

juice of dark-coloured berries. Her face must be the same colour! Concerned eyes looked at Rosa but the woman laughed.

'Don't you be a worritin', Rosa Mullin knows what 'er be about. A few washin's in warm water will see that skin o' yourn fair as ever it be; but them pretty eyes...' She pulled her lip once more, looking hard at Regan. 'There be naught will change the colour o' them. There only be one thing for it.' She released the lip. 'If we gets to talk to them o' the village then you keeps your 'ead lowered an' your tongue still, if any folk questions I'll a tell you be slow o' mind. Now for the hair.' Turning to the step of the caravan she caught up a square of black cloth and with a deft movement wrapped it around Regan's head, pulling it low on the brow. 'That be better than a bright neckerchief, don't want no more attention than must be.'

How would she not draw attention dressed as she was! Was Rosa not hoping for too much? Regan felt the whole world would stare at her.

'Now you keeps that shawl close around, and remember, should anybody ask to buy a ribbon you says nuthin' but nudge me wi' the basket; folk'll just tek it you be simple.' Pushing a shallow basket holding a host of pretty ribbons and laces, Rosa took up the larger basket of pegs and with no more ado strode away from the caravan and out into the lane.

Abberley was so much like Putley. Walking past small thatch-roofed houses, their gardens a knot of flowers, Regan felt tears prick her throat. She had visited that village often with her mother.

Why had it all gone so wrong? What had induced her mother to marry a man such as Sherwyn Huntley was? Had he dazzled her so much she had no idea of how ruthless he could be? Dazzled or duped? Rosa was silent for a moment; Regan let her thoughts run on. Had her mother ever truly loved Huntley, or had that marriage been the result of some entirely different emotion?

'We be comin' along o' the 'igh Street.'

Rosa's voice cut across her mental questioning. Regan glanced ahead, seeing a street busy with shoppers.

'You keeps that 'ead low like I told!' Rosa reminded her with a sharp hiss. She walked ahead, halting where a women stood outside a baker's shop.

'Buy pegs from a poor gypsy girl.' Rosa held out the basket. 'Tuppence a dozen be all I asks.'

'I've no use for pegs and no time for gypsies neither!' Cherry-strewn bonnet bobbing, a black-garbed woman turned a shrewish shoulder.

'Then mebbes a ribbon, a gift for an unwed daughter, one who ran away from 'ome, over a year gone.'

A swift drawn breath was the answer; Rosa smiled as the woman stalked off. 'Don't cost no copper to be civil, but ill manners carries their own price. Mebbe that one will think twice afore snappin' at a body again.' Then with a wink at Regan she moved on along the street.

'Buy pegs from a gypsy.' Rosa chanted the words at passers-by. 'Buy pegs from a gypsy an' you'll 'ave good luck.'

'May I look at your ribbons?' Attractive in yellow muslin, a cream straw bonnet tied over dark hair with a wide band of yellow tulle, a young girl stepped away from several older women all listening to one who was speaking rapidly, while darting glances at a mail coach halted at the further side of the street.

'I heard it for myself.' The woman's voice, though supposedly hushed in confidence, came clearly to Regan. 'It was in Marston grocer store. The driver came in while I was ordering supplies for the Lodge. Mr Marston asked would I excuse him for a moment while he took delivery of the village post. Well,' the woman looked from one to the other of her listeners, 'I wasn't eaves-dropping, I don't be that kind, but the shop don't be large, I couldn't help but overhear.'

'So you couldn't help but listen, but what was it you listened to?' Less patient than her neigh-bours, a stringy woman dressed entirely in black, a matching bonnet perched dangerously on top of a knot of steel-grey hair, put the demand in not so hushed voice.

'It were to do with what I heard the master and mistress along of the Lodge talking about a few days since. They had been to Ross-on-Wye and on the way back had spent a little time at Hellen House out along of somewheres called Much Marcle. Well, while there it seems they heard of a fire breakin' out at some place the name of Woodford, and Woodford be the name I heard spoke by that post driver; he said there'd been a fire, that the whole house had burned completely.'

The whole of Woodford House burned comp-letely! Holding the basket of ribbons Regan's hands trembled.

'Let me 'elp you my pretty.' Smiling at the young girl intent on the ribbons, Rosa took the basket, thrusting herself between Regan and the girl. 'Pink be a colour of a match to your cheeks, an' it'll set off that lovely hair o' yourn, or mebbes green, the green o' your bright eyes.'

'I don't know, I really cannot choose between them.'

'Then why not tek both?' Rosa draped the shiny satin over her fingers. 'They be nought but a penny apiece, what be a penny when it adds to beauty such as you be blessed wi'.'

'Burned complete you says?'

Distinct over Rosa's soft cajoling the words drove into Regan's brain.

'That be what that post driver says, and he don't be likely to get things wrong!' Aggrieved at having her word questioned, the informer hitched her basket high on her arm as she prepared to walk away.

'Hold you there, Hetty.' One of the women caught at the sleeve of Hetty's coat. 'Did your folk along of the Lodge say if any folk were hurt by cause of that fire?'

'I heard the master and mistress say no more than I've said.' The woman sniffed displeasure.

Indignation, warranted or otherwise, was not to be allowed to cut off a welcome item of gossip. Such did not reach Abberley every day. This obvious in her tone, another of the women joined the debate.

'Of course you would not hear your people say any more.' The second woman smiled understandingly. 'You would not linger to hear private conversation.'

'Perhaps the green, no ... the pink ... oh dear, I really do not know which is the prettier.'

Standing in front of Rosa, her gaze centred on the array of ribbons, the girl was oblivious of Rosa's hand reaching to squeeze Regan's arm; and Regan, wholly attuned to the conversation of the women, was also unaware of the hand intended to warn her against speaking.

'Like you says, I don't make a purpose of listening to what don't be my concern.' Hetty sniffed again.

'That be to your praise; don't be many having the same position as you holds has the same principles.' The oil smoothed troubled waters; Hetty's grip on her basket relaxed. Mollified by the commendation she glanced across to where Rosa and Regan appeared intent on the girl fingering a variety of ribbons. Then, content the gypsies were not listening, she resumed her party piece.

'Well...' She paused, enjoying her moment of drama to the full. 'It was while I was taking fresh tea to the afternoon table, not that I intended to listen...'

'Of course not Hetty... God forbid it be ever thought!'

Encouraged by yet more flattery of her character, Hetty continued. 'Well as I say, I were carrying a tray of tea into the drawing room and the master and mistress were speaking of a fire. Some fine house so it sounded. Tragic were the word the master used; tragic the loss of a home, but when the fire which destroyed it also burned

156

a body to death then that tragedy were doubled.'

'Tek the two my pretty lady, tek two ribbons an' the gypsy will read of your palm an' not ask a farthin' for the doin' o' it.' Rosa's offer, laughingly made, covered the gasp Regan could not withhold. 'You like to know what the future 'as for you, I be certain.'

How had she held back the tears, how had she managed to keep her tongue still?

Sitting once more on the step of the caravan, Regan buried her face in her hands.

15

'Mother said I was to come, Mrs Mullin.'

Rosa smiled at a girl who seemed of an age with Regan. Star's low growl kept her standing some way off from the caravan. 'You are welcome.' Then she gave a curt order to the dog which sank belly first onto the ground and added, 'Come you close an' tek a sup o' tea.'

Murmuring her thanks, and with several side glances to where Regan sat on the steps of the prettily painted wagon, the girl came to the fire, her blue skirts covering the stump of tree she sat on.

'It were after bein' along o' Abberley, talk 'eard there were not the same as I'd 'eard along o' ...' She paused, glancing again at Regan. 'Well, it were just not the same.'

'What talk do that be?' Rosa handed the girl a

tin mug filled with tea poured from the steaming kettle.

'I don't know as I should speak more.'

'If it be your mother sent you, girl, then you best be sayin' what it be you were meant to say, for Rebecca Turley won't brook no goin' against 'er word.' Unheard by any except for Star whose head had lifted, ears pointed expectantly, Joab had returned from tethering the horse and giving it its nightly feed.

'You be right in that.' The girl laughed. 'Mother be 'er own law an' we chavvies abides by it or risks a birch broom about the backside.'

'Rebecca Turley knows a strong 'and be needed wi' children, though I doubts that leads to a broom teken' to 'er racklies.'

The laugh rang out once more, brown eyes dancing as they swung to Joab.

'Girl or lad, Mr Mullin, we all pays the piper should Mother's word not be followed, though I grant 'er don't lay the broom to us girls.'

Joab's own deep-throated laugh joined that of the girl seated at his fire. 'Then young Sara, if you don't feel minded to pay no piper tonight you 'ad best say what it is Rebecca sent you to say.'

Holding the mug between her hands, dark head lowered, the girl murmured, 'The gaujo.'

'Regan don't be o' Romany blood, but 'er be a friend o' Joab an' Rosa Mullin, that were enough for your father an' it seems it be acceptable to Rebecca or 'er never would 'ave 'ad you come to this camp.' Rosa's rebuke was sharp against the hush of approaching night.

'I meant no slight, Mrs Mullin.' Soft in its

158

apology the reply came swiftly. 'It were just ... just I don't want to be the cause o' addin' sorrow to that already carried.'

'A sorrow shared be a sorrow 'alved,' Rosa answered more gently. 'If what you come about be aught to do wi' Regan then I says you speak it now where 'er can 'ave the hearin' o' it.'

'It were when we were along o' Putley way. I called at a fine 'ouse thinkin' to sell a ribbon or two to the maids there. Well, seein' they wanted none I minded to try a bit o' dukkerin'.' She glanced at Regan. 'That be a tellin' o' fortunes.' Then at Regan's nod of understanding she went on, 'it were while I was a readin' o' a woman's palm I 'eard others talkin' in the kitchen; talkin' of a fire which had burned what they called a summer 'ouse, burned it almost complete they said, and along o' it a body, that o' a young lad.'

Regan's swift gasp broke the flow of the girl's speech but Rosa urged her on.

'I d'ain't hear much after that for them other women they looked to where I was dukkerin' and they lowered their voices, but I did hear the mention o' police an' then of summat found on that poor burned body.'

'Summat ... what summat?'

Rosa's demand was met with silence. She looked at Joab, the dog now at his heels. 'You knows, don't you? You knows what it be sticks to the girl's tongue.'

'I knows.' Joab nodded. 'Same as I knows it be best Sara speaks it for 'erself. It be all right my racklie.' He smiled at the silent girl, her eyes fixed to her cup avoiding Rosa's stare. 'Regan knows you will speak no lie.'

Coming down from her seat on the step of the caravan, Regan asked quietly, 'Woodford? Was it Woodford House you called at?'

The girl's head lifted, her eyes fastening on Regan's. 'I don't 'ave the knowin' o' letters so I couldn't tell them set in the wall along o' them tall gates, but I does 'ave ears an' they be sharp. Them women a talkin' low so the gypsy wouldn't 'ear, but Sara Turley 'eard; her 'eared them say the body in that summer 'ouse was charred an' unrecognisable, but the police they 'ad found a ring, a gold ring with the letters S.T. engraved on it.'

S.T. Saul Trent! Regan's senses reeled, blending dark earth with scarlet-purple sky. Saul had been burned to death – Rosa's 'vision' had proved true!

Catching the stumbling Regan, Rosa helped her return to the step where she seated her gently. The shock of what had been said had the girl near to fainting but it had come as no surprise to Rosa Mullin; the 'sight' might not always reveal as much as it could, often it left gaps that gave rise to conjecture, but what it did bring never proved wrong.

Handing her cup to Rosa, the girl Sara spoke quietly. 'I 'pologises for the upsettin', Mrs Mullin, I told Mother as 'ow that might be the result, but her would 'ave it that I come.'

'Rebecca made a wise decision, an' I be sure that the 'earing of what you 'ave said will prove to settle Regan's mind as to what 'er does in future days, it...' Rosa's reply faded, warned into silence by her husband's hand.

'Quiet!' Joab spoke low to the dog which stood

160

facing the shadows forming beyond the rim of firelight. Hair bristling along its back, ears sharp against the half light, it continued its warning growl. 'Quiet,' Joab repeated, 'I know 'e be there, I've 'ad the knowin' o' that all along.'

'It be me, Mr Mullin, Ben Turley.' From among the tall grass a figure rose, solid against the mauve and pearl of evening. 'Mother said I was to see Sara safe 'ere an' then back to our wagon, but Sara said the gaujo...' He halted embarrassed at using a word which minutes ago had caused Rosa to speak sharply, then continued, 'Sara said the girl sharin' camp along o' you might not want a man...'

'That were understandin' o' you, Ben Turley,' Joab answered as the younger man broke off again. 'You give our regard to your mother an' thank 'er for the sendin' o' your sister.'

The two having left, Rosa steeped the valerian leaves she had collected fresh from the hedgerow when returning from Abberley village, leaving them a few minutes in hot water. Then handing a cup of it to Regan sat with her while she drank it. Valerian tea was a remedy much used among the Romany for the easing of stress and helping to bring on restful sleep, and the girl sitting beside her needed both.

'Drink it down my racklie,' she murmured. 'It'll do naught but good, sleep be what you needs.'

Sleep! Regan sipped, not tasting the liquid in her mouth. How would she ever sleep again! How would she ever ban those words from her mind!

'...a body, that o' a young lad ... a ring, a gold ring ... the letters S.T ...'

Unwanted, the words spoken by Sara Turley

161

returned: words Regan knew would remain with her forever.

'You ought not to have come here!' Sherwyn Huntley looked irately at his visitor.

'Not come!' Draped carelessly on a brocaded sofa, Myles Wentworth affected a frown. 'But would that not have seemed strange? A good friend and business partner failing to call, to offer his condolence in this unhappy time; surely that would have given rise to speculation.'

He was right of course. Sherwyn acknowledged the sense of the argument but lost none of the feeling of ill temper. The staff here at Woodford would notice Wentworth's failure to call, and gossip had a way of spreading to the village, then beyond; and gossip, any sort of gossip concerning this house, was the last thing he wanted.

'So.' Myles flicked an imaginary speck from elegant tailored trousers. 'The admirable inspector of constabulary was satisfied with his inquiry?'

'Perfectly.'

'And the body? Why waste that which would have sold? Even soiled goods bring a tidy profit when sold through the right channels.'

'Profit!' Heavy with sarcasm the retort snorted across the room. 'If you could for one moment think of anything but your pocket you would realise the true profit behind that action.'

With the merest raising of an eyebrow, the plucking of a trouser crease, Myles Wentworth replied with equal sarcasm, 'Perhaps you would enlighten me.'

Glancing first at the closed door, Sherwyn

moved from where he stood at the fireplace, taking a chair facing the man he would rather had stayed away.

'Yes.' It came quietly. 'I will enlighten you for it appears you haven't the wherewithal to think it out for yourself. Dressing that boy in clothes belonging to Saul Trent, placing a signet ring with the initial S.T. on his finger was the one certain way of bringing any police search for him to an end. As far as they, or any others, are concerned, the boy burned in that fire was my stepson; could you have devised a better plan?'

'Mmm.' Myles pursed an attractive mouth. 'But surely they, the inspector I mean, will ask questions as to why, if it were your stepson, did he not come to the house, why choose the summer house?'

There had been a constant stream of sympathy cards all of which had had of necessity to be replied to, and of course he had been forced to spend time with the callers with their commiserations, but with this question of Wentworth's, Sherwyn felt the tension ease. That had been the most satisfying part of the whole charade! A self-regarding smile curving his lips, he nodded. 'The question was posed, but it was put by me. I asked why Saul would choose to go to the summer house?'

'And?'

'And.' Huntley's smile remained. 'The inspector furnished a very plausible reason. He said it was certainly an extension of a boyish adventure, to spend a night in the garden before having to face a possibly – and very rightly – displeased stepfather. He further surmised the boy woke in the night, and probably scared by the darkness lit the lamp he would know was always kept there, then he likely stumbled, being still half asleep, fell and knocked his head against the table. Most likely he stunned himself while at the same time sending the lighted oil lamp crashing to the ground resulting in the fire.'

'How accommodating of the inspector, and as you say very plausible.'

'The coroner thought so, he returned a verdict of death by misadventure, and that marks the end of one part of our problem; the police will no longer be looking for Saul and therefore will have no cause to come further to this house.'

Myles rose, a lazy languid movement. 'All very neat, Huntley, but what of the second half of the problem, what of the stepdaughter?'

What of Regan Trent? The thought which the whole morning had plagued Sherwyn Huntley's mind returned. The efforts he had employed to track her down had so far failed; what if she decided to go to the police? It could prove awkward, especially so after the business of her brother.

'Have you heard anything from those you hired to search for her? No!' Myles answered his own query, 'I see you have not, in which case will the admirable inspector not wonder as to her absence? Would not any sister, especially one devoted as Regan, be present at the funeral of a brother?'

He thought he was so clever! Acid contempt flaring, Sherwyn rose to pour two glasses of brandy from a decanter set on a side table. So astute! Holding the decanter a moment longer he

164

subdued the disdain flashing in his eyes though the taste of it remained in his throat.

'There will be no enquiry as to Regan's absence.' He turned, the very movement a sneer. 'Unlike yourself, Myles, I think everything through before taking an action of any kind, I weigh up the benefits, and definitely the disadvantages, of all I say or do. In this measure I have informed the police, and friends with whom I have been in contact since the disappearance of my stepson, that Regan is at present with relatives on the Continent, and that it is my wish she remain there for the next few months in order to avoid the pain of what is happening presently at Woodford, until she feels she can return.'

'How very thoughtful!'

Handing the other man a glass, Sherwyn noted the snideness of the remark, his reply matching it. 'The inspector of police thought so!'

Accepting the brandy, Myles swallowed half before answering. 'Then there is no more to worry over.'

No more to worry over! That was ever the verdict of a fool! Sherwyn submerged his true feelings with a mouthful of brandy saying as he swallowed, 'That, Myles, is not the case. We have every need to worry: Regan Trent could at any time make contact with the police, with her father's lawyer or any other person her family knew. Therefore it is imperative we continue to search for her.'

'Then here's to success.'

Success! Sherwyn watched alcohol disappear into his visitor's mouth. There would be success all right ... for Sherwyn Huntley!

16

She had been offered the chance of a safe return to Woodford. As she sat beside Rosa, the caravan moving at a gentle pace, Regan's mind roved back over the past. The valerian tea had brought sleep but at its departure the turmoil of thoughts had returned. Her brother was dead, Saul was dead, burned to death in the summer house they had played in, that same summer house where she had lain drowsy in the summer heat, where she had overheard her mother and Sherwyn Huntley talking.

'...*what if Regan should become pregnant?*'

'...*not all things are a result of willingness...*'

And it had not happened willingly. The peg she was attempting to fashion fell from trembling fingers, a hot tide of shame flooding into her cheeks. Sherwyn Huntley had done what those words spoken to her mother had implied: he had raped her daughter!

There had been no pity in him then, no re-morse, and in the hush of dawn, in the solitude of the bender tent, she had realised there would be none at her return to Woodford. What Sher-wyn Huntley had done would be done again and still again, she would be subjected to his vileness until the object of it was achieved. And once it was achieved, what of her then? The answer had come as before, whispering out of the silence and the soft darkness.

'*...she will follow the path taken by her mother...*'

Huntley would not settle for a fortune; all that should have belonged to Regan Trent would not be enough. He would take her life as well. It had been then she had made her decision. She would not return to Woodford. But Huntley would not give up, he would continue to hunt her as hounds hunt a fox.

'If that peg be finished set it wi' the rest in the basket an' let's be away into the town.' Already having descended the caravan steps, Rosa tied a bright red neckerchief around her head, her dark hair caught in one thick plait left to hang low over one shoulder.

'Mind you stays close.' Rosa handed across the shallow basket filled with a multi-coloured selection of ribbons. 'It be the time o' the fair and the place'll be bustlin' wi' all kind o' folk, but there will be some will pay mind to a fair-skinned racklie, so it pays to take care.'

Folk would take notice of a fair-complexioned girl being in the company of gypsies, but that was a chance she had to take. Taking the ribbons, Regan fell into step beside Rosa.

In the weeks of travelling she had learned a little of the strange Romany language and some of their ways, but most of all she had learned of their kindness, of loyalty not just to their own but to any who, like herself, had been taken into their community. Now again Rosa was being careful of her protection.

'*Be you sure?*' That had been Rosa's question that morning when the use of colour to darken her skin had been refused. From now on she would use no more berry juice, nor would she dress as a gypsy. From today she would wear her own clothing.

'*You'll draw the eye,*' Rosa had warned. '*You be playin' right into that varmint's 'ands.*'

'*He will find me sooner or later.*' Regan had made her own quiet reply. '*But he will not find me with the Mullins.*'

'*Then 'e won't find you nowheres, cos Joab an' me don't be lettin' you travel alone!*'

There had been a tussle of words yet even as they had been spoken Regan had felt that Rosa too sensed parting was near.

She could not go on accepting their hospitality, she could not continue day after day taking food they worked hard to earn. The fact she contributed nothing was worry enough, but that of having Rosa and Joab risk imprisonment on her behalf was worse. It would be hard leaving the couple she had come to hold dear, but it was that very love which said she must no longer expose them to the spite of Sherwyn Huntley.

Rosa of course had objected, Joab also declaring her '*being along o' them brought no 'ardship, it were easy a feedin' of three as it were of two.*'

But finally they had accepted her decision. Today she would accompany Rosa into the town, after that they would each go their own way.

But what way would that be? Despite the warmth of the day Regan felt a tremor run along her veins. She had no money, and she certainly would accept none from Rosa or from Joab. So what would she do? Where would she find lodging she could not pay for? Not even the workhouse would take a young, healthy woman, strong enough to make her own living.

'We goes to the fairground first.' Rosa broke in on Regan's thoughts. 'Reckon there'll be a number o' folk there by this time, should be I'll get a nice bit o' dukkerin' an' you be like to sell a ribbon or two.'

With heaven's help she would earn her bread today, but tomorrow, and the rest of her tomorrows? Would heaven help with those?

She had been to fairs before but never one such as she was seeing now. Those she had visited with her parents had been so different. Held on the village green, they had been gentler. True there had been the calls of tinkers plying their trade, the sing-song voices of pedlars advertising the delights of a pretty brooch or necklace, of ribbons or posies of wild flowers, 'For your pretty lady an' only a penny.' Her father had smiled then reached into his pocket, handing the pedlar the penny while she, Regan, had gazed wide-eyed into a large basket not knowing which ribbon or pin to choose. And there had been jugglers and tumblers, their performances so exciting to a child, but this! This was something she had never envisaged on those visits to the fairs at Putley.

She felt, bemused by the noise of steam engines powering roundabouts, king and queen swing boats, their passengers squealing as the giant cages swung dangerously near to overturning; her breath caught at the sight of an elaborate Calliope, its façade ornamented with life-sized figures of

169

nymphs whose ample charms were barely hidden by painted flimsy draperies, its music blaring so loud it almost drowned the shouts of barkers calling their goods, of sideshow entertainers singing and dancing to fiddle and drum, the roar of a large crowd of people urging on pugilists, those bare-knuckled boxers, cheeks running with blood and eyes half closed from huge purple bruises.

Caught by the glare of hissing gaslights, the loud vibrant music, the air heady with the intoxication of promised delights, Regan was entranced. Her basket hung forgotten on her arm and she walked as in a dream, her glance flitting from one noisy distraction to another, dancing over them like a moth around a lighted candle.

'Now ain't that a sight! A pretty wench with a basket of ribbons, makes a man's blood run does that.'

Caught by the elbow, the force of it pulling her off her feet, Regan was held against a man, his laugh coarse as he drew her closer.

'That's what I calls friendly.'

His arms had pulled her tight against heaving flesh, the throb of flesh she had felt once before, and in that instant the delight which had held her spellbound vanished. Pushing against the figure gripping her she cried out but it was lost in the hubbub of noise.

'Take care! Stay close!' Too late Rosa's words returned to her mind.

Twisting, she tried to free herself of the man's hold, of the leering face beginning to descend toward her own, but her struggles only served to intensify his emotions.

'I thinks you and me should find ourselves a quiet little spot somewheres.'

Beer-soaked breath fanning her face, Regan felt her stomach turn. There was no mistaking what he had in mind. Crying out again she turned her mouth away.

'You wants to play does you!' The laugh rasped again. 'Well I ain't against that but how about a little kiss or two first.'

'How about I grabs you by that which be swingin' amid your legs an' squeezes 'em 'til the tears run!'

The basket, empty of pegs, whistled through the air, the thud of it hitting the side of the man's head lost among general noise, but several passers-by witnessing the blow paused to catcall and cheer seeing the debacle as one more event to be enjoyed.

The blow took him by surprise and the man's hold broke, the suddenness of it sending Regan stumbling as he pitched forwards.

'Steady, wench.' A woman in the crowd stretched out a hand to prevent Regan from falling. 'That one be a nasty bugger, you best find your man afore 'e finds 'is feet.'

Her mind reeling, Regan murmured her thanks then turned as the voice of her attacker roared over the strident sounds coming from every angle.

Righted on his feet, head drawn low to his shoulders, he snorted like an enraged bull, hands held claw-like before him. Eyes blazing with drunken fury, he glared at a figure standing staring back at him.

'You bloody gypsy bitch!'

171

The roar erupted, adding to the delight of a fast-gathering crowd who cheered even louder at the answer.

'A gypsy bitch sees off any vermin an' that be includin' of the two-legged kind.'

'You tell 'em...'

'...give 'im another but 'arder this time...'

Thoroughly enjoying this added spectacle, onlookers shouted for it to continue.

'Gypsy trollop!' Eyes spewing temper, fingers opening and closing uncontrollably, the man took a step forwards. 'Bloody filth, I'll rip your bloody 'ead off!'

'It be needin' a man to do that an' you don't be no man!' Defiant, the answer, loud and clear, slipped into a moment of quiet as the music of the Calliope changed. As the music began to regain volume another voice was heard, this low and full of anger.

'Hey diddikai ... you've tried threatenin' of a gypsy bitch now try a threatenin' of the dog!'

At the edge of the crowd, his yellow neckerchief tied loosely about his throat, shirt open to the chest, Joab stood with hands on hips.

'Well?' Joab's head lifted to an angle which reflected gleams of gaslight in the ebony of his eyes like dark fire. 'Well?' he demanded again. 'Be it a man I be lookin' at or just melalo mush, black filth, for it be only men of that kind assaults one woman and threatens the next. That be courage of a gaujo!' Dark fire flared as his hands dropped to his sides with a deceptive ease. 'But do it stretch to fightin' wi' a Romany man?'

Unmistakable, the challenge hung in the air

172

seeming to blot out all sound in Regan's ears. This was her fault. Had she kept her wits about her, not let her mind become dazzled by the excitement of the fair, this would not have happened.

'Joab, no!' She started forward but was held back by the same woman's hand which had prevented her falling to the ground.

'Stay clear of 'em, wench.' The words were quiet against Regan's ear. 'Don't do to get in the way of men fightin'.'

'But it's my fault... Joab must not fight on my account.'

'He'll be fightin' for what he loves.' The woman's hand tightened as Regan made to pull away. 'You would see that if you only open your eyes. That gypsy woman be his wife and no man worthy of the title sees her insulted and him just standing by and tekin' no action; you bide still and let matters tek their course.'

'Dirty bloody gyppo!'

The shout sent a ripple of expectation through the assembled crowd. A fight they didn't have to pay to watch inside the boxing booth! A match between a gypsy and a drunk, this was a treat indeed.

'Filth, scum!' The man snarled, his rage-filled eyes fastened on Joab. 'I be goin' to cut your bloody balls off and mek that bitch o' yourn cook 'em.'

Where had the knife come from? Regan had not seen it drawn yet it was there in the man's hand, the long blade glinting silver death. Joab! She darted a glance to where he stood. Joab must turn away, he could be injured – he could be killed! Breathless at the thought, Regan could only stare.

'Watch him, chap, it be a dirty fighter uses a knife.'

Among the watching group someone else had seen the blade and called a warning to Joab; but he stood as before with hands loose at his sides, the fire in his eyes the only evidence of anger.

'I'll mek 'er cook 'em then I'll stuff 'em down 'er filthy gypsy throat!'

Even as he spoke the man lunged forward lifting the knife above his head, but to Regan frozen with fear for her friends it seemed everything was taking place in slow motion. The knife rose leisurely, its bearer moving with a lazy unhurried step; and Joab ... Joab's glance had gone behind his protagonist, gone to where Star was crouched low to the ground, bared teeth wet and yellow, eyes gleaming chips of jet.

'Stay!'

Joab's lips moved soundlessly, his glance returning to the other man with an almost imperceptible movement that had Regan wanting to scream; yet still the dream-like scene went on. Heavy, dull, almost lethargic the man moved toward Joab, the knife already held above his head rising slowly higher while his mouth widened in a protracted soundless snarl.

Joab had no weapon! Horror held Regan motionless but could not still her mind. He had forbidden Star to protect him! Why could he not see the danger he was in? Why did he stand there when he could grab Rosa and disappear into the crowd?

The knife was descending! Regan's heart lurched, pushing sickness into her throat. It was level with Joab's face ... it was moving toward his chest! Move! She screamed silently, run Joab! Gripped by her own fear, unable to tear her eyes away, she watched the slowly moving scene.

At a snail's pace the knife lowered, bringing the pointed tip towards the bronzed chest. The assailant's mouth opened yet again, a delayed torpid snarl that had no sound for Regan, and yet Joab remained still.

He would die! Regan's mind swirled. Joab would die and it would be her fault! It should be her facing that man, she should be the one answerable to his fury, she should intervene! The thought returning some measure of sense to her mind she tried to prise loose the hand on her arm but the grip only tightened.

'Wait, wench!' Soft beneath the invasion of sound once more filling her world Regan heard the words, 'Wait, watch the gypsy, he be a smart one.'

'Watch the gypsy.' It was all she could do, her gaze refused to be drawn away from Joab. Caught as if in some nightmare Regan watched the knife, watched the arm delivering death. 'Run Joab, run please.' It was a cry, sounding only in her heart. Momentarily caught by the glow of yellow gas-light the knife blade glistened, the menace of it thickening the terror which held Regan mesmerised, then so slowly it seemed not to move it dropped lower, and lower still. 'Joab, for God's sake run!' The words like those others spoken deep inside never reached her tongue. Then the knife was gone, disappeared from her sight, lost between the two figures. Had it plunged into Joab's chest? Was it driving deep into his heart? Choking on a scream of guilt and fear Regan tore at the fingers holding her, then all of a sudden they loosed and the woman was pointing. Regan lived her nightmare. Joab would fall, his chest would be covered with blood, and the knife, the knife would be deep in his heart.

'I said he were smart and so he be.' Beside Regan the woman smiled but Regan failed to see or hear, her attention still riveted on the two men.

'Good for you, gyppo,' a shout emanated from somewhere in the background, 'that no-good 'as bin askin' to get 'is arse kicked for a long time!'

A hail of laughter followed the call but as quickly it was drowned under a wave of indrawn breath which reached through the miasma clouding Regan's senses, bringing her sharply back to reality. In that second she saw Joab's arm flash upwards, saw the knife glitter in a silver arc as it was flung from his hand, heard the one word 'guard' as it fell to where Star stood, every muscle tense, the hair of his back erect as a thousand steel pins; no other man would take up that blade. Then Joab's arm dropped, striking his opponent across the back and as the man grunted he grabbed his arm and twisting his own body sideways sent him somersaulting through the air, the same graceful movement bringing him to stand with legs akimbo over his would-be killer.

'Well my diddikai friend.' Joab looked down at the man lying between his feet. 'The frying pan be ready, so tell me, whose balls are to be cooked, mine ... or yours?'

No anger accompanied the words, no threat. It seemed merely a question, but it was a deception belied by the black fire that was Joab's stare. Ringed by onlookers whose appreciative calls praised the skill by which he had despatched his attacker, Joab paid them no heed, but to the man on the ground said quietly, 'Whose will it be? The choosin' be yourn, but you makes it here an' now!'

Joab moved from straddling the man. Less than a yard from him he waited. For a brief moment the man lay still. Winded from the fall he stared up at Joab with eyes spewing hate.

'We ain't finished,' he muttered, 'you'll be comin' to Wednesbury again, but next time you won't be leavin'!'

A soft whistle had Star pick up the knife. Carrying it to where Joab pointed the dog dropped it beside the hand of the man still lying on the ground, then at Joab's tilt of the head it resumed its watch from the edge of the crowd.

'It don't be the way of the Romany to let a matter go unsettled.' Joab spoke in the same quiet voice but beneath the velvet lay hardened steel. 'There be your weapon, tek it up the dog won't touch you, tek it up and let's finish this now.'

'Go on, get up!'

Smelling a further entertainment the calls and jeers of the watching crowd began again.

'Ar, get you up!'

'You 'eard what the bloke said,' a voice louder than the rest shouted over the sound of a hurdy-gurdy. Hung by a stout strap about the neck of yet another pedlar who relentlessly turned a

177

handle attached to one side of a closed wooden box, it churned out a medley of tinny music. Unrewarded except by demands to 'sling your 'ook', the musician moved on.

''E won't fight.' A woman's voice rose as the hurdy-gurdy man turned away. ''E be like 'is trousers, full o' nuthin' but wind!'

'Reckon you be right, missis, won't no woman tickle that forra tanner!'

As if borne on the tide of laughter erupting from the crowd the fallen man was on his feet.

'Bloody gypsy bastard!'

Every acid syllable was spat at Joab, then with a swiftness which brought hoots of derision he turned to push his way between jeering on-lookers and was gone, lost into the night.

17

She had never felt so desolate. Regan watched the pretty painted caravan roll away around the bend of a narrow track, squeezing back tears as it passed from sight. Even at the death of her mother, that awful intense pain had beneath it a grain of comfort for she had been in surroundings familiar since childhood; but here she was utterly and completely alone, alone in a place so totally foreign to Woodford and its gentle countryside surroundings it could have been a different world.

'You don't be goin' to stay 'ere?' Rosa's words on hearing she would no longer travel with Joab and

herself had been filled with doubt. This town she had called Wednesbury, with its smoke and grime, its soul-destroying poverty so evident in drawn features and bent backs, was no fit place for a woman brought up as she had been, given the best of everything.

The best of everything! Regan drew her coat around her. Did that 'best' include a stepfather who had murdered a wife and raped a stepdaughter? Did it include a fiancé who wanted her only for her property? That was what Woodford had held for her, how then could this town hold worse?

'It don't be what you be used to, you won't never be able to settle 'ere, you'll never live in this grime!

Had those next words of Rosa made her decide to remain here? Had that given birth to the idea in her mind? Living among coal mines, iron manufacturers and streets of tiny houses blackened by a continuous pall of grey smoke rising from hundreds of houses each with its workshop was so very different to all she had ever known; would Sherwyn Huntley also be of the opinion she could not live here? So sure he would not even bother to have his minions search such a town? Rosa had been dubious of that, claiming it would be safer for her to travel on with them, to put as wide a distance as possible between herself and her tormentor. But that had been another reason for refusing to go on. That debacle at the fair had drawn a sizeable crowd, many shouting encouragement and congratulation to Joab; it had been an unlooked-for entertainment talk of which had been loud. And talk passed from mouth to mouth, so gossip might eventually reach the ears of Sherwyn Huntley. If that happened, if he got to know of a fair-haired young woman travelling with a gypsy couple, then he would not rest until he found them, and Joab would not defeat Huntley as easily as he had that man at the fair. That had been the final deciding factor. Rosa and Joab had risked enough on her behalf; she would not have them risk more.

'Tek this my racklie, tie it to any tree along a track-way, to any gatepost, its message will be sent. No matter where in the country the wagon o'Joab Mullin be restin' word'll reach it. The Romany be family an' it be many a'tween 'em, they 'ave thousands of eyes and ears. They travels wherever a path leads an' they looks out for one another an' for a gaujo accepted as you 'ave been accepted. So keep you this, an' should it be you 'ave need o' Rosa Mullin then you tie it as I've told an' I'll a come.'

Taking a slip of yellow ribbon from her pocket Regan held it to her lips, tears she could no longer hold back tracing lines down her cheeks.

'There has been no further enquiry?'

'None.' Sherwyn Huntley answered the man opposite. 'The police and magistrate were convinced of the dead boy's identity – after all who else could be wearing Saul Trent's clothes?'

'Clothes are not everything.'

Clothes are not everything! That coming from Myles Wentworth, a dandy if ever there was one! Sherwyn Huntley's answer was carefully bland. 'Perhaps not, but the ring was; there could be no argument as to that.'

'A masterly touch.'

Never one to disguise his talent for organising life to suit himself, Huntley made no effort to hide that light under a bushel now. It would do no harm to have Wentworth kept aware of which of them had the brains. Eyebrows raising slightly he returned coolly, 'Had you expected anything other?'

The man was so supercilious, so cocksure! Myles hid the surge of anger in a swallow of brandy. But one day Mr Sherwyn Huntley was going to receive a nasty shock, and that day would be soon. Then it would be seen who truly had the touch of a master!

'The package we sent last week.' He changed the subject abruptly. 'It seems to have met with appreciation, so much so I have received a request for several of the same.'

'Impossible!' Huntley sat up sharply, his glance whipping around a room furnished with velvet-covered armchairs and small mahogany tables set in secluded alcoves, lit by gasoliers which lent a heavily shaded light.

'Nothing is impossible.' Myles held up his glass, summoning a man dressed in a black suit and an immaculate shirt of brilliant white.

'I have told you before—'

'So you have,' Myles cut in smoothly. 'And I have told you. Business as it is now does not give me the returns I require; a fellow of my standing needs money, lots of money, and I intend to have it.'

'Not that way.'

'What better way?' Taking his glass from a silver tray held deferentially by the returning waiter,

Myles smiled over the brim. 'The goods are easily acquired, the purchase is relatively low cost and resale price is high.'

Irritated by argument he had heard only too often in recent weeks, Sherwyn Huntley glared at the face smiling so confidently. 'It is too risky,' he hissed through set teeth, 'it isn't exactly like taking cattle to market.'

'No.' Myles held up the glass, admiring the pinpoints of light flickering in its depths. 'Not like taking cattle to market, more like lambs to the slaughter.'

'Quiet you fool! Even the walls in this place have ears! Do you want them all to hear our business?'

'Only you Huntley ... only you!' Myles lowered the glass, the urbane smile already gone. 'I want you to hear clearly: either we sell more goods or I take a larger percent; the ball, my dear fellow, or should I say "balls", are in your court.'

The crudeness of the remark not lost on him, Sherwyn frowned contempt. Wentworth was fast becoming a liability, a liability he neither wanted nor could afford.

'The goods are easily acquired.' Irritation flared into resentment. Wentworth was a fool to think like that. The game they played was a game of chance far more serious than a hand of cards or a bet on horses. Selling young boys into sexual slavery carried the penalty of death; and Sherwyn Huntley had no intention of paying that or any other penalty, neither would he allow Wentworth a larger proportion of profit.

'Gentlemen...'

His line of thought disturbed, Sherwyn Huntley glanced at the woman come to stand in their alcove. Dressed in deepest amber taffeta, her waist cinched by corsets, breasts high above a plunging décolleté neckline, she smiled at them with painted lips.

'I hope you did not find the wait too tiring. I wanted to make quite certain my new, er ... acquisitions met the exacting standard required by my most valued clients. I trust you will find I have overlooked nothing.'

'The evening I know will be perfect as always, Mrs Langley. We shall be well content, is that not so, Huntley?'

Well content! Following the rustling skirts leading the way up red-carpeted stairs, Sherwyn Huntley felt no trace of that emotion. The anticipated evening of pleasuring himself with a young boy, the exhilaration of the feel of young flesh beneath his hands, of being first to enter that tight little channel, had been dulled by Wentworth's demand for money. Dulled but not eliminated! Entering a room lit only by candles he cast a glance to where a lad of young years stared at him through the flickering light. No, not eliminated.

She had to go on trying. Weary from hours of walking, depressed by so many sharp-tongued women telling they wanted 'no pegs nor no hawkers a' wastin' of their time', of others saying they would 'set the dogs on yer', Regan paused beside a smoke-blackened house, one of a long identical line. Houses! She glanced at the drab exteriors. They were so small, how could people

183

live in such dark tiny homes! But they did, and judging by the children she had seen in communal yards made to serve six and even, eight of these houses, the families living in them were by no means few in number.

She had tried all day to sell the pegs Rosa had insisted she take. *'You 'ave to eat'*, Rosa had declared after Regan's adamant refusal to accept money, *'you can sleep under the hedge or in a doorway, that won't see the killn' of you, but a body can't live on naught but air, it needs the puttin' o' food in the belly, so if it be you won't tek a few pence then tek you this basket o' pegs, somebody will 'ave the buyin' o' 'em.'*

Somebody would buy them! Except they had not. Not a single person had so much as looked at them. Easing the basket from one arm to the other she made to speak to a woman emerging from the building she had leaned against. Wrapped in dark shawl pulled partly across her face the woman pushed the outstretched hand away muttering words unintelligible to Regan, but she understood the meaning behind them: the woman wanted no pegs!

Stomach rumbling from hunger, Regan glanced at a sky turned suddenly crimson. It was beautiful, a wide swathe of gold-edged carmine lustrous against the purple-grey of approaching night. Night! A puzzled frown nestling between her brows, she watched the dazzling display. It was not due to the setting sun, for the sun had not shown itself all day through the heavy pall of acrid smoke and there were no brilliant sparks, no sound of fireworks which usually accompanied a bonfire lit to celebrate some public holiday. What then was it had turned half of the sky to fire?

'You ain't seen that afore 'ave you?'

Drawn from the beauty paraded above her head, Regan glanced to where the question came from. A boy looking to be about ten years old, was watching her with intent, almost piercing eyes.

'No.' Regan shook her head. 'No, I have not seen that before, what is the cause?'

'Cause?' The face, smudged with soot, creased with speculation, then smiled. 'You means what be doin' it? That be the glow from the ironworks. They be openin' the furnaces.'

'Opening the furnaces?'

'You don't know nuthin', do yer. They 'as to open the furnaces so they can bring out the crucibles, an' afore yer asks,' the lad grinned widely, 'crucibles be like great big pots, they 'olds the metal that 'as to be smelted.'

'And you'll be 'oldin' your backside, Alfie Jeavons, should you keep your mother waitin' much longer for that bread.'

'Just goin', Mrs Radley.' The boy turned his grin to the woman come to stand on the doorstep. 'Mebbes yer should tell this one not to go standin' with 'er eyes on the sky ... I could've made off wi' that basket afore 'er knowed it.'

'Get away with you!' The woman aimed a hand, missing the boy's dodging head, then as he raced off down the street added. 'He be right though, you should look to what you be about, ain't everybody in this town as honest as young Alfie Jeavons, there be them as would tek the sugar out of your tea an' then come back for the spoon.'

'I'm afraid I was rather taken by the sky, it

185

turned red so suddenly.'

'Ar, it be a sight.' The woman glanced skyward. 'It be about the only thing o' beauty this town can boast but it be beauty born of men's sweat an' women's tears. But then...' she sighed, 'that be the lot of most folk in the Black Country. Seems the Lord turned his back an' give the place to the devil for it be the regions of hell the men of Wednesbury works in. But I must bide by the advice I just give to Alfie an' not dawdle here a tekin' of your time an' a wasting of my own.'

'Wait please!' The half cry had the woman pause. 'Please.' Regan spoke rapidly, needing to get her question put before the woman changed her mind and went indoors, 'Would you ... would you buy some pegs? Twopence a dozen is all I ask.'

'Pegs!' A laugh rang across the darkening street. 'Wench, I sells pegs meself.' The woman's grey head nodded toward the wall against which Regan had leaned. She now saw the window of the house displayed a variety of articles. It was a shop! The last dregs of hope sank into the abyss of despair that was her stomach. This shop sold pegs, and there must be other small shops such as this in other parts of the town; this was why she had been driven from every door. There was no place left to try!

'I see.' Regan lifted the basket higher on her arm. 'Thank you for speaking with me, ma'am; I wish you goodnight.'

Who was this young woman she had called back? Libby Radley looked at the forlorn figure sitting by her kitchen fire. It was the girl she had caught from falling yesterday evening at the fair, the one she had prevented from intervening between that gypsy man and Bert Tanks the local lout. But this one was no gypsy; she was *with* them but she wasn't *one* of them. Libby poured tea into thick china cups and stirred each one thoughtfully. The girl's colouring denied any relationship; she was fair as those gypsy folk were dark, her skin was pale cream where they were deeply coloured by sun and weather. She had by her own admission spent weeks travelling with them, but her speech, her manner, they were not of the road.

So why *was* she on the road? Handing Regan a cup, then taking a second one from the cloth-covered table, Libby carried it from the kitchen, taking it up a narrow staircase. Pausing before a closed door she glanced back at the stairs. Was the wench at her fireside running from some crime, had she broken the law and was trying to avoid the penalty? Or did her crime carry a penalty not so easily avoided, had she tumbled to a man and found her belly not as empty as the third finger of her left hand? Was that girl drooping in her chair carrying a bastard child? Was the father a gypsy who had refused to stand by his own deed, was that the reason she was no longer travelling along of them? A sound within the bedroom interrupted the string of questions and Libby entered the room.

A young woman, and a man not many years ahead of her! Looking down at the sleeping figure Libby placed a gentle hand on the dark brown hair. One left to fend for herself, the other wanting only to fend for himself. Tears she could not shed

187

pricking against her eyelids, Libby turned back to the stairs. Heaven did not always smile but the devil sometimes afforded opportunity. If the wench she had left alone were no more than a common thief then she would be gone, and the cash box on the table gone along of her!

Why had she, Libby Radley, always so careful about putting that box away out of sight, why had she left it on the table? That young woman had only to reach out her hand; with her young legs she could be out of the house and away before any folk round about were called on for help. Reaching the foot of the stairs, the cup of hot tea still in her hand, Libby hesitated. Her brain had told her what she was doing, that she was leaving that box with the week's takings where it could be easily stolen, her mind had warned of her the foolishness of such an act, yet something inside of her, something deeper, had kept her from locking the box away.

You be a fool, Libby Radley, to go a leavin' of that box! Yes, I be a fool, Libby answered her own remonstrance. But there be times it teks a fool to find the truth!

18

The box had not disappeared. It held the same amount of cash as before she had carried that cup upstairs. And it were the same now. Tying the strings of a cotton apron over black skirts Libby took up the box she had allowed to stand all night on the table of her kitchen cum living room. The wench had been asleep when she had come into the room from the stairs, the tea she had been given still on the hob of the blackleaded grate which shone from its twice-weekly polish with Zebo. She had thought to waken her, to see her from the house. Taking up the cash box Libby smiled at her own soft-heartedness. She ought to have turned thought into practice but the sight of that head resting against the chair, the feet stretched to the warmth of the fire and the sound of rain beating steadily against the window had made her reject all idea of turning the young woman back out onto the street. Instead she had covered her with a heavy shawl and left her to sleep.

Sleep! Crossing to the side of the room which also served as a shop, Libby drew closed the heavy green chenille curtain which afforded the living quarter some measure of privacy. If only Libby Radley could sleep; just one night without waking, without the pain! Holding the box against her chest, she stared over the medley of packets and boxes crowded onto the wide shelves a neighbour had erected around and within the window to hold the display of goods, letting her gaze travel into the dull rain-soaked morning. Why had it all been snatched away from her? What terrible wrong had she done that heaven must punish her as it had? Seventeen and loved by Zeb she had been as happy a girl as ever walked to an altar. Then had come Daniel, the child who would add to that love, would increase their happiness a hundredfold. The love had remained. Libby stared, seeing not the grey of the sky but the face of the man she had loved for so long, a face whose eyes glistened with the tears which had filled them on that night twenty-three years ago, the night their son had been born with twisted legs. Yes, the love had lived on but so had the pain; the pain of watching the child drag himself where others ran and jumped, of watching Daniel and knowing beneath his smile sadness was death to his heart. They had made no other child, the risk of another born crippled as the first was a risk neither wished to take: and then, one month before their son's tenth birthday, Zeb, the husband of her soul, had died beneath a fall of coal. An accident, they happened in all coal mines! That had been her only comfort from Lea Brook Colliery; words which would not feed her son. And she had been left with a choice, the poorhouse for Daniel who could not care for himself during the long hours she would have to leave him in order to earn them both a living. She had looked at him sitting in the chair his father had made for him, almost lost among the shadows in that house of mourning, had seen the look in those brown eyes, a look which seemed to read the words of her mind and at the same time to speak forgiveness.

But she had not signed Daniel into the poorhouse. Though penniless except for a week's rent money to be paid to the colliery, she had determined nothing would separate her from the child she loved beyond reckoning. And so she had sold every stick of furniture apart from that so lovingly crafted chair. Sold every stick, every cloth, every spare garment. The blare of a wind siren echoing along the damp streets summoning folk to their work recalled Libby to the present. Placing the cash box beneath a trestle bench serving as a counter her glance rested on her left hand. Bare as was that of the wench still on the other side of the curtain; bare of ring but not of memory, no, never of memory! Losing herself a moment longer she brushed the finger where her wedding ring had been. It had been the last thing to go. Knowing that to pawn it was to lose it for she would not have money enough to redeem the pledge in the time allowed, needing every farthing if she were to keep her son, that last treasure had gone, but the love which had placed it on her finger, that would never be lost.

'A nasty mornin', Libby, don't say as I won't be glad when my rounds be done, though I be thinkin' it'll be as wet a fetchin' in of the cows for the next milkin'.'

Straightening, Libby smiled at the dairy farmer heaving heavy metal churns into the small space set aside among chests and sacks. 'Give it an hour or so and who knows, the sun might shine.'

'Ar.' Churns in place the farmer pulled the flat cap he wore more firmly onto his brow. 'It might, Libby, it might.' He brushed away a raindrop which had dripped from the peak of his cap onto his nose. 'Though with the smoke a goin' up outta all these chimneys I doubts we'd ever a notice of it.'

What would it be like to live in a place where the air was free of coal dust, where the smoke of so many iron foundries, of the hundreds of tiny workshops attached to almost every house in Wednesbury, did not blot out the blue of the sky with a pall of grey, the stench of it clogging the throat as it did the nostrils? Helping carry several empty churns to the cart standing outside Libby patted the flank of the patient horse. Would living in such surroundings have helped Daniel? That was a question she had put to herself over the years and as with every asking the answer came the same: nothing could ever help her son!

A lull in the morning tide of men calling for half an ounce of shag tobacco, a box of Swan Vesta matches or a clay pipe, of women buried in thin shawls out of breath with running the length of several streets for a loaf of yesterday's bread they could buy for a penny halfpenny, Libby returned to the living room, closing the dividing curtain behind her. Now, hands on hips, she watched the young woman busily washing the hearth, a newly banked fire breathing wisps of smoke into the chimney.

'There be no need of your doin' that.'

Coming with unintended sharpness the words had Regan spin about.

'I...' she faltered, 'I wanted to show my appreciation.'

'Ar!' Hands still holding to her hips, Libby responded quickly. 'That be as it might, but a word be all the thanks it teks! Don't be no call for you to go a skivvyin'.'

'I'm sorry.' Regan rose to her feet, glancing embarrassedly at her wet hands. 'I had no wish to offend, it is just that I wanted to show my gratitude for your allowing me to stay the night in your home, for the food you have given me.'

'What be given were given with a good 'eart. Libby Radley don't be a woman who looks for payment in return for the helpin' of another either in kind nor coin; the Lord above sees the doin' and if it be He deems it worthy then the repayin' will be the work of His hand, so let that be it and all about it!'

Almost the words spoken by Rosa. Thought of the gypsy woman and her brusque kindness bringing a lump to her throat, Regan took up the bucket and cloth she had been using. 'I will empty the water and then I will be on my way.' Half the sentence drifted behind her as she went into the cupboard-sized scullery.

Found her way about then! Libby watched the slender figure disappear, and heard the door to the yard open. The wench hadn't simply sat a warmin' of her toes while the shop was busy. But it had been right what were said about there bein' no need of her workin' in payment of a night spent at a fireside! Slight guilt at speaking so sharply brought a flush of warmth to Libby's lined features. Grabbing the kettle from the trivet Regan had swung back over the fire she muttered against the feeling which had surged in her breast. 'I stands by what I says, it be for the Almighty to decide should a kindness deserve the thankin' an' that be Him will pay its due!'

It had been a blessing she had not looked for and one certainly not expected. Regan returned the bucket to its place beside the scullery door, rinsed the cloth and draped it over the bucket to dry, then held her hands under the pump, the coldness of the water making her catch her breath. It had been presumptuous of her to dust the room and see to washing the hearth without asking permission; she had wanted only to show thanks yet instead had annoyed the woman who had provided her with a place of warmth and a meal of hot porridge. How long, if at all, would it prove before she ate another hot meal? Hands tingling from their icy douche she glanced at the metal sky darkened yet further from the perpetual clouds of smoke. Why had she chosen to stay in this forlorn town, why had she not listened to Joab and Rosa and continued on with them? Because you could no longer prevail upon good nature! Regan heard the answer whisper in her mind. The couple had befriended and protected her but that could not have gone on; if Sherwyn Huntley had discovered they had sheltered her, perhaps had been the cause of her not being found sooner, the full force of his anger and spite would have come crashing down upon them.

'You stands there much longer an' you' be a catchin' of your death!' Libby had come to stand at the scullery door.

'I was thinking.'

'Ar, so was I.' Libby glanced at the small hands, the fingers red with cold. 'I were a thinkin' I had no call to go a soundin' off at you. It were right good your washin' of the hearth an' a wiping away of dust. I 'pologises for my sharp tongue. Now...' She turned abruptly back toward the living room. 'Lessen you wants them fingers a sufferin' from the chilblains you'll come inside an' warm 'em.'

194

Warming herself would only exacerbate the coldness of the streets. Following Libby, Regan suppressed a shiver. She would offer her regrets once more for the liberties she had taken and leave.

'Not afore you've 'ad a cup of tea.' Libby dismissed the idea out of hand. 'Ain't nuthin' but social in tekin' a cup of tea.'

It would be welcome. Regan watched the cups being taken from a pine dresser which demanded most of the space allocated as living room. Perhaps being warmed inside as well as out would serve to keep away the bite of a morning seeming to herald the early frost, or was it the chill of a vanquished sun, its heat repelled by a blanket of dark grey smoke?

'There be milk in the jug an' sugar in the basin.' Indicating the dresser with a movement of the hand Libby stirred the teapot then filled the cups.

Three cups! A vague memory brushed Regan's mind. Had there been three cups last evening? Had she really seen what she appeared to be remembering now? Had this woman carried a cup of tea to an upstairs room or had that been a figment of imagination, the result of a tired mind? But she was not tired now, and the third teacup was most definitely not imagined.

'Yes, there be three.' Libby had noticed the glance playing speculatively over the cups. 'One apiece for you an' meself, the other be for Daniel ... Daniel be my son.'

Setting basin and jug on the table Regan unwittingly echoed her surprise. 'Your son? But I thought–'

'Cos you 'eard no sound other than my words you thought I lived here all alone.' Stirring sugar into the cups Libby shook her head. 'That don't be so. Daniel, my lad, be upstairs an' afore you goes a questionin' of the reason he don't go a comin' into the living room it be cos he can't, Daniel be crippled in both legs.'

The look of sympathy immediately showing on Regan's face brought a weary smile to that of the older woman. ''Twere the Lord's will.' Libby took up one of the cups, standing a moment with it in her hands. 'Daniel were born with twisted legs. We had hoped, his father and me, that doctors could somehow help, that there might be a way of straightenin' our boy and we spent every penny we could spare in followin' that dream; but that were all it were, a dream, and now it be gone.'

'But you and his father...'

'Don't be no father, not since a fall of coal buried him in the pit along of Lea Brook, there be just a mother now to look to Daniel an' that I'll do so long as breath be in my body.'

A crippled child and no husband to help with the caring of him! Listening to the tread of boots on bare wooden stairs, sympathy welled afresh in Regan. Life had a cruelty beyond belief, a pitilessness which could strike in many ways, bring the heartbreak of a child struck from birth, a husband snatched to his death in the dark bowels of the earth ... and a mother murdered, a brother burned to death!

'Drink your tea, it won't ward off the chills should you leave it stand to get cold as water in the pump.' Libby had caught the sob coming soft from the throat of the young woman standing at her table. It were as she had thought last night, this wench were runnin' from somethin' an' that somethin' had her near to breakin'.

'Would you bide here against a body comin' to the shop? It'll tek no more than a minute for me to bring this to Daniel, they'll understand if you asks 'em to wait.'

There had been no time to answer, to tell the woman she had no experience of serving in a shop.

'Be you there, Mrs Radley?'

Coming from beyond the curtain the call had Regan return her cup to the table, her hand suddenly shaking nervously. What if the customer could not wait, what if he or she went elsewhere to buy?

'...every penny we could spare...'

Should that customer take business to another shop then there would be even less to spend on a crippled boy! Drawing a deep breath Regan walked across to the curtain. If whoever stood at the other side of the counter was a regular visitor to the shop then chance was they would be familiar with where various goods were kept.

That were smartly done. Libby smiled as the girl who came to buy a pennyworth of tea hurried from the shop, the door clanging shut behind her. True, the youngster were well used with seeing the small packages of tea, wrapped in a screw of paper and placed on a shelf close by the counter, prepared for sale in the odd quiet moments of the day, so the child could easily point out where the packets were kept; but even so this wench she had given a night's shelter to had managed well enough, tekin' care to count four halfpennies change into the small hand before taking the silver threepenny piece handed across the counter and dropping it into the cash box placed beneath.

Relieved she had understood the strange-sounding jumble of words the child had mumbled as she had stared across a counter which hid everything below the level of a squat nose, Regan breathed a light sigh. She had not realised that 'a pennuth o' tay' meant a pennyworth of tea, not until a dirt-stained finger had pointed to where a neat pile of small paper packages stood piled together, the girl repeating, 'A pennuth o' tay, I be come forra pennuth o' tay.' She had passed over the required purchase and smiled into a pair of bright blue eyes which in turn registered suspicion not tempered as the halfpennies were counted one by one into a palm, fingers snapping over them with the speed of a striking shark.

'That be Poppy Jeavons, Alfie's sister and the second o' five, her be young but her don't 'ave no buttons missin'.' Libby laughed at the look of confusion that met her. 'Come you back this side o' the curtain,' she said. 'I'll explain while you finishes o' that cup of tea.'

'My lad asked would you pass a word with him afore you goes on your way?' Libby paused, seeing the quick lift of the head as Regan pulled on her coat. 'But o' course that be a delayin' of you an' I won't 'ave you put to no bother. I'll tell him you was in a 'urry to be off.'

In a hurry to be off to where? Regan's fingers fumbled with the cord frogging which formed the coat's small buttonholes. She had nowhere to hurry to, but even if she had she would not refuse to speak with the boy. How could she, after the kindness she had been shown? Buttons fastened, Regan smiled at the woman watching her. Between wide streaks of silver, wisps of hair which might once have been deeply brown now trailed like pale sand. The severe style, coiled into a knot pinned to the nape of the neck, emphasised the drawn features, the lines tracing a face Regan realised must be prematurely aged with care and worry. Regan looked into eyes which in younger and happier times would have gleamed like chestnuts in autumn but which now were dulled from past sadness and ever-present sorrow.

'I am not in any hurry.' Regan's smile deepened. 'I would very much like to speak with your son.'

That smile were genuine. Libby turned towards the door giving onto the stairs. Life had shown her too many charlatans, too many pretending interest only for that interest to be in what they could get for themselves; but this wench! Somehow she felt this wench to be different.

'Shop!' Accompanied by a slap on the counter the loud call was followed by, 'Tea up!'

Her feet already on the second stair, Libby sighed her frustration. 'That be the salesman for the tea, come for my order. Best not keep him waitin', Daniel will understand you was kept from visitin' cos of shop business.'

'I will wait in the street until you have finished your business then perhaps you will take me to see your son.'

199

Her would wait in the street! That were somethin' no other had offered, they 'ad more like wanted to sit waitin' in the livin' room, their eyes rakin' over every bit an' bob a calculatin' what might be slipped into a pocket or 'neath a skirt.

'There be no need of you a standin' in the street,' Libby answered as the call from beyond the curtain came louder than before, 'you go on up, the lad be in the room on the left, his door don't be closed.'

Would the boy be bright and full of enquiry as Saul had been prior to their mother marrying a second time? He had been happy then, eager to share in all that happened at Woodford, filled with mischief but never deliberately causing hurt or unhappiness to others. That had been Sherwyn Huntley's domain! He had brought nothing but unhappiness, he had drained the joy of life from Saul as he had drained it from the mother and the sister. And now Saul was dead.

'I would much prefer you come into the room, I like to see the folk I speak with.'

Drawn from her reverie Regan looked towards the one door standing open onto the tiny landing. The voice was deep, deep as Saul's had been when last he had been home.

Suddenly the tiny landing was gone and Regan was in a sun-filled garden.

'*It is perfectly natural...*'

Soft tones she knew so well caressed the golden peace.

'*Your voice is breaking.*'

The page of memory flipped and Regan smiled as the young boy, arms and legs gangly as a colt, jumped to catch at a branch curving from a leaf-laden tree.

'*Breaking? What…?*'

The reply halted, the young face flushing with embarrassment as the cadences of his voice switched suddenly, dropping from the high pitch of boyhood, becoming the husky promise of baritone.

'*What does it mean?*'

The gentle laugh came from the figure now standing beneath the tree into which the boy had clambered.

'*It means, my darling, you are leaving childhood behind, you are becoming a man.*'

But Saul, the boy laughing down at her, had not become a man, he had never left childhood; Saul had burned to death while still a boy!

'Saul!' The cry was wrenched from her by the twist of her heart as Regan reached for the people only her mind showed.

'My name is not Saul, it's Daniel; please won't you come in.'

Like wiping chalk from a board the sound cleared the pictures from her mind and Regan stood again on the minute landing, its white-washed walls bare of ornament.

'I … I was unsure of the room.' Though the white lie covered her hesitation, Regan coloured slightly at the telling. The boy must think she had come to speak with him at the insistence of his mother.

'It's the one with the open door.'

Was he young as Saul had been? But then maybe he was a little older; this voice was not croaky nor did it fall suddenly into depths. Mentally querying the age of the boy she had come to spend a few moments with, Regan stepped into the room then stared in surprise. The figure smiling at her from a narrow wood-framed bed was not a boy, he was a man!

19

'This be the finest to be had, I wouldn't bring naught but the best for Libby Radley.'

It was coming from beyond the curtain. Closing the stairs door behind her Regan glanced across the cramped space which must provide living room and kitchen.

'I could have sold this a dozen times over but I thought no ... if anybody deserves to have the finest quality tea for the price then it be Libby Radley.' Strong and confident, the voice reached through the mask of curtain. 'When a salesman has a customer such as you be then he looks to bring her the best bargain he can.'

Uncomfortable at what seemed like listening to a private conversation, Regan turned towards the scullery. There was bound to be a rear entrance leading from the yard onto a street running past the back of the house. Halfway to the scullery she hesitated. Leaving this way, without thanking the woman who had been so kind, felt wrong; but to eavesdrop on a business transaction! That also was wrong. There was only one way. Giving a warning cough she stepped quickly into the shop area, her goodbye already on her lips.

'This be top quality tea, it be the kind you don't get the chance of buying very often for the big firms gets first grab. I tell you there is no better tea than–' Interrupted by the appearance of Regan the masculine voice halted in midsentence, the short florid-faced speaker turning from a wooden chest he had been bending over.

'Excuse me.' Regan glanced at Libby. 'I did not want to leave without once more thanking you for your kindness.'

'You be welcome to another cup o' tea.'

The woman's generosity had been stretched too far already, she would not impose further. She shook her head. 'Thank you, but I will be on my way.' Regan nodded a silent good morning to the salesman.

'You wouldn't be so ready to refuse a cup should you have a tasting of this.' The florid face broke into a too-eager smile, the man tapping the rim of the chest with a podgy finger before returning his glance to Libby. 'That applies to the rest of your customers once they gets a tasting, you'll have folk coming from all about to buy this for it's tea of quality.'

Glancing at the contents of the chest as she edged her way around it to reach the shop entrance Regan came to a sudden halt. 'The tea in this chest is of the finest quality?' She glanced at the man.

'Don't get no better.' The thick mouth stretched even wider. 'Come from the best plantations in India did this.'

'Really?' Regan did not return the smile.

'From Darjeeling, but then a woman don't be expected to bother her head–'

'This tea was not grown in the foothills of the Himalayas,' Regan cut in firmly, 'Nor is it, as you claim, the highest quality. In fact this is a very inferior quality.'

The too-wide smile snapped away, the small inset eyes taking on an angry gleam. 'Inferior,' the word choked from a tight mouth, 'you best stay out of what you don't know.'

'But I do know.' Regan faced the man, whose anger was his turning florid face to crimson. 'I know the tea in this chest is far from fresh. Take a handful.' She glanced at Libby, who was watching, a questioning frown adding to the lines etching her face. 'Fresh tea will have the leaf spring quickly back after being squeezed whereas older tea will crumble.'

'You don't have no knowledge of tea, no woman be allowed–'

'This one do!' Libby's hands went to her hips, her face registering challenge. 'I says try what her says.'

'Don't be no test.'

'If it be no test then why be shy of the doin'? Well, Libby Radley don't be shy.' Quick as her retort Libby scooped a handful of the tea, glaring at the salesman when it crumbled to black powder. 'The very best eh!' She threw the crumbled remains back into the chest. 'If that be best Dar ... Dar ... whatever you called it then I says God 'elp the worst.'

'It is not from Darjeeling.' Regan looked firmly at the scarlet-faced salesman. 'It is my opinion this tea was not grown there nor in Assam, in fact I would say it was not from Northern India but from the south of that country, namely the Nilgiri region.'

'You would say! You would say!' he snarled. 'What does a woman know about anything!'

'I know about tea!' Regan's rejoinder was quiet but her look denoted confidence. 'And I know that what little amount of tea you are offering here is a hybrid, a mixture of leaves not always originating in one country, and apart from that the contents of this chest are mostly fannings and dust. This is the residue left after the gradings, that is the sorting of the finished or dried leaves into Pekoe, or Broken Pekoe, this being an attribution of leaf size. Exposure to oxygen reduces moisture in the leaf, thus the last proves little more than sweepings from the beds of the grading trays; but some traders disregard the poor quality of fannings adding them to some teas in order to give the impression of large quantity when in reality there is very little either of quantity or of quality.'

'And that be your idea of the best!' Libby snorted at the red-faced man. 'That be the bargain you be bringin' along of Libby Radley? Well, you let Libby Radley tell you the outcome of your "kind thought", you teks that there tea chest outta my shop afore it finds its way up your arse, and don't bring yourself back 'ere, not ever again lessen you fancies a swim in the cut!'

Pushed aside by a glowering salesman, Regan caught at the counter then as the door banged at his back turned to Libby.

'You don't say nothin'!' Libby's smile added

crease to crease. 'I've had thought of that one afore, of the goods he offers not bein' all they was cracked up to be, you 'ave simply proved it. Now come you up and tell my Daniel all that's passed, it'll bring a smile to his face.'

'When did this arrive?' Sherwyn Huntley addressed the man standing before his desk in the study at Woodford House.

The man who had replaced Edward Sanders as butler watched his employer. Whatever was written on that one sheet of paper had rattled Mr Sherwyn Huntley, that had been clearly announced by the drain of colour from his face and the fingers tightening as he had read. Now as he demanded to be informed as to the time of the letter arriving his eyes were blazing fires of wrath. 'I cannot be certain, sir.' He answered the question solemnly.

'Not certain! You cannot be certain! What am I to deduce from that?' Low as the rumbles of an approaching storm, Sherwyn Huntley's words rolled slowly from his lips.

He had been warned by those below stairs, those who had worked longest in this house, warned of Huntley's decaying temper, but the reason for it was not spoken of. Oh, the question had been asked but always a reply had either been vague or not forthcoming at all. Now it seemed one more flash fire was about to threaten. Why? What could be in that letter to make Huntley glare like a cornered rat? That was one more question to be mulled over in the butler's pantry. Now, with the deferential air of the servant who must see nothing, do nothing, think nothing but obey without question, the manservant replied.

'Only that which I deduced myself, sir, that the letter was delivered here by some means other than the Post Office for the envelope bears no stamp and neither did it come with the rest of the morning post.'

Hand-delivered! But by whom? Huntley glanced again at the letter, a frisson of anxiety tingling along his nerves. There had to be an answer! Submerging anger beneath a false layer of calm he laid the paper on the desk, careful to conceal the contents by resting both hands over it. He had employed this man for the simple reason he had not lived or worked anywhere near Woodford and therefore would have no knowledge of what had taken place in this house; that was now in the past, no more young boys would be brought here. But Regan Trent, she would be brought back and when she was, Woodford would witness one more *accident*.

'So where was this found if not among the regular post?'

No hint of anxiety showed either in his voice or in the glance Huntley lifted once again to his servant, a man who had behaved impeccably in his duties yet with whom he was still not entirely easy.

'The kitchen maid discovered it when she opened the kitchen door,' the butler replied. 'It had been placed on the step with a stone to hold it there.'

Was that a complete account? Once the butler was dismissed, Sherwyn Huntley snatched up the sheet of paper, rage rekindling as he read it through again. Who could know ... who the hell could possibly know! Yet somebody did, and that somebody was playing his own game.

... a 'undred pund...

Ill-formed letters dragged across the soiled paper.

...I knows what you and wentuth be doin' and the young uns you does it along of...

Volcanic, Huntley's anger burned hot behind his eyes.

...ifun you don't want no others to know then pay wot be asked ifun you chooses not to pay then the pulice will 'ear.

Blackmail! Huntley's closed first slammed down. Some bastard was blackmailing him! The swine had chosen the wrong game; it was one he would regret.

But regret could only follow after being caught and this letter gave no indication of where to look or who to look for; the only instruction being to leave the money outside the gate set in the boundary wall toward the rear of the estate. That gate was rarely used! Dropping the sheet of paper Huntley rose, going to stare from the window out across the wide expanse of well-kept grounds. The gate a little way from the burned-out summer house ... a gate very few people knew existed and even less used. But the staff here would know of it. Staff! Teeth clenched, he returned to the desk and snatched up the letter. That butler would have been told of the fire and the body found burned to a cinder, he would surely have gone there out of morbid curiosity. Had he walked further and discovered the gate and that given him the idea of blackmail? Yet if no one in the house had told him of that other business then how... Sanders! With the crash of thunder it boomed in his mind. Was the man who had brought this letter to the study a friend or relative of Edward Sanders? Were they in league with one another? Maybe a sure way was to put that one hundred pounds in the specified place ... and then to keep watch.

'My lad certainly enjoyed a listenin' to that.' Libby Radley followed the slender figure down the stairs. 'Ain't often there be a lightening of his day.'

He had smiled. A picture of a pale face, dark-rimmed eyes wide above hollow cheeks, flashed into Regan's mind and her heart twisted with pity. How long had he lain in that bed with no hope of ever leaving it again? How did he stand the heartache of knowing he would no more feel the sun on his face or the ground beneath his feet? It had to be heartbreaking for him; and for his mother. In the few hours since meeting Libby Radley she had seen the answer etched deep on the woman's face.

'Yes, Daniel enjoyed it though I wouldn't go a sayin' of the same for that salesman, he went out of here with his tail a' tween his legs right enough.'

'I should not have spoken.' Regan blushed,

ashamed of her interference.

'Not spoken.' Libby laughed. 'Why wench, I be right glad you did, why I'd 'ave paid a shillin' any day to witness what I seen today. I should've had more sense than listen to that toe-rag in the first place for folk who says they be after sellin' you summat for your own good never 'ave anythin' worth the sellin', an' that tea certainly weren't worth they buyin', you proved that.'

'Nevertheless, it was none of my business.'

'Mebbes not, but Libby Radley be thankful you med it so an' now I thinks we could share a sup of tea while the shop be quiet ... ooh, I should 'ave held me tongue!' Libby smiled as a call from beyond the curtain summoned her. 'No rest for the wicked as they say. Brew a pot, there's a good wench, I'll be back afore you knows I be gone.'

Loath to refuse the request Regan spooned tea into a dark brown earthenware teapot, then pressing her coat close to her body with one hand so it would not come into contact with the soot-blackened kettle she poured boiling water onto the tea leaves.

'No rest for the wicked!'

The words seemed to echo in the gentle hiss of steam rising from the teapot. Regan glanced toward the dividing curtain as a third voice heralded yet another customer. Little rest, but it was certain there was no wickedness in Libby Radley.

'I thanks you for stayin'.' Libby's voice betrayed the weariness in her body. 'You 'ave been a big help a tekin' of trays up to Daniel, them there stairs can be a bit of a struggle some days.'

210

She had been glad to help yet had known to stay so long was against her better judgement. And so it had proved for darkness had fallen. It would have been difficult finding a place to sleep had she left this house while it was still day; now it would be virtually impossible, yet she had to try. Reaching for the coat she had hung on a peg alongside the door to the stairs, Regan slipped it on.

From her seat beside the hearth Libby watched the young woman whose company had made the long day more bearable. It had been obvious there were no history of housework or tending a sickroom in her upbringin'. It were patently clear her had never touched a pot except mebbe while a travellin' along of them gypsies yet the wench had done all that were asked and without so much as a frown. Libby's thoughts matched the fastening of Regan's coat buttons, one following the other. This wench had been reared to a soft bed and a home where everything were done wi'out her liftin' of a hand. So her being here in Wednesbury pointed to only one thing, her were running from that home. But why to this town? Why leave the gypsies? The questions were not new, the reasoning not fresh; these and many others had churned her mind during the hours of night and again today and it were a fact Daniel were wondering the same though, like herself, he hadn't put his thought into words.

'Will you say goodbye to Daniel for me?'

'You be set on goin' then?'

'Yes.' Her reply tight, Regan fought her rising anxiety at the prospect of walking streets by night.

'Might a body ask to where it be you've put

211

your mind to goin'?'

Where? Regan avoided the eyes she knew watched her. If only she knew, if only there was a place she could go to, a place where she might feel safe.

'You don't 'ave nowheres to go, that be Libby Radley's thinkin', but should her be mistook then you tells her so right now.'

What good could come from lying? Regan turned towards the curtain draping off the closed shop.

'My old mother used to say, silence speaks a thousand words,' Libby said as Regan crossed the living room, 'and that be what you 'ave done; mekin' no answer were answer in itself. You don't 'ave no place other than the streets, that be the truth don't it?'

One hand drawing aside the curtain, Regan looked back to the woman who sat with both feet resting on the hearth. 'Yes,' she said quietly, 'that is the truth.'

'I knowed it!' Libby nodded forcefully. 'Same as I knows it don't be safe for you to go a roamin' the night, like as not you'll find y'self at the bottom of a pit shaft ... or more like some poor man will 'ave the findin' of you for you falls down a mine shaft then you don't live to climb out; so you let that curtain be and set that coat back on the peg.'

'But...'

'Libby Radley don't listen to buts, now you do as you be bid while I goes to settle Daniel for the night.'

20

'Sir finds it to his liking?'

Waving the hovering tailor aside, Myles Wentworth surveyed his reflection in a long cheval mirror. Yes, it was to his liking ... very much so.

Hands clasped together, the tailor watched his client twist and turn examining every angle. Examining and with luck admiring, for should the suit not be satisfactory then it might not be bought at all; this was not the type of wear often called for in Worcester.

'I have to say, sir,' he said as he stepped forward, careful to avoid blocking the other man's view of the mirror, 'you have exceptional taste in clothes, very exceptional indeed, and with your physique, and the style ... one can only say you will dominate the evening.'

'It is rather splendid.' Myles Wentworth lapped up the compliments like a cat lapping cream.

'I must say, sir, when you brought your sketch to me I felt ... well, I felt...'

'It was too much of a difference?'

'No, oh no, not that, sir.' The tailor squirmed, fearing the sudden loss to his pocket. 'I simply meant it was such a sophistication of style, but now I see I was wrong to harbour doubt. The suit is most becoming, but...'

'But!' Myles stared past his own reflection to the face displayed at the mirror's edge.

'But,' the face smiled ingratiatingly, 'sir must be prepared for the stir he will create, he will be the centre of attention, he will draw everyone's glance.'

That was the intention. Myles's glance returned to his reflection. That was the reason for his designing so radically different a style of evening dress. He would no longer follow the dictates of fashion, he would create them. This was simply the beginning, but what a beginning! His glance ran over the silk-covered reveres of the black silk alpaca coat whose spoon-shaped tails reached to just above the knee. So different to the much longer square-cut skirts of the usual evening suit, and the sleeves! He extended one arm, surveying the cut with added pleasure. He had dispensed with the buttoned cuff, leaving a smooth neat line to the wrist, and employing a narrow turnback to the waistcoat cut high where others were cut with a deep V-shaped front and wide, wide turnback ... that was the touch of genius.

'Sir is to be congratulated, his design is a work of art, a veritable work of art.' The tailor twittered like a nervous sparrow. 'So elegant, so very becoming. Sir has such flair. I declare every man of quality will be wanting such an evening suit though I doubt any will wear it with the same aplomb as yourself, sir.'

Flattery! But truthful nevertheless. Myles touched a silk revere. Soon men of worth would want to dress like Myles Wentworth. This town, though, was not the place for a man wishing to be seen in the best society; that place was London. But an address in London, an address which

214

would comply with status, that would cost money. Even so Myles smiled again into the mirror. Hadn't he proved there were ways of making money!

'You kept watch, you stayed there the whole of the night?'

'Yes Mr 'Untley sir, I done just like you told me.'

'That cannot be so!' Sherwyn Huntley rounded on the stable hand.

Aware of his employer's easily aroused temper the man answered nervously. 'I ... I did stop there sir, right where you said I should.'

'But you saw no one, you heard nothing!' Sherwyn rasped caustically, every sense telling him the man was lying.

'Nobody.' The groom shook his head vigorously. 'D'ain't nobody come nowheres near to the gate, not all night they d'ain't.'

Yet the money was gone. Had it been helped on its way by the man he was speaking with now? But he had not been given the true reason for his vigil and neither had he been told the resting place of that hundred pounds; no one other than Sherwyn Huntley knew of it. He had let it be known to the staff that he had received information a burglar had paid a visit to the house of a friend and in consequence decided that in addition to giving that information to the police he had deemed it as well to post a night watch on the rear gate leading into the grounds, thus avoiding a burglary being committed at Woodford House.

The ruse might have worked but the plan most

certainly had not! Sherwyn slammed the handles of his riding whip against a stall, causing the horse inside it to rear in fright. The man had been in a perfect position, the tree he had sat in looked right over that wall, it was impossible not to see anyone approaching, especially as the night had boasted a high bright moon. That was supposing he *had* sat there all night. Anger getting the upper hand, Sherwyn glared at the man. 'I believe you to be lying,' he snarled, 'and there is no place in my employ for a liar. You will leave at once.'

There would be speculation, gossip among the staff and more in the village. Sherwyn strode from the stables, storming without a word through the house and up the stairs to his room. A groom of long standing to be dismissed as that one had been dismissed was bound to give rise to talk. Let them talk! Throwing off his riding coat, kicking it aside, he dropped to a chair, his temper unabated. What was a bloody stable hand against a hundred pounds!

But that would not be all. The blackmailer had the scent of success and he would not be content with a sniff. The money he had taken would not last indefinitely; sooner or later he would return for more. A tap on the door announced that a servant waited on the other side of it and he barked permission to enter.

'The inspector of police wishes to speak with you.'

This was all he needed! Sherwyn glared at his butler. 'What does he want?'

'He failed to advise me of that, sir.'

The very politeness of the answer, the man's

attitude, both added to Sherwyn's irritation. Maybe he should give this one the same treatment he had given that groom, get rid of him now, today!

'Will I tell him you will see him, sir?'

'You can tell him to wait, and you, you can pull off my boots.'

Bathed and dressed in dark business suit, his temper now under control, Sherwyn looked at the clock on the mantel above his bedroom fireplace. A little under forty minutes! The inspector of police would find it better to ask for an appointment should be feel the need to visit again.

'Inspector...' Entering the drawing room, he smiled at the man sitting in a deep brocaded chair. 'I am so sorry to keep you waiting, the mud of horse riding, it takes some removing. I trust you have been provided with refreshment.'

'Your man did ask, sir, but I refused.'

'As long as you were asked,' Sherwyn answered, taking a chair facing his visitor. 'Now, tell me what I may do for you?'

'I won't be takin' much of your time, Mr Huntley, just routine, a routine enquiry, nothing more.'

'Routine enquiry?' Sherwyn frowned.

'Just so.' The inspector nodded. 'Routine 'as to be observed even though we down at the station knows it to be a waste of time calling here.'

'A waste of time, Inspector?'

Taking a notebook from the pocket of his coat the inspector flipped it open. 'As I says, sir, a waste of time but procedure has to be followed. There were an accident to a carriage coming in from the

217

London road.' He looked at the notebook reading from a page. 'Female, aged about twenty years. Five foot two inches in height, slender of build, fair hair, blue eyes. No distinguishing marks. I wondered did that match a description of your stepdaughter?'

'Well yes, it does.' Nerves tingling, Sherwyn sat forward in his chair. 'I would say it matched very well, but has the woman not said who she is?'

Closing the notebook the police inspector returned it to his pocket before answering. 'That was impossible, the young woman was killed, outright so the doctor informed me. I'm sorry to have bothered you seeing as I know your stepdaughter to be staying abroad with relatives, but I repeat, procedure has to be followed. Your stepdaughter is still with relatives on the Continent, Mr Huntley?'

Was the dead woman Regan Trent? Had she been on the way back to Woodford? If it was her then... Sherwyn drew a quick breath, then what would become of her father's legacy?

'I...' He swallowed hard, hoping it would appear to be fear of what might have happened to Regan rather than what might happen to her money. 'I have had no communication from Regan.' He rose to stand at the fireplace, keeping his back turned to the policeman until he could adopt a suitable look of worry. 'She has not written in almost a month, but surely she would have informed me had she decided to return home.'

Rising to his feet the inspector waited a moment, seeing the distress obvious on the other man's face, then said, 'So you can't be sure Miss

218

Trent be still with relatives? In that case I have to ask, Mr Huntley, would you be prepared to come to the mortuary to see if the woman taken from the scene of the accident be your stepdaughter?'

The wench were gone. Folding a sheet of news-paper through and through again Libby Radley let her mind wander. Truth to tell there had been a part – a large part – of herself had said the wench shouldn't go, but then common sense, helped by Daniel, had got the upper hand. But still it were a worry. Reaching for the knife with which she cut soap or halved wax candles, the cost of one often being too much for the folk of Woden Passage, she drew the sharp blade along the carefully measured folds. Daniel had liked the wench. After separating the cut paper, placing the small squares in a neat stack, she reached for the basin she had filled with tea taken from a large wooden container.

It had been a surprise to hear Daniel say the wench should go. Carefully filling the bowl of a spoon she had long since ensured held exactly one ounce of tea leaves she began to wrap the 'twist of tay' regularly called for.

She had expected him to say it were kinder to have Regan... She paused, frowning slightly. He had called her Regan almost from the first, a smile on his face each time, as if saying her name left a taste of sweetness on his lips, had he...? Fingers holding the spoon trembled, spilling tiny snippets of black leaf into the square of paper. Could Daniel have feelings for the wench?

'No! Oh dear God, no!' Libby's hand dropped

to the counter, her words falling soft as the tea leaves spilling over its surface. 'My lad be sufferin' enough wi'out addin' more to his misery, don't give him more heartache! Lord in Your mercy don't let him love that wench for it'll bring naught but sorrow...'

'Talkin' to y'self, Libby Radley, that be a bad sign, not that these parts sees any other.'

'Well, you knows how it is, Sarah, talkin' to y'self be the best way of holdin' conversation, you don't get to ruffle the feelin's of nobody but y'self.' Scooping spilled tea from the counter into her hand Libby turned toward, a bin holding an assortment of empty cartons.

'Hey!' Worn-out shawl dropping from her head the woman reached a hand across the narrow counter. 'Don't go a' throwin' out o' that tay, there be naught amiss wi' it.'

If only the same could be said of Daniel, if only there were naught amiss with him.

'There be a good penny wuth o' tay there.' Libby turned back to the woman.

'A penny for a twist scooped from the counter, I won't go offerin' nobody a bad bargain.'

'What be bad about a scoopin' o' tay?'

'What be bad, Sarah, be the fact that cleaned as my counter be every mornin' it don't go to say as there don't be a speck o' dust restin' on it, an' I won't go sellin' tainted goods.'

'Tainted!' Sarah snorted. 'This town lives an' breathes dust, an' that 'eavy wi' soot an' smoke so a spot o' tay flavoured wi' a little bit more won't be noticed.'

'That I won't argue wi' Sarah, Wednesbury be

220

choked wi' smoke an' soot like you says, but to ask folk a penny for what I knows be not the best ... well, that I won't do.'

'So what will y'tek forrit?' Sarah Jeavons watched the scoop of leaves once more heading for the waste bin. 'Would you consider a 'alf penny?'

Would she sell the tea for a halfpenny? Libby transferred the scoop of tea leaves into a square of paper, twisting the four corners to make a small bag shape. Sarah Jeavons was poor as a church mouse. Working alongside the men from early hours to others just as early, making nails for which a Birmingham nail master paid less than threepence a hundred, meant her having to think almost the same number of times before spending so much as a farthing. She would willingly give the woman the tea. But though Sarah Jeavons were beset with poverty the woman had pride. Twisting the corners of the square of paper a final time Libby handed it across the counter saying, 'That be a 'a'penny, Sarah.' She would not detract from the one thing life had not yet robbed Sarah Jeavons entirely of, a comforting cup of tea.

Left alone once more Libby returned to packaging tiny amounts of tea. Life robbed many folk, and here in a town given to coal mining, the making of iron and the forging of nails, that robbery was rife, especially so when accidents robbed a family of a breadwinner as it had robbed her of a husband, or of crippled a man so his limbs were useless as those of her lad. But Daniel had suffered no crushing beneath a fall of coal, had had no iron crucible lifted with molten metal drop onto his legs. His suffering had begun long

221

before, when he watched children his own age run and jump while the deteriorating strength of his twisted limbs kept him confined in a chair.

And now the strength was gone from his heart. Tears blurring the print of paper squares to a dark smudge, Libby's fingers stilled. The courage which had sustained him had ebbed with the years, fading as strength faded from his body and she, his mother, had watched it go. That was hardest of all. Tears she ignored dripped onto the stilled hands. A mother watching her only child suffer and being unable to do anything to alter it; and now if Daniel harboured a feeling other than friendship for Regan Trent then that suffering could only be increased.

'Why?' she murmured brokenly. 'Why, Lord? Why my lad? What did Zeb an' me do to rouse Your anger? Why visit it on an unborn child?'

One by one the questions slipped into the silence, and one by one silence answered them.

21

Outside the mortuary Sherwyn Huntley breathed long and deep.

'Can be dauntin' viewin' a dead body any time, but circumstances such as this makes it that much more harrowin'; I can only thank you for your assistance, Mr Huntley, and apologise for the ordeal you've been put through.'

'An ordeal indeed!' Drawing a handkerchief

from the pocket of his overcoat Sherwyn put it to his face, wiping away beads of moisture as he dragged in another long breath.

'It don't be easy work for anybody,' the inspector sympathised, 'but with folk such as yourself, parent or guardian, them as loves the ones they be asked to identify, then the task be even harder.'

'It had to be done.' Sherwyn dabbed at tight lips.

'Yes sir, it had to be done. But it be over now, there'll be no need for us to be troubling you further. Will I have the constable call for a hansom?'

With his eyes tight shut Sherwyn took a moment to answer and when he did the words trembled. 'No...' The eyelids lifted. 'No I ... thank you but I think I will walk, the evening air helps settle the nerves.'

'I understand. Once again, Mr Huntley, our thanks for the giving of your time. Goodnight, sir.'

An almost imperceptible nod informed the waiting constable their business was done. The inspector replaced the hat he had removed as a sign of respect for the dead and along with his junior officer walked away.

Above the doorway of a drab building the dull yellow light of a solitary lamp flickered over the one word set into the brickwork: Mortuary.

Ordeal was not the word he would have chosen to describe what he had just undergone; he would have rather used the word 'hell'.

The handkerchief still against his mouth, Sherwyn Huntley watched with a sideways glance the figures of the two policemen receding along the dismal alleyway. Not too soon, he must not let go too quickly, should that inspector look back at him he must see a man caught yet in the grip of stress. And yes, he had been caught, but more than stress, it had been fear, real fear.

Behind the handkerchief the tight mouth eventually relaxed. What he had gone through, his 'ordeal', had not been fear of what might have happened to Regan Trent but rather what would happen to her money.

'*...only to the children of his blood...*'

Fingers tight about the handkerchief crumpled it into a ball.

'*...the said Regan Trent...*'

But that was not all the information he had wrung from Marcia Trent regarding her late husband's will. Jasper Trent, it seemed, had anticipated that his wife might not be living out the remainder of her years in widowhood and whether from retribution or plain malice had included one more instruction in his will, that in the event of his children dying unwed then his estate in its entirety would be given to charity. With Regan Trent dead he lost everything.

When the figures of the policemen were lost from sight he snapped his hand to his side, allowing the handkerchief to fall to the ground.

Regan Trent! Teeth clenched, temper rising, he turned away from the small grim-faced building, his steps echoing along the dark narrow street. Regan Trent was the root of his problem; but it was a problem he would solve. 'Charity begins at home.' Turning the corner of Bank Street, leaving the dismal alley and stepping onto the High Street, Sherwyn glanced along its length. That home would be his!

'Can I get a cab f' you, sir?'

'What!' Unaware of the figure coming to walk beside him, Sherwyn snapped, showing the frustration still boiling inside him.

'A cab.' The figure stepped into the light from a street gas lamp which threw a long silhouette across the roadway. 'Can I get you a 'ansom, sir?'

'No, I...' Sherwyn let the rest of his refusal remain unspoken. The face was pleasant; no, it was handsome, the smile becoming. The clothes had seen better days, the boots also. He let his glance slide over what the street light showed. The offspring of some workman or other and one not exactly rolling in wealth. He glanced again at the face, the hopeful smile. Becoming! A stir fluttered deep in his stomach ... very becoming!

'There be no trains for London at this time o' night.' Pre-empting refusal of his offer to fetch a hansom the attractive smile flashed again.

Watching it, the aggression which had riled Sherwyn's mind only moments before gave way completely to a newer more pleasant emotion, the tension catching at him now being the tension of promised pleasure. Nodding permission for the youngster to hail a cab he smiled to himself. Maybe calling for a hansom might not be the only way for this lad to earn himself a coin.

A farmhouse, she might be given a cup of water here. Shading her eyes from the slant of morning sun, Regan looked across a field of ripening wheat. She had thought Wednesbury a town of nothing but coal mines and manufactories, it had

225

seemed while walking through its streets that the only thing which grew in the smoke-laden air was chimneys; but here, beyond the town with its mass of tiny dark houses, was beautiful country-side. Staring at the golden stalks swaying to the rhythm of a breeze she felt a tug to her heart. The fields of Woodford would be golden with corn, the meadows bright with scarlet poppies, the orchards heavy with fruit and over it all the heady scent of hops ripening on tall vines. Woodford! A prick of emotion moistened her eyes.

She had so loved her home, its quiet peaceful beauty. She had thought to live there with the man she had loved, with Myles Wentworth, but that, like so many more things, had proved an empty dream.

Myles Wentworth! He had stepped into her life, his charm and elegant manner sweeping her off her feet. She had been so wonderfully happy, so ecstatic at thought of becoming his wife. But then the dream had been snatched from her, the bubble of happiness in which she had floated had exploded all around her. Why had she not seen? Her hand falling to her side Regan stared at a scene which had suddenly become Woodford, at a woman walking beside a younger woman, this one laughing as she caught a strand of honey-gold hair blown across her face. The older woman smiling; but not with her eyes, the smile did not reach the eyes.

She should have known then. She should have realised her mother's unhappiness. The spider of reproach spun the thread of censure, binding Regan ever more tightly, drawing her deep into the web of self-blame.

Filled with her own happiness she had not noticed the shadow in her mother's eyes. Not until it was too late!

Of course you must have your wrap, it will take no more than a couple of minutes for me to fetch it.'

Regan watched the picture her mind showed, heard the silent words.

'No, Mother, I will not have you walk to the village without it. The air is warm now but it can so quickly become cold.'

The girl's laughter had ceased as the older woman shivered slightly, then with no more discussion she was walking back towards a graceful stone house.

It had welcomed her in, the house seeming to hold her in its loving arms. Drawn on shadows of memory, the pictures unfolded.

Halfway up the stairway leading from the large hall the slender golden-haired figure paused, listening for a few seconds to the sound of a quiet laugh, a laugh she knew so well.

'Myles!' she whispered in delight; she peered over the gleaming banister but there was no movement below. But he *was* here. Her slight bemused frown vanished at the sound of another quieter, husky laugh followed by the sound of men talking in a room above. With a smile of elation the girl moved on up to the wide landing. To the left a door stood slightly ajar. It led to a room the master of the house had set aside for his own personal use. The figure standing silently at the stairhead looked towards it.

'I thought they would never go, I wanted to chase

them away with my whip.'

Throaty as it had sounded then so it sounded now, the answer as clear in her memory.

She had listened to that voice, the eager beat of her heart blotting out all but the sheer joy of seeing Myles, of spending a few minutes with him, of hoping he would walk with her to the village.

'But they have gone and we can indulge in the pleasure we both enjoy so much.'

The reply had been made by her stepfather, the usual brittle tone harsh and quick as if made on rapidly indrawn breath. But who was it had gone thus leaving them to a pleasure they enjoyed so much? And why was it one they only enjoyed when alone together? Each question in its turn raised fresh ones. She had glanced in the opposite direction. Her mother's bedroom was furthest along the corridor, it would be the work of a moment to run and get her wrap.

That moment of indecision, that second of hesitation! If she had not delayed, if she had gone to her mother's room she would not have suffered that pain, not witnessed that awful scene.

The jaws of her mental trap biting viciously Regan shuddered but the scene she watched went on.

'Now!'

Hoarse and guttural, the growl had passed through the slightly open door.

'Now Myles … do it now!'

The fervour, the passion throbbing in the visceral cry! She had never heard the like. Thought of the wrap vanishing from her mind she had turned again to the room kept solely for the use of her stepfather. What was it caused that fever-ish, almost frenzied cry? What was it Myles should do? Was he ill? The last was too much to bear thinking of; she had gone quickly along the corridor to push open the door.

That was when she had learned the truth; that was the moment she had begun to realise why her mother had asked her to leave Woodford, to know the root of the shadows in Marcia Trent's eyes.

They had not heard her come, had not seen her standing in the doorway, her eyes wide with horror.

Both naked, they had stood. Sherwyn Huntley, eyes closed, had drawn loud rapid breaths while Myles Wentworth had laughed softly before touching the other man's throat with his mouth then slowly, so very slowly, he had trailed his tongue over chest and stomach as he dropped to his knees.

Her mind blank from horror and disgust, her limbs suddenly bereft of use, she had watched, seen the gleam of light sparkle on the copper-coloured hair, seen it mingle with metallic grey as Myles had pressed his face close into the older man's groin; and Huntley had groaned as passion contorted his features.

She had not wanted to watch, had not wanted to see. But movement had been denied her, brain frozen with what she was seeing had held her chained to the spot, gripping her fast as memory gripped her now.

'Now Myles...'

Huntley's naked body had jerked spasmodically.

'Now damn you ... now!'

229

Myles had drawn back his head, a soft laugh voluptuous in his throat. For a moment he had looked up at the face, the eyes pressed hard shut, the thin-lipped mouth apart, then...

Regan felt again the spear of shock which had lanced her that day, the same sickening disgust.

Then he had placed both hands on Huntley's hips, pushing him backwards.

But Myles did not stand, he did not turn away!

Watching what had coloured so many sleepless hours, loathing became solid in Regan's mouth.

One step. Huntley had taken one step back then the hands on his hips had stilled him, Huntley's naked body once more juddering at the touch of Myles Wentworth's lips against his navel, the kiss pressed gently to the tip of a hard thrusting column of flesh. Then with yet another soft hedonistic laugh, Myles had taken the jerking column into his mouth.

She had cried out then, cried out at the debauchery taking place before her eyes, and she had fled from the doorway, run headlong down the stairs, her ears filled with the mocking laughter of the man she was to marry.

'Steady, steady, nobody is about to hurt you.' Somewhere amid the nightmare of her mind Regan heard the words but revulsion pulsing in her brain kept all from her except fear, fear of the man whose abhorrent practices she had witnessed, fear of the one who had raped her.

'No, not again ... not again!' The barrier closing her off from reality made her scream as a hand closed over her arm. Striking out in panic she

230

cried again, feeling herself caught in a steel grip.

'It's all right, you are perfectly safe, it's all right!'

Quietly firm, strong yet gentle, the words dispelled the terror clouding her mind and slowly as if awakening from sleep Regan returned to the present.

'The way you were running I thought all the devils in hell must be at your heels.' The hand dropped away then immediately returned to her elbow, steadying her as she swayed.

'Take a breath, you will be fine in a moment.'

Not quite free of the miasma of disgust and terror, Regan freed her arm sharply.

'Sorry, but I saw no other way than to hold you if you were to be prevented from falling headlong into the ditch.'

The coolness of the reply did not register; Regan lifted a face still full of the fear memory had revived. 'I...' She paused, fighting the impact of memories which had drawn her so deep into yesterday. 'I wasn't thinking.'

'That is one thing we can both be sure of, but next time you decide to go for a horseless gallop you might choose to do so over more suitable terrain. I don't imagine the farmer takes kindly to his crops being trampled.'

Reason returned fully and Regan looked about her, her glance following a trail of broken wheat stems.

'Oh.' Dismay replaced the look of fear. 'Did I do that?'

A chuckle followed the question then, 'Not all of it. I helped, I will accept my half of the blame.'

Blame! Regan glanced again at the trodden

231

stems weaving a dark line amid the gold. Of course there was blame but it was all hers, the damage done to the wheat was due to her, to allowing her nightmare to get the better of her.

'So, if you tell me where it was, or is, you were going I will take you there.' The tall figure smiled.

Regan shook her head. 'Thank you for keeping me from the ditch, but there is no necessity for you to do more. I am quite recovered.'

Recovered from what? Watching the slender figure hurry away along the hedge-lined lane Grant Eversley pursed his lips thoughtfully. All the devils in hell? Or one not yet resident there?

22

Libby Radley paused over the tedious task of keeping her books. The shop she could run, while also caring for her bedridden son, never owing the strain to be too much, though in her inner heart, and only there, would she admit that this was no longer the truth; the stairs gave her problems with breathing, up and down a dozen times in the day had her near-exhausted, while the nights afforded no real rest. Daniel needed care during those long hours and there was no one other than herself to give it. Even so, she could, God willing, cope, but the business of figures! She breathed tired sigh in the silent living room and set the pen beside the bottle of blue ink she always stood on a large plate to guard against spills on the heavy chenille cloth;

ink were the very devil to wash out. Daniel had kept the books. Leaning against the back of the wooden kitchen chair Libby's eyes closed.

From being a lad at school he had been good at number, balancing what he called debit and credit, seeing deliveries of goods matched what had been ordered. But it had all gradually become too tiring. Oh, he hadn't said so. Libby's eyelids lifted sharply as in defence of her son. Daniel had never once said the task were too much, but a mother's eyes saw many things they were perhaps not meant to, like hers now saw the feeling Daniel had for that wench. It were not shown in words, not in gesture, but the truth shone in his eyes, in the smile which had lit his pale drawn face whenever she entered his room. It was the smile, the look in those eyes, was Libby Radley's worry. Bookkeeping could be right or not, what did it matter when in a few months... She caught at the thought, holding it tight in her mind, refusing to let it go further.

The shop, everything she had, was naught when set against her son's happiness. But how could he be happy loving where love was not returned? And it couldn't be. That wench had been friendly, genuine kindness had smiled in her eyes, but love!

Rising from the table, Libby crossed to the stairs. She shook her head as she climbed wearily, pausing on the tiny square of landing to get her breath. No, never love! Did Daniel realise this? Her glance went to the door of her son's room; Libby felt the question tug at her heart. Of course he must. Daniel Radley was crippled in body but

233

his mind was whole; reason would have told him what it told his mother: but where was reason when loved walked in? As if the question drained strength from her, Libby's hand clutched at the banister. Her son must never expect his own feelings to be mirrored by a complete stranger nor by any wench, for none would devote herself to a cripple unable to leave his bed. Daniel had accepted this, he, it had been, had told the girl she should go. Sadness a sharp pain in her chest, Libby stood a moment longer. Where had he found the strength of mind, of heart? Why had he told Regan Trent to go when it was plain to see he wanted her to stay?

That headlong flight across the field, had it dislodged the money from her pocket? Had it dropped without her being aware of it? Anxiety added to her breathlessness; Regan touched the pocket of her coat, relief coursing through her, as she felt the small hard object still nestled inside. Libby Radley had placed the money on the table then had gone into the shop half of the living room. She ought not to have left it there, left it where it could so easily be taken, beside a basket of pegs! A tinge of colour crept into her cheeks as Regan's fingers closed about the money she had taken from that table, leaving behind a basket of pegs she had found no sale for. It had been quite deliberately done. Libby Radley had purposely left the money, as the means by which the young woman she had provided with food and shelter could move on.

Regan walked on towards the house she had

234

seen across the wheat field. Deep inside she had known she should not take that money, that she should leave as she had come; but with nothing with which to pay for food and shelter temptation had proved the stronger. Now she was at the further side of the town, those coins pressed against her hand.

Had Daniel put the idea to his mother? Had he proposed she offer money and had Libby, thinking it might be somewhat awkward offering charity so openly, left those coins solely for that purpose? Regan's steps slowed as she neared the farmhouse. What did Daniel and his mother think now?

They had sat sharing an evening cup of tea, Libby, Daniel and herself and it had been Daniel had broached the subject of her moving on. *'Was there some place definite she was headed for?'* He had asked the question. How could she tell him there was not, that there was no place for her to go, no friend to whom she could turn? To do that would appear she was appealing further to their charity. In the event she had given no reply. Was she agreeable to employment? Daniel's second question had taken her by surprise. The frown which had accompanied the word now brought a further flood of warmth to her cheeks.

'Employment in a town which knows no means of work other than the mining of coal or the production of iron and nails ... I know absolutely nothing of either industry, how then could I hope to gain employment?'

They had listened to her reply, Libby nodding her head, Daniel resting against his pillows.

'Should it be employment be offered and that not in

coal mine or factory, would you consider taking it?'

Daniel had watched her face as he had put that next question.

Pushing open a gate leading into a wide yard, setting a group of hens squawking at the invasion, Regan remembered the intelligent, perceptive look. Had he known her answer before she had given it? Had he thought her silence at the first of his questions then her negative response to the second a way of avoiding the taking of employment? Was this the true reason behind Libby's leaving money on the table? Had tenderness of heart made Daniel ask his mother to find a way of helping Regan Trent leave Wednesbury?

It had been an unfortunate incident but no more than that. Sherwyn Huntley sat in the first-class compartment of the train taking him to Worcester. There had been no report of it in the newspapers which meant either it had not been brought to the notice of the police or that admirable institution had chosen not to investigate. Whichever way, it suited him.

'Country is going to the dogs!' On the seat opposite a man dressed in severe dark suit, a high starched collar and dark tie muttered irascibly, turning the page of his morning newspaper. 'Don't know what things are coming to, damned foreign exchange be down again! And there be signs of unrest in Africa, Cecil Rhodes don't be hard enough on them damned fuzzy-wuzzies! Send in the Army be what I say; a taste of British steel will soon have them natives in their place!'

His glance firmly on the window, Huntley

ignored the irritable grumblings. He had been meticulous in his scanning of the daily journals though common sense said there would be no complaint, street whores abounded in every city and that of Worcester was no exception; and whores paid for their services, whether male or female, made no protest ... not if they expected to continue in that trade.

It had been an unexpected diversion in an evening so utterly devoid of pleasure. It would have been suspicious to say the least had he refused the police officer's request he visit that mortuary. Lord, it had played havoc with his nerves! The thought of the body recovered from the wreckage of an accident being that of his stepdaughter had worried him the remainder of the day; it raised the possibility of her inheritance benefiting someone other than himself. That, and only that, had plagued his mind: how to ensure that he, Sherwyn Huntley, and not some damned charitable organisation, inherit Jasper Trent's money and business.

It had been a day of plan and counter-plan. Sherwyn continued to ignore the indignant mutterings from across the compartment. He had sat for hours in the study, ideas coming and going, one discarded in favour of another, none providing an answer he felt to be foolproof. The only real comfort had been the thought that the dead woman might not be Regan Trent, that the fortune which had smiled in bringing him the girl's mother would smile on him again.

And so it had! Both hands resting on his cane, Sherwyn Huntley felt the warm glow of satisfaction. The body had been that of a stranger. He had been given time yet to find her. But where was she? A frisson of displeasure caused his fingers to tighten over the cane's silver knob. He had had men search for her since finding her gone from that locked bedroom, a room he had believed to have only one key. But that belief had been misguided; someone else had also held a key, but who? Which of the staff of Woodford House? That also was something yet to be discovered as were the whereabouts of Edward Sanders, but once the culprit was known, silencing him or her together with that man, forever, would result in the same emotion he would feel in dealing the same fate to the mistress they had thought to rescue: pure pleasure.

Almost as much pleasure as had been enjoyed in the hour after leaving the mortuary. Relaxed in the comfort of the first-class compartment, Sherwyn indulged the memory, enjoying the euphoric flick of his senses, the swift jerk of muscles at the base of his stomach.

The lad had asked could he fetch a hansom. Had there been something else, some other question in the smile which had flashed across that comely face? Of course there had, and it had found its answer.

He had refused the offer to call a cab, but that other offer, the unspoken invitation, that had not been refused.

'P'raps sir be lookin' for some entertainment?'

The quick reply following the withdrawing of permission to hail a cab had been said casually but Sherwyn had recognised the wealth of worldly knowledge which had echoed beneath it. This was a lad of the streets, one perhaps not unversed in certain ways of life.

'*Might be you 'ave a fancy for company...*'

The lad had tried again, the hope of a coin driving him to speak.

'*I knows a 'otel, it be dependable, I means ain't no woman there will blab 'er mouth, could be a pleasant way o' spendin' the evenin'.*'

Any way would be a relief after being in that mortuary! The reply had flashed into his mind but he had not spoken it; instead he had walked on.

'*Don't be far from 'ere...*'

The lad had walked beside him.

'*...tek no more than five minutes, it be 'igh class, ain't no cheap doxies in this place, they be clean, they don't none of 'em 'ave the pox.*'

Worldly wise indeed! His glance firmly on the window, Sherwyn smiled to himself. Wise enough to understand the terse reply.

'*I am not interested in visiting a hotel, neither am I interested in procuring the services of a woman.*'

'*Don't 'ave to be a 'otel, nor do it 'ave to be a woman, there be ways an' there be other ways a man might tek 'is enjoyment.*'

The light of street lamps had illuminated the youth, the handsome face, the fetching smile, the mouth opening wide and suggestive.

'*Won't cost no more 'n 'alf a sovereign.*'

The tongue had licked over the lips, a moist sensuous inviting slide, while the eyes had issued their own husky summons.

'Foregate Street station, sir.'

Sherwyn glanced towards the doorway of the compartment, at the uniformed attendant with one hand touching a peaked cap, then waiting while the traveller with a newspaper folded it meticulously and muttered to the conductor to 'bring the valise', he followed the irate passenger to the platform.

'*There be no trains for London at this time o'night.*'

Leaving the railway station Sherwyn signalled a waiting hansom, his thoughts dwelling on that night a week ago.

He had not enlightened the lad about the fact that London was not his destination. Let him believe the man he hoped to take to a high-class brothel was from that city; a close tongue was always the safer and nowhere was it more difficult to find a person than in that great maw, especially when the one looked for did not live there.

'*You won't be disappointed, it be 'igh class like I says.*'

High-class! Sherwyn smiled to himself. That little street whore could have no idea of the true meaning of such a description. Not that it had mattered, for he had no intention of visiting any bawdy house of whatever 'class'. But he had intended to 'tek 'is enjoyment'.

Glancing from the window of the cab, a sign high on the wall of a building caught his eye. 'Broad Street'. They had turned along there and on into Bridge Street. It was there he, Sherwyn, had called a halt. He would not continue further; it was obvious no hotel was anywhere near and he could spare no more time; but should he meet a constable on the way back to the railway station

240

he would find enough time to complain of being solicited by a youth he could most definitely identify!

'*Don't need no 'otel for a mouth job.*'

Moonlight had glistened on the eyes turned to his, on the tongue once more sliding in and out of the mouth.

In the privacy of the hansom, Sherwyn placed his tall silk hat over the flesh beginning to stiffen as it had stiffened watching that tongue.

'*The river be close by…*'

The lad had reached out, his hand brushing the thickening column he guessed to be thrusting against the trousers of the man watching him.

'*…be dark under the bridge…*'

The tongue had curled over the lower lip, lapping like a cat lapping cream, then with invitation blatant in those eyes the boy's lips had parted, the mouth widening in a slow sensuous movement. His every movement had been designed to promise, to entice.

'*…won't nobody see under there.*'

The lad had stepped away and he had followed. Beneath the hat Sherwyn's hardening flesh jerked at the memory.

They had stood hidden in the deep shadow of the bridge the boy releasing the buttons of his client's tightly fitting trousers, but the slide to his knees had never been accomplished. Sherwyn Huntley's desire had not been for a mouth job.

The lad had not been prepared. Sherwyn stared through the window but saw only the remembered glint of moonlight on a satin-smooth river, the figure he spun so it faced away from him.

'*I don't do that, I ain't 'avin' no buggery!*'
'*You do what I pay you to do!*'

His rasping reply had followed the shove which made the boy's head hit the stone fabric of the wall, the hand he flung behind him clutching at Sherwyn's sleeve before a blow from the walking cane rendered him near-senseless.

But Sherwyn Huntley's senses had not been dulled! In his mind's eye he watched the night-time scene while the physical flesh throbbed. He had dragged the unresisting figure to where the structure of the bridge began its gentle rise, had leaned it across the low stone parapet, then one snatch had ripped away the thin trousers, another tearing the ragged shirt. The boy's bottom had showed pale in the light of the yellow moon. He had stared at it for the moment it had taken to free his pulsing flesh then had thrust it into that warm seductive orifice. Though dazed from the double blow to his head the boy had cried his pain, a sound which had added to the intoxication of entering where the cry had told no entry had been made before.

To be the first! Teeth clenching against the demand of his loins, against the sheer hedonism such a cry ever aroused in him, Sherwyn Huntley lived again the heady satisfaction. It was always good to be the first.

And it had been good then! Heedless of sound or movement from the passing streets, Sherwyn Huntley saw only the pictures in his mind, heard only the raucous sound of his own breath, the slap of flesh against flesh as he thrust deep into that delightful cavern, the rhythmic thud on thud that was a head hitting stone.

Passion slaked, he stepped clear of the half-naked youth, quickly refastening the buttons of his trousers. But the boy did not move. Sherwyn stared at the lifelike scene his mind conjured, saw himself take a coin from his pocket and throw it at the feet of the small figure now a slumped heap on the ground. But there was no attempt to take it, no movement of any sort; no sound!

No movement other than the soft murmur of the river lapping gently against its banks, no sound other than the agitated squawk of a duck menaced by a silent hunter. It had set his pulses beating. Was there someone nearby? Someone who had watched that rape? He stood listening intently, his gaze penetrating the silvered darkness of the night, but nothing more marred the velvet silence.

Silence! It was that had caused him to glance again at the figure lying where it had fallen. Why didn't he move? Why didn't he take the money he had earned? A poke to the spine with the silver-topped cane brought no response so he thrust a boot at the naked bottom. That too had no effect.

'Bank Street, sir.'

The voice of the driver of the hansom announcing his destination brought the present rushing in, bringing with it a rapid termination to the pulsing at the base of Sherwyn's stomach.

'Will I wait, sir?'

He nodded yes, replaced the silk hat on his head and walked steadily towards an imposing brick building.

A second, more vicious, thrust of his boot had

resulted in silence. He had glared at the figure. What game was the boy playing? Then, bending over him, turning the head, his hand had felt a warm stickiness. He had looked into the face. The eyes had been wide open, staring back at him, and above them above them the wide gash of a caved-in skull!

The boy was dead! It had taken a full minute to recover from the shock then all the agility of a cunning mind had come into play. No one had seen them beneath the bridge, no witness could tell who was responsible for rape, for death ... except perhaps the half-sovereign lying beside the body. Only a relatively wealthy client would pay so much for a few minutes of pleasure. Half a sovereign would raise doubt as to the boy selling himself to a man from the working classes. That had been a risk easily avoided. He had picked up the coin, slipping it into his pocket. Now there was nothing to indicate the rape of a street whore had been carried out by any but another of the same kind.

Entering the bank through a door swung wide by a deferential doorkeeper, Sherwyn Huntley smiled to himself. No risk, expense and nothing to point to Sherwyn Huntley being a rapist and a killer!

23

'I am sorry to have taken so long a time, I had difficulty in finding the way, I … I do not find the speech of the people easy to understand.'

'That don't be surprisin', Darlaston folk 'ave a dialect all their own an' that altering from town to town; folk 'ere in Wednesbury don't talk same as do folk from Cradley, and them along of Dudley be different to them of Bloxwich, and ain't none of 'em easy to understand. It be the way wherever you goes in the Black Country; I wonders you found your way at all.'

She had wondered, not whether or not the wench would find her way but rather was it the last would be seen of her in Woden Passage, her and the money gone from the table.

'Be my reckonin' folk you spoke to d'ain't 'ave the understandin' of y'self,' Libby Radley kept her thoughts hidden, 'they don't be used with hearin' folk speak the way you does, could sound like a foreign language to many hereabouts.'

'I did have to repeat my questions several times.' Regan smiled.

'I thinks likely you 'ad to ask 'm more'n several, and then probably tax your brain unravellin' what it were they said in the answerin', but you managed in the end.'

Reaching into her pocket bringing out an envelope and several coins Regan handed them to the woman whose face had clearly shown surprise seeing who it was had entered the shop a few minutes previously. Libby Radley had not expected her to return. Regan felt disappointment weigh heavy in her chest. Libby Radley must have thought she would steal the money and leave Wednesbury as quickly as she could, and Daniel … he also must have had the same conviction, they had both believed her a thief! She betrayed no sign of this thought as she looked evenly at the woman she respected and who had so quickly found a place in her heart, the woman who it seemed had no trust in her.

'Please…' She swallowed on the word. 'Please count the money I have handed to you, I would have you see all is correct before I leave.'

There was no animosity in the tone. Libby read the contents of the paper but her mind was on the young woman facing her. No anger for the way she had been used, but there was hurt, hurt in the voice and in the eyes. The wench knew. Taking a box from a drawer of the dresser Libby dropped the uncounted coins into it. Regan Trent knew the placing of that money on the table had been a test, a way of finding the character of her, but what had it said of the character of Libby Radley?

Closing the drawer with the box inside it, Libby took a moment with her thoughts. It had been a thimble rig she had played on this wench, a cheap underhand trick. But it had bounced back, it was Libby Radley had come out the worse for it, now it was for Libby Radley to apologise.

'It all is in order?' Regan's stifled words reached across sudden stillness.

'What?' Roused from the depth of thought, Libby answered frowning. 'Oh, the money you means! Yes, that be as it should.'

'You did not count it!'

There were tears in that answer, tears where there should be reprimand, hurt where there should be blame! Conscience pricking, Libby turned. 'There be no need,' she said. Then making no attempt to excuse what she had done went on. 'My askin' of you to go along of that farm so as to save me the walk were only part truth, the other part were to see would you come back or would you tek away with the money. It were a shabby trick an' I don't be above the sayin' of it. You 'ave my apologies an' them *do* be sincere though I don't ask you go a forgivin' of what I done across you for I knows that can't be, all I does ask is you hold no rebuke in your 'eart for Daniel for he played no part.'

'I have no rebuke for Daniel nor for yourself. Your asking me to take money to that farmer gave me the opportunity to repay in some small part the kindness and hospitality shown me in this house and that is something I thank both you and your son for; please would you tell Daniel that.'

It would have been understandable had the wench rattled and raved but to be offering thanks! Self-reproach a sting to her veins Libby could only answer quietly. 'That be somethin' he would rather come from your tongue than mine; would you give a few minutes for the tellin'?'

A few minutes talking with Daniel! She had enjoyed the times they had chatted together, she would enjoy it now but she must forgo that pleasure; to sit with him was merely delaying the inevitable. 'I'm sorry.' Regan shook her head. 'I have to go.'

'Ar, well if you 'as to go then you 'as to go, but 'ere in Wednesbury we likes to share a cup wi' a friend afore they leaves.'

A friend! Regan felt the rush of tears. It was not philanthropy she wanted, not aid which succoured the body but that which nourished the heart, the charity of friendship; friendship she had shared with Rosa and Joab Mullin.

'Look, wench.' Libby stared over the teapot held in her hands. 'I be far from proud of what were done today an' though I tells you I be sorry I knows that won't mek no amends but I ask a kindness where none be due, that be you says farewell to Daniel, don't leave him with the thinkin' it were 'imself be the cause of you goin' from Wednesbury.'

'Daniel!' Regan glanced first toward the door leading onto the staircase then back to Libby. 'Why would Daniel think that?'

Cos he has feelings for you! That was what must never be said. Libby bent to replace the teapot on the trivet swung close to the fire, the thought ironbound in her mind. 'There were folk would come a visitin',' she straightened but remained staring into the fire, 'lads he were friends with, an' sometimes wenches. They would come an' spend an hour or two sittin' along of him in this room but gradually the times they come grew less an' the minutes they stayed got fewer until eventually they d'ain't come at all. I tried to tell 'im them lads an' wenches was too teken with workin' the

248

long hours us sort of folk 'ave to work in order to live, but Daniel he felt otherwise, he believed it were sight of 'im, his twisted legs and body a wastin' away, it were that they couldn't stomach and so they stopped comin' altogether. I seen the pain in his eyes, heard the misery he tried to hide an' I begs you now, don't add another thorn to the crown he wears.'

'Blame there is, but it can't all be borne by my mother.' Daniel Radley's smiled served only to emphasise the thinness of his face. 'I must take fair share...'

'No Daniel, naught of it were your doin'!'

'A mother protecting her son.' Daniel smiled again. 'But as she always taught, truth is the best protection, and the truth, Regan, is it was me and not my mother was the instigation behind asking you go to Meadow Farm, to take money for the purchase of oats and barley, it was myself put your honesty to question and that will always cause me shame.'

Leaning forward in the chair drawn to the bedside Regan touched the hand resting on the cover. 'I hope not, Daniel, it was a kindness in itself for it provided me with a way of showing my gratitude for the help you and your mother have given me, it afforded me the means of returning that kindness. I only wish it were more I could have done.'

'Then stay!' Long fingers closed about Regan's own. 'If you mean what you say, if it be you really want to help then stay here along of Mother and me.'

249

In bewilderment Regan looked at Libby, the woman saying quickly, 'I knows what be in your mind, be it Daniel Radley alone be offerin' you a place? But I tells you Libby Radley be offerin' the same.'

A place to stay! Relief rushed at Regan then as swiftly became the voice of reason. Daniel and his mother were acting out of guilt for having put her integrity to the test; this was yet one more way of saying they were sorry, but it was a way too far.

'Me an' Daniel 'ave talked matters over.' Sensing the thought behind the absence of answer Libby Radley went on. 'We talked of how you sent that salesman packin' the other day, how you said that tea he vowed were the best quality to be had were naught but the sweepin's up, of the quickness with which you've picked up the way o' things in the shop, well I ... we reckoned that be help o' the sort we be needin'.'

'I think what my mother be trying to say is would you consider working here, assisting with the shop those times she is here looking to me?'

'Don't go an answerin 'til you've 'eard the all.' Libby glanced at her son, at the hand still holding to Regan's. 'It be employment will pay little wage, the shop don't be mekin' a fortune, but along of the job comes board an' lodgin'.'

Board and lodging! Bewilderment returned to Regan's face, showing clearly in the look turned to Libby. The only place to sleep was the living room and grateful as she had been for that the practice could not go on indefinitely.

The explanation however continued. 'This 'ouse be what Wednesbury folk call end of terrace, that bein' so it had a small piece of ground to one side, ground left empty of anythin' other than bricks an' rubble. That were what decided me on the buyin' o' it for I reckoned in time to 'ave a room built so Daniel could 'ave privacy to talk with friends. Folk were kind, men givin' the time they weren't at the pit or the forge to build that room, the women a sewin' o' a cushion or a curtain so it were made pleasant. Now that room don't be used for naught but the storin' o' boxes. A couple of hours an' a bit o' elbow grease an' it could be pretty as ever it were. Should you be choosin' to bide 'ere then that room be yourn for as long as you wants.'

'Regan.' Daniel smiled into eyes starry with moisture. 'We would both like you to stay.'

''Er be livin' in that storeroom, I knows cos I've seen 'er light the lamp times after the shop's bin shut.'

'You sees too much forra little 'un, Poppy Jeavons!'

'I don't be no peeper, Mrs Radley.' Blue eyes blazed defensively across the shop counter. 'I don't go a spyin' on folk, I sees that lamp from the window when I be away to bed, an' I sees the one who lights it, that be 'ow I knows you 'as a lodger.'

Reaching for the pennyworth of tea the child had come to purchase, Libby set it on the counter. 'So you knows that does you!' she said, hiding a smile. 'Do you also know what'll 'appen should I mention that window-gazin' to your mother?'

'Ar.' The girl nodded, brown hair flopping over her brow. 'I knows, my backside'll be redder than

251

a tomarter … you won't say it will ya Mrs Radley, you won't go a tellin' o' me mother will ya?'

Taking several coins from the box beneath the counter Libby shook her head. 'You be safe enough this time.' She counted change into the outstretched palm. 'But you mind to keep that nose o' yourn away from windows in future.'

Her customer gone, Libby stared into the shadow the anaemic yellow glow of the single gas lamp seemed to accentuate. The girl had said what everybody living in Woden Passage already knew; nothing remained a secret in the Passage nor the maze of streets surrounding it. A lodger was nothing new here, but one whose manner of speech was so clearly different to their own, that had caused a stir.

''Er talks like the vicar along o' St Bart's.'

'Ain't never 'eard a body talk like 'er does, it be right bay-windowed an' no mistek.'

No there was no mistaking that Regan Trent's way of speaking was that of someone who had enjoyed a better life.

'I ain't never 'eard the like 'ceptin that time that fella come from Himley to order iron railin's for the Earl o' Dudley's estate.'

Women gossiping over the counter, men calling for tobacco or a box of matches as they passed on their way to work, all of them spoke of Regan. But did they speak of her other than here in this shop? Of course they did!

Her mind answering the question it had asked, Libby crossed to the door, slipping the bolt into position. Gossip was the only thing free in life for folk whose lives were given to labour.

Turning off the jet of gas feeding the lamp, Libby watched its mantle fade, the yellowness which illuminated the shop quickly swallowed by eager shadow. Labour! Standing in the room lit now only by the beams of a pallid moon, Libby sighed. Work was the god of poor folk, a god who demanded they labour every hour of every day, the god they must worship in order to live, and gossip was the only thing which did not take a farthing of the money they laboured to earn. Was it any wonder then they indulged in it?

Once her sight had adjusted to the semi-darkness, Libby walked towards the living area of the room.

She could not blame folk for talking.

One hand reached to the curtain dividing living room from shop, then she paused.

But who had they talked to? Who else might know Regan Trent lodged at this house?

There had been no explanation from the wench as to what brought her to Wednesbury and only one question asked by Libby Radley: 'Is there a child on the way?'

The answer had been 'No,' and the truth of it she had accepted but the quick pain flashing across those eyes had told another story. Could that story be of a man, a man whose advances had been re-fused, a man not prepared to take 'no' for an answer?

Supper over, Libby folded the tablecloth, placing it back in a drawer of the dresser.

No man of working class would approach a woman of means, none would expect a wealthy woman to marry beneath her and certainly none in his right mind would dare forcing her to lie with him. Was it then somebody of her own class were a threat to her?

It was obvious Regan Trent had been reared to a good life, one cushioned by wealth. What then if not threat of rape would have driven her to leave it?

'Let me put the dishes away and then I will bank the fire for the night.'

A girl used to the comfort money provided, but this one had settled without complaint to a life which held little of the luxury she must have known. Libby looked at the girl coming from the scullery, a tray stacked with freshly washed dishes in her hands.

'The fire can wait.' Decision made before she knew what it boded, Libby shook her head. 'Set them crocks down an' come you to the fire, there be somethin' I feels should be said.'

A frown of enquiry flicking between her brows, Regan moved to set the tray on the table.

'Don't be nothin' you've done wrong, wench, so you can wipe that frown from your face.'

'Daniel … is it Daniel?' Anxiety had Regan's hands tremble, rattling the dishes on the tray.

'No, it don't be Daniel.' Libby's smile was warm but quickly gone. 'Now do like I says and set them crocks down afore you drops the lot. It be somethin' young Poppy Jeavons said when her come to fetch tea.' Libby began again as Regan sank to a chair. 'Her said about the lamp in your room, how her watched it bein' lit an' of seeing yourself movin' around inside. That of itself be of no concern but talk of you livin' in this house be a worry.'

A worry! Regan's nerves twanged. Was Libby about to tell her she must leave?

'Folk talk,' Libby was speaking on, 'that be only natural, just as it be they'll talk of you, of any stranger comin' to live in Woden Passage, that don't be neither 'ere nor there as far as I'm concerned, but I does fear talk of you could spread across all o' Wednesbury an' possibly beyond. What I be sayin' is this, be there somebody might be searchin' for you, somebody you be anxious shouldn't find you?'

Regan's hands twisted in her lap. Her being here was inviting harm to Libby and to Daniel, the same harm that had hung over Rosa and Joab while she had travelled with them. It was certain Sherwyn Huntley was still searching for her, that he would never stop searching, and most definitely he would take revenge on any who had helped her evade him.

'I...' She paused, not wanting to say what she knew she must. 'I have been foolish staying here–'

'Foolish!' Libby interrupted sharply, 'what be foolish about tekin' employment? Of keeping y'self from the workhouse? I sees naught foolish in that!'

'You don't understand–'

'I understands this,' Libby intervened again, 'you be runnin' from somethin' and that somethin' be more'n 'ard words; tell me that belief be wrong!' Waiting a few moments for a reply Libby shook her head when that reply didn't come. 'No, it don't be wrong, but you does if you thinks runnin' be the way to solve the problem. You

255

can't run forever, wench, there comes a day when it has to stop.'

'I … he…' Regan pressed her hands to her face, the words refusing to come.

He! Libby's mind caught at the word. So her thinkin' were right, some man was at the back of Regan Trent's leavin' her home, a man she feared yet.

She took Regan's hands, easing them from her face, her next words gentle with understanding. 'Regan wench,' she said softly, 'I be a woman of years, I've had the seein' of many evils of this world and the one I knows you holds inside won't 'ave the shockin' of me but lockin' it deep will 'ave it fester an' breed, it'll grow and grow 'til it destroys all quality of life. I don't be a woman to pry and I don't be askin' that which don't be my business but this much I do say. A trouble shared be a trouble halved. The tellin' of it can be a healin' in itself, it can't wash a wound nor will it wipe away the scar, only time can see the fading of that. Think on my words, wench, and think on these as well. You be welcome in my house and it'll be woe betide any who comes a lookin' for you 'ere!'

Curling her fingers into the gnarled ones spread over her own, clutching tight for support, Regan looked at the lined face.

'There be no need of more.' Libby spoke quickly. 'What be said be said and that be all about it!'

Swallowing against the tears in her throat, her answer a whisper, Regan stood up. 'There is a need. If I am to remain here then you should know all that it implies, and so should Daniel.'

256

24

'It be sin enough for any man to go forcin' hisself on a young wench, God knows it be, but to poison 'er mother then go orderin' the killin' of a lad ... eeh!' The look on Libby's face showed the incomprehension in her mind. 'What kind of varmint is that stepfather of yourn?'

'But Saul, your brother, died in an accident, that is what you said!'

There be fire ... a boy looked on by the Angel o' Death.

Loud as though Rosa spoke at her side the words rang in Regan's head.

Speaking quietly, Daniel repeated the statement which Regan had not answered. 'Saul died as the result of a fire in the summer house.'

Rosa's words still sounding in her ears, Regan could only nod.

'There be no question about that?'

Regan shook her head then, hands clasped tight together, told of Rosa's vision, adding, 'It was some nights later another gypsy girl, Sara Turley, came to the Mullin camp; she told of visiting Putley Village and of going to a large stone-built house. It was while she was there she heard the servants speaking of a body being discovered in the summer house and of there being a ring on one of its fingers, a ring with the initials S.T. Saul had a signet ring with those same initials. He had obviously returned to Woodford House.'

'But why set hisself there in that summer 'ouse?' Libby wondered. 'I means why d'ain't he go into the main 'ouse?'

'I have asked myself the same many times,' Regan answered. 'I know Saul was afraid of Sherwyn Huntley, that must have been the root of his running away from school, but when he found it difficult being so alone he returned home and waited in the summer house. Knowing it was a favourite escape of mine he must have thought I would find him there and possibly shield him from Huntley's wrath; I can only assume he must have fallen asleep and on waking perhaps knocked over the lamp, thus causing the fire which killed him. There can be no other explanation.'

'It be said Romanies 'ave second sight, that there Rosa Mullin certainly does,' Libby said as Regan finished speaking. 'Her were right about there bein' a fire, the only pity of that is it were a lad died instead of that swine of a stepfather. There be no justice in heaven, not when a man such as him be left to live while a lad be let to die!' Nor when it has a mother made to watch her only child die a little more every day! Libby glanced at her son, her heart twisting at the sight of pale drawn features and wasted body.

'So the death of your brother leaves yourself as the only obstacle to Sherwyn Huntley getting his hands on your father's legacy and that he intended to overcome by forcing you into marriage with Myles Wentworth.'

'I couldn't, Daniel, not after...' Colour flooding her face Regan struggled with the vivid rush of

258

memory. 'I told him nothing would make me marry Myles after witnessing what I had.'

'It were then he raped you!' Libby's blunt intervention heightened the flare in Regan's cheeks.

'He was adamant I become Myles Wentworth's wife.' Distress kept Regan's reply painfully quiet. 'When I refused, when I told him he could never force me to agree, then...'

'...*girls as well as boys have to be taught to obey ... to do with as I please ... most certainly be repeated...*'

Regan's knuckles showed white against the horror of her thoughts.

'It be all right wench, no need to go tellin' it again.'

'He laughed.' Almost as if Libby had not spoken, Regan continued to whisper. 'He said he would take his pleasure the way he preferred, that it was a pleasant deviation.'

The way he preferred. The man had taken her as a dog takes a bitch! Libby's glance played over the girl sitting tense as an iron rod. Rape was terrible enough for any woman but abuse in such a way was destroying to the soul.

'He threatened to repeat his abuse until I became pregnant.'

A shudder from deep inside made her voice tremble. 'He said carrying a child which would be born a bastard would prove too much, that I would be glad to marry Myles in order to keep the name of Trent untarnished by scandal.'

'Untarnished!' Libby spat contempt. 'He be the one that be tarnished, his mind be black wi' it!'

Propped against his pillows Daniel Radley watched the colour risen in Regan's cheeks, saw misery paint its shadows over her face, the shame which held her gaze lowered from his own. Regan Trent was in hell and the doors were still shut, doors which would never open should her stepfather find her.

'Do there be no let out? I mean be there no way to stop what 'Untley be about? I means your father ... d'ain't he mek no provision to safeguard what were intended for his kin?'

'There was one.' Regan's look remained on her hands. 'I overheard Myles and Huntley talking. It appears a condition in my father's will states that in order to claim any inheritance I must sign in the presence of his lawyer.'

'I don't reckon that to be a lake he'll drown in, slime floats on dirty water!'

His mother was right. The man Regan had described would not allow the matter of a signature stand in his way.

'Marriage,' he glanced at his mother then back to the girl sitting on the opposite side of his bed, 'marriage grants complete control of a woman's property to the husband in which case it would be Wentworth, not Huntley, would hold the purse strings.'

'So that swine of a stepfather wouldn't be gettin' of anythin' after all.'

'I wouldn't think that to be Huntley's idea,' Daniel answered his mother. 'It be my reckoning his plan to be himself and Wentworth to divide everything equally between them.'

'An' what of Regan, what equal share might her be gettin'?'

Regan heard the answer echo in her brain.

'...I shall recommend Myles try the same.'

Sherwyn Huntley slammed the letter down on the desk, his lips white with anger. Each week it was the same, each report a facsimile of the one before. 'Investigation has so far failed to reveal...'

Failed to reveal! Failed to reveal! It was a man and a girl was being searched for, not a needle in a haystack! But it might as well be a needle for all the progress the weeks of enquiry had resulted in. He snatched at the letter, ripping it then hurling the pieces to the floor. People didn't just disappear; Edwards Sanders had to be somewhere, and Regan? She too could not vanish into thin air yet that was all the so-called investigation had come up with, thin air; the men set to find her had found not a trace. But she had to be found. Fists clenched, he stared at the shredded paper. Her signature was vital, without it he could say goodbye to all of this, all of what Jasper Trent had built up, the money and business murder had twice brought a step closer. Too close to lose now! Regan Trent must be found, and then? Avarice glinted coldly in his eyes as he glanced about the comfortable room. Murder was not so hard to do!

'Your pardon, sir.' A polite tap had heralded the manservant's entry into the study.

'Mr Wentworth is in the hall, he asks to see you.'

Wentworth! Sherwyn's irritation flared afresh. What was it had the peacock from its nest so early in the day! With a curt nod indicating assent, he resumed his reading of the morning mail, ignoring his visitor until a kick at the fire irons demanded attention.

'When did you receive this?' Sherywn looked up from reading the letter which had been thrust at him.

'This morning.' Myles Wentworth's reply was agitated as the rapid movements of his hands. 'I thought it best to bring it over right away.'

'Do you know who might have sent it?'

'I've no idea.' Myles swung away from the desk. 'As you see there is no signature, no address.'

'Neither is there any stamp.' Sherwyn masked a rising apprehension, glancing again at the envelope which had contained the non-too-clean sheet of cheap notepaper. 'Which would indicate...' He dropped the letter onto the brilliantly polished surface of the desk and wiped his hands on a spotless linen handkerchief, before throwing it from him as though it carried leprosy. 'It was delivered by hand; did your man not inform you as to the time of its arrival!'

The significance of this, a reprimand more than a question, was not lost on Myles. 'It came during the night,' he responded crustily, 'the entire household were abed. Whoever brought that left it on the step of the kitchen door with a stone to hold it against it being swept away by any night breeze. It was found there by the maid opening the door to the delivery of milk.'

No signature! No return address! A frisson of alarm rippled through Sherwyn's veins. The letter Wentworth had received held all the hallmarks of the one he himself had been sent, a letter demanding money in return for silence. That had made two. The ice of vengeance hardened in his stomach. That made two people yet to be destroyed if

262

his life were to remain one of comfort.

'No signature and no address,' he repeated aloud, 'and you have no idea who is behind it.'

Sunlight streaming from a tall window sent copper-coloured sparks darting as Myles spun to face the man regarding him with a stone-hard glare. 'None,' he snapped, 'it could have been anybody.'

'Not anybody, Myles.' Metallic as the stare the response rang sharply. 'Not just *anybody* can have the knowledge that letter implies, it has to be some person you have talked with.'

For a moment Myles met the accusation with silence, then, 'Are you saying *I* have told somebody ... are you saying I am that stupid!'

Above the anxiety churning his stomach Sherwyn Huntley's stare was smooth as frozen water. 'That, my dear Myles, is the cross you are burdened with. You see I *know* it is not any word of mine has brought this about, the same as I *know* your tongue is ever loosened by drink; therefore only your carelessness can be responsible. However what is done cannot be undone, it remains only to deal with this unpleasant state of affairs.'

Was Wentworth's carelessness responsible for his loss of one hundred pounds! The thought with its attendant bile remaining silent, Sherwyn watched the younger man's face, the frown drawing the handsome brows together, the flash of worry darken the hazel eyes.

'You mean pay?'

'Do you know any other way?'

'For Christ's sake Huntley ... you know I can't pay, you know I don't have the kind of money that letter is asking! Look at it!' Grabbing the letter Myles pushed it back across the desk. 'Look at it, it is not only myself is referred to.'

… I knows what you and Untlee be doin, same as I be knowin what comes of them young uns you does it to…

I knows what you and Wentwuth be doin an the young uns you does it along of.

Words the fires of rage had branded in his mind seemed now to dance beside those on the paper. Sherwyn's acid glance took in the soiled note-paper, the ill-formed letters scrawled across it.

…a undred pund…

The words stared back, taunting insolent words.

…ifn you chooses not to pay then the pulice will ear.

The two letters were near-identical. Grammar was almost non-existent, punctuation totally so and the spelling of names and words pointed to a person of poor education. Not Myles's usual style of company, not a member of the gentry; but then Myles Wentworth did not always take his pleasure with those of his own class. One of the boys taken from an orphanage? Sherwyn's anger fastened on the thought. Not only the gentry had ears, nor did they alone have tongues.

'See!' Myles stabbed a finger at the paper Huntley had let fall. 'See, it names you.'

Huntley's mouth tightened, his glacial stare

fastening on the younger man. 'Meaning?'

'You know damn well!' Myles retorted. 'If the person who wrote that letter carries through with the threat of informing the police then it is you will stand in the dock alongside of me.'

'Then you have no other choice than to pay, at least no other choice until the one who is behind this extortion reveals himself.'

A laugh more of fear than despair caught in his throat as Myles turned to stand before the fireplace.

'Pay!' The half-laugh choked, 'With what? I've told you I don't have the money.'

'So what do you suggest?'

'Suggest?' Across the separating space Myles Wentworth's look became suddenly brittle. 'I don't *suggest,* I advise. I *advise* you to provide the necessary, a loan against our next sale; you can recover it from my share of the proceeds.'

It was certain Wentworth did not have a hundred pounds; this conceited dandy, this affected fop of a man let money run through his hands like a waterfall sliding from a cliff! Yet the proviso he had voiced was equally certain. The demand left unmet was an open invitation to trouble, but once paid would that see the end of any threat?

Rising to his feet Sherwyn Huntley took a calf-skin wallet from the pocket of his coat, extracting several banknotes. The answer required no speaking!

'Make certain you are not seen.' He watched Myles grab the money eagerly. 'Make equally certain watch – discreet watch – is kept on the place of collection. The blackguard who has written this has to be caught, caught and silenced!'

Caught and silenced! In the hansom taking him to the railroad station Myles Wentworth touched the lapel of his dove-grey silk mohair coat. His most recent purchase and the most expensive. The tailor had stroked the special order of cloth as if it were sacred and well it might be, considering the cost of a single yard. Five pounds. Myles's fingers caressed the smooth, soft material. Five pounds a yard, that was more money than some folk could hope to earn from months of menial labour, and assuredly Huntley's staff skivvied for no more. Yet Huntley had paid for this. Myles leaned comfortably against the upholstered seat. The man thought himself a paragon of good sense, so astute, so shrewd-witted.

'Station, sir!'

The cab drew to a halt and Myles alighted. Dropping a coin into the driver's hand he walked into the station, his mind still reviewing the events at Woodford House.

The so-capable Sherwyn Huntley! Sitting in the first-class gentleman's waiting room Myles drew heavily on his Havana cigar. Always a step ahead of the pack. But he had not been a step ahead today. Behind a cloud of cigar smoke Myles Wentworth's eyes held the shadow of a sneer. True, Huntley had played his cards cleverly, but Wentworth had played the winning hand; he'd scooped the prize, his clever associate standing the loss.

A long smooth breath carried the thin veil of cigar smoke high towards the ceiling of the waiting room. And the man called him a fool!

The shadow of a sneer became a smile. But it was Huntley had been the fool, it was he had paid that hundred pounds.

It had been easier than could have been imagined. The smile deepening with the thought, Myles threw the remnant of cigar into the fireplace as the train steamed noisily alongside the platform. Nodding amiably to the station attendant rushing to open the door of a first-class compartment he settled to a window seat. It had been a smart move on his part arriving at Woodford in a hansom rather than his own carriage and pair, it had added credence to the claim of being without funds; a claim Myles Wentworth's future was never truthfully to know again.

It had been so easy! Satisfaction glowing warm within him Myles stared through the window. Huntley had shown remarkably little resistance to the loan of a hundred pounds, but then he had seen the consequences of not doing so, consequences Sherwyn Huntley despite his abilities for deception would be unable to escape, for if not convicted of child molestation and rape by the courts, the damage done regarding his standing in society would be insurmountable. Huntley could not contemplate the risk of that and so he had paid.

Just as he would pay again!

The thought warmed his heart as Myles watched the passing landscape, the greenery of fields seemingly overlain by the grey-white of steam blowing back from the train engine.

There had been no mention of any previous demand. Huntley had not once spoken of a similarly worded letter delivered to Woodford House. That had been a stroke of genius wording both letters in the same uneducated fashion; it had Huntley's search for the blackmailer entirely off the scent. Blackmail! A dirty word. Myles's satisfaction deepened. But money, earned by whatever method, was spendable and his future would be well-cushioned with it.

Being so conversant with the grounds of Woodford House and knowing Huntley as he did had proved most fortunate. It had taken no depth of reasoning to ascertain watch would be placed on that rear gate, that the one set to watch would not stand in the open where he would be clearly visible, nor would he take up station until darkness fell. It had been simply a matter of waiting and that had not proved long. Worn out by a day's toil the man perched in the tree had fallen asleep. He had not seen the figure glide swiftly along the shadowed wall to take the package held down by a stone; he had not seen Myles Wentworth!

25

There was no getting away from fact. Libby Radley wrapped penny portions of tea. The wench were clever; it were not just knowing the qualities of tea her father had taught, or of many other commodities folk needed, he had also taught the use of number. She did the accounts in a fraction of the time it had taken herself, and always she did them with Daniel looking on.

Daniel! Libby's hands stilled. They had talked together, herself and Daniel, the times Regan was out on some errand and each time the talk had returned to the question of marriage. Marriage to someone else would see her safe from the threat of Huntley and Wentworth, he said. But marriage to who? Was Daniel thinking that man to be himself? He must realise! Libby's fingers tightened about the scrap of paper. He must know nothing but sorrow would come of a match such as that, the mental pain of being with a woman he could be no real husband to would be a thousand times more hurtful than that of his twisted limbs! But Daniel were no child, he were a man grown and as such need pay no heed to aught but his own thinking.

'I'll be tekin' of one o' them packets.' A woman close-wrapped in a shawl, the corners tied beneath thin breasts, entered the shop. 'An' I be wantin' a quarter-pound o' pearl barley an' the same o' oats.'

'Sound like y'be cooking' grorty puddin'.'

Already counting coins onto the counter the woman nodded. 'Ar, it'll be thin o' meat, tuppence don't buy no more'n a few bits o' scrag but oats an' barley along wi' 'alf a dozen o' potatoes fills the bellies o' little uns.'

While their mother eats nothing! Libby glanced at her customer. There were so many of her ilk in Wednesbury, men and women struggling to keep a family, toiling day and most of the night, the result often not enough to afford them a decent meal, and sometimes, as with this woman, no meal at all.

269

The 'Truck Act', a law passed by Parliament a few years before, had banned the practice of paying workers with tokens, metal discs with the name of foundry or employer stamped on front and back, the value of which could only be redeemed by buying goods in a shop owned by that same employer. But it had done little to help the folk still having to frequent those shops for the price of goods had risen accordingly. She had kept her own prices low as she could but not every woman in the town could take time to come to Woden Passage, and those who did scurried in and out like shadows, scarcely passing the time of day.

A heavy step heralding a customer Libby glanced towards the door, then recognising the man said sharply, 'I told you not to come 'ere no more, I wants no dealin's wi' the likes o' you!'

'You wants no dealin' with me!' The response came as a sneer; the man crossed to the counter. 'P'raps you'll have a change of mind.'

'And p'raps I won't!' Libby's hand slapped the counter. 'You come a sellin' tea you said were finest to be had ... and it were fine, so fine it were naught but dust; y'would 'ave teken my money for that rubbish.'

'You could have sold it on, folk hereabout have so much soot and smoke on their tongues they wouldn't know the difference were you to sell them the soil that tea were grown in.'

Libby's tightening mouth showed resentment at the retort. 'I would know,' she said. 'Wednesbury folk works 'ard for their money, too 'ard for it to be given for sweepin's of tea dust or for anythin' else that lyin' mouth o' yourn says be fine.'

270

'Sweepin's.' Close to the counter the man's smile was cold. 'That were the word that wench used, her with the fancy way of talkin'. Where is the wench?' He glanced towards the curtain closing off the living-room area. 'Is her still here? Don't bother answerin' for I know her is.'

'Be naught to do wi' you, be none o' your business where that wench might be!'

'But I can make it my business, and if I does then Libby Radley could be finding 'erself out of business ... permanently. I knows who it is you've given lodging to and I knows them as be searchin' for her; it'll tek no more than a word to bring them here and I tell you they won't deal kindly wi' you, so you tek your pick, either you deals with me or you deals with them who be lookin' for that wench, and remember that son of yourn, wi'out a place to live what'll become of him, the workhouse be what it says, a place of work, it don't tek in no cripples so it would be the madhouse for him. Think of that when next you needs to stock this shop – think of your son in the asylum for the insane!'

A sound at the door had the man draw back but the threat in his eyes gleamed across the counter.

'Right you be then Mrs Radley, I'll be bringin' your order this time next month.' He touched his hat, adding, 'Thank you for your business.' Then turning to leave he glanced at the figure still standing in the doorway.

'He tried sellin' me a chest o' tea that were naught but dust.' Libby set the cups she had filled on the wooden tray.

'Was that what he was doing when I came in?'

'No.' Libby shook her head. 'That were some time back, if it 'adn't bin for Regan then I'd 'ave bought it not knowin' it were rubbish.'

'Regan?' Deep brown eyes regarded Libby.

'Be a wench I took in off the streets, 'ad travelled wi' some gypsy couple.'

'And she knew about tea?'

'Knowed about a lot more'n tea.' Libby smiled as her visitor picked up the tray. 'That wench 'as a good 'ead on her shoulders, it just be a pity...' She broke off, following up the stairs in silence.

'Have you met Regan?' Daniel looked at the man at his bedside. One man who of all his childhood friends still visited regularly.

'No.' Grant Eversley shook his head. 'But your mother said she knows tea.'

Daniel's eyes flicked to his mother. 'Quite enjoys the tellin' of that does Mother; and has her told you Regan knows a deal about other things beside tea?'

A call from below summoned Libby to the shop.

'So tell me of this Regan,' Grant Eversley said as Libby left the bedroom. 'She sounds quite intriguing.'

Intriguing had hardly been the word, baffling would be a more fitting description. Grant Eversley listened to Daniel while his mind asked a string of questions. What was an obviously educated woman doing travelling with gypsies? Why choose Wednesbury as the place to part company with them? What had she got to hide? More than that, what did she hope to gain? Inveigling her way into this house, worming into the affections of a crippled man and a woman who had no other child to pass her business to, could be for no other purpose than to take all she could get.

'Daniel,' he said as the other man finished speaking. 'You and Libby, you know nothing of this woman.'

'I know this.' Daniel's smile said he understood his friend's concern. 'Regan talks to me not as to somebody of crippled wit but as to a man sound as yourself. You don't understand what that means to me, to be looked at through eyes not filled with pity, not striving to hide revulsion, but eyes holding warmth and laughter. Regan brings that to me, she brings life into this room.'

Life and what else? Grant Eversley watched the face of the man in the bed, the nuances of emotion cross the pale face, the strength of feeling livening tired eyes. Had this Regan woman awakened more than the echoes of life in the heart of Daniel Radley? Had she also awakened love?

Had Libby Radley seen in the face of her son that same thing he had seen? After he left, Grant Eversley's thoughts ranged over his visit to the house in Woden Passage. Did Daniel's mother harbour the same thoughts which had filled his mind while listening to Daniel? Did she also think her son to be in love with the woman they both named simply Regan? He did love her, there was no question of it; and the woman! Unless she were blind or a fool then she too must have seen it, and from what he had learned she was neither. That then answered all his questions: the woman was a schemer! With Daniel Radley hopelessly in love with her then robbing the Radleys of all they

273

had would be child's play.

'Of course it was an accident!' Sherwyn Huntley's angry reply ruffled the silence of his private club, bringing looks of annoyance from members engrossed in reading their newspapers.

'Damned awkward if you ask me.'

'But I am not asking you.' Ice-cold eyes regarded the man nursing a brandy goblet in his hands.

'Neither was the delightful Mrs Russell.' Myles Wentworth indulged an inner satisfaction at seeing a dull flush rise to the other man's face. True, Huntley had caused the proprietress of that "house of pleasure" to be no longer welcoming but that was a price willingly paid for the pleasure of seeing Huntley squirm. Glancing over the rim of the half-filled goblet he said, 'She asks we no longer frequent her establishment.'

'So take your enjoyment elsewhere, or will that, along with everything else, prove beyond your capabilities!' Huntley snapped again ignoring the aggrieved 'tuts' coming from the readers.

If you but knew the extent, the full range, of those capabilities my friend ... but you won't. Myles Wentworth flicked a manicured hand over expensively tailored midnight-blue alpaca. The jacket had cost a packet, but then where one packet had been obtained another would be forthcoming. Two hundred pounds paid to a blackmailer the identity of whom Sherwyn Huntley was no nearer discovering than he had been weeks ago! An identity he would never discover!

The free hand waved in a flippant, slightly disparaging gesture designed to achieve a further riffling of Huntley's temper. Huntley was worried, so much so this next tactic could only succeed.

'I've already found a replacement for Mrs Russell's house.' He sipped then dabbed a napkin elegantly to the corners of his mouth. 'You might try the new place.'

'I shall try no new place. I shall continue as before.'

'But Mrs Russell...'

'I do not care what that woman says, I shall avail myself of that place whenever and as often as I wish; the woman well knows what will happen to her should the practices carried on there be brought to the attention of the police.'

Myles lowered his own voice. 'In that case I feel I should warn you.'

Ice which seconds before had frozen the eyes fastened on Wentworth seemed suddenly to flow downwards, cooling the red fire of anger burning in Huntley's cheeks while an unmistakable edge marked the, 'Warn me ... of what?'

Huntley was anxious. Sipping again, Myles Wentworth tasted satisfaction more than he tasted brandy. Beneath the displeasure, the show of bravado, there was a definite anxiety. Lifting a leg across the knee of the other, fingers tapping a custom-made soft leather shoe, Myles's mind revelled in what would come next. Huntley feared he had troubles now, but wait a few days and he would really experience the full meaning of the word. His glance on the expensive shoe, he said quietly, 'This is not the place.'

'This is as good a place as any.' Huntley glared. 'Say what you have to say, I wouldn't want you to choke on the enjoyment!'

Tut tut Sherwyn, we really are nervous! Myles continued, his features showing none of the amusement inside. 'Look,' he said quietly, 'I'm sure it will all come to nothing, Mrs Russell ... well, she will handle it but you ... you should stay clear.'

Every fibre an icicle Sherwyn Huntley regarded the younger man lounging elegantly in the deep leather armchair. Wentworth was enjoying this, he was revelling in every moment. But the winds of change could blow in different directions and when they did this ostentatious clown would be carried away in the blast! Controlling both nerves and temper he took a slim cheroot from a silver case and lit it.

'Mrs Russell?' Slipping the silver case back into his coat pocket he looked at Myles. 'What is it that woman can handle?'

Fingers brushing his shoe Myles hesitated, a pause which while entirely false was totally enjoyable. Let the so competent Sherwyn Huntley stew in his own juice!

'Well?' Huntley blew a stream of smoke, the action appearing one of nonchalance to any who might observe it. Myles was not deceived. He was not finished yet, the fruit of revenge was delectable, it was to be eaten slowly. 'I went to see her,' he answered, not looking up. 'I thought perhaps to find out if anything had come of that ... that accident.'

'And?' Sherwyn's glacial demand hid the sudden quiver running along his every vein.

Now for the *coup de grâce*. Lowering his foot to

the floor Myles gratified his senses with another slightly longer hesitation, then, 'Bad news I'm afraid.' Placing the goblet on the table set between the armchairs he took a long breath as though allowing himself respite from what must be said, of appearing to search for a way of saying it though he knew every syllable by heart. 'It,' he glanced about the room before going on, 'it seems someone knows what took place there that night, someone who knows what really happened, someone who is asking for money.'

Someone was asking for money. Another blackmailer! Closeted in his bedroom, Sherwyn Huntley seethed. How could anyone have seen? Yet Wentworth had said... Wentworth! Huntley seized on the name. Had he lied about there being someone claiming knowledge of that night? Was it a figment of his foolish mind? And what of the Russell woman, if indeed she had been approached, if demand had been made for money wouldn't it have been wiser for her to come here to Woodford, to speak directly with himself, not to send word with Wentworth?

But then Wentworth had suggested he bring that news to Woodford. His arrival here was a regular occurrence and anyone seeing him would pay no particular attention but should a woman visit, a woman never seen here before, then that would be bound to draw attention from the staff. It was the better way. Sherwyn admitted the reasonableness though it relieved none of the rage blistering his mind.

A letter. Wentworth had said the Russell

woman had been contacted by letter. A rough uneducated hand had demanded fifty pounds. Money Russell had declared be paid by the one responsible for...

It had been an accident! Anger with himself adding to that at being blackmailed yet again Sherwyn brought a fist hard down onto the arm of his chair. Christ, it had been an accident, he had not meant it to happen!

If only he had said no. But that was so easily said while so difficult to do, temptation was a harsh mistress; and she had prove her mastery.

'You should see for yourself.'

Wentworth's words returned to echo in Sherwyn's head. *'This delivery is worth twice what others have gone for, let me bring the goods to you so you can judge for yourself.'*

'No, I said no more were to be brought to Woodford.'

His own answer heard clearly in his mind, Sherwyn's fist clenched. He should have left it at that! Told Wentworth to make the sale as usual! But Wentworth had been persuasive.

'I would prefer you view the goods, have your opinion as to the asking price; it will more than settle the loan you made me.'

The return of the hundred pounds! That had gone further than Wentworth's praise of the latest acquisition and when he had suggested the Russell establishment as the viewing pen then there had been no more refusal.

It had been the same room, that ultra-private room on the top floor of the elegant house, the room kept for patrons with especial tastes. Wentworth had already arrived.

Fingers bunched tightly, Sherwyn stared at pictures forming in his mind.

Wentworth and the boy! Dressed in plain jacket and trousers, blue eyes glazing from liberal swallows from a brandy flask, a wide smile showing good teeth, a wealth of bronze curls touching the brow of a fetchingly handsome face, the youngster held all the promise of a budding Greek god. Wentworth had been correct in his assumption: this one would realise a healthy profit. Wentworth had also seen the reaction the sight of the pretty youth had provoked in Sherwyn Huntley, the flicker of desire flash across his eyes, the soft intake of breath as he looked at the smiling figure.

It had been almost two months since the episode at that bridge, two months in which he had not indulged in this most special pleasure.

Deep within his mind the thought tried to rise, to soothe the moment by providing an excuse, but another stronger one rose above it.

'*We could take a slightly lower profit.*'

Had it been deliberately said? Had Wentworth judged perhaps his debt would be wiped clean this way?

'*A few pounds, Sherwyn, what is that against an evening of enjoyment?*'

Wentworth had smiled as he had said it, a smile of invitation, one which had been accepted.

They had plied the boy with brandy, then when he was almost asleep on his feet had stripped away his clothes before laying him face down on the bed.

If only he had not cried out!

Despite the harsh life he had endured in

Burnford Home for Orphan Boys the lad had a fine body, straight limbs and fine shoulders. Spreadeagled on the bed the sight had fuelled the desire already flaming along every vein.

Unaware of his harsh intake of breath Sherwyn watched as memory unfolded in his mind.

It had been too long! The last time had been so many weeks ago!

Lust, powerful and overriding, had taken control. Naked, he joined the giggling figure on the bed, covering it with his own; then as he entered that warm orifice the giggling had given way to a cry. But he had not stopped; he could not stop. The need for satisfaction, the lust had become a craving as he had thrust deeper, and the cry had become a scream of pain.

That was when he had slipped a hand beneath the boy's head, a hand which covered the mouth.

One hand beneath the head, the other pressing down on the shoulder. The boy was pinned beneath him and he, his own head arching back with the frenzy of climax, had snatched that other head, his own gasp of fulfilment drowning the snap as the boy's neck broke.

As if the sound were real, Sherwyn started from the chair, but though the pictures vanished from his mind thoughts continued.

They had dressed the boy, he and Wentworth. Then first ensuring no one was to be seen they had pitched him head first down the stairs. Russell had claimed the boy had been an employee of hers, a lad she had hired to work in the scullery, that he must have stolen brandy from the wine cellar and while drunk had missed his footing and fallen to his death.

It had been a plausible explanation. Anger returning Sherwyn kicked at the chair. The magistrate had accepted it!

An orphan; a boy who had already been a financial burden on the state; further investigation would simply add to that burden; so the verdict had been clear. 'Accidental death due to a fall whilst under the influence of alcohol.'

It had all passed over so smoothly. 'So why now?' One fist crashed into another as Sherwyn's question cracked against the silence of the room. Why now were things going wrong?

26

'Regan?'

As she left the butcher's shop Regan's blood froze. The call from across the street, it sounded so like her own name. But it could not be, no one outside of Woden Passage knew what she was named. It was no more than nerves, they had been on edge from Libby telling her of that salesman saying he knew those who searched for her. Again she had determined to leave Libby's house for fear of what might become of the man's threat. But Daniel had asked that she stay.

Her being here in Wednesbury at all spoke of her having left her home, her speech verifying it had been a home very different to the one she shared in Woden Passage; the rest he had said was

281

no more than guesswork on the part of a man peeved at being found in a lie. He had also said it was improbable the man would know anything of Huntley or Wentworth and that she should stay where she had friends and anyway those living in the streets close about were wary of strangers, especially any who came asking questions, so should it be someone did come then there would be plenty of warning; time would be then to disappear from the Passage. But running before the stable door opened, well... Daniel had smiled, that was the action of a stupid horse. She had known what he meant, she should wait and see. But waiting meant worrying. *'It'll be that way wherever you goes, leavin' 'ere won't mek life no easier, you far better bide wi' Daniel an' me.'*

Libby's advice had been practical common sense. Anywhere and everywhere she might go worry and fear would be constant companions. She had tried less and less to leave the house, to be seen in the streets, but Libby must close the shop losing custom while she came to the market. She could have stayed in the shop; children who came in place of their mothers would solemnly point to the goods they shopped for, their eyes asking how was it a 'grown-up' didn't know for herself where everything was kept or how much it cost? But even with children time in Woden Passage was money, the longer they were away from the workplace the less money they had to live on, so she had elected to visit the market. It had seemed more sensible; Libby could serve people in a fraction of the time it would take herself, yet each errand that took her away from the house was filled with fears of being discovered. Maybe, as Daniel had assured her, that salesman had lied when saying what he had, but she could not lie to herself. Huntley would have people looking for her and he would never give up until she was found.

'Regan ... Regan Trent!'

Coming a second time the call jangled every nerve. It was her name being shouted across the High Street. There was no mistaking what she heard, she had been found!

Desperation chasing all else from her mind she darted between market stalls oblivious to the annoyance of women pushed aside, the shouts of stall-keepers to 'watch where you be goin'!' her only thought being to get away.

'Running again, a hobby, Miss...?'

Caught by strong arms, Regan vented her fear in a cry but far from releasing her the arms tightened.

'Running across a field is one thing,' a voice spoke quietly, 'but running amok among those market stalls is something else again. There are folk don't take kindly to being shoved aside.'

Fear paramount Regan pushed against the body close to her own, her voice cracking with dread. 'I won't ... I won't go back, please ... he will...'

The devils of hell! Grant Eversley held the quivering girl. Seemed they were once more on the loose!

'You don't have to go anywhere you have no wish to go,' he said, 'though I do recommend getting off the street. A woman in tears might be nothing new to Wednesbury but still it does not

283

fail to draw attention.'

It had made no impression; the girl had obviously not heard a word. Grant Eversley felt the tremors running through the slight figure. Where would she not go back? Who was 'he'? And what was it that 'he' would do?

Question riding on question he held firmly to Regan. What was needed right now was a soothing cup of tea.

'Regan – Regan Trent!'

Glancing across the head against his chest Grant Eversley frowned at the figure coming towards them then at Regan slumped barely conscious in his arms.

'I'm sorry, it weren't my intention to frighten her.'

No? Well you've done a pretty good job all the same! thought Grant Eversley to himself as he helped Regan to a seat in a quiet corner of the coffee house then requested tea and scones from an attentive waitress.

Shamefaced, Regan smiled into worried eyes. 'It was not your fault, I...'

'It were my fault! I should never have called out as I did, it were just I was so astonished, I never thought to see you in Wednesbury, not never in a million years.'

'Nor I you.'

'But how? I mean how come you be here?'

She would explain later but first she must thank the man who had thought to help, who now watched her with questions in his eyes.

'There was no ditch to fall into, but at the rate you were going you could have made the Tame, now a swim in *that* river was to be avoided.'

There was a smile in the voice but not in the eyes, they were full of 'why?' and behind that something else. Suddenly aware of a prickle along her veins Regan blushed. 'I have to thank you yet again, Mr...'

'Eversley, Grant Eversley.'

'Mr Eversley, it was kind of you to come to my assistance but there is no further need, I will not keep you from your business.'

'You might at least take a cup of tea, a courtesy only, Miss Trent. How did I know your name?' Grant Eversley caught the frown as Regan rose to her feet. 'I heard it called across the street.'

'That were my doing, it were real thoughtless I realises as much now but right then I thought of nothing except was the woman I looked at Regan Trent, and well ... it just came out, I'm real sorry, miss.'

'Don't be.' A smile touched Regan's mouth. 'I am so glad you saw me and even more glad you followed when I was stupid enough to run before ascertaining who it was calling my name.'

'You thought it might be–'

'Yes.' Regan's swift reply cutting off the rest she turned again to the man whose presence she was so alarmingly aware of. 'Ann is ... is a friend, we ... we lost contact a while ago.'

There had been hesitation, a pause which said 'friend' was perhaps not the full description. Logging the thought for future reference Grant Eversley smiled at the woman sitting alongside Regan. 'Then as a friend perhaps Ann,' he waited for the nod which gave permission for his use of the name, then went on, 'will prevail upon you to accept the offer of tea.'

Good manners had insisted she also accept that offer. Dressing for bed Regan remembered strong handsome features, arms holding her so securely. Grant Eversley had asked no reason for her dashing madly between market stalls but the fact of his wondering had registered in cool grey eyes.

Ann Searson had taken note of the curt reply which had prevented her speaking of Sherwyn Huntley and had made no further reference to how it was her former mistress came to be in Wednesbury. But all of that had been revealed later, Ann insisting they walk back to Woden Passage together.

'*Eh, Miss Regan.*' Ann had shaken her head as the explanation ended. '*To think of you being along of gypsies, I don't know whether to laugh or cry.*'

Regan had smiled into the mirror Libby had found for her room. '*Certainly not cry,*' she had assured Ann and it had been truthfully said. Tears would never find a place in her remembering of Joab and Rosa Mullin.

But how come Ann was in this town? The question had been asked just as Libby had come to stand in the doorway of the tiny shop, her expression a dire warning to the woman beside Regan. It had taken a moment to say Ann was a trusted friend and even less of a moment for Libby to retort, '*Then a friend shouldn't be kept a standin' where all ears be a listenin'.*'

They had taken to each other almost immediately, Libby and Ann. Regan's hand moved

286

mechanically, braiding shining hair, fastening the end of both plaits with a snippet of yellow cloth. Yellow ribbon! The past rushed silently into the present.

'Tek this, my racklie, tie it to any tree along a trackway, to any gatepost, its message will be sent ... the Romany be family...'

Rosa and Joab had been like family to her, a family she had come to love as she loved her parents and brother. Like that family the Mullins too were gone, but hopefully not forever. Opening a drawer of the chest Libby had also found for her Regan took out the length of yellow ribbon Rosa had given her. Maybe one day they might meet again.

Ann had been doubtful as to that. Returning the ribbon to the drawer Regan climbed into bed. But she had not been doubtful about Sherwyn Huntley and Myles Wentworth wanting to get Regan back to Woodford.

They had sat, the three of them, in Libby's small living room and it had been Libby had returned the conversation to Ann.

''Ow be it you comes to be in the Black Country?' The direct question had come with an equally. direct stare but Ann had not hesitated in answering it had been on the advice of Mr Sanders.

'Do that be the Sanders Regan tells might 'ave put that key in the cupboard?'

Ann had nodded, saying the butler had told her of that and she had many nights fallen asleep wondering had it been found, and if so had it been Huntley had done the finding?

'I had to inform Mr Sanders of my dismissal from

Woodford House...'

Pulling the bedclothes to her chin Regan listened to the words repeating in her mind.

'I told him I were feared for you, feared of what that stepfather might do, that was when the key were told of, the key your mother asked be put in your wardrobe. He asked then did I have relatives, a place I could go to and when I said there were nowhere and nobody he told me of Wednesbury. Seemed he lived here before going to work along of some big house. He said Wednesbury were a town black with smoke but folk here were for most part kind and good-hearted.'

'Ar, he got that right enough,' Libby had answered, *'but what folk give you a place to settle?'*

Ann had not smiled at that. She ate and slept in a barn, one meal and a bed of straw her wage for a full day's labour.

'You don't need a goin' o' namin' namesl!' Libby had exclaimed. *'I reckons I can do that for you. Be it the Billin's place out along o' Lea Brook?'* Then at Ann's nod she had gone on to say Zebediah Billings and his wife Clara were noted throughout the town for their miserly ways, that it was a wonder the straw dealer had included a meal at all in his repayment of work no matter the hours it took.

Libby had left them then, carrying tea upstairs to Daniel, and on her return had said she had no opposition to Ann sharing Regan's room for the night and come tomorrow she would see about finding her another means of employment.

Turning off the lamp Regan listened to the rhythm of Ann's quiet breathing. Heaven had returned a friend to her.

It was proving a most profitable venture. Leaving the tailor's shop Myles Wentworth touched his silk hat, treating two middle-aged women to his most dazzling smile. Profit was what pleased him most and this was so easily got. Waving away the hopeful driver of a hansom cab he strode easily along Foregate Street. He had chosen to travel by train for a very simple reason. This was where the money demanded by that letter was to be brought, money in exchange for keeping silent about a murder. That was what Huntley believed. Someone would be waiting close to the railway station at Worcester to receive that fifty pounds. Fifty pounds! Myles's inner smile was almost hedonistic. It was only a quarter of what had been paid already, but a little caution was better than a lot of grief. Huntley had paid each time and he would pay next time also, only next time the demand would double.

Huntley had checked the story given to him and yes, Mrs Russell had corroborated it. She had received a letter threatening to report the killing of a young lad unless fifty pounds were brought to the entrance of Worcester train station, then had followed date and time of payment. A rough, uneducated hand, and no, she had no idea who it could be.

Of course she had no idea, but then who would have?

'...it be fifty pun or that fancy gent be gettin' o' a visit from the pulice...'

Really Myles, you would make a very fine actor! Feeling smug, he approached the station.

He had made the case it be himself rather than

Huntley pay over the money, had said it best Huntley not be seen anywhere in the vicinity of Worcester station in case the threat of informing the constabulary had in fact been carried through. Should the police be waiting when Huntley made to pay over the money then it would be tantamount to a confession, whereas Myles Wentworth was simply visiting his tailor.

Huntley had swallowed it. Walking onto the platform Myles almost laughed. Fifty pounds had paid for a very handsome evening suit.

27

Slipping the bolt across the door giving onto the street Libby paused in turning off the lamp which shed no more than a dull gleam over the shelves and counter of the shop as a burst of laughter came from overhead. It had been so many years since her son had laughed that way, so very long. But with the coming of that young woman laughter had returned; if only – but no, she must not even think such a thing. But then it would mean a permanent home for the wench, a house to call her own and the business, though small, would provide her with a living for all of her years.

She knew her son. Libby moved into the living area of the one room. His laugh hid a hurt, one his mother could not soothe. Half a man! Quick tears stinging her eyes she lifted the steaming kettle from the bracket swung over the fire.

Heaven had given her son the pain of being only half a man, and heaven alone could relieve it.

'Let me do that.'

Kettle in one hand, the other wiping tears from her cheeks, Libby straightened. She had not heard the light tread at her back.

'It be done now, wench,' she answered, not yet turning to face Regan. 'But you could fetch milk from the scullery, the jug there be empty.'

Should she say what preyed so often on her mind? Libby took cups from the dresser. Should she talk to the wench ... talk to Daniel? What if the wench said no? With Regan's return, jug in hand, Libby forced the thoughts away. There were time yet, there were time. But as the familiar pain bit beneath her breast Libby knew that time grew even shorter.

'I don't know much more than yourself.' Regan shook her head as she answered Ann's question. 'Mr Sanders left Woodford shortly after you did.'

'Did he send you no word of where he might be?'

'No ... well, he may have written.'

'But by that time, supposing he did write, you yourself were gone.'

'I would have liked to thank him for putting that key in my wardrobe but without an address that is not possible.'

'I shouldn't worry.' Ann's hand touched Regan's sympathetically. 'Mr Sanders knows you better than to judge you ungrateful, and with you yourself disappearing from the house he's in the same boat. He can't write to you if he don't know where you be; I wonder if he returned to that other house?'

Libby had sat listening to the two young women but now she spoke, her voice sharp with warning. 'Things be best the way they be! You says this stepfather and his crony be a lookin' for you an' though I doubts John Sutton would break a confidence there be more ears than his at Sutton Place an' more tongues, any one of which might carry a tale to Woodford if'n they thought the master there likely to pay 'em a sovereign or two.'

'Sutton Place!' Regan glanced enquiringly at Libby. 'Is that where Mr Sanders went on leaving Wednesbury? Do you know the owner?'

'Yes, I knows him though it be only in passin' as you might say. Years back John Sutton come to the colliery along of Lea Brook, come that same day my Zeb were killed. He had wanted to see what it were like workin' in the earth's belly, how coal were ripped from her veins; insisted on goin' down in the cage. He were no more'n a few yards so we was told later, no more'n that from the coal face when it come tumblin' in. Edward Sanders were workin' near along and experience tellin' him the rumble of sound meant the face were giving way he flung hisself at John Sutton pulling him out of the way just as the tunnel ahead caved in. The man were thankful, he offered Edward Sanders a place in his own home; talk after were that he done well there, so well I were surprised when I were told of his leavin', 'eard no more of him after that. Eh, who would 'ave thought a coal miner's son to become a butler! An' to your father, life teks some strange turns.'

'And then for him to go leaving Woodford,' Ann put in, 'but then it could be he were sent packing same way I was, that there Huntley telling him to go.'

Somehow she did not think so. Regan's thoughts swung to the past. Knowing the man who had served her parents, had been so kind to herself and to Saul and who, it had often seemed, had the same deep dislike of Sherwyn Huntley she herself felt, it was far more likely Edward Sanders had resigned from his post at Woodford.

'It don't matter none whether he were sacked or went from that 'ouse of his own accord, but it do matter you should go a askin' after him for word gets word and it would tek only one to reach the ears o' that Huntley to bring him to Woden Passage; so think on that the pair o' you. Remember what Libby Radley be a sayin', a rattling tongue meks a loud noise.'

Had one already rattled? While Regan was seeing Ann off at the door Libby stared into the fire. That salesman had threatened and his job took him to parts other than Wednesbury. Had it taken him to Putley? Had he called at a house the name o' Woodford? Had he talked to the master there?

Was it already too late for the wench she had grown so fond of? Glancing at the girl coming from the other side of the dividing curtain Libby was suddenly sure of one thing.

She must do that which ever more often entered her thoughts.

She must speak with Daniel.

The weekly accounts finished, Regan smiled at the

293

man propped against his pillows. There was colour in his cheeks and a smile on his mouth. Daniel Radley seemed a little happier these past days, a little more interested in life around him. 'I think that calls for a cup of tea.' She closed the black bound ledger. 'Will you join me, Mr Radley?'

Including his head, his smile spreading to his eyes, Daniel answered. 'My pleasure is in sharing your company, Miss Trent.'

Rising to her feet, Regan dropped a curtsy, laughing as she replied, 'I thank you, Mr Radley.'

'Perhaps I should call some other time!'

The coolness of tone had Regan turn quickly, a surge of pink rising in her face as she met a cold hostile stare.

'I am interrupting, that is most bad-mannered. Forgive me Daniel, some other time.'

'Grant.' Daniel's smile reached to the tall figure standing at the open door.

'Mr Eversley.' Regan nodded politely. 'I was about to fetch Daniel some tea, could I bring you some?'

'No thank you.' Curt in his refusal, Grant Eversley switched his glance to the man in the bed. 'I would like to talk with you, Daniel, if you feel up to it.'

He had not asked her to leave Daniel's room but his eyes, his aloof manner, had said the words for him.

Reaching the living room Regan offered the accounts book to Libby. 'Ain't no need for me to go lookin' at it, if Daniel an' y'self say the figures be good then they be good.'

'You really ought to go through them, perhaps

you and Daniel...'

'He knows what a job I 'ave a understandin' of number.' Libby shook her head. 'If he be satisfied then I be satisfied so set that book back in the drawer.'

Colour still high in her cheeks Regan paused before turning back to the woman sitting at the fireside.

'Mr...' She hesitated, the name seeming almost to burn her lips, 'Mr Eversley refused the offer of tea. Should I wait before making Daniel some?'

'Ar, wench.' Libby nodded. 'Best let it wait; them two gets to talkin' and all else be forgot.'

'They have been friends a long time?'

'Since boyhood.' Libby glanced toward the stairs. 'Grant Eversley and Daniel were close as brothers, seemed they even thought alike. Grant, he would sit and play chess or just talk with my lad while the others they kicked a ball or swung a bat. Come to Woden Passage every day did that lad but then his father's passin' meant givin' more of his time to his business and so visitin' of this 'ouse be less often, but 'e comes when 'e can. Be one o' the best be Grant Eversley, a body can trust in 'is word.'

Carrying the kettle into the scullery Regan filled it with water she had earlier brought from the pump in the yard, then turned to blow out the candle standing in a jar.

'Be one o' the best be Grant Eversley, a body can trust in 'is word.'

Libby's words echoing in her mind Regan stared at the slim golden flame.

A body could also trust in his look. She blew on

the candle the rush of darkness hiding the look which came to her eyes.

Grant Eversley's look had spoken his feelings clearly as could any words. It had said he held no liking for Regan Trent.

'You must be mistaken, the man can have no earthly reason to hold a dislike of you.' Ann Searson looked up from cutting squares of newspaper into which Regan was measuring tea. 'If he has taken a dislike to anybody then it'll be me.'

Regan frowned. 'Why would Grant Eversley take a dislike to you?'

'Cos of the way I scared you that day in the town. He fair stabbed me with those eyes of his. Mind...' She grinned. 'They are handsome eyes, in fact he is a very handsome man, don't you agree, miss?'

'I thought we both agreed that you no longer address me as miss. We are no longer mistress and maid, we are friends, Ann, and I wish you to use my name as I use yours.'

'I always felt we were friends.' Ann smiled over the large pair of scissors. 'You treated me fair, not like that snotty-nosed Huntley. If ever anybody deserved to be hated it were him, he made my blood creep; and as for Myles Wentworth! It isn't my place to say this, Mi– Regan, but I am right glad you decided against marrying with him, I doubt he would have brought you happiness. He were a man too taken with himself, if you know what I mean, he seemed to have just one love and that were Myles Wentworth. What kind of husband would he make a woman, he would spend too

296

much time worrying were her clothes more fashionable, more eye-catching than his own.'

Her glance firmly on the tea Regan resisted the giggle rising to her throat. 'Isn't that a little harsh?'

'Harsh my foot!' Ann retorted. 'It's the truth. The man is a dandy, his way isn't natural to a man.' Scissors resting on a folded sheet of newspaper, Ann fell silent then said quietly. 'I don't know how to explain but...' She hesitated, a touch of colour staining her face. 'It wasn't just the way he had of dressing, it was something else.'

Something else! Regan's nerves jarred. Had Ann noticed what she herself had seen?

'It was hearing the stable lads one day I was passing. I heard the name "Wentworth" and what with you being engaged to him,' Ann's glance lifted defiantly, 'well, I listened. They were talking of the way Myles Wentworth looked at them whenever he came to the house, then one of them laughed and said it were the kind of look a man gives to a woman he wants to take to bed. I thought they were simply being bawdy about a man, that it was jealousy of his wealth and would have dismissed what they said as being just that, but then the head groom spoke. Maybe you recall his voice was very gruff, there was no mistaking it. *"You lot stay clear o' Myles Wentworth..."* were the words he said, *"that one would sooner lie wi' a man than wi' a woman."* I watched him more closely after hearing that and though it might be wrong of me to say, his attitude whenever a man was present just ... it just didn't seem to be as it should. What I'm trying to say is it would have been more appropriate for a woman, that is the reason of my

297

saying I was glad you no longer intend to marry him. I hope you understand I couldn't bear to think of you tied for life to a man like that.'

Life would not have been very long!

Sleep a distant stranger, Regan stared at moon-cast shadows drifting like pale silk about the walls of her room. Ann Searson could not have known Sherwyn Huntley's avowed intention had been his stepdaughter become the wife of Myles Wentworth, and equally strong his vow she would die soon after.

He would still have people searching for her, that fact was not open to question. Beyond the window whose curtain she had drawn aside after putting out the lamp, patches of silvered cloud floated across a charcoal sky. The sky had never had this degree of blackness over Woodford; almost every night a myriad stars could be seen from her bedroom window and no smell of coal dust and chimney smoke clogged the throat, but Woodford was no longer the pleasant-smiling place of her childhood. It too held a darkness, a choking presence infinitely more threatening than a smoke-blackened sky. It held Sherwyn Huntley, a man who would not rest until he owned all which had once belonged to Jasper Trent and until Regan Trent was dead!

Would he come tomorrow? The next day? Dread was a constant companion; helping in the house, going on some errand for Libby, talking with Daniel or Ann, the fear of being found was always there, always a second behind every thought, the only certainty being that he would come.

28

'The pay for nails bin dropped agen, I tells ya Libby, them nailmasters along o' Brummajum got no mind o' folk sweatin' all hours at a forge, they be filled wi' only one thought, the mekin' o' profit – an' it be bugger anybody else, it don't matter none to nail-masters whose kids suffer from an empty belly.'

The shawl loaned by Libby pulled low over her brow, Regan descended the low rise of ground leading from the town's one flour mill.

The words had reached past the barrier of heavy chenille closing off the living space from that of the shop, the tears beneath them clear as though they lay on Sarah Jeavons's thin cheeks. Sympathy welled in Regan. The woman had darted in and out of the shop running in Libby's words 'like a shadder afore the sun'. It was an apt description. Sarah Jeavons was worn as a shadow as were most women of Wednesbury toiling as they must every hour to help feed a family.

Reaching the market place Regan skirted the busy square, walking quickly along the Shambles lined with butchers' stalls where the calls of vendors failed to drown the words of Libby still sounding in her mind.

'...ain't no 'elpin' of it, wench, them nailmasters be a rulin' o' the roost, it be a case o' tek what they offers or do wi'out, an' the Jeavonses can't do wi'out, no matter 'ow little be offered, they must tek it or see their

little 'uns took into the workhouse.'

But there was a way of helping. A small way but with people as poor as the Jeavons's the smallest fraction of help must be welcome. She had toyed with the idea for weeks but had said nothing, for fear of being thought of as interfering in that which did not concern her. Yet surely poverty and the suffering it caused was the business of everyone.

The rumble of iron wheels coupled with the indignant blare of a horn startled Regan, making her step sharply from the path of an approaching tram.

'Them don't be things to go a dawdlin' in front of, nor do Holyhead Road be a cart track, you needs keep your mind on where ya feet be a tekin' of ya!'

The sharply spoken warning followed the woman crossing hurriedly as the tram rattled past, but then as the quieter narrower streets were reached, Regan's mind became once more occupied with thought.

She had been on the verge of speaking with Libby, of telling her of the idea as she had told it to Ann. Her friend had listened, had said it was excellent, that she should discuss it with Libby. But was Ann being over-enthusiastic? Would Libby be resentful?

'I guessed it were you.'

Caught by the arm, the swiftness of it loosing the shawl from her fingers, Regan's brain screamed one word: Huntley!

'Yes, I guessed it were you.' The voice grated close to her ear. Sherwyn Huntley's voice?

300

'I saw you crossing the market place, the shawl hid the face but it couldn't hide you completely, couldn't hide the figure I remember so well.'

It had happened! The thing she dreaded above all else, the horror that was never far from her – Sherwyn Huntley had found her! The finality of it drummed in her brain, beat in her throat yet beneath it revulsion lent her strength.

'Let me go!' Regan tried to push free but the lock on her arm remained tight.

Held tight against the man who had caught her she looked into eyes vicious with revenge, while hard and spite-filled as the eyes the voice hissed, 'Now why would I do that when you can bring me what I want?'

'I won't, no matter what you threaten I won't ever sign.'

'Sign?' The laugh rattled like breaking ice. 'No signing of yours is necessary to what I want, that will be given by another.'

Another? Fear-trapped though her mind was, the word eased its way. Another? Who was it could give Huntley what he wanted? Who if not herself could sign that Trent inheritance over to him?

'You thought maybe I would forget, leave you in peace, but that were wrong.'

Venom darkened the face Regan stared at as the man thrust her to arm's length.

'It were very wrong if you expected I would forget the bitch who told Libby Radley the tea I offered for sale was naught but sweepings! Nor did I forget the rest. I've done what I promised to do, I've told them who searches for you where it is you can be found.'

301

Thrown against a smoke-crusted wall Regan stared after the figure striding away along the empty street. It had not been Sherwyn Huntley, but now he knew where she was then he would not be long in coming to Woden Passage.

'There be something plaguing her mind, I can see it in her eyes.' Daniel Radley toyed with the meal his mother had brought to him.

That made two minds being plagued, with her own as well. Libby kept the thought silent.

'You say it was nothing happened at the flour mill?' Daniel pushed the tray away.

'Her said that her paid the money I sent to pay for them sacks o' flour, then after a pleasant exchange o' words made 'er way back 'ere.'

'Then if nothing went amiss at the mill it must be something happened between there and her reaching this house. The question is … what?'

'Well, ain't no use in askin'!' Libby took the tray. 'Like yourself I seen there were summat upsettin' of 'er soon as 'er got back. I asked what it were but got no answer other than 'er were anxious at the time it 'ad took a gettin' to the mill along of Brunswick Hill an' back; course I knowed that d'ain't be reason but I couldn't go forcin' the truth.'

She was right. Daniel watched the black-skirted figure of his mother leave his room. Regan Trent had given the same answer to his own question. She had denied being worried or upset, but the gleam in those lovely eyes had been the glitter of fear, the fear he had seen there once before, the time she had told of being raped. Had she met that

302

man again? Was her stepfather here in Wednesbury?

Leaning back against his pillows Daniel glanced
at the window, at a sky becoming crimson with the
glow of furnace doors being opened. If only he
could walk maybe then he could be of some use,
but that longing would never be realised. But
Grant Eversley could walk!

Scarlet streams engulfing the grey of approaching night spilled a warmth of colour across
the room but for once Daniel did not watch the
glory of its progress.

Grant Eversley could walk! The thought ran
before a host of questions. Ought he to ask help of
Grant Eversley? Was it right to break a confidence?
Hadn't Regan Trent spoken of her circumstances
only in the belief they would not go beyond this
house? Yet if by breaking that confidence Regan
could be helped was it then right to say nothing?

'I asked were you sleeping but your mother
assured me you were awake.'

'Grant!' Daniel turned his glance to the
doorway. 'Now if that isn't coincidence!'

Grant Eversley's handsome face wreathed in a
smile. 'Coincidence ... and there I was imagining
you might welcome an old friend.'

'You are always welcome.' Daniel returned the
smile. 'I say coincidence for the simple reason I
was just thinking about you.'

Settled in the chair kept close to the bed Grant
raised an enquiring eyebrow. 'Thoughts of me,
now what brought those on?'

'Regan,' Daniel answered bluntly. 'Regan Trent.'

Grant concealed his reaction of suddenly

tautening senses and waited.

'You know who I mean,' Daniel pressed on, 'the girl you spoke with in this room a few nights ago.'

He knew. Senses twanged like stretched twine. He knew the young woman his friend spoke of, he knew why she had chosen to remain in this house, what she hoped to gain ... or had she gained it already? Daniel Radley was more than taken with the girl, was he now going to confide that he had spoken with her, offered her more than friendship? Had the conniving Miss Trent's pretty net caught its prey?

'I spoke to her...'

He had not misjudged, it was as he thought! Grant felt his mouth dry.

'...today after she returned from the flour mill, Mother could tell something was amiss. Regan said nothing untoward had happened but when she came to bring me some tea I also could see... There was fear in her eyes, Grant, real fear.'

Real fear? Or a good piece of play-acting? Daniel was a cripple but he wasn't a fool; surely he realised Regan Trent was no more than a grasping opportunist.

'She had been frightened, Grant, I mean really frightened, I was afraid she would leave there and then.'

So she came to you in tears and you couldn't see past them, you couldn't see she was playing you like a fish! Each thought a burning drip of acid in his mind, Grant Eversley's lips compressed, holding back criticism of the man whose friendship he valued.

He had kept his silence. Grant Eversley stared absently from a window overlooking a canal lined with several narrow boats waiting to pull into the wharf.

He had listened to Daniel, listened to him tell of the reasons Regan Trent had given for her being in Wednesbury, of a stepfather who had killed her mother, who had intended to kill her young brother and who had stated positively the same would happen to her following an enforced marriage to a man she hated. Lies? His glance followed the departure of a newly loaded boat. That had yet to be proven to his, if not to Daniel's, satisfaction. Was the young woman his friend so admired truly what she claimed, a woman driven from her home for fear of a marriage she did not want? Or simply one with her eye to the main chance? Yet if she were the latter, a fortune hunter, would she not have set her sights higher than a small general shop in the Black Country? His brain telling him there was a great deal of common sense in the reasoning he pushed it adamantly away.

Regan Trent was clever, clever enough to know that oak trees started life as an acorn; her acorn was Libby Radley's shop, and when her oak tree was flourishing what then of Libby's crippled son? The beautiful Miss Trent would have no more need of him.

'The *Queen* be up from Liverpool, Mr Eversley, will I 'ave 'er pull into the basin afore the others or would you 'ave 'er wait?'

'What?' Disconcerted by the interruption to his thoughts Grant blinked, bringing his concentration to the present. 'The *Queen,* she's carrying sugar isn't she?'

'That an' several barrels o' rum brought in from the West Indies, thought y'might prefer they be passed on afore word gets about; be a temptation do liquor, wouldn't be first cargo to be away wi' the fairies.'

Grant smiled at that but knew the truth of it. Snatching from boats moored for the night, stealing some or all of their cargo was not unknown, and rum was as strong a temptation as it was a drink. Glancing once more at the string of boats he turned to the man awaiting his instruction. 'Where is it bound?'

'Docket be 'ere, sir.'

Taking the paper from his wharf foreman Grant read quickly, his glance running a second time over the name of the buyer. 'Jasper Trent. Importer of Quality Foods.'

Jasper Trent. Importer! Eversley Transport had moved goods for that firm on many occasions.

Daniel's account of that girl had included the information that her father's business had been the importation of goods from several parts of the world. She had certainly known the quality of that tea! But was she Jasper Trent's daughter?

'Shall I push the *Queen* through, sir?'

'Yes.' Grant handed back the paper. 'We wouldn't want a visit from the fairies.'

When the foreman had gone Grant turned again to the window. Regan Trent ... a girl running from home? Or one driven from it by a man who on marrying Trent's widow had become responsible for the entire Trent estate? Whichever was the truth one thing was glaringly obvious: Regan Trent was a young woman bent on taking the home and living of Libby Radley. Watching the narrow boat whose name *Midland Queen* was emblazoned along its tiny cabin ease into the basin, Grant Eversley's mouth thinned to a line. The only way of her doing that was by marrying Libby's son!

'Fairies' were not the only means by which a man could lose his all, neither would Daniel be the first susceptible man to fall for the wiles of a beautiful woman. But when it ended in disaster, as it must, Daniel Radley would lose more than a home, more than money: he would lose what little respect for self he still had; his mind as well as his body would be crippled and Daniel Radley was not a man could live with that.

But Daniel had made no mention of having proposed marriage. If he had asked Regan Trent to become his wife he surely would have said as much.

Grant turned from the window, his brain going rapidly over the conversation.

It was not too late!

Thin lips relaxing into the essence of a smile, he reached for his hat.

Daniel Radley was not so deeply enmeshed he could not be cut free. The artful Miss Trent might yet have to find some other fly to lure into her web!

'How can you be sure!'

The words Sherwyn Huntley had spat at their last meeting ran in Myles Wentworth's mind. The answer was simple, he could be sure because he would be writing no more letters to the Russell woman, no more threats concerning the unfortunate 'accident' which had happened in her establishment. It had been his intention to repeat the demand for money and then repeat it again, but Huntley hadn't accepted his assurance that they'd heard the last of the person who claimed to have witnessed that boy being flung down the stairs.

'If you paid over that fifty pounds then you have seen the face of the one who took it...'

Anger had bristled in every word. Myles turned the page of a newspaper in a show of reading but it was the words in his mind which seemed to flow across the paper.

'...if you saw the face then you can identify...'

Huntley had paused then, his eyes had hardened and the heat of anger had turned to a lethal coldness.

The next had been a slow deliberate thrust. An accusation?

'...if you handed over that money...'

If! If! If! Myles's hands tightened on the newspaper. Huntley was suspicious. He had had time to think over that demand, the way it had been made, the fact it had been conducted via two other people rather than being made directly to himself and he had come up with his own proposal: *'Blackmailers can be found!'*

He had said that, his stare that of a snake.

'They can also be eliminated.'

Huntley was determined no more threat of blackmail would be made against him and Huntley never set aside anything which would benefit Huntley!

The meeting had ended eventually with the vow that *if Myles Wentworth did not find the culprit then Sherwyn Huntley would.*

Christ, what was he to do! Huntley would not let go, and if he found out...

'Bit of a bad business, wouldn't you say, Wentworth? I say, sorry old chap, I never thought to startle you.'

'I ... I was half asleep.' Myles blustered, covering the sudden jerk of his hands with a lie. 'Late night at the tables.'

Across from Myles an elderly man nodded. 'Cards, they've swallowed many a night and many a fortune besides; wouldn't surprise me if it were gambling were the back of this.'

Conversation was the last thing he wanted but walking away without answering would create speculation. Resigned to the fact he must answer, Myles lowered his own paper.

'Mebbe you haven't come across it yet.' The man tapped his paper. 'Be on the second page, but I see you are not reading the same newspaper as myself. Here, take mine.'

Rudeness would have availed him nothing. Walking from club to waiting carriage Myles smiled to himself. But reading that report in the newspaper could very well do just the opposite.

'I thought 'er to be settled, I thought 'er content biding along o' Daniel an' me.'

'She was content.'

'Was! Was!' Libby Radley's face showed confusion. 'That be it, the wench *were* content yet that be the case no longer, there be summat changed 'er mind but what? Daniel nor me 'ave said aught to 'urt.'

It was nothing Daniel or Libby had said. Ann Searson watched the older woman going to answer the call of a customer come into the shop. Regan had not spoken to her of that man grabbing her in the street, of what he had said about informing Huntley of her whereabouts.

'He will come here, Ann, come to Woden Passage.'

Regan had explained when they had stood at the door saying goodnight.

'Huntley will come here to this house. You know his spite, his cruelty, you know he would not hesitate to harm Libby and Daniel; I cannot stand the thought of that, Ann.'

There was no credible argument against that. Ann glanced towards the door opening onto the staircase, at the girl stepping into the living room.

29

He could be here in Wednesbury at this very moment, Sherwyn Huntley could be just around the next bend; maybe he had watched her leave the house and was following, waiting until reaching a spot where there were fewer people to witness his abduction of her. A spot such as this! Reaching the end of Camp Street Regan's nerves tingled at the prospect of crossing the expanse of empty heath that stretched to the Shambles. An empty stretch of land would be Huntley's choice.

Wrapped in the borrowed shawl, Regan forced herself to go on.

Libby had said she would come to the meat stalls herself. She would close the shop for an hour and come herself to the market, that there was no need of Regan running her errands.

But there was need. How could she stay in the house knowing every minute the shop was closed meant a few pennies of lost business, pennies Libby Radley could ill afford to lose; and so she had insisted it was herself would come to buy meat.

'Be sure y'goes only to 'Ollington's stall, 'is meat be the best.'

Hollington's! Libby had stressed her preference, but which butcher's stall was Hollington's?

''Ow be that for a fine bit o' rump, tender as a babby's bottom be that, a few spuds and an onion or two set along of it will 'ave that 'usband of yourn feel like a new man.'

'Ain't a new man I be needin', Bert 'Ollington, be truer to say I could do wi' a bit less o' the old 'un; I 'ave enough kids wi'out the invitin' o' another, so just you set that rump aside an' put me some scrag end.'

Bert Hollington! The banter guided Regan as she walked along the Shambles. That was the name Libby had specified. Joining the several women waiting their turn to be served, the shawl half across her face, she glanced nervously towards the wider market place.

'Scrag end!' The butcher laughed. 'I be surprised at you, Polly, I would 'ave thought you to 'ave treated your 'usband to a bit o' the best, after all y' can't do too much for a good man.'

'No, but 'e can go doin' too much to a good woman a' I ain't a tekin' o' no risks.' The woman's tart reply bringing a roar of laughter from the ruddy-complexioned man he turned to his next customer.

How long had it been since she told that salesman the tea he was offering Libby was no more than sweepings? Huddled in the shawl, Regan's thoughts turned inward.

'...*it were very wrong if you expected I would forget...*'

The words had been like blows, the face dark with anger.

'*I've done what I promised to do ... told them who searches for you where you can be found...*'

Had he informed Huntley that same week? Had he taken longer than a week? Was Huntley deliberately postponing coming to Wednesbury? That would be so like him. Exulting in the knowledge that she must be living every day in fear of being discovered would have kept him from coming immediately; but was that period of waiting ended? Had his appetite for torment from a distance outlived its enjoyment?

'...would never 'ave thought that, don't be like Libby Radley to judge a character wrong.'

'Well, 'er judged wrong wi' that 'un! Next time Libby Radley comes askin' aught of me, 'er be like to get answers which won't please.'

The name penetrated the tumult of Regan's mind. This woman was speaking of Libby!

'But you said the wench were polite an' clean in 'er ways.'

'An' that were so.' The woman fumbled in a black cloth purse. "Er were so 'elpful an' tidy an' with 'er keepin' no late hour a comin' in at night I thought meself to 'ave a good lodger.'

Purchases wrapped, the butcher took money the woman held out to him, asking as he counted change:

'So what 'appened to change your opinion?'

'Her be gone be what 'appened!' The woman watched each coin being dropped into her hand. 'Ain't been sight nor sign o' Ann Searson not for five nights, gone wi'out a word 'er 'as; I tells you, Bert 'Ollington, if that wench be the kind Libby Radley thinks to be a good lodger then the next one as comes along 'er can tek in 'erself same as 'er did the wench who be livin' along o' 'er now.'

Ann had not been seen at her lodging for five nights! With her own purchases in the basket held over one arm, the shawl clutched across her nose, Regan walked away from the stall. There had to be a mistake, she had misheard what had been said, the woman must have been speaking of a different Ann.

'Ain't been sight nor sign o' Ann Searson.'

The words echoed clear in Regan's head. There was no denying the name she had heard, but it did not have to be her friend, there could be another woman of the name Ann Searson living in Wednesbury. But it had been coupled with that of Libby Radley – and the woman had also mentioned Ann Searson being her lodger.

'The shop has a rush of orders, seems every woman in the town is wanting a new bonnet. I couldn't but offer to work late so I won't be visiting you or the

Radleys for a time.'

Ann had smiled when saying that. There had been nothing in her manner, nothing in the way she spoke to indicate she had thoughts of leaving Wednesbury. Regan's nerves fluttered like leaves in a wind. Ann would never go without saying goodbye to Libby and to Daniel, nor would she keep such an intention from her friend; that left only one conclusion, Huntley! He had seen Ann, he had snatched her from the town ... for what reason? Ann Searson could do him no harm, but then Sherwyn Huntley needed no reason ... and she, Regan, could no longer find reason to believe that man was not already present in the town.

Immersed in the misery of her own thoughts Regan did not notice the figure step from among the shoppers, was unaware of it turning to follow along the row of meat stalls shadowing her path toward the open heath, had no conscious sense of the footsteps close behind until...

'Regan Trent.'

Stabbing into her brain, slicing away every thought, chilling the blood in her veins, the voice of a man!

'I don't know if you are who you claim to be nor do I care. Neither do I know why you chose this particular town as a stopping-off point, for that is all Wednesbury is to you, isn't it, Miss Trent? And once you have what you need you will be off and no matter the people you hurt in the process. Well let me tell you this, Libby and Daniel Radley will not be among that company.'

She had tried to speak, to ask what it was she was guilty of, what she had done or said could

314

arouse such anger, but every attempt at protest had been snapped aside.

'You have Libby fooled, you have Daniel moon-eyed, but I see more plainly, and now I offer you this advice. Do not think to use Daniel in order to take his mother's business. Attempt it, Miss Trent, and you will regret you ever saw Wednesbury!'

The words had been said so quietly but the anger in those grey eyes had shouted. Trembling from the experience Regan stood in the small living room. She had thought the voice saying her name had been that of Sherwyn Huntley, that it was her guardian whose hands had fastened on her, twisting her to face him. His anger she could have understood, but that which had been directed at her a few minutes ago, the undisguised threat in Grant Eversley's words to her, defied comprehension.

Why had he chosen to speak to her in the street? Why not here in Libby's house?

Hands shaking, Regan removed the shawl and hung it up.

Why would Grant Eversley think she intended to take away Libby's livelihood? That she would cause Daniel any hurt? Yet the idea had been blatant in his threat.

'There y'be wench.' Libby smiled as she came from the stairs. 'I were beginnin' to think you'd lost the way.'

'I ... there were several women waiting to be served.'

'An' Bert 'Ollington canting with every one of 'em I don't doubt. Be a wonder how that man sells anythin' the way he goes on; can talk the hind

315

leg off a stone donkey could Bert 'Ollington.'

Please let someone come into the shop, let a customer call Libby away long enough for the trembling to stop! The silent plea went unanswered; Regan had to reply or arouse Libby's suspicions that all had not gone as it should on that trip to the market.

'There...' she faltered, 'there seemed to be rather a lot of news being passed.'

'News!' Libby chuckled. 'Gossip more like. I tells you, wench, it be only the peak on his cap keeps Bert 'Ollington's tongue from bein' sunburned. But I don't be much better a standin' talking instead o' gettin' that there meat into the stewjar.'

Strength of mind which had carried Regan back to the house drained as Libby went into the scullery and with a sob she sank to a chair.

Grant Eversley had not tried to hide his dislike whenever their paths had crossed. Regan stared blankly across the room. He had given her tea the day Ann's call had startled her but that was an act of charity, a kindness of heart; it was something he would have done for any woman in those same circumstances, it had not been done out of any other regard. There was no reason the man *should* like her! Regan's brain argued against a misery which seemed to have seeped into her very bones. They had exchanged barely a dozen words during any of their meetings yet somehow he had formed the opinion she was no better than a thief.

There was no reason why Grant Eversley should like her!

The words rang again in her mind and this time

316

they were met with a question in her heart.

Why did that hurt so much?

'You've been maudlin' all day, be it your month-lies causin' you pain?'

Setting down the stewjar she had lifted from the oven Libby looked across the table at the girl selecting cutlery from a drawer of the dresser.

Spoons and forks held in her hands, Regan stared at the drawer. She had seen Libby's frown several times since her return from buying meat from the Shambles, a frown which had quest-ioned the lack of a smile, but until now it had not found expression in words.

'There be Siedlitz powders on the back shelf o' the shop, go get y'self one while I brews a pot o' tea; a drink an' a powder afore you goes to bed an' the pain'll be gone come mornin'.'

Tears suddenly smarting Regan closed the drawer. Libby was kindness itself. How could anyone think of cheating her? Yet Grant Eversley thought she was.

'I knows well them pains, they makes a body miserable.'

'I ... I am not in pain.'

Libby turned from lifting the teapot from the bracket swung against the fire. 'Oh!' she said. 'So it don't be no monthly a troublin' of you. Then what do it be?'

Answering truthfully could only increase the misery which had been with her since that meet-ing. The Radleys had long been friends of Grant Eversley where she had known them for just a few months, yet even that short time had been enough

317

for her to learn that Libby's outspoken way would not allow Grant Eversley's words to go unchallenged and that might well lead to friction between them. As she set forks and spoons on the table Regan's lips tightened. She would not come between friends.

'Look, wench.' Libby set the teapot down with a thud. 'I knows there be somethin' botherin' you, I seen it the minute you got back from runnin' that errand this mornin'. It don't do no good to go denyin' what be plain wrote across your face so you best speak it now.'

Across the table Regan's look pronounced the end of all denial. 'It...' Regan hesitated, fears of endangering the friendship which existed between Libby and Grant Eversley grabbing at her tongue.

'It?' Deep drawn as plough lines Libby's frown settled across her brow.

There was no way but to tell. Regan drew a deep breath. Perhaps if she spoke with a laugh, passed the whole conversation off as no more than an amusing joke. But Grant Eversley had not been amused and he had certainly not intended she take his words as a joke.

'It was something Mr Eversley said.' Pretending to straighten already neatly positioned cutlery, Regan avoided looking into eyes she knew watched her. 'I met him this morning, he ... he was of the opinion I would soon be leaving Wednesbury and wanted to wish me well.'

It was a lie. Regan turned and took cups from the dresser. That was not what Grant Eversley had said. He had virtually warned her she must leave this town.

'*...do not think to use Daniel in order to take his mother's business...*'

The words seemed to throb in the quiet room.

'He thought you to be a leavin'? Now why would he go a thinkin' that?'

Forcing what she hoped was a flippant laugh, Regan replied. 'Who can say what Mr Eversley thinks.'

'I can,' Libby answered firmly. 'Or I thought I could. Grant Eversley be like a son to me, I always thought I knowed his mind, but this ... well it fair has me flummoxed. There's a reason somewhere an' I'll be askin' of it when next we meets.'

Wheeling about, Regan's exclaimed, 'No!' was out before she could prevent it.

'I knowed there be more to your maudlin' than you've spoken on.' Libby's frown grew even deeper. 'So wench, if'n you don't want me a questionin' of Grant Eversley you'll tell me the rest of what passed between the two of you.'

'Left you says, up an' left the town wi'out a word, an' Grant were of the opinion you would be a doin' of the same; well if that don't mek the babby piddle its trousers! But how come Grant knowed when we d'ain't?'

Collecting dishes and placing them on the wooden tray kept Regan's glance from meeting that of the woman she had deliberately lied to. Grant Eversley had made no mention of Ann. What if he said as much to Libby should she question him? It had been thoughtless telling such a lie, but that thought had been the only one

319

to present itself, and now she must keep up the pretence.

'He said he had heard it being spoken of while he was in the town.' Cutlery set beside the dishes Regan picked up the tray, carrying it quickly into the scullery.

'I be goin' out.' Libby tied the corners of her shawl beneath her breasts as Regan turned from washing plates. 'If anybody comes needin' aught from the shop they'll point you to where it be kept an' tell you the price of it; I've spoken wi' Daniel, he won't be wantin' nothing afore I gets back.'

She should have told Libby the truth, confessed the lies spoken about Grant Eversley. But there had been no time, Libby had swept from the house almost before her last word was said. It had all been so underhand. Sitting beside the fire, Regan stared at the glowing coals. Now Libby had gone to confront the man. She had not said as much, but where else would she be going? And Grant Eversley – what would he say? Would he tell Libby it was all lies or–

The sound of the shop door being opened chased away the thoughts. Rising to answer the summons of a customer, Regan's breath caught in her throat as the heavy chenille curtain was drawn aside.

Black bonnet perched high on the updrawn knot of greying hair, arms clasped beneath her shawl Libby waited while the steam tram lumbered past, then, side-buttoned boots clattering on close-packed setts, crossed Victoria Street.

So Ann Searson had just up and gone without

so much as a word! Grant Eversley had heard it gossiped over, but had he heard the reason? Libby Radley would have the hearing of it ... and it would be the truth.

Turning into Haworth Street she glanced at the houses. Joined together in a long dark ribbon, chimneys like skeletal fingers poking a smoke-laden sky, they stretched away on both sides.

Midway along the length of the street, curtains of every house having twitched as she passed, Libby stepped into one of several entries, each of which she knew served as access to each of a dozen houses, six being to each side. But she would not knock on a dozen doors, she needed to knock on just one!

'It be Mrs Radley.'

'Ar, it be Libby Radley.' Libby stared fixedly at the woman come to stand beside the lad who had answered the door.

'What be you wantin'?' Defensively hard, the words hit out at Libby.

'What I don't be wantin' is for this lad to hear what I be about, so you best send 'im some-wheres.'

'Don't you be a tellin' me what I needs or needn't be a doin' wi' my own!' snapped the woman, who made to step back into the scullery.

Libby stuck out her boot to prevent the door being slammed shut as she snapped in return, 'Not yet, Gertie, you don't go closin' no door on Libby Radley afore her be ready to go, an' I ain't ready, not 'til I've 'ad words wi' that 'usband of yourn.'

''E ain't in.'

''E ain't in!' A hand shot from beneath the shawl and Libby pushed hard at the door, sending it wide on its hinges. 'Then I'll wait along of his comin'.'

'Close the door, woman, don't want the rest o' the street a listenin' to y'business!'

'I've come to ask what it be sent Ann Searson runnin' from this 'ouse?' Standing in a living room even tinier than her own, Libby returned the stare of a man dressed in striped twill shirt open to the chest and trousers held about a paunchy waist with a heavy buckled belt, his greasy mutton-chop whiskers almost meeting beneath his chin.

''Er give no reason an' I'll be givin' you none!'

'Then I'll give it to you,' Libby answered the woman, though her stare remained on the man's face. 'This don't be the first time, does it, Naylor Fox? Not the first young wench you've tried puttin' y'filthy 'ands on; there's been talk of your doings along of women in the town, talk I should 'ave given mind to when Ann Searson said her had teken lodging 'ere cos of Sally Picken 'aving let the room I told the wench of; but out of Christian charity I put talk of you down to spiteful gossip. Now I don't 'ave no morsel of Christian charity left in me but I 'ave a tongue. I intend findin' Ann Searson and if her speaks of that which I sees from your face be truth, that it were your filthy mauling of her had her run from this 'ouse, then there'll be nowheres you can hide.

'Fox you be by name and Fox you might be by nature, an' quick as them creatures. But you won't be quick enough to escape the men I tell of your filth, they will hunt you down and when they catches up with you there won't be that left swingin' atwixt your legs to trouble any wench with!'

30

She was to gather her belongings, the bits and pieces of clothing Libby had bought for her from pawnshop or market stall must be collected by morning, that was when she was to vacate the room built onto the side of the house. What had brought about this change in Daniel?

Shaking yet from the abruptness of it all Regan felt tears spill warmly onto her cheeks.

Was it something Grant Eversley had said to him, had he met Libby, heard from her the lies which had been told then repeated them to Daniel?

He had swept from the house in the same manner with which he had arrived. Regan stared at the chenille curtain still quivering from being snatched aside. He had glanced at her, his grey eyes cold and hard as granite, then without a word had gone up to Daniel's room.

She had heard their voices, Daniel quiet and passive as always, that of Grant Eversley firm and authoritative. Had the two friends been having something of a disagreement? Wishing not to eavesdrop she had gone into the yard, spinning out time by slowly filling a bucket with coal, then spinning out yet more by washing her hands several times at the pump. She had been standing before the fire warming fingers deadened by the sharp bite of near-freezing water when Grant Eversley had come from Daniel's room. He had looked at her, his stare openly hostile, then in a voice of gravel had told her of Daniel's decision.

Daniel's decision – or Grant Eversley's decision? They had been friends for near enough all of their lives. His friendship was cherished by Libby and by her son and in consequence must have influence with both. That influence must have persuaded Daniel she should be sent from this house. Grant Eversley had given her no opportunity to explain that she had no desire to take anything away from Daniel and his mother, given her no chance to apologise for having lied about him. But then Grant Eversley would want no apology; he simply wanted her gone.

In his carriage driving to Burnford House for Orphan Boys, Myles Wentworth's smile was one of pure satisfaction. Fate had played him kindly. It had been a bit of a sticky moment those few weeks back but Lady Luck had smiled at him; Lord, she had taken him in her arms and kissed him! Huntley had been unwilling to believe they had heard the last from the person claiming to have watched them pitch that boy headlong down the stairs of the Russell establishment; in fact the man had been downright suspicious.

Sherwyn Huntley was a man without mercy; nothing mattered other than his own well-being and peace of mind and he had certainly lacked peace of mind the day they had discussed the paying off of that second blackmailer.

How to convince Huntley the money had indeed gone to a third person? That had caused himself a few hours of worry. Huntley was too shrewd a bird to fly off with only one worm; he would know a blackmailer would come and come again, the demand for money repeated time upon time, and like a bird he would peck and peck until the final worm was unearthed: Huntley would not give in until he had the blackmailer in his hands. Then they would fasten tight about the throat.

But that danger had passed. Myles flicked a gloved finger across the black velvet lapel of his immaculate dove-grey overcoat. It had melted away the moment he had read the newspaper loaned to him at his club.

The relief had been overwhelming, but not so overwhelming he had bought his saviour a glass of something by way of a thank-you. That would perhaps have shown the relief which had swept through him upon reading that article of news, relief Myles Wentworth could not afford to display.

A photograph of a swarthy-looking middle-aged man had accompanied some half column of print stating he had been discovered in a wood, that he had been dead for some days and was probably the victim of robbery seeing his pockets were totally empty. It had all been of little interest until the part of the report which asked could anyone identify the dead man?

The request had pealed like thanksgiving bells in his mind, had sung a hymn of gratitude.

He could identify the man, though he had never seen him.

He could identify ... but not to the police.

Flicking the rein Myles indulged the returning warmth of achievement, of his own undoubted expertise.

He had purchased a copy of that newspaper, had taken it to Woodford House and there placed it on the desk of Sherwyn Huntley.

This was the man to whom he had paid that blackmail demand. He had slammed a hand to the newspaper. *This* was the man! It had been said with conviction; why have it said otherwise? Myles glanced at the passing countryside, trees and fields coated in the purity of winter frosts. Hadn't Huntley himself said if the money had been handed over then the face of the one accepting it had been seen. Of course, so it had. Myles smiled, remembering his reply.

'I could not forget the face that looked at me, the man who snatched the money from my hand, it is that face, the one you are looking at now!'

There had been no more 'ifs', no more innuendo, no question of the money being paid. Huntley could no longer question the word of Myles Wentworth; after all Huntley had not been the one to meet his blackmailer, he had not seen the face of the man who threatened him.

Except he had!

Myles's glance fell on the dreary building rising dark and forbidding among the pristine whiteness.

Sherwyn Huntley had met his blackmailer many times. The supposed culprit had, of necessity, been 'disposed' of. The dead man of the photograph had served that purpose; but the other, the one who had actually placed a letter on the step of the kitchen of Woodford House, had not been disposed of, and he was certainly not dead.

Alighting from the carriage, passing it in the care of a ragged hunchback youth, Myles entered the stark, unwelcoming Burnford House for Orphan Boys.

'I wants a word, wench.'

Regan turned to face the woman who spoke, unhappiness flooding through her as she met the look in Libby's eyes. Sorrow, regret? No that was not what played there, nor was it anger. She had dreaded Libby's return to the house, of having to own to the lies she had told, but she had owned them. Libby had listened in silence then, still not speaking, had gone upstairs to her son's room. Now she stood here in the room given over to the girl she had taken in off the streets and her eyes gleamed determination.

'Leave what you be doin' and come you back to the livin' room, there be somethin' I wants to say an' it best be said sooner than later!'

Libby had gone upstairs to her son; he must have asked that his mother ensure Regan vacate this room; was that the reason of the determination in those faded brown eyes or was it something else had been said to her, by Grant Eversley?

'I...' Regan hesitated, fighting between tears at the thought of having hurt two people she had grown to love, and anger at the man who judged her a thief, and a parasite, 'I should just finish here, Daniel asked...'

'I knows what Daniel asked,' Libby answered tersely. 'But you don't 'ave to go breakin' your neck a doin' of it, right now it be my word wants the hearin' of.'

She had not waited for any other answer, but had turned on her heel, black skirts rustling as she had led the way to the living room.

'Mrs Radley, I–'

'Mrs Radley?' At the fireside Libby turned. 'Mrs Radley? Be we strangers again?'

'No.' Regan shook her head. 'I thought... Oh, I don't know what I think!'

'Then let me tell you what I think, what it is I've been a thinkin' of for many a week from your comin' to this house.' Motioning for Regan to be seated before seating herself in a facing chair Libby stared into the fire then softly, as if speaking to herself, went on. 'Daniel were born wi' crippled legs but now he be crippled in the soul, there be a great sorrow in him, a sorrow a mother cannot heal. I watched it grow, watched it swallow him up until he took to his bed completely. I watches him in the day and I feels his heart break, I listens in the night and I hears his soul cry. He be a man in torment and his mother knows her own torment, for her knows life for her can't be many years more.'

'Libby!'

'No, wench.' Libby turned from gazing at the fire. 'I be gettin' old and generous as the Lord be there has to be an end to every life.'

'But not yours ... not for a long time.'

'Time will be what the good Lord sets it to be.' Libby's hand stroked the head of the girl who had flung herself to her knees beside the chair. 'Whether it be long or short for Libby Radley don't give her no cause for sorrow, it be her son be the only worry. I don't want Daniel taken into no poorhouse nor no institution for the insane where it be like he would be put. His mind be sound as any but that would 'ave no bearin' should he be left wi' nobody to care what become of 'im. That be the fear has played in Libby Radley's mind, fear of her son being thrown from his home, and that be the core of what I would speak with you about. I will sign over to you this house and business in return for your marrying with Daniel.'

'Marry Daniel!' Surprise had Regan sit back on her heels.

'It would be marriage in naught but name.' Libby's eyes glinted tears. 'My Daniel would ask no more than the care and friendship you shows him now; as for yourself though Woden Passage don't be the sort of place saw your upbringin', it don't 'old the danger of Woodford.'

The danger of Woodford! Regan's fingers tightened on the hand she had clasped between her own. Maybe that danger was no longer just in Woodord; perhaps it was here in Wednesbury. That salesman had said he had informed Sherwyn Huntley of her whereabouts so it could not be long before her stepfather arrived to take her back.

'You need give no answer this minute.' Libby's smile was sad behind the soft gleam of tears. 'I knows you still be of no age to speak for yourself, but while you thinks on what be put to you I would 'ave you think on this: which would be the better life, living in this house as the wife of Daniel Radley or bein' dragged back to a life subjected to the rule of a man who thinks naught

329

of rapin' young boys nor of doin' the same to his own stepchild?'

'But I heard it in the meat market, I heard a woman say you had left Wednesbury.' Delight and puzzlement mixed together shone in the look Regan beamed at the figure come to stand in Libby's small living room.

'Not Wednesbury.' Ann Searson returned the smile. 'Just from that house.'

'I ought never to 'ave let you bide a night there.' Libby's taut mouth displayed self-condemnation. 'I should 'ave fetched you away that first night.'

'You were not to know.'

'Mebbe not *know*,' Libby returned with a shake of the head, 'but after what others said I shouldn't never 'ave agreed to you a lodgin' along of Naylor Fox.'

'It doesn't always do to listen to gossip.' Ann smiled, releasing herself from Regan's hug. 'It rarely turns out to be truth.'

'Often not.' Libby nodded. 'But this be all truth, Naylor Fox won't be settin' a hand on no woman other than the one he be married to for he knows the upshot, he ain't simply been told the consequences he's had the promise of it, and Libby Radley don't be one to go breakin' of her promise.'

'But if you have not slept at your lodging where have you spent the nights?' Regan spoke her concern. 'And why not come share your problem with me?'

'I felt you had troubles enough, Regan, without putting mine to them, besides,' Ann turned her glance to the older-woman, 'I couldn't tell you,

330

Libby, not after you had been kind enough to get me employment so...'

'So!' Libby intervened, 'you slept on the floor of the back-room of that shop, you let y'self in through a window after the place closed for the night an' there you stayed 'til just afore the shop opened the next mornin'; but you can tell Regan all about it while her helps you finish a tekin' of your things from the side room.'

'Daniel has said you are to move?' Ann's question echoed her disbelief as she followed Regan to the small annexe. 'But why? I don't understand, I thought the two of you were such good friends.'

'Not so good a friend as Grant Eversley!'

'Eversley ... what's he got to do with it?'

Why had she blurted that out! Annoyed with herself, Regan snatched clothing from a drawer. She had not intended to speak of him; in fact the less said of Grant Eversley the better!

'Come on, I want to know! What is Grant Eversley to do with your being turned out of this house? Just what is it he said to Daniel?'

Maybe it'd be best to confide all to Ann, it might help her get things straight in her own mind.

Taking the clothing from Regan's hands, setting it aside before drawing her to sit beside her on the narrow bed, Ann said quietly, 'Don't matter the leaving of Woden Passage for we will be leaving together, but that won't be 'til I hears all.'

'I don't know what he said to Daniel.' Her voice quiet as that of her friend, Regan explained what had passed between herself and Grant Eversley that morning, of his sweeping into the house minutes after Libby had left on what turned out to

331

be the business of finding whether or not Ann had truly up and left Wednesbury without saying goodbye, his going straight to Daniel's room without a word to herself and leaving in the same manner.

'He said that!' Chestnut eyes glittered flames of anger. 'He called you a thief!'

'Not in so many words.'

'They might not have come from his mouth but they were in his mind, Lord I'll give the man what for–'

'No!' Regan caught the hand striking the bed. 'No Ann, you will say nothing.'

'But the Radleys!' Ann protested, 'Eversley must have told them his stupid suspicions, that has to be the reason of their wanting you gone, but you have to tell them...'

'No.' Regan interrupted again. 'I will not speak against Mr Eversley, not to Daniel or his mother. I could not live with the knowledge I was the cause of ending their friendship, and you, Ann, you must promise not to tell them.'

'Mebbe they know already, p'raps Eversley doesn't have the same principles as yourself, could be he didn't mind spreading lies.'

'Could that be why...' Half-finished, the question hung in the air.

'Could *what* be why? What's the rest of it?' Hackles already raised by the accusations levelled at her friend, Ann's anger bubbled. 'You might as well tell me cos unless you do I go to the Radleys right now.'

'No.' Regan swung round. 'You promised!'

'I made no such promise, and even if I had it wouldn't bother me none to break it. You best understand, Ann Searson don't be a woman to stand idle while a good friend is slandered, especially not when the one pointing the finger knows bugg– nothing at all about her.'

'It ... it's really nothing to fuss about, a few days and it will be forgotten.'

'Not by me!' Her face mutinous, Ann snatched the bundle of linen, throwing it down beside the neater pile on the bed, then rounded on Regan grabbing her by the wrist. 'We are going to sort this out now, and if the Radleys don't give no answer then it's Mr Grant Eversley will be getting a visit!'

'Wait ... please.' Regan drew back. 'I will tell you but this time I must have your spoken promise, cross your heart Ann, swear you will never divulge any of what you have heard or may yet hear spoken of in this room, that it will remain a secret between the two of us.'

'But surely if it involves Libby or Daniel...'

'Swear it, Ann!'

Masked by the demanding rise in Regan's voice a sound beyond the door went unobserved.

'It was when you said Mr Eversley could already have told Libby and Daniel his suspicion of my being a fortune hunter...'

'Fortune! I hardly calls a half-room shop in a poky back street a fortune.'

'It is Libby's fortune.' Regan's rebuke was gentle. 'It is all she and Daniel have and though I am not happy at being accused of intending to steal it from them, I applaud Mr Eversley for protecting the interest of his friends.'

'So you *do* think he said as much to the Radleys!'

'I have said I do not know but...'

'But?'

Gathering the scattered items of underclothing, folding each with slow deliberate movements, Regan breathed deeply before saying, 'Before you came into the house Libby asked... Libby asked would I marry Daniel in return for her giving her business to me!'

'Marry! Marry Daniel!'

Beyond the door an intake of breath was drowned by Ann's loud exclamation.

'She said she was aware I am not yet of age but asked me to think which would be better for me once I could choose for myself, was it a life here with Daniel or a life with Sherwyn Huntley.'

'Choose for yourself!' Ann flung back. 'You know there'll never be free choice, not while Huntley be around, and coming of age won't alter things; one way or another he will take all that is rightfully yours, house, business, money, everything to the very last farthing, and if the only way of doing it is by killing you then he won't stop at that, but if you are married to Daniel, if you are already the wife of another man, then Huntley can have no hold over you, so you have to say yes.'

On the other side of the door a figure stood silent.

'Taken back to Woodford, being subjected to the horror Sherwyn Huntley practised on me, also being forced into marriage with Myles Wentworth: hateful though that choice is it is the one I make. I love Daniel, but it is the kind of love I had for my brother; I would not take that to Daniel in marriage, I could not hurt him in that or any other

334

way, but this I do vow: so long as I live Daniel Radley will never be deprived of his home.'

Soundless as leaves falling on mossy grass the figure in the narrow passage connecting the annexe to the house moved away.

31

Wentworth had flair not only in his choice of dress but also in the choice of entertainment. Sitting in a first-class compartment of the train Sherwyn Huntley smiled to himself. The latest purchase from Burnford Home for Orphan Boys had proved satisfactory in every way. Blue-eyed, handsome features, a mop of sand-brown curls, he had expressed his gratitude at being rescued from that morbid institution. Rescued! Sherwyn shifted his gaze to the passing countryside. He could not have thought of a less apt description had he pondered all day. True, the boy was free of that orphanage but the life he was now destined to lead held no real freedom. Maybe he would not find it too terrible while his looks lasted, for a handsome lad draws wealthy clients; but once the looks were gone, when his body was being sold to any man with tuppence enough to pay... But that was not Sherwyn Huntley's problem. Opening the door of the carriage as the train steamed into the station, Sherwyn touched his hat, politely offering his hand to a portly, much befeathered matron, alighting behind him.

He had thought maybe he would patronise the establishment of Mrs Russell given what had occurred following his last visit there but on seeing the boy Wentworth had procured the idea had vanished. The Russell woman would hold her tongue; after all any whiff of scandal would harm her more than it would harm the owner of Woodford House. She would lose not only her reputation but her living while earning herself a prison sentence; whereas a man ... a few months and the sowing of wild oats was forgotten. She had raised no more argument. The very private room on the top floor of the house had been made available along with the usual disposal of the 'toy' once the game was finished.

Leaving the station, climbing into a waiting hansom, Sherwyn settled to the drive to Woodford, satisfaction glowing inside him. All in all the process worked very well. Wentworth brought in the 'goods', no doubt having paid less for them than he stated. But that was of no real consequence, a small overcharge being compensated by a little extra on the resale price, a price maybe not always happily paid, but paid nevertheless. It was a profitable business, and one which would be safeguarded should the so-fashionable Mr Wentworth try adding too much to his own share; Wentworth was useful but he was not irreplaceable.

This also must be safeguarded. Descending from the hansom Sherwyn ran a glance over the graceful stone house. At all costs this would remain his. But finding Regan Trent and eliminating her was the only sure way.

Why had she not yet been found! Irritation

replacing the glow of pleasure he thrust hat and cane into the hands of his butler, then removing his overcoat, leaving it to drop onto the floor, stalked upstairs to his room.

Those men had been searching for months. He untied his silk cravat, throwing it onto the bed. Folk didn't just disappear from the face of the earth. Not unless they were dead. Fingers pausing on the buttons of his shirt, Sherwyn indulged the thought. That had to be why she had not been found, Regan Trent was dead. But he had heard nothing of a young woman's body being dis-covered, seen no photograph in the newspaper. Surely there would have been some report? But then maybe not! Smug in the thought Sherwyn released the rest of the buttons. Dead bodies were not always found, especially if thrown into some pit or disused quarry. That was what had hap-pened. Throwing off shirt and trousers he walked into his bathroom, dismissing a manservant add-ing cologne to the bathwater.

She was dead. Settling into the perfumed water, he breathed deeply. And Sherwyn Huntley was alive, alive to live the comfortable life of country squire and wealthy businessman, alive to enjoy more of the pleasures his evening had afforded.

It had been delightful. Closing his eyes, resting his head against the rim of the bathtub, Sherwyn watched the pictures floating in his mind.

Wentworth, naked, his manhood proud as a stallion, had led the pretty boy, naked also except for the strip of silk halter about the neck, into the private room. They would play a game. The youngster had giggled, the effects of brandy dousing any refusal. They would play a game and he could win a sovereign or even more. The promise of money had brought a wide smile to that pretty mouth, a mouth which moments later had been put to very different use.

Beneath the warm water Sherwyn's flesh jerked. Wentworth had brought the boy close.

Sherwyn's manhood throbbed again. Wentworth had pressed the boy to his knees then had passed the silken neck cord about Sherwyn's own waist.

Memory vivid, demanding, Sherwyn sucked air deep into his lungs.

Wentworth had laughed softly as he pulled on the silk drawing his 'captives' closer, closer until mouth touched erect flesh.

Those lips had felt so sweet.

Lust driving as it had driven then flared hot in Sherwyn's veins.

The mouth had parted, the wet tip of a tongue touching, almost licking the swollen head of the penis jerking against it; then as the boy had joined in Wentworth's laugh the pulsing flesh had slipped inside that warm wet mouth.

Memories and nature taking their demanded reward, Sherwyn stepped contentedly from the bath.

Yes, Sherwyn Huntley led a most enjoyable life, a life he would continue to lead.

'You thought what?' Libby's glance scanned the faces of the two young women standing in the living room. 'You thought Daniel an' me to be tellin' you to go, to leave this house altogether? Eh wench, had that been in my mind would I 'ave gone lookin' for Ann? Would I 'ave gone tellin' her to come to Woden Passage once her work along of that millinery shop be over for the day?'

'But the room,' Regan looked confused, 'Daniel asked my things be taken from the annexe.'

'I ain't a denyin' of that,' Libby replied, 'nor will Daniel when we speaks with 'im. Yes, he asks to 'ave that side room for his own usin' but that don't go to say you two must find lodgin' elsewheres.'

'Two?' It was Ann's question.

Lifting a large dish from the oven and placing it on a folded cloth she had set at a corner of the table to protect the scrubbed wood surface, it was a moment before Libby replied.

'That be what I said. Daniel an' me be of a mind, the pair of you will live along of this house, that is if you be willin' to share that bedroom Daniel be a leavin', so...'

The rest of what Libby intended to say was lost in Ann's happy cry as she hugged the older woman; Regan's thoughts remained with the prospect of Daniel suddenly wanting to change his room. What was the motive? What was the thinking behind it? Then as she watched the two women embrace the answer came. The annexe was to serve as a private space for Daniel and his wife – for Daniel and herself! Libby must be certain in her mind the reply when given would be yes: Regan Trent would marry her son. They both had to be told, it was unfair to let them continue to think she would become wife to Daniel.

'Libby.' She looked at the woman disentangling herself from Ann's hug. 'Libby, what you asked earlier...'

'Don't be need to go further for I knows what it is you be goin' to say, you can't be wife to my son.'

'Libby, I...'

'No, wench.' Libby shook her head, lamplight gilding silver streaks softening them to pale gold. 'I were wrong in askin', I knowed that from seein' the look which come to your face and I 'pologises for causin' you sorrow, but...' A film of spreading tears once more had the tired eyes gleam like freshly ripened chestnuts. 'There be one thing I would ask and that be for you not to tell my Daniel of what I put to you; I would shield him from hearin' aloud what the heart inside him tells, Daniel Radley won't never know the special love which binds man and woman together. It be that kind of love I knows you don't be able to give but for so long as you bides 'ere then p'raps my Daniel can know the love of a sister.'

Rounding the table Regan flung her arms about Libby. 'He knows that love already,' she declared, 'I love Daniel the way I still love Saul, nothing will ever change that.'

Turning from Libby and Regan, Ann Searson hid the tears risen swiftly to her own eyes. Daniel Radley would have the love of two sisters.

Perhaps he had been too hard. Sitting in his office overlooking the wharf busy with loading and un-loading narrow boats, Grant Eversley wrestled with feelings of self-reproof. Daniel Radley had long been a friend. As boys they had shared the same interests, they had laughed and talked, made plans for what they'd do together once they were grown, and though those plans had never materialised, the friendship had remained solid. But how solid was it now? It had been her fault, the fault of that girl Libby Radley had taken into her home! No, that wasn't true! Exasperated with himself, he pushed from the chair, pacing the small room like a caged lion. He had told himself Regan Trent had been the cause of the angry words he had thrown at Daniel, that beneath it all was the thought she was no more than a thief ... a thief with a beautiful face. Yet all the time he had harangued Daniel he had known the blame lay with himself.

Yet it had not stopped him! For all his brain had shouted he was wrong he still had not stopped, and all the while Daniel had made no answer. Damn the man! Grant's fist hit the desk hard. Damn him, why hadn't he argued back, why hadn't he said it was no business of Grant Eversley's what went on in the Radley household. It would have made things easier to shoulder right now. Crossing to the window Grant looked at the scene below. Normally the wharf and its canal traffic would have all of his concentration but today he looked on it with blank eyes and a mind concerned only with the friendship his own stupidity might have cost him. Might! He reached out a hand to the window letting his weight fall against it. There could be no 'might' about it; after what he had said to Daniel Radley there would no longer be a welcome for him in Woden Passage.

'You come sit down, wench, you've worked 'ard enough for one day, what be left will keep 'til mornin'.'

341

'I will take Daniel's tray to him first.'

'No you won't.' Ann Searson turned from hanging her coat alongside Libby's shawl. 'I have to say hello to Daniel so I can take the tray along of me.'

'Her be good to Daniel.' Libby smiled as Ann left the living room. 'Her be the same way with 'im as you does, talks to 'im like there be no difference 'twixt 'im and any other man.'

'That is because there is no difference.'

Soft with the pain of years Libby's answer was quiet. 'You be a good wench, Regan, you and Ann both, you've come to be like daughters and like daughters you would spare me pain, but no lie, whatever the meanin' be at back of it, no lie can cover what I sees every day. My son be a cripple and that be the difference. Maybe it meks no odds to the way you and Ann looks on 'im, but don't you see, wench, it be the way he looks on 'imself, that be where the difference lies, he can't live a life other men live and that is the knife in his heart, the agony in his soul while the agony in his mother's be fear of what will become of 'im once you and Ann be gone.'

'Ann Searson won't be gone, not 'til you and Daniel give her marching orders.' Ann had re-entered the living room.

'Then you be 'ere for keeps, wench, cos don't Daniel nor me wants to part wi' either of you.'

'Speakin' of Daniel, he asked me to show this to the both of you.' Her smile wide, Ann set a newspaper on the table.

'That be more'n a week old.' Libby frowned.

'And ready to be cut up for wrapping tea. Daniel knows that but says you are both to go through it again before cutting it.'

The frown still creasing her forehead, Libby scanned the first couple of pages then, 'Well I go to the bottom of our stairs!'

The local expression of surprise brought a smile to the young women watching.

Libby's hand smacked the paper. ''Ow could I 'ave missed that? If this don't be a turn-up! 'Ere,' she passed the paper to Regan, 'read that, wench, and tell me don't that be a turn-up!'

The salesman who had threatened to expose her whereabouts to Sherwyn Huntley was in prison. Regan stared at the photograph in the newspaper. He would not be able to threaten her again.

Libby took the paper, snorting scathingly. 'Serves 'im right, deserves every one of them fifteen years 'ard labour! Were it left to me 'stead of that there judge he would 'ave gotten another fifteen and them every bit as 'ard; robbin' poor folk were easy to 'im, so easy he decides to try robbin' his employers, but he stuck his dirty fingers in the pot a mite too deep and they got bit.'

'You won't have to worry about him any more, the place he is in he won't be able to go see Sherwyn Huntley so that lifts another worry from your mind.'

'I can't be sure of that, Ann.' Regan glanced at the paper still in Libby's hands. 'That newspaper is several days old, and that salesman's threat was made some time previous to the date printed on it, so how can we know the man did not contact Huntley during that time?'

'You can't be sure.' Libby laid the paper aside. 'Can't none of we be sure, but goin' on what I've 'eard of the 'Untley I thinks if word of you be already given to him then he would 'ave come lookin' for you long afore now.'

'Mmm.' Ann nodded. 'There's a great deal of sense in what Libby says, I think we can forget Mr Sherwyn Huntley.'

Maybe Ann could! Regan met her friend's smile. But she could not afford that luxury. Neither would the man who played the caring stepfather forget her. Regan Trent alive was a threat to the life he enjoyed being master of Woodford, his hands alone holding the reins of both house and business; it was a way of life he had killed for, and he would kill again in order to maintain it.

32

'You should speak with Daniel, tell him what it is has been in your mind these past weeks.' Ann Searson returned the heavy flat iron to the trivet, drawing it close against the fire to reheat. 'After all,' she went on as she straightened then turned to face Regan, 'it isn't like you would be takin' charge, not like ordering things be done.'

No she would not be giving any order, but even so Daniel might resent what she said. Regan silently folded laundry carried in from the washing line strung across the yard. Daniel had seemed different since that last visit of Grant Eversley, he was friendly as before yet there was something, some indefinable something, she felt whenever they were together *Since that last visit of Grant Eversley:* the words sprang back.

He had stormed from the house without so much as a look in her direction, and that was when the change in Daniel had begun. Had Grant Eversley told Daniel of his suspicions? Told him Regan Trent was a fortune hunter interested only in taking his livelihood? Certainly the two men had exchanged hard words, that had not been difficult to infer, and Grant Eversley's failure to call at Woden Passage following that exchange signified a rift. Regan's hands tightened on the cloth she was folding. The one real friend Daniel had! Had that friendship ended because of her?

'I says you should go to him now while Libby is in with him, let them both hear what you've been thinking.'

'An' what be it you've bin a thinkin'?' Neither of them had heard Libby come into the living room; now they met her enquiring look with rapidly colouring cheeks.

'It ... it was nothing.' Regan turned away, putting the folded cloth into a drawer of the dresser.

'If it be nothin' then why be it you pair have faces redder than the breast of a robin?' Waiting several moments for the reply which did not come Libby's hands went decisively to her hips, her eyes demandingly sharp. 'Well! I be a waitin'! What be it you feels you can't go a sayin'?'

Taking the iron from the trivet Ann spat onto its flat surface, nodding satisfaction at the quick sizzle. 'It's an idea Regan had ... we both had.' Wiping the iron on a spare piece of cloth she proceeded to press the cotton apron laid ready

345

on the thick blanket spread over the table to protect it from the heat of the iron.

'Idea?' Libby nodded. 'What idea might that be?'

'Please.' Regan shut the drawer, her fingers staying on the handle. 'It was just an idea, it is not my place to tell you or Daniel–'

'Let me be the judge o' that,' Libby intervened. 'Now out wi' it, ideas good or bad be best talked on, left inside they gives no benefit.'

She had not expected this! Embarrassed by the situation she was caught in Regan felt the colour deepen further in her face. It was not like she was a member of Libby's family; it was impertinence to even think what she had, much more so to dream of speaking it.

'Will you tell or do I?' Plonking the still-hot iron on an upturned saucer Ann stared across the table.

There could be no avoiding it. Regan's throat tightened. Libby must also know of Grant Eversley's accusation. What had been told to Daniel would have been repeated by him to his mother; now hearing what had been discussed with Ann could only serve to confirm that man's belief, to confirm suspicion Regan Trent was intent on robbing mother and son.

'Wait!' Libby stepped forwards, her hands lowering to her sides. 'What be about to be said should 'ave the hearin' o' Daniel seein' as you spoke of 'im along o' meself, so set that iron in the hearth 'til talkin' be done.'

'It … it was just a thought.'

'Then let's be hearing it.' Daniel Radley smiled

346

at the girl sitting at his bedside, her fingers nervously twining one about another.

'It was with the women coming into the shop, they are always in such a hurry.'

'That be cos of when comin' 'ere they don't be workin', an' that in its turn means less money to feed their families – a woman can mek upwards of several dozen nails an' a lad p'raps as many in the time teken to run to this place so it speaks for itself why they scarce stays long enough to say what it is they be after buyin', an' scarce ever gives time to chattin'. Time be food to the women o' Woden Passage an' what don't be earned don't be ate.'

'Which was what gave rise to the idea of taking goods to them rather than having them come to the shop.' Having at last spoken of what she had in mind, Regan went on. 'I've noticed how many times women or their children have to return to the shop for items forgotten in the haste of returning to their work, and this loss of earning does indirectly add to the cost of a purchase.'

'I understands that,' from the further side of her son's bed Libby swung her head slowly, 'but they 'as to fetch what be needed, ain't no other way, I can 'ardly go humpin' stuff to each an' every 'ouse in the Passage.'

'But there is another way.' Regan's eyes stayed on Daniel. 'A small cart carrying twists of tea, sugar, in fact most of the goods those women come for.'

'A cart you says, wench ... I ain't no cart 'oss! I can no more pull a cart than hump a pack on me back!'

'I don't think Regan had that in mind.' Daniel

347

smiled at his mother's indignation.

'Then what do 'er 'ave in mind?'

This was the part she least wanted to enlarge upon. Questions involving the private lives of others was not Libby's idea of conversation. Enthusiasm fading, Regan fell silent.

'What Regan won't say is this.' Ann spoke up. 'Enquire from the family of a lad you can trust how much he earns in one morning and pay the same for that lad to deliver goods to any house which orders them.'

'That be all well an' good,' Libby frowned, 'but profits don't be so much they'll pay a lad to go a deliverin' stuff to folk.'

'We talked about that.' Ann paused, Regan's glance catching at her, then continued adamantly, 'It might as well be all said as half! We spoke together on that same thing and I said the money I can pay for being here could ... well part of it could pay a lad a morning's wage.'

'But that be throwin' money away, where be the profit o' that!'

'I think I see where the advantage be.' Daniel's lips pursed, his brain working rapidly. 'If people can order what they want, if they can be certain of it being brought to them so they have no need to leave the work which brings their living, that has to be an advantage.'

'To them, ar, I don't be a arguin' on that, but where be the benefit to the Radleys?'

Self-conscious because of her own silence, Regan began awkwardly. 'There ... there may be very little, maybe the issue is not worth discussing.'

'That is the first bad idea I've known you have.' Daniel chuckled. 'I think it be a damn good one. Think on it, Mother, folk in Woden Passage gets to talk with them from other streets about, and what one woman finds beneficial another will try. If it takes off then the business you do now could double, even treble.'

'I have no doubt of it, Daniel.' Enthusiasm gleamed in the smile Ann turned on the man who sat propped on pillows. 'Like Regan said, penny twists of tea wrapped in newspaper replaced by small packets holding perhaps several ounces, sugar packaged the same way, each of those could stand a farthing added to the purchase price once the value of home delivery became recognised, and that need not be the all of it. Radley's could supply so many other things; but let Regan explain.'

'I was really thinking of my father, what he taught me regarding business.' Regan's gaze held fast to her fingers, white with tension as they lay clasped in her lap. 'He said the best method lay in buying materials in bulk: take a whole crop, eliminate any middleman and you can sell to a customer at a lower price while still maintaining a small profit; but more important to any business was quality, my father said if the standard of quality was kept high then goods would sell themselves, consequently business would expand.'

'Buyin' in bulk!' Libby shook her head. 'I don't see 'ow we can be a buyin' o' stuff in bulk.'

'Not everything, and not right away.' Regan looked up. 'But twice now you have sent me along to Bescot Farm to buy a couple of sacks of barley

349

or to pay for the same number of sacks of wheat to be sent along to the mill for grinding into flour, several journeys where one could suffice.'

'You don't be mekin' sense, wench...'

'Regan is mekin' sense, Mother,' Daniel interrupted. 'What she is saying is guarantee to buy a full crop provided the price be fair, that way be better than tekin' a sack or two at a time. The assurance of their cereals having a market would be welcome to Bescot Farm.'

'Mebbe it would,' Libby frowned again, 'but what would I do wi' a whole crop o' wheat?'

'Time.' Ann laughed. 'Isn't that be what this entire conversation is about! We all know the time it takes to make bread, we also know that for almost every woman hereabouts that is time could be spent making nails and so helping to keep her family. If you, Libby, have some of the wheat milled then baked into loaves, then send them out on the cart I'm sure they will go.'

'Ar, but who do we gets to mek loaves? Seems you forgot that.'

'No.' Ann shook her head. 'We did not forget. I can bake bread and Regan is a quick learner. We will make your loaves, at least we will until "Radley's Best Baked Bread" is selling all over Wednesbury.'

'Sellin' all over Wednesbury, that'd be a fine day, though I reckons that be dreamin'; no, it were a bit o' fun to talk on but it best be left at that, it best be just talk.'

'But it must be worth a try.'

'No wench, it don't.' The catch in Libby's voice betrayed the holding back of tears in the answer given to Ann. 'Ain't no use in wishin' for the moon nor in settin' faith along o' dreams for dreams be painful, we all knows they can't never come true.'

She had not looked at Daniel when saying those words yet he was the dream Libby spoke of. Regan watched the older woman, the lined mouth drawn tight against deep felt pain. The dream in which her son would walk again lay broken in her heart.

'Mother.' Daniel caught a rough work-worn hand, cradling it between both of his own. 'It be better to hold a dream than live a life empty of all hope. It might be that dream won't come true, that the happiness it brings be over and gone in no more than it teks time to tell, but a single minute of joy, of hope, is worth eternity in a life that knows only the emptiness of sorrow.'

The emptiness of sorrow! The hand cradled in Daniel's curled about the thin fingers. Her son had known more than a fair share of that and no doubt life held yet more for him. But talking with Regan and Ann, discussing the practicality of delivering groceries to the homes of folk, had brought a gleam to his eyes, a smile to his mouth. What would happen to that smile, though, once these two moved on?

'The business is yours, Mother, you are the one has worked for it, yours must be the decision.'

Daniel's voice broke into her thoughts and Libby looked at the beloved face. The smile, the gleam in the eyes, they said he wanted to follow the course set out by Regan Trent; would it prove yet one more walk along the paths of sorrow?

'*...a single minute of joy...*'

Libby's heart wrenched. Would she risk her

351

business, her livelihood, to give her son that minute? Yes, she would risk her very soul.

'Then the decision be made.' She smiled. 'Though don't you go askin' me to mek no cart!'

'Daniel was all for it but Libby wasn't so enthusiastic.' Dark hair brushed to a sable gleam Ann set to plaiting it, her fingers expertly weaving the silken strands over and under each other.

Her own hair plaited and tied with slips of lavender ribbon, a gift Ann had bought from the millinery shop, Regan slipped her cotton nightgown over her head, which prevented her from answering but did not exclude thought. Libby had not been enthusiastic; rightly she was concerned the venture would result in loss of income, but she had seen what Ann and herself had seen, the glint of interest in Daniel's eyes, and that had persuaded her to say yes. But if it did fail, if Libby lost! Beneath the folds of nightgown Regan's eyes pressed hard shut. Why had she spoken of that method of selling! Why talk of it even to Ann! Maybe she could speak with Libby tomorrow, ask her to reconsider. Drawing the gown over her body Regan knew even now what the answer would be. Libby had seen the spark in Daniel's eyes; could it be a spark of hope had been lit in the woman's heart? Hope that in some way her son might come to walk again? Oh Lord! A sob caught in her throat as Regan's heart cried her remorse. Please, not that! To have revived hope where there could be none was unforgivable.

'I haven't seen Daniel lively as he was tonight.' Ann tied off the raven plaits. 'He really was

352

interested and that can only do him good – he even said he would see to having a cart made.'

'Ann.' Regan, her eyes dark with concern, looked at the girl tidying brushes and comb atop the chest of drawers which must also serve as a wash stand. 'Ann, what if the whole thing proves a disaster, if it causes yet more heartache for Libby. I couldn't live with that! I have to tell her I was wrong, I have to tell Daniel...'

'And take away the straw you have handed him!' Ann turned quickly. 'That is what it is, Regan, a straw he can cling to. Don't you see, Daniel needs to be needed, he needs to be involved and this can do it for him. So maybe it fails! But if it can give him a few weeks of pleasure, of feeling alive again, then let him live it.'

'But it is his livelihood we are risking, his and Libby's, we have no right to do that.'

Across the small bedroom Ann's warm brown eyes glistened, her voice as she answered soft as the sigh of a breeze. 'Do we have the right to deny him happiness, for that is what I saw in his face, Regan, happiness. Let him know it, Regan, if only for a short time.'

'But...'

'Shh!' Ann smiled. 'I know what it is you are about to say but Daniel and Libby will not starve, not while Ann Searson can work.'

Ann had been so definite. Sleepless, Regan watched the pearl of dawn start to disperse the shadows shrouding the small room. If only she herself could feel she had not led the Radleys into doing something which would bring harm to them. 'I didn't mean them harm.' The whisper

353

was so quiet it was scarcely a breath yet it seemed to be heard stilling the silver beams of moonlight which had played on the window pane to splashes of bright paint, heard by the very silence of night, silence which found sound in Regan's heart.

'...*listen to advice*...'

Gentle as a kiss of love it murmured in her head, brushed against her ears.

'...*weigh it carefully in your mind then act for yourself*...'

Her father's words. Regan strove to hold on to the murmurs already being recalled into silence. That had ever been his advice, and her father had never directed her wrongly. Could it be he was advising her now, telling her to depend upon her beliefs rather than her fears? And she did believe in herself, beneath all she had said of bringing disaster to Libby and Daniel, beneath her own mistrust, still she believed.

'Thank you, Father.' In the darkness Regan smiled. 'Thank you.'

33

Regan had been embarrassed to speak, to say how in her estimation shop sales could benefit from the introduction of a delivery service. Alone in his room Daniel smiled at the thought. Yet benefit they had. It had taken no time at all for the venture to take off; the knowledge of Libby Radley's constant fairness in her dealings, and the time the new service saved them, meant that the women of Woden Passage had readily availed themselves of it; now due to word of mouth the service was spreading further across the town.

Sarah Jeavons had been dubious at the idea of her son leaving the nailmaking even for a couple of hours, the prospect of less income a worry. But that worry vanished in the pride of knowing it was her Alfie was being trusted to take each order correctly and to bring back the payments made weekly. The boy too had been proud, it had shone in his face when he and his mother had come to discuss the part-time employment, so proud he had taken it upon himself to paint the slogan 'Radley's Tea' on both sides of the handcart; and who set out the spelling for him? There was no halfpenny prize for guessing; Daniel smiled again. The two young women who had come to live beneath his mother's roof were just as helpful to Alfie as he to the Radleys, spending an hour or so each evening teaching him reading and number. They both worked so very hard, Ann coming from her place at the milliner's shop only to stand long into the night making bread, Regan beside her even though she also laboured all day.

She had been more relaxed since learning of that salesman's imprisonment, she smiled more often yet behind the smile could be glimpsed a sadness. Her mother? Yes; her brother? Of course! The girl would feel sorrow at such dreadful loss: but the sadness in those beautiful eyes was a new one, not brought to Woden Passage with her, but acquired here. In the town – or in this house?

Closing the accounts book, Daniel sat back in

the chair. He had first noticed that look following Grant Eversley's last visit; he had feared Regan had been subjected to the same anger Grant had shown in speaking with him, but Regan had said the man had not spoken to her at all. What had Grant so bitter? So full of anger?

That had been almost as much a shock as had been his words. Grant had never, not even when they were boys growing together, shown bitterness or let anger get the better of him. So why now? What had brought about the change in him? What had him so riled he had almost spat each word, words which had been painful to hear?

His head sinking to rest on the back of the chair Daniel allowed memories of that evening to flood back.

'*...you couldn't face up to it...*'

Painful, hurtful words, yet ones which had borne the ring of truth. They had been hard to hear, but as hard to say, that much had been obvious from the look Grant Eversley could not hide, a look which said he too was hurting. Now it seemed the long friendship they had enjoyed was at an end for Grant had paid no visit since that night. Libby must have wondered why that was but she had asked no question and he, Daniel, had offered no explanation.

Eyelids closing, Daniel relived the moment. Grant Eversley had stood beside his bed, anger glittering like a live thing in his eyes.

'*... you couldn't face what you in your stupid pride believed...*'

Harsh as blows the words which had snapped then resounded in Daniel's brain.

'*...what you expected your life to become, one which no woman would want to share as wife to a cripple. So you gave up. Yes, you bloody fool! You gave up!* You *told yourself your legs would no longer carry you,* you *told yourself you were no real man,* you *and nobody else! You couldn't face up to that, so you took the coward's way out by taking to your bed, by hiding yourself away in this room; no matter it was left to your mother to work to feed and keep you, the burden left for her to carry regardless of the weight: but now the truth has come home to you, hasn't it, Daniel? Another truth you find you must hide, that truth being you are in love with Regan Trent...*'

Yes, it had been the truth. Fingers tightening about the arms of the chair Daniel watched the images floating in his mind: himself opening his mouth to answer, Grant Eversley angrily cutting him off before the first word could come.

'*...no need to admit it!*'

'*...it's plain for all to see, you are in love with the girl ... so fight for her, face the one truth we both know, get up out of that bed and walk!*'

Daniel opened his eyes and stared at the window, its curtains drawn against the night.

'*...you are in love with the girl...*'

Truth? Yes it was the truth Grant Eversley had flung at him, but only Daniel Radley knew the extent of it.

'Radley's Tea'. Driving along Upper High Street towards the George Hotel, Grant Eversley smiled grimly to himself. It seemed the girl was succeeding in her plan. A small change, a slight alteration here and there, was that the way she intended to take away Libby's business? And if she did so then Grant Eversley could be as much to blame as anyone, for he knew what Regan Trent was about. He had gone to visit Daniel with every intention of telling him the same, yet he had not. He had seen the shine in those so recently lacklustre eyes and determination had failed, anger lending a new twist, a turnabout which had him accusing his friend, of saying things to Daniel he had never thought to say and all the while refusing to own to the reason he knew in his heart, that hurt so deeply, the real feelings he had come to have for the girl.

Bringing the carriage to a halt at the front of the hotel Grant's smile became grimmer. There was nothing so fickle as Fate; but Fate could be played at her own game, and right now Grant Eversley was her adversary. In one minute he could put an end to that girl's ambitions, he could bring to a halt the threat he saw hanging over Libby Radley's head. And Daniel? What would the trump card Grant Eversley held in his hand do for Daniel Radley? For a moment the sad-eyed face of his friend crossed his inner vision, and in that brief second Grant felt his purpose falter, but as quickly it returned in strength. What he was about to do would no doubt cause Daniel some hurt but in the long run it would save him a great deal of heartache, pain he would realise only when Regan Trent, having achieved her goal, had no further use for him or his mother.

Alighting from the carriage, nodding to the ostler hurrying forward to take the vehicle round to the rear yard, Grant fought off self-reproof.

Yes, Daniel would suffer for a while, but better to suffer the sting of lost love than a lost livelihood.

Entering the smart building the resolution he had made earlier in the day hardened. He had failed his childhood friend once, now he had been given the chance to rectify that: he would not fail Daniel a second time.

The letter had arrived two days ago. Following a waiter toward the dining room Grant's mind recalled the words written flourishingly across a page of headed notepaper. Would he oblige the sender by 'taking lunch at the George Hotel'. The request was not unusual in itself; business was often discussed over lunch or dinner; it was not the content of the letter had afforded surprise, but the signature.

'Mr Eversley, good of you to spare the time...'

At the table to which Grant was conducted a man rose, extending a hand. 'Allow me to introduce myself, Sherwyn Huntley.

'We have done business on several occasions in the past, a practice I hope to continue, but one I also am in hope of expanding.'

Grasping the extended hand, Grant cast a swift glance over the man he had come into town to meet. Metallic grey hair, neatly cut beard and sideburns, well-cut suit; in fact he carried all the hallmarks of a successful businessman ... so what was it about Sherwyn Huntley he instinctively disliked?

'Let me explain.'

After Grant had ordered from the menu, Huntley went on. 'It is my intention to increase my imports. There is an ever-increasing demand for the produce of the West Indies, a demand I intend to fulfil, and that is my reason for asking you to meet me.'

Accepting a glass of fine Chablis, Grant listened without interruption to the other man outline his plans for the further development of his business.

'The sole charter of a narrow boat!' Grant looked at his table companion. 'That could be arranged provided of course I was informed well ahead of your cargo arriving at the docks. I say this for the reason that boats are regularly in use. It would not be feasible to refuse to transport goods for customers of long standing; that, you will agree, would be a sure way of losing them for good.'

'Then we can do business, Mr Eversley, that is most pleasing. One meeting has arranged a satisfactory outcome so much more pleasantly and so much more quickly than would a series of written communications, do you not agree?'

'I find it preferable to meet any new associate face to face; having some contact, however small, is always conducive to business.'

His answer had not added to the pleasantness Huntley had claimed to be experiencing! Grant caught the look flash in dark eyes. Sherwyn Huntley did not care to be reminded of any shortcomings in the matter of business etiquette.

'You are referring to my replacing the late Jasper Trent.' The reply sounded tight-lipped. 'You have my apologies for not presenting myself sooner; I regret any oversight but family matters can sometimes override those of business. I hope my lack of manners will not detract from the pleasure of this, or future, meetings.'

Pleasure! Grant met the look which totally denied the words.

'My wife.' Sherwyn ignored the waiter placing brandy before him. 'She was often ill. I am afraid my concern for her overrode any other.'

'I trust Mrs Huntley is completely recovered.'

How would he answer that? Grant waved away the proffered drink. Would it bear out what Daniel had told him?

'Mrs Trent ... my wife, she ... she died several months ago...'

The broken voice, the downcast eyes, genuine? Or a genuinely masterful act?

'My condolences,' Grant replied though some inner feeling seemed to say the man speaking to him felt no regret at the loss. Could that be because the death of that woman was what he had wanted ... wanted enough to kill her himself?

'*...he poisoned his wife, said so himself to Regan...*'

Daniel's words echoed in Grant's brain.

'*...said it were also his intention to kill the brother, and that the same would happen to her following marriage to a man the name of Wentworth.*'

No man would confess openly to murder! That had to be false, invented by the girl calling herself Regan Trent in the hope of lending credence to her story. Grant almost spat the word aloud: the only credence it lent was to the fact she lied.

'It was a dreadful blow, then when my stepson was tragically killed in a fire at Woodford only a few weeks later I ... I felt no desire to continue; all interest in business, in fact in everything, deserted me.'

361

'Happily you managed to overcome those feelings.'

'Life had to go on, Mr Eversley, not so much for oneself as for others.'

No doubt it was meant to sound credible but the man could well have been reading from some penny dreadful. Grant swallowed the cynicism sitting like a stone in his throat. He had not believed the tale dished out to Libby and Daniel, yet somehow he believed even less of what he was hearing now. Both accounts tallied in some aspects, but Huntley had made no reference to any stepdaughter.

'When a man is involved not only with immediate family but also with the wider family of business he cannot afford the luxury of thinking only of himself.' Drinking the last of his brandy, Huntley patted his lips with a pristine napkin. 'That was a reality I was forced to accept. By allowing myself to sink into a decline, to neglect business would bring hardship to others as well as possibly to my stepdaughter.'

The man might well have read his thoughts! Masking the wry smile evoked by the thought Grant managed an enquiring, 'Stepdaughter?'

'Regan.' Rising from the table Sherwyn Huntley's blackbird eyes fastened on Grant's. 'Regan Trent, the daughter of my late wife.'

So there was a Regan Trent! Grant followed the other man from the dining room. But was she living on the Continent as Huntley claimed, or in Woden Passage as that girl claimed?

'Losing my wife came as a great shock to me.' After donning his coat, Huntley took hat, gloves and silver-topped cane from the cloakroom attendant. 'Imagine then the effect upon her daughter, a young girl of twenty years. I feared for her sanity, so much so I decided to send her to the Continent to stay a while with family there. I thought the presence of female company would be beneficial.'

Standing at the entrance of the hotel awaiting the arrival of his carriage, Grant heard the questions speaking in his mind. Beneficial! To whom? Was having his stepdaughter absent on the Continent easier for her or for Sherwyn Huntley? Or was it more simply a ruse? A lie told so as to cover a girl's running away from home? For the first time Grant felt a touch of doubt about Libby Radley's lodger having lied. Aloud he said, 'I trust Miss Trent is recovered.'

To the right of the hotel the irate shouts of a carter followed another cutting across his path as his cart came up from Union Street to turn along Upper High Street, the resulting narrowly avoided collision causing a shawl-draped figure to step sharply back from the edge of the pavement.

'That were a lucky escape.' Another woman equally draped in heavy shawl but with a black bonnet perched atop a knot of brown hair caught the slighter figure steadying it. 'I sees that silly bugger done frightened the life outta you, you be right pale; you sure you be all right?'

'Yes ... yes thank you. It took me by surprise, no more than that.'

'Do you be sure?' The bonneted figure glared angrily after the carts. 'It be a danger crossing the road 'ereabouts, a body needs keep sharp what wi' 'avin' five ways to watch; the good Lord give folk two eyes only so why there should be five roads all a crossin' at one spot 'as the beatin' o' me, an' the eyes the good Lord give this body tells 'er you be shaken bad; just you come along into 'ere, they'll give you summat for the relievin' o' shock.'

'No, thank you but there is no need.' Resisting the hand which would have drawn her into 'Boots Cash Chemist' situated on the same corner of the Five Ways the slighter woman shook her head.

'I suppose you knows your own feelin's better'n I does!' Words drifting behind her the woman who had stopped to help moved on, her dark-clothed figure instantly swallowed up by others garbed in the same fashion, milling like so many beetles among market stalls erected on both sides of the road. This thoroughfare also accommo-dated the steel rails along which a heavy steam tram was lumbering towards the stop further on at the White Horse.

But it was not in the direction of Lower High Street the figure at the corner of the busy cross-roads looked, nor the blare of the tram horn warn-ing people out of its way which made her face blanch and the breath catch in her throat.

'Damned wagons!'

Turning to glare at the offending vehicle Sher-wyn Huntley did not notice the figure drawing a shawl protectively lower over a frightened face, eyes wide and terror-filled staring across to where he stood.

Brushing freshly raised dust from his coat Huntley snapped instruction to the maroon-uniformed doorman to send for a hansom. Then as a boy raced off toward the High Bullen he glanced at Grant, saying blithely as though no interruption had delayed an answer to the question posed a minute before, 'Miss Trent is recovered, I thank you.'

'Your stepdaughter is here with you? She also is visiting Wednesbury?' The answer to that question could provide the answer to the mystery of the girl living in the house of Libby Radley! Holding Huntley's cold stare Grant maintained a look of innocent enquiry.

Pulling on fine pigskin gloves, Sherwyn removed his glance from that of his lunch guest. The man asked altogether too many questions but failing to answer could point only to incivility. Smoothing each finger of the expensive gloves in turn he deliberately took time before answering. 'Regrettably not. She is at present still on the Continent, but she will be returning home to Woodford very soon when she will marry her fiancé; my stepdaughter is to become Mrs Myles Wentworth.'

Stepping into the hansom Sherwyn Huntley once again did not notice the shawl draped young woman drawing back against the wall of a chemist's shop as his vehicle passed by, and stepping into his own hansom cab neither did Grant Eversley; he also had not seen the face of Regan Trent.

His stepdaughter was abroad recovering from the shock of losing her mother; she was to return shortly to marry Myles Wentworth. Returning to the wharf Grant stared from his office window at the narrow boats awaiting their turn to despatch cargo.

Daniel had mentioned a man of that same name, a man Regan Trent was to marry! It could not be coincidence. The girl living in Woden Passage had gleaned certain information, then used it to suit her own purpose; but what Daniel had told him of her tallied completely with what Sherwyn Huntley had said during that meeting. Completely? Then how come that sojourn on the Continent? Or that proposed marriage? Was it Huntley lying or the girl?

Indecision as to the truth of the matter had prevented him from speaking to Huntley of the girl living with Libby Radley, had once more caused him to fail in that self-made promise to Daniel

But why! Why had he not revealed her whereabouts? If the girl were a fraud then her lies were best exposed. *If* the girl were a fraud! Beyond the window it seemed the slender figure of a young girl stood looking up at him, honey-gold hair glinting in the rays of the afternoon sun cradling the lovely face. That was why he had not given her over to Huntley. Grant winced at the intensity of feeling suddenly rushing in every vein, feelings he had not expected, those he ought not to have for the girl Daniel Radley loved!

'The *Brummajum Maid* be in from Liverpool.'

The interruption dispersing the vision in his mind, Grant turned to face his wharf foreman.

'Her be carryin' more of that brought up on the *Queen*, that be two deliveries within days of one another, seems Trent be buildin' up on imports of the stuff.'

Not Trent! Grant took the docket held out for his inspection. Jasper Trent. Importer of Fine

Quality Goods.

The heading on the transport docket stared boldly. But that logo no longer applied. Grant tapped the paper against the tips of his fingers. Huntley, the man he had lunched with, had taken over the running of the Trent business completely, so why not his name on these papers? Unless – he glanced again at the docket – unless the daughter of Jasper Trent stood in the way!

'Would you 'ave it pushed on along of Worcester same as before, sir?'

'Yes.' Grant nodded, then as the other man left the office returned to gaze from the window.

Just which was lying, Huntley or the girl calling herself Regan Trent? Huntley had not appeared in any way distressed as might have been expected of a man whose stepdaughter had run away, especially if that stepdaughter was the key to everything. That either meant Huntley had spoken truthfully or that he was an expert in the art of lying!

He should go to Woden Passage, confront the girl there with Daniel and Libby present to hear her reply; face her with the news he had met and talked with the man she claimed was her stepfather and guardian. To do so would protect Daniel from a deeper hurt, that of finding the girl he was in love with wanted only his mother's shop.

Now who was the liar! Frustrated by the emotions riding inside him he struck the wood of the window frame. If he truly had Daniel Radley's well-being at heart he would have spoken out when last he had visited Woden Passage. Now it was too late. He could tell himself it was for

Daniel's sake he would not go to that house, it was Daniel's feelings he wished to spare. Returning to his desk he slumped into the chair, the fingers of both hands gripping the armrests. He could tell himself all of that but that too would be a lie. You fool, Grant Eversley! A laugh soft and cynical trapped itself in his throat.

You damned fool, you have got yourself caught in the same trap as Daniel Radley!

34

It had been him, it had been Sherwyn Huntley she had seen standing before the entrance of that hotel, and with him Grant Eversley! Limbs still trembling from shock Regan held onto the table in Libby's living room. She had watched Huntley climb into a hansom cab, watched him drive away from the hotel. She had stared after the passing hansom, fear blazing in her mind. He could have come to Wednesbury for one purpose only: to take her back to Woodford. The salesman? No, he couldn't be the one who had told where she could be found; as Ann had said had that been the case then Huntley would have come for her weeks ago. But there was no need for further surmise. With her own eyes she had seen who it was had revealed where she was living. Hadn't she witnessed Grant Eversley shaking the hand of the man who had raped her? A man who would do the same again!

It had been made so very plain! Grant Eversley

harboured no liking for her, he saw her only as a thief bent on robbing the Radleys.

'...*do not think to use Daniel in order to take his mother's business...*'

Words which had stabbed before stabbed afresh. Why would Grant Eversley think that? What reason had she given him to think she would treat the Radleys so?

'...*attempt it and you will regret you ever saw Wednesbury...*'

He could have spoken in no harsher a tone, in no more definite terms. He wanted her gone from Woden Passage, from this town, from the life of Libby and Daniel, and had achieved his aims by contacting Sherwyn Huntley.

Sounds of the shop door opening made her hold her breath. Regan glanced at the chenille curtain. It concealed the sight of her in the tiny living space but it could be no barrier to the man who, knowing she was here, would have no compunction in snatching it aside, then striding through Libby's house until he found what he came to collect.

Regan breathed out in relief as she listened to Alfie Jeavons who had returned to the shop for fresh supplies. This time it was not Sherwyn Huntley, but who was to say he would not be the next person to enter the shop?

She ought not to have returned to this house. She should have left Wednesbury the moment she saw Huntley. Being found here would cause the man to vent his spite on the Radleys; but then, given that Grant Eversley had already informed him of who it was had helped and sheltered her, it was certain Huntley would do just that; he would not forgo the opportunity of proving himself the master.

But she had carried the money with which Libby had entrusted her to take to Bescot Farm, money to pay for wheat and barley. To have left the town with it would prove Grant Eversley's opinion of her, and mark her a thief.

Beyond the curtain Alfie Jeavons laughed. The boy was delighted with his job of delivering and taking orders for groceries. Emotion thickened in Regan's throat. She had done at least some little good for the people of Woden Passage.

'I'll load the cart now if that be all right, Mrs Radley, then soon as I've had a bite to eat I'll see about deliverin' 'em.'

The boy had finished talking with Libby. Regan glanced quickly in the direction of the shop. Unless a customer came in immediately Libby would come to the living room expecting to hear the transaction with Bescot Farm had been completed then demand to know why it had not. But she could not tell why, Libby nor Daniel must never know the reason for that nor who had been the author of her leaving this house; she would not bring disharmony between the Radleys and Grant Eversley.

Taking the coins from the pocket of her skirt she set them on the table, then removing the shawl Libby had loaned returned it to its peg.

They had been so kind to her. Despite herself Regan's glanced turned toward the annexe. If only she could explain; tell Daniel and his mother of the feelings she held for them.

From the other side of the dividing curtain Alfie's cheerful call was followed by the sound of the door closing behind him.

'I love you both, please forgive...'

Her whisper soft as her tears Regan slipped silently out through the scullery door.

'I were serving of a customer when her come 'ome, I thought then her 'ad been a bit soon in gettin' back from Bescot but that there money does the explainin', Regan d'ain't never go to that farm.' Libby Radley's drawn brows expressed anxiety she had attempted to keep from showing in her voice.

'But why wouldn't she go there? It's not like she said there was ever any unpleasantness ... that she disliked the farmer.'

'I wouldn't expect her to 'ave dislike of that lad along o' Bescot nor of his wife.' Libby shook her head. 'I've 'ad the knowin' o' both since they was born, wouldn't neither of 'em say boo to a goose lessen it be their own.'

'She said nothing when she came in?' What more was she hoping to hear? Libby had said several times that Regan had not spoken.

Aware of the girl's anxiety, Libby returned patiently, 'I told you, Ann wench, Regan spoke not one word but went straight through to the livin' room. I were busy wi' young Alfie, the lad be bringin' of that many orders from folk wide o' the Passage it took some time to weigh an' wrap different goods so by the time I did get to come in 'ere ... well I thought the wench were upstairs or yet again talkin' wi' Daniel. I never had no thought of her runnin' off, her seemed settled, especially after that there salesman were put outta the way, her were such a friend to Daniel.'

Such a friend to Daniel! Each the crack of a pistol, Libby's words rang in Ann's mind. Such a friend – but not a friend of the standing of Grant Eversley! It could only be he had caused Regan to leave without a word to anyone. He had as good as told her to quit this town that day he had confronted her in the Shambles; maybe he had done so again today, met Regan going to Bescot and repeated his threat more vehemently! Anger hot in her throat, Ann buttoned the coat she had not taken off after coming into the house.

'I'll just have a run up to the market place, maybe someone there has seen Regan.' Half of her words got lost in her rush from the house. Ann's thoughts raced in keeping with the clatter of her boots; it was no market place she was about to visit, and no stall-holder she intended speaking with. Ann Searson wanted words with only one man, and he would feel the full sting of her tongue!

In the study of Woodford House Sherwyn Huntley ran his eyes over a letter received a few days previously. It confirmed his order for twenty extra barrels of rum, delivery to be made – he checked the calendar on his desk then the date on the letter – a month from today. Perfect! Replacing the letter in a file lying on the desk he returned the same to the wall safe tucked behind an oil painting of the royal family. A month was ample time in which to arrange that special unloading at Liverpool docks, the surreptitious removal of those extra barrels to a waiting narrow boat leaving Excise men none the wiser as to their ever having been part of any cargo. That rum would realise a hefty profit on resale to hotels and ale houses, profit which would fit nicely into the pocket of Sherwyn Huntley. The owner of that narrow boat would be as ignorant of what it carried as would Her Majesty's Customs: cover those barrels with a tarred canvas, overlay that with chests of sugar, cocoa beans and half a dozen other commodities brought to Liverpool and he would never know rum was aboard.

There had probably been no need for a personal meeting with Grant Eversley but caution ever proved preferable to regret. Turning from the safe Sherwyn sneered to himself. The boat owner had not questioned the sole hiring of a vessel which was to proceed directly and with all cargo to Worcester; but then Eversley was like the town he lived in, mindlessly dull, devoid of thought for anything other than iron and coal; he would certainly have none concerning the smuggling of liquor: that took brains and Grant Eversley had precious little of those, although not many men had the intelligence of Sherwyn Huntley.

'Mr Myles Wentworth, sir, I have asked him to wait in the drawing room.'

Nodding to the manservant come to the study Sherwyn's self-congratulatory feeling evaporated. He liked this butler less than he had Edward Sanders. Where had that man disappeared to? Like a mole disappearing down a hole he had, like Regan Trent, vanished. Regan Trent! His mood darkening he walked to the sitting room. That girl supposed herself free, supposed her tracks well and truly covered; but no one, much less a woman, should ever suppose of Sherwyn Huntley!

'Some unwelcome news I'm afraid,' Myles said as Sherwyn entered the room.

'You have heard again from that blackmailer?'

He had thought to claim so. Myles Wentworth dropped into an elegant Hepplewhite chair. He had thought to use that trick but it might not be to his advantage just yet; Huntley was still raw at being taken twice by a 'blackmailer'. Keep that business for another day? Yes... Myles smiled to himself. But that day would not be too long away; after all the world of fashion changed quickly and keeping abreast of it emptied a man's pockets equally rapidly. Beneath a well-rehearsed air of annoyance, he answered, 'Not blackmail. I think you may be certain we have heard the last from that swine whoever it might be.'

'If not blackmail then what? What is the unwelcome news you have to convey?'

'Doesn't a man get offered a drink in this house?' Myles watched the other man scowl as he handed across a goblet half-filled with brandy. Huntley was easily irritated and he enjoyed pricking the man's skin.

Sipping deliberately slowly, allowing the drink to remain long seconds on his tongue, Myles felt the growing displeasure of his host.

'Well!' Huntley's infuriated bark shot across the quiet room. 'Say what you came to say or get the hell out of my house!'

Holding the goblet Myles's thoughts danced quick as the points of light reflecting in the rich

374

amber of its contents. His house! Had Huntley forgotten, it was Regan Trent to whom Woodford truly belonged, and as yet Regan Trent was missing? But one prick of the skin at a time. Myles sipped again. That way the pleasure lasted longer.

'Burnford,' he answered, savoured droplets slipping past his throat. 'There'll be no more collections from that place for some time, if ever again.'

Standing before the fireplace Huntley frowned. 'Go on!'

Resting the glass on one knee Myles replied, 'Ulrick, the governor of the orphanage, is being replaced. Told me so today when I collected a certain purchase; did not confide the reason though I suspect the fellow's greed got the better of him and he has been caught with his fingers in the cash box. Money!' Above the rim of the beautifully cut crystal goblet hazel eyes gleamed amusement. 'It is the root of so much evil.'

'And that of a sizeable profit, all of which is lost or have you forgotten that!'

'It has not escaped my notice, the same as your failure to find Regan Trent has not escaped it.' Myles returned sarcasm with sarcasm. 'It will very soon be her twenty-first birthday ... but perhaps that has escaped *your* notice.'

It had not! Mouth tight with anger Sherwyn Huntley stared at the exquisite Bokhara carpet. He had not forgotten Regan Trent's birthday nor its implications.

Without her signature this house and all which went with it, all he had schemed and killed for, could slip from his grasp; but he would not allow that to happen. What could not be achieved one way must be achieved some other way. Come the twenty-first birthday of Regan Trent her guardian Sherwyn Huntley would become sole owner of the Trent inheritance. And Wentworth? Like the girl, should she show up at any time after that birth date, Wentworth would die!

'Be a young woman on the wharf, says her be wantin' to see yourself.'

A young woman! The rush of feeling which had burned his senses once before burned again, bringing a faint bloom of colour to Grant Eversley's face. Was it her, the young woman he found almost constantly in his thoughts? But it could not be that girl, why would she wish to speak with him?

'Says her don't be movin' off this wharf 'til her 'as spoke wi' you, sir, and if truth be said then I've no fancy for tellin' you won't 'ave the seein' of her; be a regular firebrand do that one.'

'Which boat is she on?' Head bent to the paper he was reading when his wharf foreman entered the office, Grant hid the emotion he knew had stained his cheeks.

'Ain't from no boat, sir.' The man watching Grant moved uneasily on his feet. This was a problem the sort of which he had not been called to deal with before and though Grant Eversley were a decent, understanding employer he might just take it in his mind to say any foreman who couldn't handle a wench couldn't handle a wharf, and that would be this foreman out of a job.

'She is not on a boat!' Grant's senses blazed again.

'Not from any as pulls into this wharf, sir, I made sure of that afore I come to you; and speakin' frankly I 'ave my doubts her be from any boat, wouldn't no boatman's wench dare speak demands of a boat owner.'

No boatman's daughter! Grant dipped a pen into a brass inkwell then signed the bottom of the paper. A young woman making demands did not sound like the person he had chastised that day in Wednesbury; she had barely answered back. Colour draining rapidly as it had come, he looked up from the desk.

'She refuses to leave?'

'Said so point blank, sir, says her'll stand at the cutside all night if need be.'

With a quick stab of regret Grant laid aside the pen. Whoever this woman demanding to speak with him was, it was most certainly not the one from Woden Passage. 'Well,' he smiled briefly, 'we can hardly have her remain standing the whole night on the canal towpath so you had best send her up.'

'Miss Searson!' Perplexed, Grant looked at the woman entering his office. 'I had not thought—'

'No, you probably didn't!' Ann cut in angrily. 'You most likely thought me to be gone from Wednesbury along with her you have driven from the town.'

'Driven—'

Grant tried to speak but again Ann's anger prevented it. 'Yes, driven!' she snapped. 'I know full well you wanted her gone!'

'I wanted who gone? For heaven's sake, girl,

377

you are making no sense.'

'Then I'll speak plain enough for you to understand.' Edged with bitterness, the words hurtled across the desk. 'You accused Regan of aiming to take Libby and Daniel Radley's living away from them, you as good as named her a thief – don't bother to deny it!' Ann raised a hand once more, stilling a reply. 'Refusing to own to what you said only makes your behaviour the more despicable. You told her should she attempt to use the Radleys to further her own ends she would regret she had ever seen Wednesbury. Well let me tell you this, Mr Grant Eversley, Regan never had any such in mind, and let me tell you this too while I be about it. Regan Trent has done more to help Daniel and his mother in the few months of her being with them than you appear to have done in your entire lifetime! But the fact of her loving them, of their both holding that same feeling for her, meant nothing to you, it is Grant Eversley knows what the Radleys should or should not feel, who or who not they should take as friend. Well, I have seen both parties and I know which I prefer, the one I would trust, and that party is not Grant Eversley!'

Anger snatching Ann's breath Grant took advantage of the pause in her tirade. 'Firstly, Miss Searson, I do not deny I warned your friend not to think of making use of the Radleys or that I told her should she do so she would regret coming to Wednesbury.'

'How very gentlemanly of you!' Ann's eyes flashed. 'I only hope Libby and Daniel still think you so now you have succeeded in driving a girl from the only home she has.'

At this blatant insult Grant drew a sharp controlling breath then asked quietly, 'What do you mean, now *I* have driven her away?'

'I mean who else can be held responsible? It was you threatened Regan, you are the one person wanted her gone, the one person apart from Sherwyn Huntley–'

'Sherwyn Huntley!' Snapped from tight lips, it halted Ann in mid-sentence. 'Tell me, Miss Searson, your friend, was she in the town centre around lunchtime today?'

Now what was he about? Ann eyed the man facing her across the heavy desk. 'I can't say as to time,' she answered warily.

'But you can say whether or not she was in the town?'

Hesitant to say definitely that of which she had no positive knowledge Ann glanced again at the face of the man she had upbraided, at the eyes suddenly dark with concern, the mouth no longer tight with anger but tense with ... with what? Was she really seeing what she thought was in those eyes or had anger bemused her senses? She could be forgiven if that were so, forgiven for imagining Grant Eversley cared.

'Miss Searson, please,' Grant urged, 'was Miss Trent in the vicinity of the market square today?'

It was in the voice as well as painted like a mask over the face... Grant Eversley *did* care, probably a lot more than he was prepared to admit! This revelation, melted Ann's anger and she answered, 'She was to have gone to Bescot Farm, so yes, I suppose she could have passed that way.'

'And you say, or were about to say, that Sherwyn Huntley is a man might hold no liking for Miss Trent, that he might wish she were not in Wednesbury.'

'*Might!*' Ann echoed scornfully. 'There is no *might* about Huntley disliking Regan: he hates her. She is the one stands in the way of his taking all that Jasper Trent left; and as for Regan being in Wednesbury, it wouldn't be different wherever she were: Huntley wants only to find her, to drag her back to Woodford where he can do to her what he did to her mother. He wants to see Regan in her grave and himself laughing over it!'

'Allow me to escort you to Libby's house.' Rounding the desk as he spoke Grant took Ann's elbow, steering her down the stairs to the yard where he called for his carriage. Climbing into the driving seat he glanced once at the young woman seated beside him. She had been right in her condemnation of him; he had spoken unjustly to Regan Trent.

Taking the reins from the stablehand he flicked them gently and as the vehicle rolled from the wharf gates said quietly. 'It was wrong of me to speak as I have to your friend. I behaved most ungraciously towards her, but you have my word, I have not seen or spoken to Miss Trent at any time today, though I am of the belief her sudden departure could have some connection with myself.'

35

He had left Ann Searson at the entrance to the shop then immediately driven away. Although he had not known Regan Trent to be in the town, had no idea she might see him in the company of Sherwyn Huntley, which had caused her to run from Woden Passage, yet still he felt responsible. Bringing the carriage to a halt Grant Eversley stared out over the scrubland of heath rapidly merging with the soft mauves and greys of evening. He had driven in every direction hoping to catch a glimpse of that slight figure but each time hope appeared about to be realised it was dashed.

If only he had not been so quick in condemning her, in virtually calling her a thief. A thief! Grant almost laughed in his self-disgust. The girl who though afraid for her safety had gone back to Woden Passage in order to return the money Libby had asked she take to Bescot Farm. No, Regan Trent was not the thief, that was Grant Eversley! He had tried to rob that girl of her good name, to take from her the one thing left to her and now he was left to face his guilt, guilt for driving away the woman Daniel Radley was in love with.

A long-drawn breath easing none of the conflict inside him Grant turned the carriage about. He had said such unforgivable things to Daniel, accused him of cowardice, a lack of moral courage, while turning a blind eye to that same fault in himself. Where had been Grant Eversley's moral courage? Where the strength of mind to own to himself that which, even as he had made those accusations, had threatened that girl? The emotion he had felt deep within him, felt yet had not courage enough to admit – love for Regan Trent!

So where was she gone? He had driven to the towns bordering this one: Dudley, West Bromwich, Walsall, Darlaston, asking folk along the way had they seen a young woman answering Regan Trent's description but none had been able to help. She could not have walked further and without money...

Thoughts which had been running freely stopped abruptly.

Money! Ann Searson had said Regan did not have money, the small amount which Libby Radley insist she was paid for assisting in the house she put every week into Libby's small cash box which held housekeeping coins; so without means of travelling on any public transport...

In the near distance, as though brushed by an angel's hand, the heavens flared bright crimson, a carmine veil thrown across the purpling sky as the furnaces of iron-making foundries were opened; but eye-catching as the sight was it made no impression on Grant Eversley. His mind remained captured by the recurring thought: *no means of travelling on public transport.*

That had to be the reason he could find no trace of Regan Trent! She had been spotted by Huntley. He had taken her back to Woodford!

The expression in Libby's eyes while listening to Grant Eversley's disclosure of his conversation with Regan softened, though her answer came without a smile. 'I can't go a holdin' of aught against you lad,' she said, 'though you should 'ave spoken to Daniel or me afore you went accusin' of that wench.'

'I realise that now.'

Was that wry look genuine? Was Grant Eversley truly sorry for what he had done, or was this simply a way of extricating himself from blame? Of retaining Libby's friendship? Not yet wholly certain, Ann's retort of 'What I can't reckon is how you could think that of Regan in the first place!' was caustic.

The wry smile playing yet on his lips Grant looked at the young woman he had driven to this house, at the defensive gleam in her chestnut eyes, a swift feeling of regret sweeping him. It was a fortunate man would have Ann Searson for a friend. Knowing the thought was wishful thinking he said quietly, 'Perhaps had I known her better...'

'Perhaps had you given yourself *time* to get to know her a little better you would have realised Regan would never willingly hurt anybody, and especially she would not hurt Libby or Daniel; you see, Mr Eversley,' Ann went on tartly, 'I *know* how Regan felt with regard to them, it was love, *real* love, that which a daughter holds for her mother, and a sister for a brother, that is what you have driven from this house!'

Stung by the words Grant's return sounded sharper than he might have wished. 'And what are your feelings, Miss Searson? What do you feel for Libby and Daniel?'

'I love them too! Libby has become as a mother to me as well as to Regan, and like Regan I love her as any daughter would; as for bringing harm to her, if for one moment I thought that might happen I would leave this house just as Regan has left it.'

Hearing the quiet sob from Libby, Grant hesitated. He had caused enough pain in this house without the possibility of more, yet the demon inside him, the demon which had driven him to accuse one young woman, now prodded again, pushing words from him.

'No doubt truthful as that is, Miss Searson, and equally pleasant to hear it is nevertheless only half an answer. My full question asked your feelings for both, yet you speak only of Libby. So I ask again: what are the feelings you hold for her son?'

Coals settling into the bed of the fire sounded loud in the sudden silence, the flare of their descent sending a shaft of light to where Ann stood, a brilliance which despite its swift death showed the rise of scarlet staining her cheeks.

'I...' she stumbled, 'I ... respect Daniel.'

'Respect!' Grant's demon jabbed once more. 'Then unlike your friend Miss Trent you do not love him?'

What was he trying to get the girl to say? Half of Grant prompted him to ask her pardon but the other half said half an answer was still all that had been given ... but half was not enough. His glance fixed firmly on the blushing face he said again. 'In this house you and Miss Trent were treated equally, you were both accepted and

384

loved by Daniel and his mother, yet while Miss Trent returned that love as a sister to Daniel you feel only respect, you do not feel love.'

Ann stared for a moment at the man it seemed taunted her, then both hands going to her face to hide tears her voice could not, murmured. 'That is not true. I do love Daniel but ... but not in the same way Regan loves him, not as a sister would. What is in my heart for Daniel is deeper and stronger than that, it reaches to the depths of my soul.'

Libby's strangled sob choked but its sound seemed to have no effect upon Grant. The smile now only in his eyes he persisted. 'You love Daniel as a woman loves a man, then why not tell him so?'

Tears she had so long forbidden squeezed through her fingers as Ann turned her back. Hands falling to her sides, staring into the red heart of the fire, she answered. 'To do that would be to have Daniel believe of me what you believed of Regan, that it was his home and shop, the security they could provide, and not himself I truly wanted. No, Mr Eversley, I will keep my silence, it will be enough just to be in the same house, to help care for him, and that I will do until the day Libby or her son tell me I must leave.'

'You love Daniel Radley as a woman loves a man? Do you love him enough to become his wife?'

At the quietly spoken question Ann's every nerve tingled. She had thought never to own to the feeling which had grown over the months, never to divulge to anyone, not even to Regan,

385

the depth of love which could have no return.

'This is a time for truth...'

At Ann's back more slowly, deeper than before a quiet voice became apprehensive, pausing as though unwilling to finish what was begun until Libby's broken sob once more disturbed the settled hush. Then it went on.

'Answer only in truth, do you love Daniel Radley enough to become his wife?'

With a cry Ann turned towards the man whose question had set her nerves pricking as if from a thousand bee stings. For a long moment she looked at the face, the eyes so intent upon her own. Then, tears a line of tiny diamonds glistening along her lashes, she walked across the room.

'Yes.' Her smile soft as her whisper she stood before him. 'Yes Daniel, I love you enough to become your wife.'

'There be no trains tonight, miss, not none to nowheres.' Brass buttons gleaming in the light of a lantern the stationmaster looked at the figure sitting alone on the one bench on the platform. She had arrived several hours before, going into the ladies' waiting room, but now the station was closing for the night and waiting rooms must be locked.

His free hand stroking side whiskers curving gracefully to meet a splendid moustache the stationmaster moved uncomfortably from one shiny booted foot to the other. This was a bit of a to-do! He stroked the whiskers again. He couldn't go a throwin' of a woman out of the station, but on the other hand he couldn't allow her to sit

386

there all night.

'Come along now, miss,' he coughed awkwardly, 'can't 'ave you sat 'ere all by y'self now can we? Like I says ain't no more trains 'til mornin'.'

Could it be her were deaf? Were that the reason of her not answering? Holding the lantern closer so that its pallid gleam fell over the pale face, the stationmaster hesitated. If the woman couldn't hear... If her didn't know there'd be no train! Should he touch her? Should he p'raps tap her on the shoulder? But that could be misconstrued! Nonplussed, he jiggled the keys held about his waist on a thick leather belt. A minute or two longer, he could give her another couple of minutes, it would take that time a lockin' of the ticket office; but were her still a sittin' when that were done then he would ... he would do what? As uncertain as ever he turned back along the platform, lantern light a small pool dancing before his feet.

'Hey there!'

The call bringing him to an abrupt halt the stationmaster lifted the lantern above his head. Didn't folk know trains didn't stop at this station after eight p.m.?

'Last train be gone,' he answered. 'Won't be nuthin' more afore the milk train in the mornin'.'

Out of reach of the lantern light a hand smacked against another. 'I see.' Disembodied by shadow a man's voice answered irritably, 'So what time will the first passenger train run to Worcester?'

'Worcester?' Keys jingled with the reply. 'That'll be the nine a.m. for London, meks a stop at Worcester. You's don't be the first enquirin' after the Worcester train this evenin', the others were a man an' a woman.'

The shadow-shrouded figure took a step forward. 'Did they take the train?'

'Can't rightly answer that seein' I was otherwise engaged. Politely speakin', sir, nature calls even a stationmaster.'

'Of course ... but surely you would know whether people boarded the train.'

'Can't say as to people.' Yellow beams, prancing over the badge sewn to a dark blue peaked hat, glinted off the highly polished brass buttons securing the matching coat of the uniform of the London, Midland and Scottish railway. 'The man did, so Bert in the tickets office tells me.'

'And the woman?'

'Ar, now that Bert d'ain't say ... an' he can't now for he be away 'ome, which is what I'd do meself if I could but get the platform empty.'

'I'm sorry.' The apology was terse. 'I did not mean to detain you.'

'Ain't y'self, sir, it be the one a sittin' on the bench be the problem. I thinks it be a matter of bein' deaf for my speakin' receives no answer; an' I can't go escortin' the person off the premises not with bein' a woman, an' with no other female to ask do the escortin' ... well it puts me in a bit of a quandary an' no mistek ... hey!'

His shout echoing after the figure pushing past him the stationmaster followed, a choice swear word muttered under his breath. Drawing level with the other man he heard the quiet, 'Thank God!'

'Ann having informed me she had no money I did not think it worthwhile to call at either of the railway stations.'

'Well, praise be you did.' For the second time in as many hours Libby listened to Grant Eversley's account of his search for Regan Trent.

'I called there merely to ask had a man and woman travelling together taken the train for Worcester. I feared Sherwyn Huntley had sighted her in the town and taken her back with him to Woodford.'

'Well again, praise be he d'ain't! I thanks you, lad, for goin' in search of Regan and bringin' her safe 'ome. Lord, when I thinks of that 'Untley my flesh fair creeps; he meks a snake seem better company!'

'I think even those creatures would shun him.' Ann's tone indicated agreement.

'Happen you be right, Ann wench.' Libby smiled. 'Now if you will see Regan to her bed I'll mek we all a cup o' tea.'

Shaking her head as Ann made to help her from the chair Grant Eversley had almost carried her to, Regan broke the silence she had maintained during the short drive from the station. 'I...' Words choking in her throat she swallowed then tried again. 'I have to thank you, Mr Eversley, for your kindness.'

Kindness! Grant felt the hot wave of self-criticism. How could she speak of kindness after the way he had treated her? It would be only reasonable if she never spoke to him again. Subduing the quick stab the thought brought with it he answered, 'I am the one must apologise, Miss

Trent, what I said to you was unforgivable.'

'You thought only to protect Libby and Daniel. Had I been in your position I would have done the same.'

'It is good of you to say so. Now I must bid you all goodnight.'

'No!' Ann moved quickly to the passage connecting the living room to the annexe. 'You can't go until we have given Regan her surprise.'

She wanted no surprise. The day had been full of stress; now she wanted only peace and solitude. But seeing Ann's face shining with happiness, Regan forced a smile, then as a figure came slowly from the shadow of the passage to stand beside Ann the smile became a cry of pure joy.

Supporting himself with a stout walking stick, his free hand on Ann's arm, Daniel Radley's laugh echoed Regan's cry. 'This be Grant's doing,' he said, glancing at his friend. 'And I'll be forever thanking him for it.'

Regan looked from one man to the other for an explanation.

'I can see you be asking yourself how?' Daniel smiled, making his way haltingly to the chair his father had made so many years before. Then, his eyes hardly leaving Ann as she helped with tea cups, he told of how Grant had caused him to realise his growing infirmity was due entirely to his own state of mind.

'I saw what I was doing not only to myself but to my mother; I saw the pain, the stress her caring for me was causing and I felt ashamed, more ashamed because I knew my legs had not become weaker, that with effort and trust in heaven I could walk. None of you asked why I wanted to return to the annexe.' He smiled again. 'I did not explain that my moving around during the night would disturb Mother in her own room, but in the annexe I would not be heard; also if I did not manage to regain my legs then there could be no further heartache for Mother because she would not know what I was about.'

'But you did succeed, you are walking! Oh Daniel, I am so happy for you.'

'That isn't all, Regan.' Daniel looked at the girl who was so obviously pleased for him, then reached a hand to Ann, drawing her beside him. 'I know Mother agrees the best be yet to tell.' He smiled. 'Ann has consented to become my wife.'

36

With her nightgown half over her head, Regan's shocked face stared through the bodice opening. 'You went to see him at his place of business!'

'Yes, and had he not been there I'd have gone along to Willingsworth House and confronted him. I wasn't going to let him get away with what he had said of you.'

'But he spoke what he believed to be the truth; he had every right to do that.'

'And I had every right to tell him he was wrong!' Hair brushed to gleaming bronze swept a chiffon cloud about neck and shoulders as Ann turned sharply. 'He might be best friend to

Daniel but you are *my* best friend and nobody is going to say wrong about you, not so long as Ann Searson can get to them.'

As her nightdress fell to her feet Regan freed her own hair, letting it lie in swathes of pale gold over her breasts, a half-smile curving her mouth as she answered. 'At least he did not throw you out.'

'And at least I didn't hit him! Though I must admit the temptation was strong. Think of the headline that would have made: "Woman strikes local businessman."'

Laughter gurgling, Ann covered her mouth with her hand when Regan pointed to the wall separating the room from that of Libby, then with her eyes glinting mischief murmured, 'It would have been worth it just to see his face.'

'And what of Sherwyn Huntley's face had he read the same headline? He would have returned here if only to satisfy himself the Ann Searson of that newspaper report was not the same Ann Searson who had served as lady's maid at Woodford.'

'Oh Lor!' Ann's eyes lost their impish gleam. 'I never thought of that. But then that's me, I never do stop to think, I go off half-cocked! Lord, Regan, I could have had Huntley finding you after all.'

'But you haven't,' Regan answered gently, the sudden distress in those brown eyes pulling at her heart. 'Now we are not going to talk of Huntley any more, I want to hear of you and Daniel; I had no idea you and he were in love, you never said anything.'

Twisting heavy strands of hair into one thick

plait, Ann's smile was far away. 'I think I loved Daniel from that first time of meeting, he was so kind, so understanding; but at the same time I thought he loved you.'

'Me!'

'Yes, you.' Ann answered the surprise. 'He always seemed so relaxed with you, so happy when you were together, truly Regan, I thought him in love with you.'

'But all the time it was Ann he loved.' Genuine happiness glowed in Regan's answer. 'I couldn't be more glad for both of you, and now with Daniel walking again–'

'It would have made no difference to me had he never got use back in his legs,' Ann cut in quickly, 'I would love him just the same. But Daniel be a proud man, so proud he never would have asked I become wife to a cripple bound to a chair. The fact of his walking is due to Grant Eversley. He is the only one found courage enough to speak to Daniel as he did, to force him to face what was buried deep inside. He was brave enough to risk losing a friendship he valued highly, to have Daniel and Libby turn their backs on him for good. I could not have found such courage. I will always be grateful to him for acting as he did; it was Grant Eversley gave Daniel back his life and brought so much happiness to my own. I was mistaken in so many things I accused him of, especially not behaving like a gentleman; I know now there are none better than Grant Eversley.'

Tired as she was, sleep evaded Regan. Ann's summation of the man was totally correct. Yes, he had spoken out of turn but it had been said only in defence of Daniel and Libby and hurtful as it had proved that day in the Shambles she had recognised that defence so had not found it in her to ostracise him.

'*I was mistaken in so many things...*'

Ann's words could so easily be her own. Turning her head towards the window Regan stared at the high yellow orb sitting in silent majesty in a darkened sky. She had thought not to have liking for the man even though upon leaving that railroad station, and again during the carriage drive back to Woden Passage, he had apologised profusely for causing her distress. Those feelings had been mistaken. Regan stared harder at the moon, wanting its brilliance to wash away realisation, but it merely highlighted it.

She did not dislike Grant Eversley! She liked him too much for her own comfort!

'It is one week to Regan Trent's twenty-first birthday, one week before we stand to lose everything; why the hell hasn't she been found!'

Huntley had asked that same question so many times ... didn't the man realise what a boor he was! Draped elegantly in a deeply winged brocaded chair Myles Wentworth watched through veiled eyes the older man pacing angrily back and forth before the fireplace of the drawing room of Woodford House. He too wanted Regan Trent found and returned to the care of her stepfather; without that happening Myles Wentworth also stood to lose a great deal – of money that was! Lowering his glance Myles admired his handmade boots. Money was all Regan Trent meant to both him and Huntley, but unlike himself Huntley would not see a penny of that girl's fortune.

By law once married a woman's all became the property of her husband; body, soul *and* property, it all belonged to him. But that husband would not be Sherwyn Huntley. Smiling to himself Myles turned a foot, admiring the shine of fashionable patent leather. The man could have her body, use it for as long as pleased him, but this house and all that went with it would be enjoyed solely by Myles Wentworth.

'Perhaps it would have been better to have waited a while longer before posting marriage banns.' Myles lifted his glance. 'I mean a wedding with no bride! You can hardly pass that off before the vicar, much less Trent's lawyer; there is that matter of Regan signing for her inheritance, or maybe that slipped your memory.'

Sherwyn Huntley's lips drew back in a cat-like snarl; he snapped to a standstill, jet-black eyes burning with fury. 'Nothing has slipped my memory!' he grated through set teeth. 'And nothing will slip from my grasp. Jasper Trent's fortune will be—'

'Mine.' Myles's quiet retort had the effect of a gun blast. 'Mine,' Myles said again, 'if, and I repeat, *if* you find Regan before she attains her majority, while you can still force her to your will; after all, should she refuse to sign, refuse in the presence of her lawyer, which given hatred of you she is likely to do, then we both can say goodbye to the Trent fortune, and frankly, Huntley, I think our little venture has already failed.'

'Really!' Losing none of their fire, Sherwyn's

eyes locked onto the figure sprawled in the chair. 'You think! That is evidently something you do not do. Were you to spend more time thinking rather than in visits to your tailor then you would realise our "little venture", as you put it, has not failed and neither do I intend that it should.'

'Then how…?'

'All in good time.' Sherwyn's mouth relaxed into an icy smile. 'All in good time.'

'All in good time.' Seated in the compartment of the train carrying him to Worcester, Myles reflected on the words. What had Huntley meant by that? Why refuse to enlarge upon it? A wedding without a bride – could he be planning a marriage by proxy? That might overcome one obstacle but what of that of Regan's signature? Surely no lawyer worth the title would settle for anything other than the girl herself doing that. Yet Huntley had seemed so sure, so confident. So much so he proposed placing an announcement of the forthcoming marriage. Huntley was cunning, but cunning enough to pull a trick like that?

Slowing into the station the train hissed steam, grey-white vapour passing across the windows like storm-driven clouds. Rising to his feet, the sudden wrench of brake against wheel had Myles bump against the only other passenger sharing the first-class compartment. Apologising for his clumsiness he smiled at a young handsome face. Attractive! He stood aside murmuring for the young man to precede him to the platform. Very attractive! Just the way he preferred.

Following the man into the street Myles

396

watched the stranger glance towards a waiting hansom. Hesitating briefly he raised his silver-topped cane, smiling to himself as the young man from the train gave an exasperated shake of his blond head.

'I've taken the last cab, it seems.' Myles let the smile show. 'Perhaps we might share it.'

'It would be a great help.' Blue eyes gleamed gratitude. 'But then I must not presume upon your kindness.'

'Glad to be of assistance. Where is it you wish to go?'

'I have an address, though this being my first time in Worcester I have no idea of whereabouts this might be.'

The first time in this city! Myles savoured the reply. Did 'first time' allude to any other activity? Quashing the stimulation the thought sent trickling through his loins he said pleasantly, 'Well, if neither of *us* knows the place you are looking for we can be fairly sure the cabbie does.'

The cab driver had known; he had also re-marked that Tallow Hill being on the further side of the canal it would be some twenty minutes before they reached that destination. The young man had protested this was too long a time but Myles had brushed it aside. Time, he had smiled, was a commodity of which he had plenty to spare.

The young man had said this was his first visit to Worcester but that did not preclude his having relatives here. Seated beside him now Myles tapped the tip of his cane against a boot, asking casually, 'You have family in Tallow Hill?'

The blond head turned quickly toward the

window. 'No.' It came with a noticeable swallow. 'I … I have no family, my aunt who reared me after my parents died of fever passed away a couple of months ago.'

'I'm sorry,' Myles murmured, feeling absolutely none of the professed emotion.

'That was the reason of my coming here to Worcester; my aunt knew I had aspirations of becoming an actor, her will stated her house and its contents be sold, the proceeds of which I should use to achieve my ambition.'

'And Tallow Hill?'

'My lodgings?' Turning from staring out of the window, the blue eyes smiled directly at Myles. 'To be truthful I have as little idea of what they may prove as I have of my chances of obtaining a position in the Swan Theatre. The address was offered by a traveller who left the train some stations back and with having no knowledge of Worcester apart from its theatre, then I felt I had no choice but to follow it up; at least – supposing I am accepted as a tenant – it will allow me a breathing space, time to look for something else.'

'Speaking of time...' Myles took a gold half-hunter watch from the pocket of his silk waist-coat, glancing briefly at the dial before slipping it back. 'If you are not pressed perhaps you might join me in a spot of luncheon.'

Agreement given with a dazzling smile Myles tapped the cab's driving seat with the cane reinstructing the driver. Mrs Russell's establishment provided an excellent luncheon. And a little after-lunch amusement? Feeling the pressure of a thigh against his own, a thigh which did not move when he, altering his position on the seat, did not pull away, what had been a mere fancy while following his companion from the station now became a positive desire.

Touching the hip flask of brandy he always carried in the pocket of his coat, Myles laughed beneath his breath.

A little after-lunch amusement?

Most definitely that!

She had promised never to divulge what had been told to her, given solemn word never to reveal that secret. Setting bread dough to rise in the warmth of the hearth Ann wrestled with a problem which had chased away sleep for several nights. A secret was a secret! She reached baked loaves from the side oven. A promise was a promise!

Flushed as much from the continued mental struggle as from the heat of the oven she brushed the back of one hand across her brow.

A secret should be kept! She tipped flour into a large pottery mixing bowl. A promise should never be broken! Adding a teaspoonful of salt to the bowl, she watched the tiny grains merge with, then entirely disappear, into the flour. That was what would happen if she remained silent. One day Sherwyn Huntley would find what he sought and when he did Regan Trent would vanish from the face of the earth as completely as the grams of salt had vanished among that flour.

But she had given her word!

Reaching for the cup in which she had mixed yeast, warm water and a little sugar then set inside the hearth so the heat of the fire would set the yeast to germinate she stared at the froth-covered contents.

'Set the devil to rise.'

That had ever been the saying of her mother and grandmother when baking bread. They had set yeast and water to germinate on a sunny windowsill or, in winter, in the warmth of the hearth, and she in her innocence had waited beside it, heart in her mouth each time a bubble burst thinking the devil would follow.

Was that not what was happening inside her? The promise she had made and now the feeling she should break it were churning together in her stomach, raising the devil of indecision and guilt.

Ann stared at the bubbles breaking on the crusty surface of the yeast mixture. She would be guilty of going back on her word, of breaking confidence with a man she respected, but then how could she ever again respect herself if she did not try to help a friend?

Yet to help one could lead to losing one!

Cup in hand, Ann turned a glance to the passageway connecting living room to annexe.

By attempting to help Regan she could lose the friendship of Libby and more than that, she could lose the respect – the love – of Daniel.

Lose the love of Daniel? Fingers tightening on the cup Ann turned to the table. Or see a friend lose her all? Biting hard on the answer she poured the yeast mixture into the bowl.

37

'Well I be beggared! That's a pretty drastic thing to ask for.' Smiling at the exclamation Grant Eversley came to stand at the shoulder of his wharf foreman.

'Oh, didn't see you there sir, sorry, I...'

'No.' Grant smiled again, 'I'd like to hear what it is has you wish to be beggared.'

'It be this 'ere.' The foreman tapped a finger against a column of the newspaper he had been reading, 'I reckons this be the reason of them kegs of brandy.'

'Kegs of brandy?' A momentary frown of recollection settled on Grant's brow.

'Ar, sir.' The workman nodded. 'Them kegs we sent along sharpish lessen the fairies paid the boat a visit ... they was for the Trent business, and as I recalls it be a fellow the name of Huntley now runs it.'

'So?'

'So that be the reason of the brandy. It be to celebrate a weddin'... and a fine party it'll be with what were sent on along of Worcester.'

'Huntley?' What had been a fleeting frown at the recollection of cargo brought weeks before on the narrow boat *Midland Queen* became stronger, drawing Grant's brows together. 'Does it give any other name?'

Folding the newspaper to fit his hand more

comfortably, using the other to trace a finger beneath a line of print, the wharf foreman read aloud. 'Mr Sherwyn 'Untley, director of "Woodford Business Enterprises", is pleased to announce the forthcoming marriage of his stepdaughter Miss Regan Trent to Mr Myles Wentworth. The ceremony–'

'May I see that?'

Interrupted yet again the foreman handed the folded newspaper to Grant. 'It be none too clean, sir,' he said apologetically, 'were given me by a boatman hauling coal, said it were wrapped about a loaf his wife bought when they passed along of Worcester.'

'Is he here now?'

'Left an hour gone, sir; would you 'ave me send after the boat? 'Ave the man brought back?'

'What?' His attention on the newspaper Grant answered vaguely then more positively. 'No ... no, I merely wished to offer to purchase the newspaper from him.'

'Ain't no need of that Mr Eversley, sir,' the other man smiled, 'he were finished with it and so be meself ... if it be you wants it then you be welcome, though like I said, it don't be none too clean.'

'...*Miss Regan Trent to Mr Myles Wentworth...*'

Back in his office overlooking the canal the words danced in Grant's mind. During their meeting at the George Hotel Huntley had said his stepdaughter was shortly to return from the Continent and then would marry a Myles Wentworth; but the girl living in Libby Radley's house also claimed to be the same Regan Trent! If this were so, and he now believed it was, how then could Huntley be proposing to give her in marriage to Wentworth?

'I thought it best to bring 'er straight on up, sir, better than 'ave 'er threaten to stand the rest of the day on the wharf.'

'What was that?' Grant looked at the man entering the office. 'Oh I see.' He rose smiling as his eye caught the figure following behind. 'Please come in, Miss Searson.'

'So you told Daniel what you intended to do.'

'Yes.' Ann nodded. 'I feared it would be he would lose all respect he had for me if I broke a vow I had made in good faith.'

Respect ... or love?

The quick drop of the head, the colour flushing into the cheeks, was answer for Grant. Ann Searson had risked losing the man she loved doing what conscience told her was wrong but the heart told her was right. Daniel Radley was indeed a lucky man!

'I had to tell him.' Ann stared at fingers twisting together in her lap. 'I wouldn't start married life with a lie on my lips. Daniel listened then said it were right I should do what I said but that I could not do it alone, he would be with me. But I couldn't have him do that!' Eyes alight with concern lifted to Grant. 'He grows a little stronger each day and the callipers you had the blacksmith make and fit to his boots give him great support, but even so I would not have him go far from the house, not so soon. It was confessing this had Daniel silent for a time, that were when I thought he would say I was to keep

403

my word, that it was best I abide by my promise.'

'But he did not?'

The light shining in her chestnut-brown eyes became one of pride and Ann shook her head. 'No,' she said quietly, 'Daniel did not say that nor did he forbid, he asked only that I first come to you. He said if anyone could help it would be you.'

'Ann...' Across the desk Grant's eyes fastened on his visitor. 'Seeing you are to become the wife of my best friend I ask the privilege of addressing you by your given name.' A quick smile giving consent he proceeded. 'I will be happy to assist in any way I can, but first,' he handed the newspaper to Ann, 'I think you should read this.'

Weighing tea, packaging each two ounces into blue paper packets printed across with the logo 'Radley's Tea' Regan glanced to where Ann was placing freshly baked bread into a large wicker basket. The bread sold well, Alfie Jeavons bringing more requests for it every day, a growing demand Ann and herself could not satisfy, yet it was a market the Radleys should not let slip past them. She had discussed this with Daniel and his mother, pointing out the probability that following marriage Daniel and Ann could have the upstairs bedroom leaving the annexe free to be turned into a bakehouse. She had further suggested the employment of two or three women who could no longer wield a hammer making nails yet could knead dough. Libby and Ann had objected. Where would she, Regan sleep?

Where indeed? Gathering several packets Regan turned to stacking them alongside others on the shelf behind the counter. That question had been in her mind even before putting her idea to the Radleys. Where *would* she sleep? She had claimed there would be no problem finding a room nearby, that the annexe was better used for a bakehouse. But that had been only part truth, the rest being she would feel herself an intruder, that Ann and Daniel should be free to live without the encumbrance of a lodger. Had she said as much then Ann would have denied it, but in the fullness of time, with maybe children to fill the home, then she would be forced to think differently.

But leaving this house! Being alone to face the fears only the kindness of Rosa and Joab Mullin, of Ann and the Radleys, had saved her from drowning in, was a prospect which had brought nightmares.

Turning to scoop the remainder of the packaged tea from the counter, her glance going to Ann standing now with both hands rubbing her back, Regan felt the quick surge of guilt. She had been so taken up with her own problem, so full of her own worries, she had not spared thought for those of Ann. How could she have been so blind! Leaving the tea packets on the counter she went quickly to where the other girl had again bent over the basket.

'Leave that.' She tugged at Ann's hands, pulling them away from the almost-filled basket. 'I will see to the rest, you go get yourself a cup of tea.'

'You can both of you come get a cup o' tea.' Libby drew aside the curtain closing off the living area.

'You go.' Regan ushered Ann towards the

405

curtain. 'I'll just finish up here then I'll be in.'

'No more'n two minutes then, pot already be filled.'

'Things will be done quicker with both of us doing it.' Ann had resisted the push designed to send her along with Libby.

This was one more excuse for keeping to herself. Her guilt dissolved into apprehension as Regan watched the figure bend once more to the basket. She had not realised until now just how many of these same excuses had been made for the last day or two, how her usually talkative friend had been so withdrawn. Had Ann too had the same thoughts about having another person share her married home? Was she fretting over how to ask Regan to find herself another lodging?

A whisper would not penetrate the heavy chenille curtain. Her hands closing over those of Ann pulling her upright, she said, 'Ann, if my being here... I mean once you and Daniel are married–'

'That will be no bother, you know that!'

The reply cut her question short. Regan held the hands tight in her own. The anaemic yellow glow of the one gas lamp battled hard to banish the gloom of shadow descending over the tiny shop and touching the eyes she looked into; it lit the worry showing deep within them and Regan's guilt flooded again. How was it she had not seen! How could she have been so selfishly blind!

'Ann,' she murmured, 'I'm so sorry... I've been thoughtless. If my staying here after you marry is not the cause of the worry I see in you then please, tell me what is; let us share as we have since finding each other in Wednesbury.'

'It–'

The jangle of the shop door being pushed open had Ann's explanation finish abruptly and as she freed her hands Regan caught the look flash across her face as she glanced towards the figure striding into the shop.

'I thought Miss Trent should see this.' Once they were seated in Libby's living room Grant Eversley held out a folded newspaper.

'That were what has been worrying me,' Ann said as Regan looked up from reading.

'You knew?' Regan asked, a confused frown settling on her brow.

'Two days since,' Ann answered, colouring slightly.

'Ann said nothing because I asked her not to.' Daniel reached out a hand to Ann. 'If anybody be to blame then it be me.'

'But this is impossible!' Regan glanced at the paper still held in her hands. '*I* am Regan Trent, you have to believe that!'

'We all believes, wench, but that don't give no answer to what be printed along o' that paper. 'Ow that there 'Untley can say it when you don't be with 'im ... well, that be a puzzle and no mistek.'

'A puzzle indeed.' Grant answered Libby but his eyes stayed on Regan. 'Though it is one he has obviously presumed to have solved.'

'Sherwyn Huntley is determined to get his hands on Regan's inheritance,' Ann put in, 'and if getting some actress to play the part of the bride is the only way of doing it then that will be what he will do; but I tell you, marriage or no marriage, it will not end his search, he will never stop looking for her.'

'But two days from now will see 'er turned twenty-one, neither 'Untley nor that other ... that Wentworth ... will be able to do anythin'!'

'Except kill her, Libby, and I know he will.' Ann looked at the older woman. 'I lived in the same house as Sherwyn Huntley, I know his sly ways, what he is capable of doing, the same as I know he would have no hesitation in killing Regan. That is the reason Daniel and I decided I should go speak with Grant.'

Ann had talked with Grant Eversley! That was the reason for this visit, the reason for showing her the report in the newspaper. For all he had brought her back from the railroad station, had apologised then and since for his attitude towards her, disbelief in her still lingered. But that was of no matter any more, Grant Eversley had no place in her life, he never would. But he does! Loud in her mind the cry answered Regan. Grant Eversley had slid silently into her heart and now he was locked inside it. She had fallen in love with a man who still thought her a liar.

Returning the newspaper across the table, Regan looked at the man every atom of her loved. When his fingers touched her own while taking the paper it seemed the world danced crazily around her, that breath no longer filled her lungs, that blood tingled in her veins. For one wild moment she imagined that hand caressing her own, those clear eyes shining with the same feelings now racing in her; then his hand withdrew, leaving the world to return to reality.

'Mr Eversley.' Tight in her throat, the words had

to be pushed from her tongue. 'I have no doubt Ann came to you asking assistance on my behalf. She and Daniel decided upon that action out of kindness. I understand your coming here, your bringing the newspaper for me to read the report of Huntley's marriage for myself. I also understand the need you felt for doing so; you wish to protect them both from someone you still perceive as a threat to their life. I assure you, Mr Eversley, you had no need. Libby, Daniel and Ann have risked too much on my account, they have exposed themselves to Sherwyn Huntley's spite and revenge for long enough, a danger that will not end with that so-called wedding, for as Ann herself said, Huntley will not give up the search, therefore I must end it. I am returning to Woodford.'

'You will marry Wentworth?'

Had the flare in those grey eyes been one of anger ... or of pain? Regan's glance fell away before the emotion in her own was seen.

'No, Mr Eversley,' she responded quietly, 'I will not marry Myles.'

His jaw tight against a tide of feelings, Grant looked at the girl whose face he found so often staring up at him from his desk, smiling at him in his sleep, a girl he wanted beside him always. But Regan Trent had no smile for him nor would she ever have love for him. Forcing down the sting of the thought he said, 'You will not marry Wentworth. . . how then do you propose to put an end to Huntley's searching?'

'Perhaps you know, Mr Eversley, that two days from now I reach the age of twenty-one, the age where the law says I can act for myself. On that day I will sign everything over to Sherwyn Huntley.'

'You'll give everthin' to that swine!' Libby's body shook with indignation. 'Eh Regan wench, you can't go a doin' of that, you can't let 'im tek all your father left for you.'

Surprised by the truth rising suddenly in her mind Regan hesitated before saying, 'There will be no pain in parting with Woodford. All happiness was ripped from that house when Sherwyn Huntley came into it, the love which it had held died along with my mother and my brother. Without them there is nothing there for me; I want no part of it.'

'You suppose going back there, signing over everything to Huntley, will see an end to all of this!' Hairbrush in hand Ann turned from the makeshift dressing table, her glance sweeping to Regan laying day clothes over the room's one chair. 'Well, I tell you the signing will be your own death warrant! Do you honestly believe that man will settle for anything other than having you follow your mother and Saul to the grave? No, Regan, he won't; he won't suffer the rest of his life being shadowed by the thought of you being alive.'

'But it will remove the shadow from your own life, yours and the Radleys, that is all I care about, Ann, nothing else.'

'But I care.' Ann banged the brush aside. 'I care, Regan, and so do Daniel and Libby. We don't want you going back there, we don't want you to leave Woden Passage.'

'*Life does not always give us what we want.*'

Lying in her bed, the answer she had given to Ann's request that she change her mind about returning to Woodford resonated in Regan's brain.

Sleepless, she stared at the moon-kissed walls of the room they shared, only now in the silence allowing the rest of what lay in her heart to be whispered in her mind. Life would not give Regan Trent the thing she most longed for, it would not give her the love of Grant Eversley.

'*Miss Trent...*'

From the soft darkness it seemed the rich voice spoke again.

'*I realise you can hold no respect for me, neither do I ask any. My behaviour these past months has been reprehensible, I know too that it is unforgivable, but believe me when I say I wish only for your safety...*'

The eyes which had looked at her then stared from the windows of memory, eyes filled with that strange indefinable something which had hurried the beat of her heart, had sent blood racing helplessly in her veins, just as thought of them was doing now. Ashamed of her feelings Regan closed her eyes but the eyes of Grant Eversley regarded her from behind closed lids, his deep voice continuing to speak in her mind.

'*...I cannot in truth expect you to trust me in saying this, but if you will allow I will do all that I can to help you.*'

He did not expect her trust! Turning her face towards the moon, Regan admitted one more truth. She would trust Grant Eversley with her life – no, she stared into the soft golden radiance feeling another radiance, one as golden and soft, flood through her body. She would trust not only her life to Grant Eversley, but her very soul.

Two days, two more days, and the waiting would be over, he would be sole master of all that Jasper Trent had intended go to his family: he, Sherwyn Huntley, would own everything. And Wentworth? A laugh of disdain echoed in the quiet drawing room. Wentworth was a fool, and he would have the reward due a fool, which was nothing. But that was simply one more plan the man was as yet unaware of.

Helping himself to a brandy then settling into a graceful armchair, Sherwyn smiled to himself. He had thought things out carefully, spent hours going over the smallest of details, thinking and rethinking each time and time again until they interacted one in perfect unison with the other. It would not fail, it *could* not fail.

A sip of brandy on his tongue, he leaned his head against the chair listening to the silence of the empty house.

He had dismissed the entire staff, telling them Woodford was to be closed while he went abroad for several months. And with the completion of what he had planned then that was what he would do. But to close the house beforehand? That too was necessary to success; with no staff there would be no observers, and therefore no one to witness what was about to take place.

38

His actor friend was proving expensive. Riding a horse hired from the livery stable adjacent to the railroad station Myles Wentworth looked towards the graceful stone house standing at the head of the tree-lined drive. Yes, his new playmate was proving heavy on the finances but then Woodford House held the answer to that problem. He had thought on previous occasions to leave a note at the kitchen door, a note saying in effect Sherwyn Huntley *must* 'pay up or else'. But there would be no 'or else'. Myles smiled confidently. Huntley would not dare risk his tastes, those little sexual proclivities, being noised abroad.

Two hundred? Myles watched the house drawing nearer. Should he have made it five hundred? The amount would be the more useful seeing the expense of his adorable little lover, but it would not have been the more sensible. Huntley was a man with problems; he was also predictable. Faced with a demand for five hundred pounds he would flatly refuse, and without the means of supporting that pretty actor then Myles Wentworth might well lose him to someone not so financially dependent. Reining in the horse, leaving it tethered at the stable, he took an envelope from his pocket, taking care to soil it with dirt from the ground before placing it halfway beneath the door of the kitchen. Then walking around to the front of the house he knocked loudly on the door.

'That is impossible ... it's madness!' Disapproval marring his handsome features, Myles Wentworth helped himself to a second brandy.

Sherwyn Huntley watched the lithe slender figure resume its position in a facing chair before replying.

'Madness, you say ... then listen to what I say. The only madness is yours if you think I will let the Trent fortune slip away from me; you will do what you are told, all of what you are told, and mistake me not, Myles, try doing anything other than what I say and you will not live long enough to taste regret.'

'But how?' Wentworth ventured again. 'I mean how can you possibly expect to get away with a scheme like that? There are bound to be people who know Regan Trent, who can identify her; oh yes, you say the ceremony is to be held in strict privacy, but you can't prevent onlookers standing at the church gate. There is every possibility of someone from the village recognising that the bride is not the young woman they expect to see; and what of Trent's lawyer? He will be sure to know it is not Trent's daughter signing that paper.'

Sherwyn blandly sipped from his glass before returning. 'Allow me to set your fears at rest. First, the bride will be wearing a veil, a cover through which, while hiding her face, she can see clearly so it need not be lifted during the church proceedings nor to sign documents produced later by the lawyer; second, Marcia told me that neither herself nor either of her children were ever allowed to be present the times Trent's lawyer called at the house, so he would not know Regan Trent from a housemaid.'

'Not removing a veil while signing the church register will appear strange enough, but in a lawyer's office! Isn't that carrying things too far?'

Holding the glass to the light of an overhead gasoliere Sherwyn watched the pinpoints of colour dart from the crystal. Explaining each point was a bore, but then he could afford to pay some small price to achieve a fortune. 'Not at all.' He glanced across at the figure draped in a matching chair. 'A young girl is allowed a certain shyness at her wedding, it is not unusual. But in the case of Regan, who has so recently lost mother and brother, the veil will be guessed to hide tears her loved ones could not share the day with her.'

He had it all cut and dried! Myles moved to pour himself yet another measure of brandy. So who was it Huntley had hired to play the bride?

Rising to his feet Sherwyn plucked the glass from the other man's hand. 'That,' he said, setting the unfinished drink aside as the question was asked, 'is something I leave entirely to you; but now I think an evening at the delightful establishment of Mrs Russell.'

He did not want to visit that place, entertaining as it had always proved. The young man he had waiting for him at Tallow Hill was infinitely more desirable, but to refuse would set Huntley pondering the reason, and should Huntley find out about this new friend he would expect to share the delights and afterwards the proceeds of a sale. But there would be no sale! Lips set resolutely together, Myles followed his host to the rear of the house. His latest acquisition was not for sale and most definitely not for sharing.

'What's this?' Opening the outer door of the kitchen Sherwyn's glance fell on the envelope lying on the step. At his back Myles Wentworth smiled. Two hundred pounds; a visit to his tailor, a short holiday with his pretty amour?

'You said this swine was dead!'

Huntley's blast scattering the pleasant thoughts Myles caught at the paper being pushed into his face. A pretence of reading allowed him a moment in which to adopt a look of surprise as he answered with a croak, 'He ... he is. That photograph in the newspaper, it was the same fellow I paid the money to.'

'Really!' Huntley's snarl rang over the quiet yard. 'Then how do you explain that?'

'I can't ... I mean ... he...' Myles stuttered while inwardly congratulating himself on his skills of deception. 'He must have told someone else.'

Snatching the sheet of paper, tearing it to bits then throwing it across the yard, Sherwyn's answer showed in his face.

'Told someone else did he! Well, whoever this someone else might be he will get nothing from me!'

The usual storm, Myles smiled to himself. But it would pass, the money would be paid; a little urging would have Huntley see sense.

'But what if this person should carry out his threat, what if he should tell...'

Unaccustomed to saddling a horse for himself

Sherwyn fumbled in the half-light of the stable but his voice carrying back to Myles, already mounted and waiting in the stable yard, was perfectly steady. 'Then that bastard will have the police on his tail for that is what I will do should one more demand find its way to this house!'

It could have gone better! Myles watched the other man lead his horse from the stable, a fist jabbing into the animal's side when it reacted to a snatch on the rein. But he would not give up just yet; Huntley had too much to lose, he would not involve the police.

Irritated by the blackmail demand, Sherwyn dug his heels into the horse's flank, swearing yet again when it reared. This was one more item to be disposed of. If only he could have disposed of Regan Trent as easily! He rode ahead while the thought returned as it often had. If he had found her there would have been no need of any charade, he would have forced her to sign for her inheritance then married her to the fop riding behind him, and shortly afterward, arranged a sad demise.

But he had not found her, so for now at least he must follow another route to the Trent fortune. But then... Despite his irritation Sherwyn smiled to himself. As the saying went, 'all roads lead to Rome', and the road Sherwyn Huntley followed would certainly prove the case.

Her coat buttoned, Ann Searson looked at the girl standing beside the table in Libby Radley's living room. They had talked of this matter well into the night, Regan determined to return to Woodford alone while she, Ann, was equally determined that

417

would not happen; now to settle any final objection! 'There is nothing you can do to stop me,' she said defiantly. 'You might as well get used to the idea, I am going to Woodford with you.'

'Accept it, Regan.' Daniel added his weight to Ann's ultimatum. 'It's best you have someone with you.'

Libby Radley held aside the heavy dividing curtain and watched the two young women dress in their coats, her heart telling her only one could return. Had she been told little under a year past Libby Radley would come to love a stranger as she would a daughter she would have said they was fools, but that was the way in her heart she felt about both of these girls. They were part of her in a way she could not explain even to herself; now the fate which had brought Regan Trent to her door was set to take her from it.

Fighting tears she felt rising to her throat, she held out her arms to Regan and as she stepped into them murmured, 'Daniel be right, havin' Ann the side of you be better than your bein' alone.' Then, despite her resolve to shed no tears, she whispered brokenly, 'I'd keep you 'ere, wench, for the Lord knows I loves you dear, but the choosin' don't rest wi' me. You've come to your decision and I must needs abide by it, though I prays that same Lord walk alongside you, that His mercy be wrapped as a cloak about you, that He allow no harm to come to the girl I wish had been my own.'

It had been hard parting from Libby. In the train carrying her and Ann to Worcester, Regan swallowed on the lump remaining stubbornly in her throat. Birthdays should be happy days but this, her twenty-first, was the most miserable she had ever known.

As she sat on the other side of the third-class compartment Ann's face was solemn. It had taken all of her persuasion to prevent Daniel accompanying them to Woodford after Grant Eversley's assistance had been refused. With Grant's departure he had tried again to get Regan to accept that the man should travel with them, be with them when they encountered Huntley; he had told her Grant Eversley would take no nonsense from that man nor any other, that Regan would stand a better chance of standing up to him given the backing of Grant; but all of Daniel's reasoning had fallen on deaf ears. Regan had remained adamant. Why? The question Ann had put to herself several times kindled afresh. Regan had been glad to take the help of those gypsy folk, the same of the Radleys, so why not that of Grant Eversley?

'Why wouldn't you allow Mr Eversley to come with us?' Annoyance at what she saw as simply pride on Regan's part made the question sharp. Then realising she had spoken aloud she followed up more gently. 'There is more to your refusing than what you said yesterday, more to your not wanting Grant at Woodford than the inconvenience it would cause him; what is it, Regan? But no, I don't need to ask, I saw for myself last night when we talked before getting to bed, the look in your eyes as you spoke of him; you feel for Grant Eversley the way I feel for Daniel, you are in love with him.'

The arrival of several passengers in the compartment spared Regan the need to answer.

Thankful for the reprieve she turned her glance to the window. Ann was right, she did love Grant Eversley, and that was the reason she could not have him meet Sherwyn Huntley. Should what Ann had seen in her eyes be seen by him, should he once suspect she cared then Grant's life would be in danger, and that she could not live with.

She had been spared answering Ann's 'you are in love with him' yet the reply beat like a drum in Regan's ears. Yes, she loved him, loved the man who had thought her a liar and a would-be cheat. He had apologised, but in his mind did he still think of her in that same way, did he even now think the story of her being the daughter of Jasper Trent to be a lie? Was the reason he had offered to come with her to Woodford so that he could lend support or to see her exposed in deceit?

'Worcester ... Worcester next stop.'

The loud call of the train attendant announcing its imminent arrival imposing on her thoughts, Regan felt her nerves tense. She had so feared being found by Sherwyn Huntley, being forced to return to Woodford with him, yet she was going there now.

'You shouldn't do this.' Halfway along the platform Ann caught Regan's arm. 'You don't have to, we can get a train back to Wednesbury. Forget it, Regan; you said Woodford holds nothing for you now your mother and brother are no longer there, so why put yourself in the hands of Huntley? You know he doesn't have an ounce of mercy in his whole body. Regan please ... let's go back.'

'That would not put an end to this.' Regan

gently removed the hand clutching at her elbow. 'You have said on several occasions Sherwyn Huntley will not relinquish his search for me and while that continues yourself and the Radleys will not be free of him, of the spite we both know him capable of; I will no longer have that cloud lie over them or over you.'

'But the threats he made! They were not just talk, not stories meant to frighten you into submission. Huntley is not that sort, he meant what he said, meant to have you locked away or else to kill you, and he will, Regan, he will, but not before he has put you through hell! You know as well as I do, Sherwyn Huntley isn't a man vengeance satisfies once, he has to taste it again and again.'

Had he not done that already? Had his raping her not been proof of his evil? A deed he had said would be repeated!

The thought resulted in a shiver which did not escape Ann, who said again, 'You must not go to that house, neither the Radleys nor myself want you to, we don't care what Huntley–'

'But I do, Ann!' Quick and firm the intervention halted the other girl. 'I care very much. I will no longer shelter behind friends. You and Daniel deserve a life of happiness together, not one blighted with the dread of some day finding Sherwyn Huntley on your doorstep. No, Ann, that threat ends today.'

In the hansom cab they took from the station every fibre of Regan was taut. Today would see the cloud of threat lifted from the people she loved but it would never lift from her until... Desperate to push the darkness from her mind she turned her gaze to the window, but the fields and hedgerows she had loved and known so well held no interest for her now. Ann had said it was not too late, that even now they could turn around, go back to Woden Passage. As the thought came so Regan pushed it away.

'There it is.' Ann leaned forwards as Woodford House came into view.

Regan did not need to see the building her heart knew every stone of. She had been so happy in this house, so loved, but with Sherwyn Huntley every last trace of that happiness had been destroyed, leaving only emptiness in its place.

What would it have been like to live there with Grant Eversley, to have known his love? A little shocked by the forwardness of the thought Regan drew herself even more tightly upright. Crying for the moon was a useless occupation!

'Where is everybody?' Ann had led the way as they looked in every room, even daring to go into Huntley's inner sanctum, the study, but that, as every other, had proved empty. Now they stood in the kitchen. 'Looks like no meal's been cooked in here for a while, every pan is washed and hung on its hook; the house might've been empty for years.'

There should be someone in the house, the cook, the butler, but the house was deserted. Equally confused, Regan watched Ann going into the butler's pantry, emerging with a shake of the head.

'Now what do we do?' Hands on hips Ann stared about. 'Suppose it's no use asking you to go back? Thought so.' She huffed as Regan shook her head, then inspiration struck. 'The lawyer, your father's lawyer, we can go see him!' She almost shouted.

'I don't think that would do much good. He does not know me, and without proof of identity, birth certificates, my father's papers, I also could be impersonating Regan Trent.'

'Impersonating!' This time it was a shout echoing in the empty room. 'That's it, that's where everybody is!'

'Where?' Regan frowned. 'Ann, you are not making any sense.'

With a laugh Ann caught Regan's hand. 'Aren't you getting married today?' Then at Regan's deepening puzzlement she added, 'The piece in the newspaper! Regan Trent is to marry Myles Wentworth. So where does a marriage take place? The church! Come on, let's see who this other Regan Trent is.'

She didn't want to see the person pretending to be her; as for Myles and Huntley, the wait before having to see them was like a reprieve from the gallows. Searching for a reasonable excuse Regan used the only one which came to mind. 'The hansom.' She glanced at the door leading off the kitchen, the door they had left open. 'We didn't ask it to wait.'

Nonplussed, Ann smiled. 'So m'lady don't have a cab, but she does have legs ... we can run!'

Heads had turned at sight of two young women, skirts flapping indiscreetly above the ankle as they raced through the small village, but Ann had not slowed down. 'We have to see her walk down the aisle,' she had laughed.

It had never seemed this far when she had walked to the church of St Luke nor had coming here been so dreaded. Chest aching from exertion, breath drawn in short rapid gasps, Regan pushed open the door.

39

'I said the ceremony was to be conducted in strict privacy!' Eyes hard with anger, Sherwyn Huntley glared around the body of the tiny village church, at two people who knelt in prayer in the rearmost pew.

The vicar followed the glance saying apologetically, 'I am sorry, Mr Huntley, this is not a private house, but a house of God; I cannot forbid worshippers to enter. Perhaps you would prefer to delay the ceremony for a while? I'm sure those people will leave shortly.'

Then again they might not! Huntley's anger deepened. Any delay, however brief, could not be afforded. The sooner he was in that lawyer's office, the signed document in his hand, the sooner he could relax. This in mind, yet careful it should seem he was mindful only of the bride's comfort, Sherwyn looked at the figure beside him, a veil reaching almost to the waist of a cream satin gown, both hands hidden by a bouquet of palest pink roses. His satisfied smile stayed inside him when with a shake of the veiled head the bride refused his offer of waiting for the church to empty.

Taking that as his cue the vicar began. 'Dearly beloved...'

Things had gone exactly as he intended they should. The intoned words of the vicar holding no interest for him, Sherwyn allowed thought to run free. Wentworth had done all he had been instructed, there had been objections but they had dissolved in the face of argument, Wentworth eventually coming to terms with what after all was the most sensible method of procedure; but then Sherwyn Huntley's plan was more than sensible, it was masterly.

'Do you, Regan, take this man for your lawfully wedded husband?'

A slight shuffle, a rustle of bouquet against satin, brought Sherwyn's glance to the bride, breath easing in his throat at the whispered, 'I do.' Had he thought for a moment the answer would be different? Of course not! Hadn't he ensured nothing could go wrong?

From the further end of the nave the sound of the church door being pushed open grated on Sherwyn's temper. He should have approached the bishop, got permission to have the church closed to any but the bridal party!

Book in hand, the vicar looked past the couple before him, his glance carrying down the nave. Then, his slightly raised tone ringing in the silence, he went on. 'If any person has just cause why these two should not be joined in holy matrimony let him speak now or forever hold his peace. Wherein–'

'I have cause!'

Coming from the rear of the church the call

halted the vicar who, presuming no objection, had already begun intoning the final act of the service. Now, the book almost falling from his hands, he stared at the figures coming from the pew.

Eyes dark with fury, Sherwyn Huntley turned to the approaching figures, his brow creasing with recognition. 'You!' He stared at Grant Eversley. 'What brings you here?'

'I wanted to be at your wedding, and seeing I received no official invitation I thought I would just turn up.'

'This is a private ceremony! We wished it attended by no one.'

'Oh I've no doubt of that,' Grant answered the bark calmly.

'Then leave – *now!*'

Clearly in a quandary as to how to handle an entirely unforeseen turn of events, the vicar dithered. 'Gentlemen please ... gentlemen ... remember, you are in the house of God.'

Ignoring him, Sherwyn grated, 'You will leave now Eversley, if you know what is good for you!'

'Thank you for the advice; did you give the same to your bride? Did you tell Regan Trent what was good for her? And Mr Wentworth, did he back out? Change his mind about marrying Miss Trent?'

'Damn you, Eversley, mind your own bloody business!'

A profanity in his church too much for the perplexed vicar, he closed the book with a bang. 'There has been an objection to this marriage,' he said testily. 'Might we hear that objection ... *without* profanity!'

Calm as before, Grant looked first at the vicar, reading the sense of injury on the flushed face. That injury would worsen yet! 'Certainly, Reverend.' He turned his glance to Huntley. 'This is not the man whose name appears on the banns posted on this church.'

'There is no law says a guardian may not marry his ward!'

Every word iced with anger, Sherwyn threw them at Grant.

'Agreed,' Grant parried. 'But then the bride standing here is not your ward, she is not Regan Trent.'

'Not Regan Trent? Then who...'

'Precisely,' Grant answered the vicar's unfinished enquiry. 'Just who is it Mr Huntley proposes to marry?'

'Perhaps we might continue in the vestry.'

'No, Reverend.' Grant shook his head. 'Not in the vestry. I say the bride remove the veil where we can all see her, that would prove my objection true or false.'

'No, she will not!' Sherwyn's outstretched arm reaching towards the bride caught the bouquet, knocking it to the ground.

Powerless to eject the contestants by force the vicar turned a sympathetic look to the cream-gowned figure. 'If you would my dear ... it will put an end to this unhappy situation.'

'She will not remove her veil.'

Perturbed as well as perplexed, the vicar looked at the fallen bouquet then lifted his glance to Grant. 'Really Mr Eversley, is this truly necessary?'

Eyes suddenly pure steel looked straight into

Huntley's. 'Yes,' Grant answered tersely. 'It is truly necessary.'

On the receiving end of that hard glance Sherwyn Huntley's own eyes narrowed. 'You are familiar with my stepdaughter; you can say if she is or is not the young woman standing here. How is that, Mr Eversley? It was certainly not in my house you have seen her for you have never been a guest there, so then the Continent maybe? That is where Regan has been for almost a year.'

'I say that is a lie, as I say this woman you are marrying is not Regan Trent. But then why do we not prove it!' Grant caught a corner of the veil, flipping it to the back of the pale blonde head.

A moment of stunned silence fell over the group standing a little way from an altar bedecked with a cross flanked on each side with tall brass candlesticks, a silence which seemed to scream across the nave, to bounce back and forth from the grey stone walls; but it was only a moment, then Huntley was speaking, his voice sharp with surprise, his face registering disbelief.

'Wentworth!' he gasped. 'Wentworth, what the hell!'

At the rear of the church a scuffle of movement followed a muffled cry but was lost beneath Sherwyn Huntley's tirade.

'I don't know what game you think you are playing, Wentworth, but I'll see you pay dearly for it!'

'Don't try that, Huntley!' Myles Wentworth's reply was a shriek. 'This game as you call it ... it was all your idea, your masterly, foolproof grand plan; I told you it was stupid, that you would

428

never get away with it!'

Wentworth could prove nothing. He was the one dressed in woman's clothing, he the one in wig and veil, he the deceiver. All of this quicksilver in his brain, Huntley snapped, 'That is a lie, but whatever you hope to gain by it...'

Snatching the wig and veil from his head Myles flung them down onto the flowers at his feet. 'What I hope to gain!' he cried, 'what *we* hope to gain, *we*, Huntley, the Trent fortune was what we hoped to gain, a fortune shared between the two of us.'

'You are out of your mind if you believe that story will get you out of the mess you have brought upon yourself,' Sherwyn snapped again. 'Now what have you done with my ward? Where is Regan?'

Again a shuffle of feet sounded from the rearmost pew and with it a quiet voice. 'Here,' it said, 'I am Regan Trent.'

Regan! It screeched along Sherwyn's nerves. She was here in this church! Despite his every effort to find her! But how? How had she managed to evade discovery yet arrive back on this of all days? Eversley? He was the one who had halted this 'wedding', he the one had claimed it was not Regan Trent wearing gown and veil, so it followed he had to be the one who had kept her hidden. Jasper Trent's money? Had its siren song sounded as sweet to Eversley as it sounded to him? Undoubtedly! Full of tension, Sherwyn glanced at the man who was turning towards the movement at the further end of the nave. That was a melody Grant Eversley would not have the pleasure of hearing to the end. Pushing the thought away, forcing a note of joy to his voice, he called, 'Regan,' at that moment moving towards the slender fair-haired figure standing in the aisle; but quick as he was Grant Eversley was quicker, his body square in front of Regan.

'Don't touch her!' Granite on ice the words ground. 'You won't touch her ever again!'

Realising the hopelessness of his own position, of convincing Regan he had wanted no part of it, Myles called, 'It was him, Regan, Huntley. He murdered your mother, he had your brother killed and after you had married me you also were to die, then your inheritance would be shared equally between him and me.' Ripping at the gown, he stared wildly at Sherwyn. 'But it didn't work out as intended, did it, Huntley? You needed Regan to sign for that inheritance but you could not find her. That was when you conceived the idea of replacing one bride with another. No one would ever know, you said. It was foolproof, you said. Well who is the fool now, Huntley?'

With one stride Sherwyn returned to the man still struggling with the gown, then struck him in the face, sending him sprawling against the vicar.

'You stupid bloody fool!' The snarl echoed through the church. 'You think Regan will believe your lies!'

Still sprawled half across the unfortunate cleric, Myles seemed all at once calm. 'Ask her,' he said quietly, 'ask her does she believe? Then tell her of the boys you violated then sold to brothels...'

Out of the shadows thrown by an overhead organ loft another figure, that of a stockily built man, stepped to Myles's side, a Myles who laughed before saying, 'Tell her of the lad you burned to death in the summer house.'

'Saul!' Hearing the cry at his back Grant Eversley turned quickly, catching Regan as she swayed.

One hand holding firm to Myles, the other fishing a small leather wallet from a pocket of his jacket, a slick practised movement flicking it open, the stocky man held it so Grant and Huntley could see.

'Police Inspector Clines,' he introduced himself, a second dexterous flip of the wrist snapping the wallet closed. 'You were correct in saying the law does not prohibit a man from marrying his ward, Mr Huntley, but it does prohibit a man marrying another man.' Glancing briefly at the vicar fluttering before the altar like a disturbed moth he continued. 'Myles Wentworth, Sherwyn Huntley, I arrest you both on the grounds of attempting an act of unlawful marriage.'

He would see no inside of a magistrate's court. Lashing the hindquarters of the carriage horse Sherwyn Huntley raced along the drive of Woodford House. That policeman had not expected one of his prisoners to escape, but then he did not reckon on Sherwyn Huntley. Leaping from the vehicle he ran into the house, making straight for the study. All was not lost, he would take Trent's papers from the safe; without them Regan could not claim a penny of her father's money, she would have no proof of identity; and there was no person could validate her claim of being Jasper Trent's daughter. Eversley no doubt would try backing such a claim, but no court would accept the word of a man who could only have known her a few months. He grabbed papers and cash from the safe then stood a moment listening for any sound. Nothing but the somnolent tick of the long-case clock in the hall marred the deep silence. It would be guessed where he had come, the police would follow, but they would not find him here.

Wentworth's horse was in the stables. He would leave the carriage where it was, take Wentworth's horse and ride to Worcester. That would not be expected, those searching for him would expect him to take a train. But he would take no train, not for several months.

Myles had left the horse saddled! For once glad of his accomplice's lack of care Sherwyn leapt onto the animal's back, his heels jabbing sharply. He would leave through the small gate set in the curtain wall and then ride through the woods. But this wasn't goodbye to Woodford, he could still get half of Trent's estate. A year? Entering the thick fringe of woodland Sherwyn smiled to himself. Perhaps a little longer, then he'd contact Regan, offer the return of the papers in exchange for half that inheritance. Half? No ... he deserved more than half; but then he must be generous to the girl, he would ask no more than three-quarters!

The smile becoming a deep-throated laugh Sherwyn was unprepared for the figures stepping onto the track in front of the horse.

Head throbbing, Sherwyn opened his eyes. What the hell had happened? One moment he had been on that horse, the next he was thrown to the ground. Some fool had stepped in front of the animal and the horse... Lord, if it had bolted! He had to find it before the police found him! Trying to rise Sherwyn felt a tug on his wrists; they were tied ... they were tied with rope staked into the ground! God Almighty, he was arched across a boulder, his legs spread apart and both feet staked the same!

'You don't be goin' nowheres.' At his back a woman's voice came quietly.

'What do you think you are doing? I'll have you hanged for this!' Sherwyn's screech sent birds flying from the trees.

''Angin' holds no 'orrors for me.' The quiet voice answered Sherwyn's enraged snarl. 'I seen all the horrors life can hold for a woman when I looked on my son, when I sponged away the marks of your rape, when I washed his body for the buryin'.'

'Mother, should we...?'

'No!' Sharp yet quiet, the denial joined the rustle of breeze-stroked leaves. 'You get yourselves away, I be needin' no more help ... what be done will be done by my 'ands. Now go, the pair o' you, I've lost one son, I'll not have another two teken by the law.'

'You will all answer to the law!'

'First, Mr 'Untley, you will answer to me, the mother of the lad you raped along of a bridge crossing the river along of Worcester, a lad whose head you smashed against the stone parapet, the lad you left dead. But the dead 'ave a way o' speakin', Mr 'Untley, and my son spoke to 'is mother.'

433

Head arching on his neck in an attempt to see the woman, Sherwyn snapped, 'You have made a mistake.'

Wrapping a cloth about Sherwyn's mouth, pulling it tight, the woman replied, 'Mistake is it? Do this be a mistake?' Moving to face her captive the woman thrust out a hand. 'Do you recognise this?'

Sherwyn felt his throat constrict. The cuff link he had lost that night bore his initials. He had not realised it was missing until he had returned home to Woodford.

'Yes, I sees you knows it. It were in my boy's 'and when his brother carried him 'ome. Yes, Mr 'Untley, his brother saw you leavin' of that place, thought you'd been there with some woman, ain't unusual for a prostitute to tek a man there; but when no woman followed a few yards behind ... well, a man be a man and my lad went to spend a copper or two, but he found no woman, he found a brother with his skull caved in. But smashing of his head don't be the all of what you done, was it?' The woman rose to her feet, drawing a smoothly rounded club from beneath wide skirts. 'You raped my lad!' The voice which had been quiet became a rasp. 'Now you be goin' to feel the pain he felt!'

No! God in heaven, no! Words which could not pass the gag screamed in Sherwyn's brain as he felt his trousers ripped away, a scream matched by one of agony as the club thrust deep.

40

She didn't want to enter that house, never wanted to step through its doors again. One hand caught in Ann's, Regan stared at the mellow stone building of her childhood. Why had her mother married Sherwyn Huntley? Had a son and a daughter not been enough to bring back happiness to her life? But that was an unfair question; love for children must be so very different to a love felt for a husband just as love for a brother was not the same as love felt for another man. She had loved her brother, loved Saul dearly, but that emotion differed greatly to that aroused by Grant Eversley. Conscious of him now, of the nearness of him walking at her side, Regan's veins flooded with warmth. In all the tumult at the church, her surprise at finding him there, she hadn't asked herself the reason of his coming, now she could not ask it, could not face the answer, 'I came as a friend.'

'Wait...'

The hand touching her arm tripped her senses more than the caution in the voice; Regan stepped closer to Ann, afraid her eyes would betray what she could not withhold from her heart.

As if sharp teeth had bitten into him Grant dropped his hand. Regan Trent could not make it more plain she did not welcome his presence. Meeting Ann's eyes he said again, 'Wait, stay here, I will see if Huntley is in the house.'

Taking Regan's tremor to be one of fear at the prospect of her stepfather being at Woodford, Ann put an arm about her friend, as Regan's glance followed the figure striding into the house.

'He can't hurt you, Regan,' she said comfortingly, 'Huntley can't do anything now you be of age. Tomorrow your father's lawyer will come and settle your affairs, then the whole thing'll be over.'

'...*the whole thing will be over.*' It clanged in Regan's mind. But it was not relief Ann's words evoked but pain, the pain of knowing there would be no further need of Grant Eversley's support. He would return to his life in Wednesbury, a life which did not include Regan Trent.

'Do you know what was in there?'

They had come to the study, Grant asking the question on seeing the rifled safe.

'No.' Regan shook her head. 'I was never shown what was kept here, nothing was spoken of.'

'Well it's clear there was something Huntley didn't want you getting hold of. Let's hope he still has whatever it is when the police catch up with him.'

'No sense in talking of that now. I think a cup of tea would be much more useful. If you, Grant, would take Regan into the drawing room I'll see about making some.'

She used his name so easily, and he Ann's. Sitting in the room her mother had so loved, Regan stole a quick look at the man who stood staring out over the gardens. Grant Eversley had become friends with Ann but for Regan Trent there would only ever be the courtesy good manners called for.

'There we are, this will soon have we all feeling

more–' The sound of the doorbell ending her words abruptly, Ann set the tea tray down with a thud.

'With your permission, Miss Trent.' Even as he asked Grant Eversley was across the room, the door closed behind him.

'We've found Sherwyn Huntley.' The police inspector's voice lowered as Grant put a finger to his lips. 'Sorry sir,' he said, 'should have realised the young ladies ... but as I says, Huntley has been found.'

'You have taken him into custody?'

'Not in the way you might think.' Meeting the quick frown of Grant's brow the inspector went on. 'Huntley is in the mortuary, he was dead when we found him.'

'Dead – how? Was he thrown?'

Darting a look past Grant, satisfying himself they weren't being overheard, the inspector shook his head. 'Were no fall from a horse killed Sherwyn Huntley. The club were still in his backside.'

'Oh my God!' Grant's exclamation of disbelief cut through the explanation. 'Who on earth could do something like that?'

'Somebody who had no intention of Huntley ever telling; we found a branch a few yards from the body, the blood upon it indicates this were the instrument used to smash his skull.'

'Miss Trent?' Grant threw a swift look behind him.

'She has to be informed, Huntley being her stepfather you understand, but it will be enough to say he is dead, no call for a young woman to hear the gory details.'

'Would you have me tell her?'

'No thank you, Mr Eversley, that be my responsibility. Rules be rules, and we have to abide by them.'

'Thrown from his horse; well I don't be hypocrite enough to say I feel sorry!' Ann said as Grant returned from showing the policeman out. 'Regan is free of him now and that is all I care about.'

Regan was all he cared about! Grant looked at the pale face. If only he could tell her, confess the love he held for her.

'I think you should go up to your room, Regan, rest for a while.'

Go up to that room, the room where she had overheard Myles and Huntley discussing how Saul was to be killed ... the room where Huntley had raped her! Sickness rose to her throat, but Regan managed a quiet refusal of Ann's suggestion. Then forcing the thought away she said, 'I have not yet thanked you Mr Eversley, for coming to Woodford. It was kind of you, but you should not neglect your business on my account.'

Was this her polite way of telling him he should go? What else could it be? Grant rose to his feet. 'It was my pleasure to be of assistance, Miss Trent, though I fear it has proved something of an intrusion.' He turned to Ann. 'Will you stay with Miss Trent until she is fully recovered? I will explain to Daniel.'

He was leaving! Her remark, innocently as it was meant, had been insulting to him! 'I...' Regan coloured, 'I did not mean to sound offensive, I meant only...' The colour flared wildly in her cheeks. Words coming falteringly she finished, 'I meant I am grateful for your coming.'

'Then perhaps you will allow me one more intrusion before I leave. One I hope will bring you as much pleasure as it brought myself.'

What had he meant? Her eyes asking the silent question of a smiling Ann, Regan turned her glance to follow Grant Eversley, then with his return to the room the breath stilled in her lungs.

'Saul!' It came at last. A whisper half of disbelief at what she saw, half of fear the vision would disappear. Blinded by tears, she watched the figure come towards her, a figure which could only be illusion. Then she was caught in a bear-hug she knew was no fantasy, the arms flung around her were those of her brother and behind him, smiling at their happiness, was Edward Sanders.

Minutes later, alone with Edward Sanders and her brother, her hand holding his as if afraid he would disappear after all, Regan listened to Sanders' quiet explanation.

'It was my doing,' he said, 'it was I who took Saul from the train. I could not risk my son returning to Woodford.'

'Your son!' Regan gasped, her grip tightening protectively over her brother's hand.

'My son.' Edward Sanders' smile was gentle. 'You will find proof of that among your father's documents. Your mother and I fell in love many years ago. She was spending the summer in Cornwall, your father being away on an extended business trip. I need tell you only that my love was so strong I could not bear being parted from her so I followed her here. It was my intention to reveal the truth to Trent, to take Marcia away

439

with me. But she could not leave you, her daughter. She knew your father would never allow her to take you so she let him believe the child she was carrying was his. It was a deception I had no liking for, but to save Marcia from the condemnation of society and the child from the stigma of bastardy I agreed to remain silent, but not to go from this house; that was when I accepted the post of butler. I could not take the woman I loved to live with me but being a servant in her house meant I could in some fashion be close to her ... and to my son.'

'But after my father died, why did you and Mother still not marry?'

'I had hoped to.' Emotion strong in him Sanders paused, then, 'I wanted nothing more than to make Marcia my wife, but then Huntley came on the scene. He told her of how he had been discussing business with Jasper when his heart attack struck, of the words he had uttered before death closed his lips: 'Saul ... not Trent... Saul not my son.' It was all Huntley needed for him to step into your father's shoes, the ultimatum being disgrace for your mother as well as that which would follow Saul the rest of his life.'

'How did my father know Saul was not his son?'

'I asked your mother the same question.' Sanders' eyes reflected an old sadness. 'She had been kneeling beside the bed, she did not hear your father enter the room but he heard her prayer asking the Lord to forgive her betrayal of her husband, to protect the son of her infidelity. To your father's credit he did not discard your mother. They would stay together, safeguard the name of Trent and the future prospects of his daughter; the boy would enjoy the benefits of that name only until attaining majority; after that date he would receive nothing. That was what would be placed in his will and with it would go a signed affidavit of Marcia's confession of adultery.'

'If Huntley knew Saul was not the son of Jasper Trent, and in view of what you've already told me I must presume he got as much from my mother, that Saul could not inherit, then why kill him?'

Looking at the two sitting close together, Edward Sanders smiled briefly. 'A logical question. Simply put, Huntley had no way of knowing, other than Marcia's word, that Saul had been disinherited. He had not witnessed the reading of Jasper's will therefore would not accept the truth of what she told him. He intended no one but himself to have Jasper Trent's estate. With Marcia's death, I realised the danger. The note I slipped beneath your door would, I hoped, lead you to finding the key Marcia had asked be placed in your wardrobe, then I enlisted the help of Ann. I gave her the address where I could be contacted, getting her solemn promise to use it if I could prove to be of help to yourself. That done I took Saul to the Isle of Wight. A week ago I received a message asking would I return to Woodford to assist in identifying Regan Trent; it was signed by Grant Eversley.'

He had contacted Edward Sanders, he had taken the trouble to write, to have the man met at the docks and brought to Worcester where a hotel room awaited him, then further arranged train

441

travel to Woodford station and a hansom cab to transport him to the church, but he was only to intervene should it transpire there was no other way of identifying the 'bride' as a fraud. He had done all that solely to help her.

Looking at Grant as he and Ann were invited back into the drawing room, Regan felt a flush of shame that she could have been so distrusting of him, thinking the offer of assistance that evening in Libby's living room had been empty words, that his help would be given merely to prove himself correct in believing she was not Regan Trent.

'Ann ... Mr Eversley,' she smiled now, 'however can I thank you both?'

How should he answer? Tell her he wanted only the smile on her lips, the happiness gleaming in those lovely aquamarine eyes? That was true, but he wanted it to be for him. Quenching the thought he returned the smile saying instead, 'Your happiness is thanks enough, Miss Trent.'

'Then allow me to add to those thanks by sharing a little of that happiness.' Taking Saul by the hand she drew him forward. 'Mr Eversley, allow me to present Saul Sanders.'

'Phew!' Ann blew a short breath after hearing a brief outline of Edwards Sanders' story. 'Like Libby would say, that be a right thimble rig and no mistake.'

'It was one Marcia Trent and I endured for the sake of her children, but now it is finished.' He turned to look directly at Saul. 'You have heard me repeat what I told you after reaching the Isle of Wight. You are my son but should you choose I relinquish that claim.'

He had grown so tall. Regan looked at the boy who in one short year had become a man. There was pride in his face, a strength of character, and in his voice a quiet determination.

Going to stand beside the man who had kidnapped him from the train he said, 'I do not relinquish that claim. I am the son of Edward Sanders, I am proud to call him father.' Then swallowing the break in his voice he went on, 'I love you, sis, I am glad of that clause which names you sole inheritor of this house and everything that goes with it. I would not have it any other way than you should have it all.'

Silent for a moment Regan looked at the boy she had mourned as dead, the boy she had thought never to see again, then with love surging in her heart she said, 'All is not enough. I want my brother and his father too if he will stay. Woodford will need a manager and Saul a representative to take his place on the board of Trent Importers of Wines and Quality Foods until his education is finished and he can take those responsibilities for himself.' Turning to smile at the man resting a hand on her brother's shoulder she asked, 'Will you do that, Mr Sanders?'

He was returning to Wednesbury. Regan gazed over gardens heavy with the scent of roses. There would be no more meeting with him. Despair had sat heavy since Grant Eversley's farewell; now it pressed her into the ground. How had this happened? How had she fallen so in love? The world seemed a place of darkness with his having left.

'Good afternoon, Miss Trent.'

He was not here, he had returned to Wednesbury. Hands clasped together, Regan resisted the urge to turn and look behind her.

'I had hoped we were friends...'

Melodious in its softness, the voice caressed the silence of the garden.

'Friends enough to wish each other well.'

She had to face the dream, dispel it, accept the reality; it was simply her mind playing tricks. She'd do it this once, drive the ghosts from her heart, as she had to if life was to be liveable. Then she turned quickly and her cry echoed in the stillness.

'I'm sorry,' Grant apologised. 'I did not mean to startle you.'

'I...' Words sticking in her throat, Regan replied stumblingly, 'I thought you left for Wednesbury.'

If she would smile at him! If her eyes would show just once she was happy to see him!

'I took Ann to the train but stayed behind to speak with a client in Worcester.' Grant doused the disappointment burning inside. 'Seeing my train is not due to leave for a while I took the liberty of calling upon you, to ascertain if all is well.'

Unhappiness churning, Regan turned back to the garden.

Grant was beside her and suddenly her hands were in his. 'Regan, what I said a moment ago was not true. I did not speak with any client. I remained in Worcester because to leave without you is to leave my heart behind. I love you Regan, nothing can alter that!'

He loved her! Her heart song rising, Regan smiled with eyes dewy with happiness. Grant Eversley loved her!

444

'I have no right to expect–'

Standing on tiptoe Regan stopped the words with her mouth, her soul answering the call of his.

Lips against her brow, Grant breathed the perfume of her hair. She had not drawn away from him, she had not refused his mouth. Arms holding her close, his mind winged back to an evening he had stood in the passage leading to the annexe in Libby Radley's house. He had gone there to speak with Daniel but, though the reason still escaped him, he had not gone upstairs to his friend's room but to the annexe.

' *...marry Daniel...*'

The words which had halted him then sounded clear in his mind, words which had stirred an anger he had found difficult to control, an anger which said he had been correct in his assumption the girl he heard speaking was a cheat. But he had been the cheat!

In the quiet of the garden, Regan in his arms, Grant could smile at the recollection.

'*...I love Daniel...*'

Memory bitter in its sweetness flowed freely.

'*...it is the kind of love I had for my brother, I would not take that to Daniel in marriage...*'

Those words had halted him, had made him hold his breath, while an incredible feeling had swept the length of him. Yes, he had been the cheat, telling himself that emotion had merely been relief Daniel was not to be used as a pawn in a trickster's game; but the only trick was the one Grant Eversley had played on himself, that of not admitting he could be in love with Regan Trent.

'Rosa's visions!'

445

The quiet murmur breaking his thoughts Grant smiled at the face lifting to his own. 'Rosa?'

'Rosa Mullin ... her visions, what she saw, the fire ... the boy ... it all happened just as she predicted.'

Telling Grant of her travelling with the Mullins, while instinctively leading him to the burned-out summer house, Regan stared at the charred ruins, Rosa's words whispering in her ears.

'Fire and water, there be fire and there be water ... a man an' a boy, a boy looked on by the Angel o' Death, a man an' a boy ... fire ... there be death in the fire!'

Seeing her tremble from watching scenes he could not see, Grant drew her again into his arms but did not try to stem memories he realised would fade the sooner for being brought into the open.

'Rosa spoke of this place...'

Quietly, held in the arms of the man she loved, Regan related the visions of Rosa ending with: 'It was fire killed a boy, a boy I thought to be Saul, and the water ... the water was the Solent that he and Mr Sanders crossed to hide from Sherwyn Huntley.'

A sparkle of happiness in her eyes replacing the darkness of the moment, Regan smiled. 'Rosa said should I want her for any reason I was to tie the yellow ribbon she gave me to a tree or bush so that its message would find them and they would return. I would like to tie that ribbon.'

'Then you will, but could the message it sends be an invitation to a wedding, *our* wedding?'

Her smile crushed beneath the press of his lips, Regan's heart gave its answer.

446

The publishers hope that this book has given you enjoyable reading. Large Print Books are especially designed to be as easy to see and hold as possible. If you wish a complete list of our books please ask at your local library or write directly to:

Magna Large Print Books
Magna House, Long Preston,
Skipton, North Yorkshire.
BD23 4ND

This Large Print Book for the partially sighted, who cannot read normal print, is published under the auspices of

THE ULVERSCROFT FOUNDATION